Praise from earl

Gone to Dallas

★ ★ ★

"A lovely work of historical fiction, eminently readable and richly embroidered with period detail. This reader gets a Louisa May Alcott feel from this first-in-a-series historical novel, and that's high praise! Laurie Moore-Moore projects a tale of decency and resourcefulness that is fundamental to the continuing identity of the American West in general and of Texas specifically."

—Paul Hobby, Founder, Genesis Park, LP and Former CEO, *Texas Monthly*

"Creative and captivating. *Gone to Dallas* is that rare debut novel you won't want to put down. Scrupulous research. Laurie Moore Moore makes history real again with a compelling story set in early Dallas, Texas. If every history class could have been this interesting, we would all have been history majors. Remarkable and memorable. Five stars!"

—Dan Gooder Richard, Author of *The Good or Evil Side: Matamoros 1846*

"*Gone to Dallas* by author Laurie Moore-Moore is an unforgettable journey into the exciting yet turbulent times of a young Texas and the town of Dallas and beyond. Well written with a cast of characters that will capture your heart with their tenacity and spirit as they journey into unknown territory. Superb writing."

—BJ Mayo: Author of *Alfie Carter* and *Sparrows of Montenegro*

"I was hooked at the very first sentence! Sara is a formidable, likable young woman supported and challenged by a whole host of engaging and interesting characters. There were plenty of twists and turns to keep me guessing. The balance of storytelling and interesting historical detail was just right—making it an entertaining and informative read. The novel is both Sara's story and the story of Dallas. So glad I read it! I'm eager to follow Sara in the sequel!"

—Debbie Botelho, Vancouver Island, Canada

"A female protagonist who's Tennessee Smart and Texas Tough! *Gone to Dallas* captures an historically accurate essence of what early Texas was like and how committed and tenacious early settlers had to be to make it—especially the women!"

—Dr. W. Arthur (Skip) Porter, President Quantum Consulting and Professor and Associate Dean for Innovation, College of Natural Science, University of Texas at Austin (retired)

"I confess. I read the "Notes on the Story's Characters" first. Even though the author warned it contained spoilers. To my delight the notes tickled my interest to meet the real historical figures salted throughout *Gone to Dallas* as the story drew me in. So few books give credit to women in the early west. *Gone to Dallas* is a strong story about even stronger women. A book I'll definitely recommend to my reading group."

—Synnove B. Granholm, retired CFO, Arlington Virginia

GONE TO DALLAS

GONE TO ~~TEXAS~~ *Dallas*

The Storekeeper
1856 – 1861

A story of migration, betrayal, challenges, and determination
salted with true Texas history

Laurie Moore-Moore

GOAT MOUNTAIN PRESS

Library of Congress Control Number: 2021914534

Paperback: ISBN 978-1-7374361-0-2
Ebook: ISBN 978-1-7374361-1-9

Book cover and interior design by Lance Buckley

DEDICATION

*To the settlers who left their homes behind and traveled to Texas
in pursuit of land and opportunity.
and
To the Plains Indians whose lives centered around the millions of buffalo.
Two brave and strong cultures unfortunately in conflict.*

On the Trail

Sara's husband had been a disappointment in life but, she had to admit, was certainly a handsome corpse.

Damn Texas! It had all seemed so romantic when Morgan Darnell had courted her in Tennessee, finally offering her a ring and convincing her that they should marry and join a Gone to Texas wagon train. "It will be a grand adventure, and we'll make our fortune," he'd said.

Momma had cried and tried to talk her out of it. "Texas is too far away, and, Sara, you're only nineteen." Sara bit her tongue and didn't remind Momma that she had married Papa at nineteen.

Papa had shaken his head sadly and said, "If you are bound and determined to do this, Punkin, at least let me set you up with some decent teams of oxen and a wagon." Dear Papa, ever the practical man.

Thank goodness for grandma, who had given her money to buy merchandise to stock the store she and Morgan hoped to open in the Three Forks area of the Trinity River, in the small settlement called Dallas. "I planned to will it to you when I died, honey. I guess you can have it early," she'd offered, with tears in her eyes.

Two weeks after the wedding, Papa helped load the newlyweds' belongings and some initial merchandise for the store into the Pennington Horse Farm's largest wagon to drive them to Memphis—the jumping-off point for the wagon train's trip to Texas.

The spring sun was warm on their backs as the wagon bumped along the dirt trail past green pastures. Riding on the back seat of the wagon, Morgan turned to Sara sitting beside him. "You've been awfully quiet for a while. Penny for your thoughts."

"I've been thinking about our store. Ever since I was a little girl, I've wanted to be a storekeeper."

"So you've told me, but why?"

"Momma took me into a store in Lexington, Tennessee, when I was little. It smelled of coffee—spicy and exotic. Momma bought coffee beans and poured them into the store's big red coffee grinder with fancy iron legs. She turned the wheels and opened a small drawer in the grinder. And there it was, perfectly ground coffee. It seemed like magic."

"Are you sure you didn't just fall in love with the coffee grinder?" Morgan chuckled.

Sara smiled. "No, it was the store. I wandered the aisles admiring every shelf—cans of different fruits in neat rows, colorful cigar boxes, barrels of flour, stacks of blankets, buckets of candy, and things I couldn't even identify. When Momma said it was time to leave, I cried. That store reappears, even now, in my dreams."

"We'll recreate that store together in Dallas, honey," Morgan said.

"That's what I'm hoping. When I was older, I talked Papa into teaching me how to keep the horse farm's books. I knew I'd need to be a good bookkeeper to run a store."

"You're going to have your dream, Sara. We're going to be storekeepers and build a good life together in Dallas."

Sara looked up at her new husband. "Yes we will. I've been arranging the shelves in my mind. What goes where. Oh, and I really want a red step stool, so I can reach the top shelves. Just think, Morgan, our very own business. Papa said we're likely to have to work from can't see to can't see. I don't care, it will be worth it."

Morgan dipped his dimpled chin and met her brown eyes. "Don't mind working from dawn to dusk, as long as we're together."

Memphis was a long, narrow city built on a sandstone bluff overlooking the Mississippi River. As they rode into town and approached the river, Sara said, "I've never seen so many riverboats and barges. And look . . ." She pointed at a string of docks piled high with bales of cotton. "Or so much cotton. Gosh, there are people everywhere. Memphis is busy as a beehive."

"How large is Memphis?" Morgan asked Sara's papa.

"Don't know for sure, but five or six years ago it had about nine thousand people. Been growin' fast, prob'ly double that now. Major river port for cotton, hogs and wheat."

"Let's see," he said, "the wagonmaker and mercantile store we want should be just around the corner." Leaving Sara and Morgan at the store to buy their covered wagon and supplies for the road, Papa went elsewhere to negotiate for four teams of oxen.

The Memphis wagonmaker assured the young couple that their wagon was strong, solid, and made of seasoned hardwood. "It should handle river crossings, but be sure to keep the slats well caulked. There are hooks for tar buckets, and I oiled the double-canvas cover. It's as rainproof as I could make it."

"Spare parts under the wagon?" Morgan bent down to look.

"Yes, and I threw in an extra wheel, water barrel, and two big coils of heavy rope for you."

Sara saw that the wagon was straight sided with a flatbed about ten feet wide and sides rising two feet high. "It looks smaller than the old Conestoga wagons."

"Yep. It's also a bit lighter than a Conestoga, but it's strong. You can pack twenty-five hundred pounds, give or take. With a load like that, you'll need four ox teams and some good luck to deal with rough roads and river crossings."

Are we trying to take too much?

The wagon seller delivered the wagon and the newlyweds to the farm where Papa had bought eight oxen. After yoking and hitching the ox teams to the new wagon, Sara and Morgan drove to an open field on a road out of Memphis where the other Texas travelers were gathering. Papa followed with the Pennington horse-farm wagon full of their supplies for the trip.

"There's a lot to load," Morgan said as they looked at the mountain of goods piled in the farm wagon. Sara made a complete list as they packed their new wagon. The least-accessible space was filled with initial merchandise intended for the Dallas store the newlyweds planned to open. They'd order more goods after arrival. Once these things were safely packed, they began to load what they'd need on the road. "We have two hundred pounds of flour, one hundred pounds of bacon, fifty pounds of coffee, twenty pounds of cornmeal, ten pounds of salt, and twenty one-pound cones of sugar wrapped in blue indigo paper," Sara said, as she pulled the pencil from where she had tucked it in the coiled braid of her light brown hair and added the items to her list.

Morgan said, "I just put in dried beans, dried fruit, chipped beef, vinegar, pickles, mustard, rice, and saleratus. Still need to pack the tea, syrup, and the cans of tomatoes you asked for."

"This is a rolling pantry for sure," Papa said as he handed Sara a box of a dozen cans of tomatoes.

Sara found a spot for the box. "What we don't use on the trail can go into store inventory."

A store clerk had helped Sara choose a kettle, fry pan, mixing bowl, coffeepot, tin plates, and cups, plus knives, forks, and spoons. "Better add a spider Dutch oven too." The store clerk held up a large, three-legged pot with a lid. "The three spider legs keep the pot above the coals."

"Hmmm . . . good idea."

"You may also want a couple of long-forked iron rods, a cross rod, and hook to hold your kettle and Dutch oven above the fire," the clerk added. "If you use sticks, you'll be pulling food out of the ashes when the sticks burn." Sara had added the suggested items to her order, along with a washtub, washboard, two flat irons, soap, starch, and two good brooms. As all this went into the wagon, Sara's list grew.

Morgan had purchased and packed items he'd need: two kerosene lamps, lamp oil, a shovel, pick, and handsaw to use on the road, an extra yoke and chains, shot, powder, caps, and pistol cartridges. Sara wrote them down as they went in the wagon.

Sara had asked for two reams of letter paper, a box of steel writing pens, ink, a half dozen memorandum books, and two dozen lead pencils. "We'll want these things for record keeping at the store."

Morgan ran his hands through his thick, blond hair, and his broad shoulders moved with laughter as he watched Sara making her list. "You are a record keeper, honey."

Papa chuckled, "She sure is—a record keeper and list maker. Has been all her life."

As they finished loading, Papa turned to speak to Morgan. Working on the other side of the wagon, Sara heard the exchange. "Young man, I'm trusting you to take care of Sara. She's still part little girl, although she has a strength she doesn't yet know exists."

"Yes sir, Mr. Pennington. I will."

Listening, Sara grinned. *I'll never be totally grown up to Papa. Always his little girl.*

Papa wasn't through with his comments. "Morgan, Sara may be only five feet, two inches tall and mighty sweet, but her temper is big and flares like a firecracker."

"Yes, sir. I've learned Sara can be feisty."

"Yep . . . Well, good luck, son. Take care of each other."

On the other side of the wagon, Sara smiled.

The wagon finally ready, Sara and her papa shared a tearful goodbye. "We'll sure miss you, Punkin. Write your momma and me soon as you can." Papa hugged Sara with tears in his eyes.

Her arms around him, Sara promised, through her tears, "I'll write as soon as we get there. I love you, Papa. Thank you for everything." He squeezed her hard, kissed her cheek, and shook Morgan's hand. He then returned to the family farm wagon with the easy-going lope of a horseman. Sara's eyes didn't leave the farm wagon until it was out of sight.

Goodbyes said, Sara and Morgan walked to the middle of the fallow field. There, they joined the other travelers for a meeting with the wagon train captain, Paul Pollard. Captain Pollard had helped organize the group and was an experienced traveler. During the '49 gold rush, he had made a trek by wagon train to California from Kentucky and had returned on horseback.

Pollard was a medium-sized man with receding brown hair, a long Roman nose, and a wide mouth. Not a handsome man, Sara thought. *Despite his looks, he carries himself with authority . . . his deep voice is strong as black coffee.* Sara thought his voice alone invited confidence. *I want to say, "Yes, sir," every time he speaks.* She smiled. *But his ears do look like they might flap in the wind.*

Captain Pollard gave them a brief idea of what to expect. "Well folks, we got twelve wagons plus four men on horseback planning to travel. We'll leave Memphis tomorrow, cross the border into Arkansas, travel southwest about 150 miles across swamps and prairies to Little Rock. Then, we turn west along the old Indian Trail of Tears through the Arkansas River bottom to Fort Smith, another 160 miles or so. There, we'll cross from Arkansas into Indian Territory."

A question came from someone in the group. "Will we be in danger in Indian Territory?"

"Don't worry. There are treaties and the Indians are peaceful at this point. The road through Indian Territory will take us a couple hundred miles through the Cherokee, Choctaw, and Chickasaw Nations to the Red River and the Colbert Ferry crossing into Texas."

"How far do we have to go in Texas to get to Dallas?"

"Once in Texas, we go down the Preston Road fifty or sixty miles to Dallas, part of the Peters Colony. The good news is some of our trails, like the Preston Road, are first-class roads."

"What are first-class roads?" The question came from the front of the crowd.

"Thirty-foot-wide dirt trails. The tree stumps in 'em are only about six inches high. Other parts of our trail will be rougher, with higher stumps, so if you have things stored under the wagon make sure you have a foot's clearance. Any of you traveling on from Dallas to Austin or San Antonio will just stay on the Preston Road."

Morgan asked, "Tree stumps?"

"Yep. There'll be plenty of tree stumps in the roads all along the way."

Another question came from the back of the crowd. "What's the land like around Dallas? As good as we've been told?"

Pollard chuckled and rubbed his clean-shaven chin. "Not sure what you've been told. We'll come into Texas through the cross timbers, a forested area some people call the 'cast-iron forest' because it's so dense. Dallas is cross timbers to the west and blackland prairie to the east. Best of both worlds, I'd say. Plenty of fertile farmland on one side, plenty of wood on the other."

Someone else in the group shouted, "How long will our trip be?"

"Hard to say. The first few days we'll shoot for twenty miles a day to settle the oxen into the routine. After that, we'll only travel about fifteen miles a day to avoid wearing them out. Also, a lot depends on the trail conditions. There will be days we can't travel due to breakdowns, weather, flooding, maybe even sickness. Oxen will have to rest some along the way, so will we. We'll waste a lot of time waiting to ford rivers. We'll spend several days in Little Rock and in Fort Smith so you can replenish supplies, fix wagons, and so on. I'd say plan on about three months, give or take.

"We'll spend tonight in the field here and have another meeting tomorrow morning before we leave. I'll be prepared to answer more questions then. We do need to decide today whether to travel on Sundays." The majority of the travelers voted to keep moving seven days a week, but to take an extra hour Sundays at noon for the reading of scriptures and the singing of hymns. Two families traveling in their wagons were not happy with this and huffily announced they would, "wait for a more religious train which would honor the Sabbath by not traveling on Sundays." That left ten wagons and the four men on horseback.

Before the meeting ended, the remaining travelers introduced themselves. Most were craftsmen looking for new opportunities in Texas. Sara jotted down names and professions in her notebook as the men introduced themselves: Captain Pollard, a cooper; Butler, a gunsmith; Sims, a watchmaker; Fisher, a tailor; Radcliff, a blacksmith; Fowler, a jeweler; Flannigan, a stonemason; Davis and Burnam, both lawyers; Thornton and Tanner, both farmers; and three bachelor brothers named Foy, dairymen who were traveling together. Morgan introduced himself as storekeeper. Two young men, who would travel on horseback, introduced themselves as the Johnson twins and didn't indicate a profession. Sara pegged them as ne'er-do-wells. Altogether twenty men, counting Morgan, two grandpas, and an adult cousin traveling with their families. Women and children weren't introduced, but based on visiting at the meeting, Sara guessed the wives and other female family members totaled thirteen or fourteen. The children were playing and never still enough to count accurately. *Maybe twenty?*

The dairymen are the most interesting of the group. They had introduced themselves as the Foy brothers: Matthew, Mark, and Luke. Someone in the group had shouted, "Where's John?" Mark Foy was quick with a response, "John is a bookkeeper back in Memphis. Didn't want to come. You can tease us all you want about our names. We're used to it. Our older sister calls us Genesis, Exodus, Leviticus, and Numbers. You probably can't top that." This generated a round of laughter.

Sara turned to Morgan. "The Foy's have a sense of humor, I like them already. Suspect I'd like their sister too. Wonder what she's named."

"Deuteronomy, maybe? Hopefully not Lamentations," Morgan's dimple appeared with his crooked grin.

Sara stifled a laugh. "Some books of the Bible just don't work as people's names, do they? Can you imagine calling, 'Ecclesiastes, supper's ready'?" By this time, they were drawing attention with their whispering and giggling. Sara lifted one finger to her lips.

That night they slept in the wagon. Morgan took Sara in his arms and whispered, "Mrs. Darnell, tomorrow we start an exciting new adventure together."

Sara kissed him, sliding her fingers into his curly blond hair and lingering over the kiss. When she pulled back, she said, "Morgan Darnell, I love you, but no man should have such beautiful, thick eyelashes. It's just not fair." Laughing, she swatted him with her pillow. Morgan tossed the pillow aside and began to tickle her ribs.

It was hard to tell who was laughing harder. "Say you love my eyelashes and I'll stop tickling."

"I do . . . oh stop . . . love . . . your lashes . . . ." The words were caught up in Sara's laughter, which quickly became hiccups. Morgan kissed her hiccups away, and they slept in each other's arms, ready for the unknown adventures that would begin the next day.

Sara had filled a trunk with three practical calico dresses, aprons, modest nightclothes, stockings, underclothing, two extra bonnets, and a straw hat. Her wedding dress, wrapped in brown kraft paper with lavender sachets, had been safely tucked in the bottom of the trunk with a nice day dress. A small hope chest contained treasures from home —carefully wrapped china, a silver tray, a family photograph, good table linens, two sets of linen sheets, and Sara's small cache of jewelry. Morgan had packed a large carpetbag with his clothing. A box contained a winter coat for him, a cape for Sara, and warm hats and scarves for each of them. A second trunk, containing towels, bed linens, pillows, and quilts, was packed for easy access on the trail. Pockets in the canvas walls of the wagons held soap, twine, matches in a large jar, buckskin strips, needles for mending leather, and an awl. The large water barrel hung on the side of the wagon. Morgan's shotgun, powder, lead-shot, were secured in a box under the wagon seat, as was his pistol.

The next morning, packed and ready, they lined up in the field with the other nine wagons and four riders bound for Texas. Each wagon had "Gone to Texas" painted on its canvas cover in foot-high black letters. Sara had clapped her hands in delight when Morgan had crossed out Texas on their sign, replacing it with "Dallas." They pointed their oxen toward the Red River—Texas's northern boundary—and were "Gone to Dallas."

Sara did not expect to arrive alone, her husband dead.

John Henry Adams came into Sara and Morgan's lives the first evening on the trail. After the wagon train had passed from Tennessee into Arkansas, and the wagons had circled for the night, Sara and Morgan heard a deep voice shouting, "Hello the wagons!" They watched as an unshaven, middle-aged man, wearing denim pants, a fringed buckskin jacket, and a wide-brimmed hat, rode into camp. He was mounted on an Indian pony and leading a pack mule. Sara and Morgan joined the crowd that gathered around him.

"Evenin' folks. Name's John Henry Adams. I'm a former Texas Ranger headed back to Texas. Gets lonely on the trail. Be mighty obliged if I could travel with you as far as Dallas. If you want to discuss my joinin' amongst yourselves, I'll just sit here on my horse for awhile."

The men from the wagons stepped aside to quietly discuss Adam's request. Sara linked her arm through Morgan's and walked over with him. "Miss Curiosity." Morgan said, looking down at her with a grin. She was the only woman in the group.

"Yes. I'm part of this trip too." Sara said.

Captain Pollard was speaking. "When we cross out of Arkansas, we'll be in Indian Territory. There are treaties, but we've been told the peace is fragile. I'm for lettin' Adams join us. I saw a muzzle-loading flintlock rifle in the scabbard on his horse, and—"

One of the Johnson twins interrupted. "Looks like he's wearing a Colt Paterson on his hip." All eyes looked back at Adams.

Pollard continued, "Yep, can't hurt to have another man along, especially an experienced frontiersman who's well armed. Everybody in favor of lettin' him join us?" Heads nodded. And with that, John Henry Adams joined the four other single men trailing the wagons on horseback.

In the first few days, Sara quickly settled into a routine. She began her days before dawn clicking though her mental list: get dressed, gather wood, start the morning cooking fire, put water on for coffee, and cook breakfast. By the time she had warmed the beans, boiled the coffee, cooked pancakes, and fried the bacon, Morgan had yoked the eight oxen and was ready for breakfast.

"This meal preparation on the ground is killing me. All morning, I'm squatting, stooping, and going back and forth between the wagon and the fire," Sara said, rubbing her lower back. Morgan put his hands on her shoulders, turned her around, and began to gently massage her back.

"Oh, that feels good, don't stop . . . ."

"I understand, honey. While you're doing all that, I'm trying to gather eight oxen that aren't eager to be back in their yokes and hitched to the wagon. I'm glad we're not goin' all the way to Oregon. No wonder they say folks arrive there exhausted."

"I guess traveling takes some getting used to." Sara held up a plate of bacon, beans, and pancakes. "The good news is your breakfast's ready."

After eating, Sara heated more water, cleaned the breakfast dishes, and hurried to fold and repack the bed makings. She realized the sun was rising and rushed to prepare something that could be eaten cold at the midday nooner meal before Captain Pollard rang his cowbell and called for the wagons to line up at six thirty to begin the day's trip. *I need to make the nooner meal the night before to save time.*

To avoid adding extra weight for the oxen to pull, Morgan and Sara usually walked. Morgan led the oxen by holding the first team's yoke. Sara walked beside or behind the wagon, collecting kindling for the cooking fires and tossing the sticks and dry weeds into a cowhide sling fastened under the back of the wagon. If wild onions or a berry patch were spotted, the word would circulate, and the ladies would congregate to pick quickly, so as not to lose track of the moving wagons.

Sara looked forward to the circling of the wagons at the end of each day. After a camping area had been selected for the night, the lead wagon would make a right-hand turn from the trail. The second wagon would turn to the left. These two wagons would move forward in a semicircle until they faced each other. The remaining seven wagons would follow, alternating to the right and left, creating a circle. The first night, Sara thought, *It's almost a parade. Add a bit of music and some flags, and it could be a celebration of a successful day.*

Each evening Morgan joined other men tying ropes to the tops of the wagon wheels to fence the gaps between the wagons, turning the circle into a corral. Once watered and allowed to graze, as many oxen as would fit were led into the corral for the night. Others joined the horses outside the circle. Since the men took turns as night guards, they also kept an eye on the livestock.

The first night on the road, Sara had said, "I thought we'd camp inside the circle rather than outside it."

"I did too. But Captain Pollard said that, since we're not traveling through dangerous territory, it's smarter to use the inside of the circle as a corral. Campin' outside the circle gives us more room. If we keep our fires burning low durin' the night, animals shouldn't bother us. We're dependent on our oxen. Corralling as many of them as possible keeps 'em safe, and we can gather 'em faster each mornin'. Guess the only worry with havin' oxen inside the circle is if somethin' causes a stampede. Our wagons could be overturned."

"That could be a disaster," Sara said.

"Yep. It could."

Traveling through the Arkansas Delta, the land was flat and marshy with occasional cypress swamps. "I've never seen cone-shaped trees like these, Morgan. They grow in the water and they must be a hundred feet tall."

"The cypress sure don't look like the trees at home, do they?" Morgan said. "Did you know the wide-flaring roots at the base of the trees are called the knees?"

"Trees with knees?" Sara laughed.

That night, sitting in the dim light of a fading campfire, Sara watched the light from the moon dance in the surrounding marsh water creating eerie colors and making ghostly shadows from the trees. *The cypress look like other-worldly creatures.* She shivered. Later, she lay listening to the occasional sounds of splashing water and the constant croaking of frogs. As she fell asleep, she wondered what creatures prowled the swamp.

Two days later, they moved into the delta prairie. Captain Pollard told them that this area was most likely the richest farmland in the state of Arkansas. "As we travel, you'll see some farms and maybe a few cotton plantations."

Sara quickly found that her evenings were as busy as the early mornings: water containers needed filling, the cooking fire had to be started, bread baked, supper prepared, fruit stewed for another day, the nooner meal prepared—to be eaten cold the next day—the bed made ready for sleep. And after all this, if it were light enough, berries or other edible plants located and picked.

Much to her distress, Sara discovered that cooking over an outdoor fire was far different than cooking on an iron stove. One evening, muttering in frustration over a badly scorched loaf of bread that was still only half cooked inside, she looked up in surprise when a woman's voice said, "Campfire cooking can be a challenge, can't it?"

Sara stood and held up her ruined loaf. "I'm not much of a cook anyway, but I had no idea how hard this would be. I don't even know what I've done wrong. By the way, I'm Mrs. Morgan Darnell, but please call me Sara."

The other woman smiled. "I'm Miss Cecilia Stewart. My sister, Effie, is Michael Butler's wife. We're just around the circle in wagon number two. There are plenty of hands to cook at our wagon because my two nieces are helping my sister, so I'm available to help you, if you'd like."

Sara sighed in relief. "Please. I'm struggling."

"Then let's see what we can do to get your supper ready. What are you planning to cook?"

As Cecilia spoke, Sara studied her. She was a slim woman, probably in her forties, with an almost musical voice. Her calico dress looked freshly pressed, and her rich, brown hair was neatly tucked into her bonnet. By comparison, Sara realized her own hair was straggling out of her bonnet. Her pinafore apron was smudged with soot from the fire, and the sash was untied and trailing behind in the dirt. *How can this woman be so neat?*

"I'm not sure what to cook . . . just knew I needed bread, so I started with it."

"Do you have any dried chipped beef?"

"Yes."

"Good. We can make a soup with the beef, canned tomatoes, and wild onions. Oh, and rice. And we'll need a small piece of bacon. Do you have those fixin's?"

"I do."

"Let's make the soup first, it can simmer while we bake the bread."

Taking Sara's large cook pot, Cecilia hung it on the pot hook above the fire and tossed in the piece of bacon. She browned the chipped beef in the small amount of bacon fat which that had accumulated in the pot. She added water, the undrained canned tomatoes, and the onions. She showed Sara how to chop the onions on brown kraft paper, using the wagon seat as a work surface. "We'll leave all this to cook for awhile. The beef will moisten and flavor the broth. Then we can throw the rice in to simmer until it is soft."

"It already smells good. Thank you so much, Cecilia."

Once the soup was bubbling in the pot, they turned their attention to the bread. Cecilia looked at Sara's ruined loaf. "You can maybe rescue some of this. If you tear off the burned portion and break the rest into bite-size chunks—even the doughy part—you can add the chunks, along with onion and some salt and pepper, to another can of tomatoes and stew it all. It will be a bit mushy but would make a good lunch even if it's not hot."

Hmm . . . wouldn't have thought of that. "It should work." Sara was feeling better about supper. *Maybe it won't be the disaster I was afraid of.*

"Let's make a pan of camp bread. It'll be quick. Are you saving your bacon grease?"

"Yes, I pour it into a big can."

"Good. We'll make bread to eat tonight with enough left to have at lunch tomorrow with the tomatoes.

Sara tried to reach a large bowl and frying pan stored in a box in the wagon. Her arms were too short.

"You are so petite, Sara. I'm pretty tall, I bet I can reach."

Soon, with the cooking utensils in hand, the bread making began. Following Cecilia's instructions, Sara mixed about four cups of flour with a couple of tablespoons of sugar, a tablespoon of salt, and two teaspoons of saleratus for leavening. She mixed in half a dozen tablespoons of the solidified bacon fat—the only shortening she had. Once that was evenly mixed with the dry ingredients, she worked in a cup of water, using her hands.

Cecilia continued her instructions. "Roll out the dough on the same brown kraft paper you used to chop the onion. If the bread picks up a bit of onion flavor, so much the better. First, flour the paper and your rolling pin a little bit so the dough doesn't stick."

"How thin should I roll it?"

"Pretty thin, about a quarter of an inch and round enough to just fit in the bottom of your skillet. You should have several rounds."

While Sara rolled the dough, Cecilia pulled hot coals to the very edge of the fire, creating a hot, flat cooking surface. Once the dough was all rolled and the coals had cooled to medium hot, Sara dropped the first round of dough into the frying pan and set it on the coals.

"It should be ready to flip in about five minutes. We'll watch to make sure it doesn't brown too fast. In the meantime, better toss the rice into the soup."

While they waited to turn the bread, Sara thanked Cecilia again. "I don't know what I'd have done without your help tonight. How did you learn to cook on a campfire?"

"I grew up in Pennsylvania, but when I was a teenager we moved to Kentucky. My mom had died, and as the oldest girl, the cooking fell to me. Like you, I could cook on a stove. Had to learn outdoor cooking by trial and error. And there was a lot of error."

"So there's hope for me?"

"Absolutely. You should have seen my first bread-making attempts. Pretty funny, although they didn't seem so at the time."

Sure enough, after being flipped and baked for another five minutes, the bread rounds came out of the pan golden brown and perfectly cooked. By then, Cecilia's family was calling her for supper.

"I'm so grateful, Cecilia. Thanks to you, Morgan and I'll have a good meal tonight instead of a disaster."

"I enjoyed cooking with you, Sara. I'll visit tomorrow to see if I can help again."

"Please. That would be wonderful!"

"Almost forgot, when you're ready to eat the bread, just slice it like a pie."

Sara watched as Cecilia walked back across the wagon circle. *I've made my first "Gone to Dallas" friend.*

At the end of each day's travel, after evening camps had been set up and suppers made and eaten, Morgan often wandered a short distance away from the circle to where many of the men gathered to visit, some playing cards, others just talking. Drinking was a pastime for a few, especially the Johnson twins, a couple of rowdy young men who—Sara had heard on the grapevine—had already picked quarrels over imagined slights.

Shortly after John Henry Adams joined the wagon train, Morgan came back from the male gathering outside the circle with stories about the man. "He was in the Battle of San Jacinto back in '36. Told me the craziest story. Said the Texicans fiddled their way to victory."

"They what?" Sara was busy pulling their quilts out of the wagon to air before bedtime and wasn't sure she'd heard Morgan clearly.

"Fiddled, you know, with fiddles. When Sam Houston was ready to march on the Mexican army, he wanted marching music. John Henry told me two fiddlers, a father and son named Davis, stepped forward and began to fiddle. Guess what they played?"

Some military march?"

"Nope." Morgan, pleased to have a surprise answer, paused for effect. "Will Ya Come to the Bower?"

Sara laughed, gave the final quilt a shake, and temporarily draped it over a bush beside the wagon. "A romantic ballad is a strange choice, but I guess it worked. The Texicans won, right?"

"Yes, and the battle lasted just eighteen minutes."

After several days with the wagon train, John Henry began to join Sara and Morgan occasionally around the evening campfire after supper. Frequently, Morgan would drink his cup of coffee, then saunter off to join the Johnson twins, who spent the evenings drinking and playing poker. One night, Morgan left to play cards, leaving John Henry and Sara talking about the day's events over the evening's final tin cups of hot coffee. Sara lifted the coffeepot from the coals on the edge of the fire to refill John Henry's cup. The flames of the fire illuminated John Henry as he blew on his coffee to cool it. His salt-and-pepper hair framed a craggy, middle-aged face. The shadows played on a nose that had been broken, maybe more than once. His skin was dark from the sun, but it was his eyebrows that captured Sara's attention. *Why*

is it that at a certain age some men's eyebrows stop sitting sedately above their eyes and take on a life of their own? Mostly gray, like the stubble on his face, John Henry's eyebrows were out of control. The individual hairs had grown long and created a wild fringe above his hazel eyes. Somehow it added to his toughness. He was how she imagined a Texas Ranger should look.

Sara refilled her own cup. "What was it like being a ranger? What did you do?"

"We spent a lot of boring time in the saddle, but it could get mighty exciting." John Henry was so soft spoken, Sara had to lean in to hear him. "After the Texas Revolution, Comanche raids increased. Soldiers were scarce as hens' teeth, not nearly enough of 'em. So, we fought Indians, rescued as many Indian captives as we could, and generally tried to maintain the peace."

"It sounds violent."

"Had to be to get the job done. I was honored to serve under Jack Coffee Hays, a fine man and fearless fighter. With his leadership, we patrolled from San Antonio north along the Colorado River and along the Texas-Mexico border. It was lawless along the border."

"What was happening?"

A gang of Mexican border jumpers rampaged on the Texas side, robbin' and murderin' at will. We were charged with stoppin' the gang—dead or alive, which we did. A corrupt Mexican army officer led the bandits and was getting rich from the spoils. I was shot in the final fight with him."

"You were shot? I've never known anyone who has been shot . . . although, there was a neighbor back in Tennessee who shot himself in the foot climbing over a fence while hunting." Sara wrinkled her brow and then pursed her lips in a thoughtful expression. She shook her head. "But I don't think that counts."

John Henry's eyebrows shot up, and his laugh was deep and genuine. "Best not say that to him, he might take offense. My wound wasn't severe. Bullet went clean through the flesh of my left arm. Healed pretty quick. Been shot more than once. Always lived to tell."

"Why did you quit rangering?"

John Henry looked down and became still. He sat so long without moving or speaking, that Sara started fidgeting with her apron strings. John Henry finally looked up, his eyes were wet. Sara doubted she'd ever seen a sadder face. His voice was hoarse and even softer, almost a whisper. "Sara," He paused and his voice broke, "cholera took my wife and fifteen-year-old daughter in Austin three years ago. It has been hard times for me since. In my grief, I lost myself in my rangerin'." His pain was almost tangible.

Sara's eyes filled with tears. She didn't know how to comfort him. "I'm so sorry, John Henry, I can't imagine how awful it must have been to lose them both."

He looked into her eyes and tried to smile. "Six months ago, I quit the Texas Rangers and just took to wandering. Trying to find myself again, I guess. It's time now to rebuild my life but not as a ranger. I don't miss the fighting and killing." He looked Sara's way. His face was lit by the crackling fire, and he gave her a small smile. "I do miss the panola."

"What in the world is panola?"

"Every ranger was given a supply of the stuff. It's parched corn that's been spiced and sweetened. Best allayer of thirst there is. Suck on a mouthful of panola and you forget you're thirsty. That's a blessing when you spend days in the saddle."

"Well, we could certainly use some panola on this trip. Aside from maybe learning to make panola, what are your plans when you get home to Texas?"

"The grief will always be with me, Sara, but it's time to make a new life. There's plenty of open grazing land near the Trinity River, and I aim to be a cattleman. Sold my land grant from fightin' in the Texas Revolution. Got me a young partner and some cow chasers rounding up a herd of wild longhorn cattle down near Mexico. They'll drive 'em up to Dallas. Hope to break some wild mustangs too. Already registered my brand. It's the T-Lazy-R. The T is for Texas and the R is for rangers."

"Lazy R?"

"Think of the R as laying on its back. That's a lazy letter in a brand. I just like the look and sound of it . . . T-Lazy-R."

A night breeze arrived to ruffle the grass around the wagons and the upper branches of the trees whipped around. The smoke of the dying fire followed the wind and their eyes started to sting. John Henry stood. "Guess I'd better meander back to my bedroll. Thanks for the company, Sara. Good night."

"Good night, John Henry. If you see Morgan, remind him that we start early tomorrow, and I need some help at the wagon before we can go to bed."

"I'll watch for him."

On another evening, watching the moon rise over the trees along a wooded creek bottom, with the sound of mockingbirds in the background, John Henry had said, "Sara, my daughter would've been just a few years younger than you, had she lived. She was smart as a whip. When she set her mind to do somethin', it got done." John Henry's voice broke. "Her momma called her 'Miss Saucy.' Lord, I miss 'em both somethin' terrible."

After a few days on the road, Sara discovered a source of milk, buttermilk, and butter. The three Foy brothers—Matthew, Mark, and Luke—traveling in wagon number seven, had two cows. Gertie and Bessie trailed behind the Foys' wagon and were milked twice a day. Morning milk, the brothers told Sara, went to fill a churn that bounced around all day, creating butter and buttermilk. Extra morning milk made the rounds to the settlers' children, alternating days between odd-numbered wagons and even-numbered wagons. Eager children met the "milkmen" each morning, standing in front of their wagons with their tin cups. The evening milking was bartered for mending or laundering services or for food. Pies topped the brothers' list of highly desired items. Lining up with several others to trade for milk and butter, Sara asked, "Would you trade several days' worth of butter and buttermilk for three brand-new sets of suspenders?" A deal was struck.

The next day Sara surprised Morgan with buttermilk biscuits, baked in the iron skillet and slathered in butter. "I traded three pair of red suspenders from our store merchandise in order to make these, just for you. Was it worth it?"

"For hot, buttered biscuits, you bet! Darlin', you're the best!" Morgan took a big bite of biscuit. Butter dripped down his chin.

"I aim to keep the man I love happy." Sara looked up at him. He had a face that caught your eye. It was . . . what was the phrase she read in art books? . . . perfectly symmetrical. He looked down at her and his thin, straight mouth turned into a dimpled smile. Her knees went weak. *How could I not fall in love with him?*

As the wagons moved through Arkansas, they arrived at the St. Francis River. Several men rode out to find the ferry or a place to ford. Sara and Cecilia joined the women carrying their kettles, washtubs, and piles of laundry to the riverbank. After building a fire, the women took turns heating water. "We'll never get washtubs full of hot water, but we can at least warm the water a bit," Cecilia said, as they took their turns adding their kettles to a fire on the riverbank. "Our hands may not chap so badly and the clothes will be a little cleaner if the water's not so cold."

Sara tucked a loose stand of hair into her bonnet. "I've already given up trying to stay clean on the trail. I wish I'd packed more clothes. The hems of my skirts stay black with dirt, and when we can wash, nothing seems to come quite clean."

Cecilia added the kettle of warm water to the river water in her washtub. "I think we are destined to be dirty until we reach Dallas."

"Yes, and it's not just clothes, it's everything. Yesterday, I bounced along on the wagon seat and stitched two new pillowcases from a bolt of dark calico fabric. Used some of what was supposed to have been store merchandise. Our white pillowcases were so disgraceful looking they are now in my ragbag."

Cecilia had rolled up her sleeves and was busy with her washboard. "At least this river has lots of big rocks where we can spread our laundry out to dry. Otherwise, we'd have to wear our wet clothes until they dried. I think the plan is to stay here for a day and rest. Maybe tonight after supper we ladies can find a place with enough privacy to bathe in the river. I think we'll have a full moon."

Sara looked up from her washing. "That would be heaven." As it turned out, the evening was used to bathe all the children in washtubs full of soapy river water and rinse them in the river. Cecilia and Sara pitched in to scrub little ones. "I think we are as wet as they are," Sara laughed as she tried to rinse a squirming toddler.

The next day the men scouting for a river crossing returned. Morgan was eager to share the news he'd heard with Sara. "They found a farm upriver, and the farmer directed them to a shallow spot with a gravel bottom where we can ford. It's closer than the St. Francis ferry, we can cross faster, and we'll save some money. He also told them it's still several days travel to the White River. Then we head southwest to Little Rock. From there, we travel along the Arkansas River all the way to Fort Smith and into Indian Territory."

Sara took a deep breath. "Indian Territory . . . I don't know whether to be excited or a bit frightened."

Morgan slipped his arm around her waist and briefly rested his chin on the top of her head. "Don't worry, sweetheart, I'm sure it will be fine."

The wagon train stayed by the river another day to let the people and livestock rest. Morgan left with most of the other men to fish and hunt. That evening fish and venison were shared among all the travelers. Sara roasted a shank of venison and made stew, saving the marrow bone for Morgan. As they ate, Sara realized the entire camp smelled of roasting meat. *What a wonderful smell!* That afternoon she had rolled out piecrust on the wagon seat and made a pie with stewed, dried apples. "It's apple-and-mosquito pie. As I was ready to roll out the piecrust, a swarm of mosquitoes arrived and covered the ball of dough. They refused to leave, so I finally had to roll it out, mosquitoes and all." Morgan ate two huge pieces.

"Thank you, Sara. Best dinner we've had on the road. I wouldn't have guessed apple-mosquito pie would be so good." He smiled, then smothered a large belch.

"Certainly sounds like you enjoyed it. Guess it's better to eat the mosquitoes than to have them terrorizing us."

The fording of the St. Francis River began smoothly. Captain Pollard made a quick inspection of each wagon in the line to be sure that loads were evenly distributed. "An uneven load can cause a wagon to tip in the water or on a slope," he told Morgan and Sara. "Looks like you are weighted too much on one side. Better balance your load and tie down anything large and loose."

Morgan and Sara were still shifting things inside their wagon when the wagons behind them were ready to ford. As Morgan lashed down the two trunks, Sara watched the wagons behind them pull around one by one, join the single file line, and drive into the narrow, gravel-bottomed river. The water just reached the tops of the large wagon wheels. After splashing across, the oxen climbed a gentle slope on the far side. The men splashed through the fast-moving water leading the oxen, while the women sat in the wagons and held the reins. With their wagon now balanced, Morgan and Sara entered the murky water as the last wagon in the line, Morgan leading the animals and Sara holding the reins.

As the wagon in front of them reached midstream, Sara looked up from adjusting the reins in her hand and saw that ahead, two-year-old Lydia Sims had crawled to the open back of her family's wagon. Sara caught her breath as the child tried to stand and toppled head over heels into the river. *Oh no!* Although not deep, the swift current swept the small girl away. Sara shouted and pointed. Morgan saw the child, dropped the ox yoke, and swam after Lydia, who was now being bounced against some large rocks. By the time he reached the rocks, she had gone under. Diving down and coming up empty-handed twice, he finally found her small, lifeless body and began to struggle to shore. Her father, who had been leading his team, finally realized what was happening and swam after Morgan. Reaching the shore, Morgan lifted two-year-old Lydia out of the water and carried her up the sloping riverbank. Mrs. Sims' screams echoed across the water. Mr. Sims' frantic attempts to revive the small girl failed. Sara sat on the wagon seat while the water flowed around her, her eyes hot with tears. *So young. She had a whole life ahead of her.*

That night in bed Sara held Morgan close. "Why couldn't I save her, Sara?" She felt his tears on her shoulder.

"You did all you could. I'm proud of you and I love you, Morgan." *He wanted so much to save her. He's a good man.* He slept all night in her arms.

The following morning the travelers stood by the edge of the trail as tiny Lydia Sims, dressed in a ruffled, white dress with bows in her curled hair, was gently placed in a roughly-made wooden box lined with a small, blue blanket. At the last moment before the box was shut, her weeping mother slipped a small homemade doll into the child's arms. She was buried under a tree, there by the side of the trail, to the sound of hymns, scriptures, and mourning doves cooing in the trees. The mother, sick with grief, wept and could not be comforted. Sara listened as Michael Butler read a verse from Psalms. Lydia's father read a poem:

> "I send you up to God, my dear,
> never again to hold you near.
> He holds you in his gentle hand,
> while I remain upon the land.
> I'll keep you in my broken heart,
> and, so you see, we'll never part."

At the end of the burial service, rocks were piled on the small grave to protect it from animals. Lydia's father then planted a small, wooden cross. Sara realized how fragile life on the trail could be. *Just yesterday little Lydia was happy and healthy. How quickly we can lose the ones we love.* The wagon train continued that afternoon, but the settlers' mood was solemn. That evening Sara joined the line of ladies bringing condolences and food to the Sims. *It's all we know to do for broken hearts.*

Two days later Lydia Sim's father crossed the circle to Sara and Morgan's wagon to thank Morgan again for his attempt to save the small girl. "My wife wants to return to Tennessee. I can't say no. We're turnin' back. My God, I wish we'd never left." He shook Morgan's hand and nodded at Sara. As they lined up for the day, the line was one wagon shorter.

After leaving the St. Francis River, the wagon train crossed Crowley's Ridge, a narrow arc of rolling hills rising more than three hundred feet out of the grassy delta flatlands, and extending north to south. The ridge was covered with oak and hickory trees and an occasional tulip tree. As Sara walked along behind the wagon, she saw mountain ferns, yellow jasmine, and a crimson flower she didn't have a name for. A soft breeze blew across the ridge and Sara realized the ridge had fewer mosquitos than down on the delta. The wagons kicked up the heavy layer of fine silt that covered the ridge's top, leaving Sara's skirts brown with dust. The first morning on the ridge, Captain Pollard had sent a message down the line with his fifteen-year-old son, Daniel, a boy who looked much like his dad, with big ears and a large nose. *He must have inherited his freckles and shock of sandy hair from his momma.* "The silt is deep up here," the boy said. "Pa says to keep wagons twice as far apart as usual. Breathing too much dust is bad for the oxen." Morgan and Sara knew that keeping the animals healthy was important. They were dependent upon them.

Sara looked down from the ridge to the delta and saw cotton fields being planted by rows of slaves. Occasionally on the ridge, they'd pass a two-story, white-columned plantation house. When the trail turned west across the L'Anguille River, Sara and Morgan were relieved to see that the river crossing was a bridge. That evening Captain Pollard announced to the group that, despite their slow travel, they had reached the sixty-four-mile post west of Memphis. "Remember, we'll continue to keep our travel to about fifteen miles a day, so we don't wear the oxen out. Let me know if yours start lookin' tired out."

Morgan had named all eight of their oxen and seemed to know which one was which. Sara hadn't mastered matching names with each animal, but she thought the two leaders looked tired. *What do we do if one dies?*

It was whiskey and poker that caused Morgan and Sara's first argument. The second night on Crowley's Ridge, Morgan staggered back to the wagon very late, red eyed, his shirt untucked, his blond hair matted under a hat on backwards, and smelling of whiskey. Sara was preparing their bed when he stumbled in. To create a sheltered sleeping space, they'd learned to raise the wagon tongue and then spread an oiled canvas sheet over it to make a kind of tent. Quilts piled over a bedroll served as a mattress. Trying to help Sara, Morgan fumbled with the sheet, tangled himself in it, fell down, and banged his head on the wagon tongue. Shouting curses at the wagon, he tried to untangle himself. Sara pulled the sheet away, "I'll do this myself. You go sit down." After Sara made their bed, she turned to find Morgan passed out against a rear wagon wheel. Tempted to dump the last of the cold coffee on him, she resisted, not wanting to deal with the stains when she next washed clothes. Instead, she tossed a ladle of water over his head. Sputtering, he struggled to stand, then stumbled his way to the front of the wagon. Sara slipped into bed.

"I lost it, Sara," he mumbled as he crawled into their makeshift tent and tried in vain to creep under a quilt beside her. "Lost, lost . . ."

The strong smell of whiskey on his breath made Sara turn her head away. "Lost what?"

"Part of our stake. You, you know, a hun'erd dollars lost . . . money . . . for the sshtore. But I'll winner . . ." he hiccuped. "Yes, I'll win it back . . . tom . . . 'rrow." He rolled over and began to snore.

He . . . what? . . . Lost the money for our store?

Sara sat up, shook him hard by the shoulder. "You did what? We agreed you'd only gamble with two dollars. How could you lose so much of our money for the store?"

"Sorry . . . sorry. Don't be mad. I'll play again, win . . . win it back." He closed his eyes.

"The dickens you can!" Sara jerked him into a sitting position, causing him to whack his head on the wagon tongue for a second time. "Give me the rest of the money. Right now! What do you think will happen to us if we arrive in Dallas penniless because you squandered our money playing some dumb card game with those two idiot Johnson boys? Did it not occur to you they probably cheat? Give me the rest of the money right this minute!"

Frowning, Morgan crawled out of their improvised tent, stood swaying, and tried to empty his pockets. Coins spilled onto the ground and rolled under the wagon. "Where'd they go?" he said, squinting at the ground.

Sara sighed. "Never mind, I'll get them."

While Sara retrieved coins, Morgan managed to climb into the wagon. After much fumbling, he dug paper money from a tin can hidden in the wagon and handed it to Sara.

"Get back in bed and go to sleep. From the looks of you, you'll have one heck of a headache tomorrow, and we have miles to cover and a creek to ford before tomorrow night."

As he crawled back into their bed, under the wagon tongue, Sara climbed into the wagon and tucked the retrieved money safely away in a tea tin buried under her brown-paper-wrapped wedding dress at the bottom of her locked trunk. She then replaced the key on its chain around her neck.

Sara resisted the urge to cry. *Thank heavens I hid Grandma's money. Wanted to surprise Morgan when we got to Dallas. Most likely, it'll be our salvation.*

The next morning, after leaving the sixty-four-mile post, Sara was still angry over the loss of their funds. Giving Morgan the silent treatment, she climbed onto the wagon seat beside him. The spring day was mild, and wild-flowers lined the rough, rocky trail, creating large patches of color. Morgan sat on the wagon seat, his head hanging. He slipped his arm around her shoulders and pulled her close. "I'm sorry about the money, honey. You're right, I was foolish."

Sara felt her anger slipping away. She remembered her momma saying, "You can't help who you fall in love with." Sara guessed that was true. She'd fallen hard for Morgan when he'd arrived in Henderson County from Nashville. He'd looked at her with blazing blue eyes, fringed with long, thick lashes, and the look had given her goosebumps. His soft lips could look either cynical, or change to a crooked, dimpled smile. He flashed that smile at her now. Sara realized she couldn't stay mad at him. *We'll just have to manage with less money. We'll find a way.*

Later that day the wagons in front of them came to a halt. Shortly, the Pollard family's oldest boy, Daniel, came running along the line of wagons. "We've broken a wheel. Pa has an extra, so we can replace it. Shouldn't take long."

"Need any help up there?" Morgan asked.

"Pa said we have more than enough hands already, but thanks for the offer."

Morgan looked at Sara with a gleam in his eyes. "Come on." He lifted her off the wagon to the ground. Grabbing her by the hand, he guided her across the rocky ground and into a clump of trees. Circling his arms around her, he pulled her close and kissed her. "I love you, Mrs. Darnell."

Releasing her, he placed his right hand over his heart and said, "I promise no more poker playin' with the Johnson twins. After all, they probably do cheat. Forgive me?"

Sara looked into his eyes. "Yes, I forgive you."

"Wait," he said with a gleam in his eyes. "I do wish to reserve the right to an occasional drink of whiskey." Then he picked her up and spun her around until they were both dizzy with spinning and laughter.

Sara wished she could stay angry with him. *Probably save me some grief down the road.*

Moving on, they turned a bit southeast to the ferry over the Mouth of Cache, a tributary of the White River. Pollard advised parents to keep small children in the wagons. "This is black bear and bobcat country. There are plenty of trees, so you may not spot the predators, but they are out there. And watch the water for water moccasins, they're poisonous."

The ferry on the Cache turned out to be a flat boat poled across the river. It was a tedious crossing. One at a time, a wagon was strapped to the flat boat and poled across. Waiting for their turn to cross, Morgan asked Pollard, "Isn't there a better way to cross? This sure is slow."

Pollard shook his head. "Nope. Be glad we don't have to remove the wheels, unpack the wagons, then send the empty wagon boxes across. Once that's done, the wheels and all the goods have to be ferried across, then the women and children. In the meantime, the men swim across with the oxen. Add the time for reassembling and repacking the wagons and hitching the oxen and it makes today's process look fast and easy."

Morgan chuckled. "I reckon I'm sorry I asked."

When the final wagon and oxen were across the Cache and safe on the shore, the settlers stepped onto the flat boat in groups to be ferried across. As they were poled across the slow-flowing current, Sara looked back to the shore and spotted a pair of black-and-white woodpeckers with long, ivory bills darting through the trees. *Beautiful.*

As the ferry reached the center of the river, Morgan pointed. "Sara, look at the size of that snake." Undulating its way across the top of the water was a long, dark snake marked with lighter bands. "It must be five feet long." Sara shivered. Almost as if aware of them watching, the snake turned its triangular-shaped head toward them and opened its mouth, as if in warning. Morgan pointed again. "Its mouth is as white as cotton."

Sara took a step back from the side of the ferry. "I'm just glad we're up here, not down there with it."

Morgan laughed. "So you don't want to go for a swim?" Sara rolled her eyes at him.

As they traveled toward Little Rock, they left the delta and rode into the Arkansas prairie. The terrain turned into flat grassland. Late in the afternoon the temperature suddenly dropped, and the air felt heavy. A mass of dark clouds crept over the sun, and the air began to smell of rain. Captain Pollard sent a message down the line with Daniel. "Pa says storm's comin' and we'd best stop now." The wagons were quickly circled, and oxen unyoked to mill restlessly in the corral made by the circle. The tall grass was whipped by the gusting wind. Jagged lines of lightning could be seen in the distance. Periodic dull booms of thunder echoed around them. Captain Pollard was working his way around the outside of the wagon circle. "Last thing we need is a stampede. It takes somethin' pretty severe to send oxen into a general scamper, but the storm comin' looks like it could build into a real doozie. Every man needs to try to keep his oxen calm. Not sure how to do that, but do the best you can." Within minutes the fury of the storm reached the small wagon circle on the prairie. Hard rain pelted down, growing into a torrent of water. Mothers gathered their children into the wagons and adults sought cover. Lightning lit the sky above them, and thunder bellowed.

Watching from inside the wagon, Sara was mesmerized. There were two gelded bull oxen in the milling herd, and tiny bolts of lightning were dancing back and forth between their horns. The few horses in the train had been secured in the circle with the oxen, and there were small balls of lightning on the horses' ears. Michael Butler, Cecilia's brother-in-law, made a run from one wagon to another, and Sara saw pea-sized lightning balls on his bushy mustache. *Wouldn't believe this if I hadn't seen it myself.*

The oxen were growing increasingly nervous. A bright flash, followed immediately by a tremendous clap of thunder, sent oxen pushing against the ropes between two wagons. Sara's heart began racing. *They're going to pull the wagons over.* Suddenly she heard a man's voice begin singing "Amazing Grace." *John Henry?*

"Sing, everyone!" John Henry called out and then continued the song. The women, then the men—even the children—began to raise their voices in song. "Again!" The hymn was repeated with the storm as accompaniment. The oxen actually seemed calmer. They weren't pushing against the ropes.

The voice now changed to several choruses of "Rock of Ages," then "Silent Night, Holy Night," and, finally, "The Old Oaken Bucket," as the oxen settled down and the storm slowly moved past. The settlers, soggy from the downpour, left their wagons and gathered around John Henry.

Questions and comments came at John Henry thick and fast.

"How did you know to do that?"

"What just happened?"

"Thank the Lord!"

"Whoa." He raised his hands. "In Mexico the vaqueros, who work the cattle, sing to 'em to keep 'em calm. Thought it might work with oxen. Sang the only four decent songs I know. Figured everybody else would know 'em too. Guess it worked."

And thank heavens it did!

Less severe spring rainstorms followed them for several days. *Rain, rain, rain. I am so sick of being wet!* Sara looked out of the wagon and watched the raindrops splash for the third day in a row. Yesterday, after several wagons got stuck in the deep mud, they had camped to wait for the rain to stop. The ground was saturated. Inside the wagon a leak spilled cold water down Sara's neck. Sara sighed and muttered in frustration to herself. "Our bed makings are wet, most of what's in the wagon is wet. I'd best figure out what we can eat without cooking." *Crackers and venison jerky again, maybe some dried apples.*

A short time later, Morgan came back from checking on the oxen. "I'm hungry, what did you fix to eat?"

"I can't cook, thanks to the rain, so our nooner meal is dried apples, crackers, and jerky. You can put some jam on the crackers for variety, if you like."

Morgan frowned, mumbled something, grabbed some jerky and crackers, and left the wagon. *Where's he going that's drier?* Suppertime was just as wet, the meal as basic, and their attitudes as dark as the stormy sky. As night fell, the rain became a roaring thunderstorm. Sara watched as the bright flashes of lightning crackled through the sky, revealing the landscape, then going dark again with a crash of thunder. They slept in the wagon on wet quilts, in wet clothes. The drumming of the rain on the canvas wagon cover made their sleep restless, while the wagon contents grew damper and damper.

The morning dawned with a brisk breeze and a light, misty drizzle. Hungry, Sara was trying to cook bacon and pancakes over a smoky fire. The mist, blowing into the fire and her skillet, was causing grease spatters and slowing her cooking. Putting a lid on the skillet and setting it aside, she quickly rummaged through the wagon and found an umbrella. When Morgan came back after checking the ox teams, she was flipping the pancakes while holding the umbrella to shelter the fire and skillet.

Cecilia, making her way around the wagon circle, pointed at the umbrella and shouted, "Smart idea, Sara!"

After breakfast the sky cleared, and the sun came out. Sara spent the rest of the morning taking everything out of the wagon and trying to find a place to set things out to dry. Morgan had gone to help unpack two wagons that were stuck, so the men could free them from the mud. By evening things were still not dry, so the decision was made to wait one more full day before traveling. Captain Pollard rang his cowbell and gathered the group. "Tomorrow things will have had time to finish drying, and we can repack the wagons. If my estimates are right," he told the group, "a week or so more of travel should take us to North Little Rock." There were murmurs of excitement. "We'll spend a couple of days resting there, make wagon repairs, reshoe oxen, if necessary, and give everyone time to take on any needed supplies. Then we'll move on toward Fort Smith and the border with Indian Territory."

The mood that night was almost celebratory. "Little Rock is pretty close to the halfway point between Memphis and Fort Smith," Morgan told Sara over supper. "We still have a ways to go, but after Little Rock, we'll be going along the Arkansas River bottom all the way to Fort Smith. It should be a good road."

"I hope it's a drier one. I feel like we've gone from one muddy pothole to another muddy pothole for most of the trip. How far from Little Rock to Fort Smith?"

"Maybe 170 miles. Probably take us twelve or thirteen days, maybe less if the weather's good."

"And from Fort Smith to Dallas?"

"I'm not sure. Captain Pollard has a map of Indian Territory, but he says we'll get detailed guidance at the border."

"Good!" *I don't want to be lost in Indian Territory.*

After repacking the wagons with their dry things, they continued on, turning toward one of the southwest trails and crossing the bridge at Bayou Meto, a small tributary of the Arkansas River.

As they crossed the bridge, Sara heard a mighty commotion and looked up to see hundreds of ducks taking to the air. Morgan grabbed his long gun from under the wagon seat and fired randomly into the midst of the flying birds. Sara heard shots from the other wagons. The wagon train stopped, and men went in search of downed ducks along the shoreline. Morgan came back shortly, opening a cloth bag to show Sara two skinned duck breasts and four small, skinned legs. "Roast duck for dinner tonight!"

No feather plucking tonight! The ducks are ready to cook.

That evening Morgan said, "Tonight the cooking fires all smell of roasting duck. I can hardly wait to eat."

After enjoying the results of the serendipitous hunt the evening before, the travelers turned their wagons southwest, skirted a low range of hills, and dropped off into the river basin where a bridge crossed over a small cypress swamp. The wagons bumped off the wooden bridge one by one. Sara was walking beside the wagon when she heard shouts from one of the wagons in front of them. All the wagons slowly came to a stop. As Sara followed others rushing to see what had happened, she heard someone say, "Samantha just dropped dead." Another voice spoke, "Can't bury her. We'll just have to roll her off the road."

Roll her off the road!? What a crass comment. She followed the voice to one of the wagons and saw that Samantha was an ox. "She seemed weak yesterday, eyes were cloudy, and she wouldn't eat last night. But I didn't expect this. Sam was a mighty fine animal. Poor thing, hate to lose her. Rest of my team is okay, but not sure they can handle the wagon with her gone."

Michael Butler spoke up. "We have an extra ox just trailin' the wagons with the other livestock. Molly's experienced, so you oughta be able to put her in Sam's place. Get a new ox in Little Rock and then give our Molly back." Problem solved, Molly was yoked, poor Sam was pushed off the trail, with the owner lamenting he couldn't give her a decent burial, and the wagon train continued.

For several days they followed the high plains between two large cypress swamps. Sara told Morgan that she had expected the swamps to smell bad, but instead the odor was simply earthy. "The breeze blew a faint scent across the trail all day. Reminded me of cedar." Past the swamps they finally reached the bank of the Arkansas River, just east of the Old Crittenden Ferry on the edge of North Little Rock. The riverside was dotted with small farms and boggy areas. The town of North Little Rock consisted of a few houses, several general stores, a blacksmith, and freight warehouses. They found a place to camp not far from the ferry. After the wagons were circled, Sara and Morgan walked down to the water. Looking south across the river to a high, rock bluff and the town of Little Rock, Sara told Morgan, "Little Rock looks like a considerable town."

"It does. Pollard says we'll camp here in North Little Rock for a few days. We can buy supplies, make necessary wagon repairs, and reshoe our oxen. When everyone's rested and ready, we'll ferry across the river. Then we'll move on to Fort Smith and the border with Indian Territory."

"I'll start a list of the supplies we need. Can we afford an oiled-canvas tent? The canvas sheet tossed over the wagon tongue doesn't work very well in the wind and rain."

"I think so. We'll buy what we need today. Tomorrow we can take a steam ferry across the river to visit Little Rock, if you like."

"Yes! I'd like that." *A visit to a town is just what we all need.*

"Day after tomorrow," Morgan said, "I'll join the line at the blacksmith. Even though we're only eight wagons, there are lots of oxen needing shoes."

They spent what was left of the day in North Little Rock recaulking the wagon, finding a small, oiled-canvas tent, and adding to their supplies. Sara replenished food items that were low and bought fresh hen eggs, which she packed in their flour barrel for safety. *Scrambled eggs for breakfast and I can make a real cake.* She also splurged on a pound of cheese and two loaves of freshly made white bread. At the end of the day, Morgan surprised her with a red step stool. Sara stood on tiptoes and threw her arms around his neck. "Oh, Morgan, thank you for remembering I wanted a red step stool for the store."

Morgan smiled. "Now you'll be able to reach our store's top shelves."

That evening they could see the riverbank was dotted with the wagons of other groups of settlers heading west. Women were busy cooking supper and the smoke of their fires drifted upward. Sara could hear the laughter of the children playing and the contrasting sound of a fiddle playing a melancholy tune. Sara sighed at the comforting thought of others traveling to start new lives. *Just like we are.*

The following day a large group of the travelers gathered to take a steamboat ferry across the Arkansas River to Little Rock. Once in town most of the men and women separated. The men headed for the taverns and other adventures, while the ladies and children enjoyed strolling the streets of the town, peering in the shop windows. Sara, Cecilia, and a small group of other women also visited the white-columned Arkansas State House. "It's a beautiful building." Sara pointed to the white columns. "Greek Revival architecture, if I remember from school."

Cecilia agreed. "Sara, where did you go to school?"

"The Covey Girls' School in Henderson County. Twenty girls boarded there, but I lived close enough to ride my horse. We studied grammar, literature, math, history, penmanship, and needlework—my least favorite subject." Sara chuckled. "I had pricked fingers the whole time."

"How long were you there?"

"Four years, ages thirteen through sixteen. Before then, Momma schooled me. My sisters go to the same school now. Momma insisted we three girls be educated. She was forever correcting our grammar and finding books for us to read, like Greek mythology."

"Your momma sounds like a wise lady."

"Yes, you'd like her." Sara's smile was wistful. *I miss her.*

Cecilia and Sara made a final stop at a general store. It was a single-story brick building with a large display window filled with a variety of things, from pretty patterned china to men's top hats. Sara wanted to see the merchandise inside. They bought small pieces of rock candy from a barrel at the front counter and wandered the store. *Neat and well organized.* Sara made a mental list of things she and Morgan needed to add to the inventory list for the store they planned to open. "Sardines, canned plums, and I can't believe we left cigars off our list."

"Important items . . ." Cecilia glanced up at the store's clock. "Oh, dear! Sara, we're gonna miss the ferry back to North Little Rock. We'd best hurry."

The ferry was loading the last passengers when they arrived. "Whew! Just in time," Sara sighed and fanned her face with her wide-brimmed straw hat. "Let's go up to the top deck. Did you know it's called the Texas deck? Don't know why, but we can see better from up there."

As the ferry moved through the river, they heard the rhythmic lapping of the water against its sides. The smoke of campfires along the approaching banks rose in ghostly plumes against a background of a sunset painting the sky with changing colors. The sky had turned gray when they docked in North Little Rock. They hurried back to the wagon circle. It seemed every-one was there—except for Morgan.

Tired of waiting and getting increasingly worried, Sara made a sandwich of jerky, watercress picked along a stream the day before, and bread sliced from the loaf she'd just bought. Finally, not sure how to set up their new tent, she made the bed as usual under the wagon tongue and tried to sleep. She was restless and sleepless, imagining all the awful things that might have happened to Morgan. *Where are you, Morgan? Are you hurt?*

Shortly after sunrise Sara was grinding the morning's coffee beans and worrying about Morgan, who was still missing, when the Johnson twins wandered up to her fire. "We've come for our money," Horace Johnson said. He was holding a deck of cards and flipping it back and forth between his hands.

"I beg your pardon? What are you talking about?"

"We won thirty dollars off a Morgan last night playin' cards in Hell's Half Acre. We tried to collect, but he said you had all the money. We want our thirty dollars." As he finished his sentence, Sara snatched the deck of cards from his fingers.

"Hey . . . what ya doin?" he sputtered.

Sara fanned the cards out in her hands, face up. She thumbed through the cards, then flipped them over and fanned them out again, thumbing through them and continuing to study them. "Well, no wonder you won. These cards are marked."

"Heck! How'd you know?" Horace's mouth knotted into a scowl.

Norman, Horace Johnson's twin, poked him in his ribs. "Shut up, Horace." But it was too late. Sara's bluff had worked.

Now I know for sure these two cheat.

"I'm sure there are other men on the wagon train who'd be interested in knowing that you have been playing with a marked deck."

"Aw, most of 'em only lost a few dollars to us, 'cept for Morgan."

"Cheating at cards is thievery." Sara stepped forward and poked Horace in the chest. "Captain Pollard warned everyone about talking politics or religion and cheating at cards. He's likely to make you leave the wagon train. So, Mr. Thief, I suggest you get busy paying back the money you've already taken." She held out her hand. Horace hesitated, glared, then reached into his sagging pocket and pulled out a wad of dirty bills and a bag of coins.

"Morgan paid you in gold and silver, so you can repay me with them as well." Sara held her breath. Horace stared at her, then angrily counted out a hundred dollars in gold and silver coins and placed them into her hands. "Thank you." *Sure glad these two aren't very smart.* "Where did you leave Morgan last night?"

Norman Johnson was happy to share bad news. "He went off with some bar girl. We saw him later, passed out drunk at the old tavern in Hell's Half Acre. He got mad when we tried to rouse him to tell him it was time for the last ferry. So we left him." With that, the brothers stomped away, muttering curses in Sara's direction.

Sara turned her back on the brothers and ran to the wagon. She was crying before she was inside. *Another woman? Drunk and more gambling? Oh, Morgan, why do you do this?*

After a few minutes, Sara dried her eyes, took a deep breath, and went in search of John Henry. She found him working with Michael Butler to remount a repaired wagon wheel. They were just finishing. Sara greeted the two men and turned to John Henry. "When you have a chance, I need your help with something, please."

"Sure, 'specially if I can talk you out of a fresh cup of coffee."

"I'm headed to the wagon and I'll put on a fresh pot."

The coffee was ready when John Henry walked up. Sara handed him a cup and wasted no time getting to the point. "Morgan didn't come home last night. The Johnson brothers say they left him drunk and passed out at the old tavern in Hell's Half Acre. What should I do, John Henry?"

John Henry frowned, bringing his eyebrows closer together. "The morning's first ferry should be coming in pretty soon. I'll go see if he's on it. If not, I'll go across, find him, and bring him back."

"I'm afraid something has happened to him. Please find him. I know he gambles and drinks more than he should, but I don't want to lose him."

John Henry took one last sip of his coffee, handed Sara the cup, and patted her shoulder. "I'm on my way. I'll find him." Tears were streaming down Sara's face. Unable to speak, she nodded.

It wasn't long before Cecilia arrived at the wagon. "John Henry told me Morgan isn't back yet. If anyone can find him, it's John Henry. In the meantime, thought you could use some company."

"Oh, Cecilia, what if he's hurt? The Johnson brothers told me he even went off drunk with some bar girl."

Cecilia put her arm around Sara's shoulders. "Let me pour us some coffee. Then come sit down with me, I brought us a couple of pieces of pie I made from some canned peaches. Dessert for breakfast might do you good this mornin'."

The ladies sat on the ground, on a folded quilt, with their pie and coffee while Cecilia tried to distract Sara with stories about her days as a schoolteacher. Sensing that Sara was exhausted from a night of worry and little sleep, Cecilia finally talked Sara into making a bed in the wagon and taking a nap. Sara slept for three hours.

In the late afternoon, John Henry returned with Morgan. He was hanging his head and wouldn't meet Sara's eyes. His clothes were rumpled and dirty and he was unsteady on his feet. *Oh, Morgan, look at you. Still half drunk!*

John Henry stood in front of Sara, hat in hand. "I found him passed out in an alley at Elm and Water Streets in Hell's Half Acre. Poured a lot of coffee down him 'til he was able to walk to the ferry. Pockets are empty. His watch is gone. Guess somebody robbed him. He doesn't remember."

Sara hugged Morgan hard and then pulled away, shaking her head. "Oh Morgan, you promised!" She turned to John Henry, "Thank you for finding him."

"Glad to help, just sorry about the circumstances." John Henry frowned and shot Morgan a sharp look. "Young man, you have a fine wife here, don't be a fool and disappoint her again." Morgan looked up. John Henry held eye contact, then turned and walked away.

Sara and Morgan stood and stared at each other. Finally Sara said, "Morgan, I can't believe you'd do this! Gambling, getting so drunk you pass out! And what were you up to with a saloon hussy, for Pete's sake!?"

Morgan shuffled his feet and looked away again.

"Look at me!" Sara put her hands on his face and turned it toward her. "How long have you been gambling?"

He moistened his lips and swallowed hard, resisting eye contact. "Since I was 'bout fifteen. I won the money for our trip to Texas by bettin' on horse races. I don't always lose."

"Why didn't you tell me that gambling is a big problem for you? That you can't stop?"

"Because I didn't think you'd like it. I was afraid you wouldn't marry me."

"Oh Morgan. You're darn right I don't like it! I also worry about your drinking. So, what do we do? I love you to pieces, but you're putting yourself and, for that matter, our livelihood at risk. I won't deal with that."

"Gamblin' tempts me, Sara. Cards, horse racing, any kind of betting. Whiskey too."

"And what about the saloon girl? How could you do that to me? Why would you do that?"

"Musta been really drunk 'cause I don't remember that part."

"Humph! You don't remember?! That's a poor excuse."

Morgan tried to put his arms around her. "But . . . Sara . . . darlin', I love you."

Sara pushed him away. "Your actions certainly don't show it. Go clean yourself up and we'll have supper. I just don't know . . . I don't . . ."

Sara turned and left him wallowing in his misery.

They were both in a quiet mood all evening. Sara made supper, and after eating, Morgan showed her how to put up their new tent. That night in bed, Morgan rolled toward her, reaching out to stroke her hair. "I'll be a better man for you, Sara . . . promise." Sara turned her face away from him. *Please let that be true. Otherwise I've made a terrible mistake.*

The blacksmith was still at work shoeing the wagon train's oxen the following day, so departure was delayed. Sara asked to go with Morgan to the blacksmith. "Oxen can't stand on three legs, so I'm curious about how they're shod."

The blacksmith, a bald, brawny, olive-skinned man in a black apron, was eager to show off his skills for Sara. "First, you gotta remember that oxen have cloven—or divided—hooves. Each hoof needs two shoes, one for each side of the hoof. You're right, they can't balance on three legs. So here's what I use." He walked over to a wooden device with ropes and large, leather slings. Sara noticed the blacksmith's little finger on his left hand was just a stump. "This is my mechanical stock." His assistant led an animal into it. The device lifted the ox off the ground and rotated it onto its side, feet extended.

"Oh my gosh!" Sara shook her head at the outlandish position of the animal.

"Now I can reach all four feet."

They watched the blacksmith nail two crescent-shaped shoes on each of the ox's four feet, whistling while he worked. Then he rotated the ox back to normal position and released it from the stock. "Don't know why, but my whistling seems to keep 'em calm." He grinned. "Tried whistling to calm my children, but it didn't work."

"What about on the trail?" Sara asked. "Can you shoe an ox without a stock to hold it?"

"Uh huh, it's just harder. You dig a trench and use ropes to turn the ox on its side or on its back and lower it into the trench. Then you can shoe it. Ox isn't too happy about it, but it works in a pinch." Sara tried to visualize an ox upside down in a trench. The scene that came to mind was a long trench with all eight of their oxen on their backs, feet waving. *What a funny sight that would be.* Sara and Morgan watched as the blacksmith finished shoeing their eight oxen. "I figure you know these big beasts have tender feet. If they break a hoof, they most likely die. Any trouble with shoes, you can make a pair of moccasins for them until you can have them shod again. Make a rawhide bag, fit it to their foot, tie it on real secure. Won't last long in muddy conditions, but it might save your ox."

"Hmm," Morgan nodded. "Good to know. Our oxen seem pretty smart. They follow my verbal commands, turn right when I say 'gee' and left with 'haw.' Respond to some gestures, too."

The blacksmith looked thoughtful for a moment. "Smart? Reckon they are just as smart as they need to be."

The next day Morgan woke Sara in the dark of night. "I know it's earlier than usual, honey, but we need to hurry if we're going to be lined up ahead of the other wagon trains wanting to cross the river." The eight wagons arrived at the ferry long before dawn, only to find three dozen wagons in line in front of them. Hours later, after an uneventful crossing on the flatboat ferry, they were finally headed out of Little Rock to the Military Road which ran west through the bottomland along the Arkansas River. Captain Pollard had been right. The road was wide and well traveled. As they walked, Morgan said, "If the road is this good all the way to Fort Smith, we should be able to make fifteen miles a day, maybe more if the oxen hold up."

The river-bottom road was almost flat, the land dotted with hardwood trees and small farms, yet they were in view of small mountains. They walked by an oxbow lake with scores of white wading birds. At the sound of the wagons the birds rose in the air, their graceful necks straining forward and wings flapping. Morgan called to her from the front of the wagon and pointed. "Look at the beaver dam."

This is pretty country. Will Dallas look like this?

That night around the fire, Sara asked Morgan why Captain Pollard had called the road the "Trail of Tears." "I can only tell you what Captain Pollard told me when I asked him. It began before we were born. Used to be Indian tribes all over the South, but in 1830 the US passed The Indian Removal Act."

"Removal?"

"Uh huh, The the government wanted the Indian land for settlement for whites, so they rounded up the Indians in what were called the 'five civilized tribes,' and marched them across the country to a new Indian Territory north of Texas. Most came through Arkansas and traveled some of the same roads we're traveling to Fort Smith. Some even traveled partway by steamboat on the Arkansas River."

"It's the Trail of Tears because they didn't want to leave their homes?"

"It's worse than that. Many were force marched in all kinds of weather. It was especially hard on the very old and young. Food supplies were short, hundreds were killed in steamboat accidents, and cholera epidemics killed others. Captain Pollard says thousands died along the way. That's why the Cherokee call it 'The Trail of Tears.' "

"I had no idea. That's awful."

Did we have the right to rip them from their homes? It feels wrong.

Two days out of Little Rock, Captain Pollard stopped the train early, and the wagon circle was formed in a clearing which had been hollowed out of the forest. In sight was a small lake. Pollard called the travelers together with the ringing of his cowbell. He was smiling ear-to-ear. "This lake is inviting us to cast for catfish. Likely to be some big ones in there. Thought we oughta take advantage of the opportunity." There were some cheers from the men. Soon the shore was lined with fishermen. Meanwhile, Sara and the other ladies, took the cornmeal and bacon grease from their wagons and started cooking fires. Soon the men were pulling in fish and cleaning them on the rocks. Morgan came back to the wagon with a small basket of large, fresh fillets. "That little lake is full of big fish!"

Sara cut each fillet in half lengthwise and dipped the fish into buttermilk from the Foys' cows, letting the fillets soak for a couple of minutes. Shaking off the excess milk, she rolled each fillet in cornmeal, mixed with a bit of flour and seasoned with salt, then dropped the fillets into her frying pan of hot grease to cook for about six minutes. Morgan's watch was gone, so she had to judge doneness by color. She drained each batch of fish on a clean cloth. As the fish cooked, Sara topped the remaining slices of white bread with cheese and toasted them over the fire. Loading their tin plates with fish, cheese toast, and wild greens, they sat on the rocks by the small lake for their banquet. Watching Morgan use a bit of cheese toast to sop up the last bit of juice from the greens, Sara said, "I didn't know fish could be so tasty." Morgan agreed with his mouth full.

That night they took their final cups of coffee to the rocks by the lake and watched the sun slowly slither below the horizon, leaving the sky alive with bands of pink changing to red, then purple. Sara cocked her head. "Listen, I hear Whip-poor-wills."

"It's a sunset concert just for you. Even the birds love you, Sara, and so do I."

The next day the wagon train stopped early again. Word went up the line that Mrs. Fowler's baby was coming. Sara had visited over laundry and picked berries with the frail, but very pregnant woman, who already had three small children. While picking berries she had told Sara, "Was 'fraid if we waited 'til the baby came, we might not find another wagon train for awhile. Didn't want to make the trip in the winter, so we signed up with this train. Hope I can make it to Texas 'afore this child arrives."

A couple of ladies experienced with deliveries immediately went to help. Two hours later word was passed from woman to woman that Mrs. Fowler's baby had died during delivery. Effie Butler, an older version of her sister Cecilia, shared the news with Sara, "They say the cord was wrapped around the child's neck. By the time the baby girl was born it was too late to save her."

"How sad." *Another little grave added to those we've seen along the trail.*

"Mr. Fowler is burying the baby now, just off the road beside a small dogwood tree. He told Captain Pollard the dogwood tree's blooms will fall on the grave. I'm told Mrs. Fowler is resting and grieving her heart out at the idea of leaving the child alone on the trail with only a wooden cross to mark her resting place."

Sara took beans and cornbread to the Fowlers along with her condolences. *Even today it is a trail of tears. The poor Fowlers.*

It was a subdued group that continued down the road that day and finally found a stopping place near water and grass for the animals. Everyone understood that too-long a delay for the dead and dying could put the lives of the living at risk. Cecilia reported that two days after her baby's death, Mrs. Fowler baked a blueberry cake for her three-year-old boy's birthday.

Life must go on.

With the weather and the road in their favor, the travelers made good time. As they travelled toward Fort Smith and Van Buren, the small town growing up across the river from the fort, they continued to see a few small farms set in forest clearings. One enterprising farmer had posted a sign on the roadside offering fresh vegetables for sale. Not knowing what might be available on the road ahead, Captain Pollard agreed to stop briefly for those who might want to buy fresh produce. The farmer's wife was happy to sell Sara a dozen eggs, some garden peas, spinach, two small bunches of radishes, and two jars of carrot jam. Thirty-five cents bought a nice supply of all three vegetables, the eggs, and the jam. When Sara returned to the wagon, Morgan looked in her basket. "Is that spinach?" Sara nodded. "Ugh! Not my favorite, but I do like radishes."

They had invited John Henry and lawyer Aaron Davis, one of the single men on horseback, to join them for supper. Sara roasted the two rabbits that John Henry had brought them earlier in the day, made cornbread, and cooked spinach topped with hard-boiled egg slices. For dessert, she baked a light cake with stewed-berry topping.

They sat cross legged on folded quilts around the fire, juggling plates on their laps. Finishing his last bite of cake, John Henry wiped his mouth, "This certainly tops what we bachelors in the back of the train fix for supper. It was wonderful, Sara, thank you."

"It was delicious," Aaron Davis echoed. "I do believe that was the best rabbit I've ever eaten. My compliments to the cook, Sara."

"I even liked the spinach," Morgan said. "The boiled eggs made all the difference."

"That's good because the leftover spinach will be our nooner tomorrow along with the last chunk of cheese."

Over coffee, while the men talked, Sara studied Aaron Davis. His short chestnut-colored hair was gray at the temples, and Sara guessed he was in his forties. John Henry had told her Davis had been a congressman in Kentucky and had political ambitions in Texas. His hazel eyes were slightly hooded under neat brows. A generous mouth, with a broad bottom lip, framed perfect white teeth that had flashed frequently with laughter during the evening.

Although he hailed from Kentucky, he had only a slight southern accent, and Sara found him well spoken. *I like him. With his formal way of speaking, he does seem like a congressman.*

When they finally reached the outskirts of the scattering of cabins called Dardanelle, Pollard called a halt and walked down the wagon line proposing that the train move on several miles before camping early. "There's a big train behind us that would like to pass. Let's stop, let them pass and get a bit ahead of us, so we don't eat their dust or have to wait for them at any ferry. We are about halfway to Fort Smith. There is a deep creek close by. We'll camp near it. The animals can water and graze, and we can rest too."

Once the wagons were circled, the ladies gathered their laundry and made a beeline for the creek. Soon Sara and Cecilia were vigorously scrubbing clothes on their washboards at the water's edge. Cecilia looked at Sara. "I wouldn't exactly call this rest. At least it's a break from walking behind the wagon. Do you think we can bathe after the laundry's done?"

Sara flipped away soap suds that had splattered from her washboard onto her forehead.

"I plan to, even if I have to bathe in these clothes." Instead, the ladies made a plan. Once the laundry was washed and spread out on the rocky shore to dry, half of them would stand guard, and the other half would bathe in their drawers and chemises. Happy to be in the first group, Sara and Cecilia stripped down to their chemises, washed their dresses, then, still in their chemises, splashed into the creek where they soaped themselves, rinsed, and washed their hair. Standing in the waist-deep water, Sara cupped her hands and sent a wave of water onto Cecilia. Dripping and laughing, Cecilia dunked Sara and the water fight began. Others joined in, splashing and laughing. *Everyone seems happy and relaxed. It feels good to laugh.*

After the water fight, the first group of bathers air dried on the shore, standing guard for the second group of bathers. When all were bathed and shampooed, and their dresses and bonnets were dry enough to wear again, they put on their shoes and stockings and returned to the wagons to discover the men had gone to another part of the creek to swim and bathe. Sara could hear their laughter in the distance. *It will be a jolly crowd around the fires tonight. Clean too.*

The next morning in camp, as she and Morgan were preparing for the day's travel, Sara looked up to see a homespun and buckskin-clad Indian, with feathers in his long braids, riding out of the trees on a paint pony. Trailing behind on another pony was a young squaw, also in buckskin. *Indians!* Both wore beaded moccasins. Their skin was mahogany, their hair almost black. The eyes the woman turned toward Sara were dark. She had a papoose strapped across her chest and long braids dangled down her back. Lagging behind the riders were two mongrel dogs. Seeing Morgan, who had been adjusting the yoke of their lead ox team, the Indian rode up to him, holding out a burlap sack. He slid from his horse and opened the sack so that Sara and Morgan could see that it held dewberries. "Sell," he said.

"Buy them, Morgan." Sara nodded at the Indian. She felt no threat from these two. Morgan reached into his pocket and pulled out the few coins it contained. He held them out in the flat of his palm. The Indian took them, handed the sack to Morgan, remounted, and the two rode away. Sara took a deep breath. "I didn't think we were in Indian Territory yet."

"We're not, but Captain Pollard told me that some Indians slipped away from the trail during removal and remained in Arkansas. I think we just met two of them."

The mongrel dogs were still in sight when Mrs. Radcliff, a small round woman with unruly red hair peeking out in all directions from her bonnet, came running up to Sara.

"Oh my, how exciting! We've just seen our first Indians on the trip. Did you see her papoose? With four children, I've spent half my life carrying babies around while trying to do my work. Think how convenient it would be to wear your babies. Of course, you don't have any yet, but your hands would be free and—" Captain Pollard rang the cowbell, signaling time to line up the wagons. "Oops! Gotta go." Mrs. Radcliff scurried back to her wagon. Sarah sighed in relief. Saved by the bell. *My, she is a chatterbox*

After a day of travel from Dardanelle, the road turned due west to Fort Smith and the town of Van Buren. Walking beside their ox teams, Morgan cracked his whip above the heads of the oxen. "This is a good road with a very gentle roll, but we are climbing a bit. Look to the south, Sara, above the trees."

Sara turned her head to see a tall, tree-covered mountain rising in the distance. "That's a big mountain. Looks taller than the big one we saw yesterday from the road in Dardanelle. Sure pretty country."

Following the road, they entered a small valley between the low mountain ranges and saw scattered, small farms. By the fifth day from Dardanelle, they left the mountain views behind and arrived at the outskirts of Fort Smith. They circled their wagons by the Arkansas River, near the border between Arkansas and Indian Territory. After a nooner of cold cornbread and beans, Morgan proposed they visit the fort. Sara agreed. "I'm eager to see it too. Let me change my bonnet for my straw hat and let's go."

As they walked toward the fort arm in arm, the breeze caught the wide brim of Sara's straw hat and sent it flying. A young, uniformed officer caught it as it blew across the ground. He stood at attention, then returned the hat to Sara with a grin and a salute. "Madame, your hat."

"Thank you for rescuing it." Sara smiled and placed it firmly back on her head.

"You were certainly Johnny on the spot," Morgan said. "Thank you."

"Strange you should say that." The officer smiled, flashing a perfect set of teeth. "Let me introduce myself. Lieutenant John Thomas Hill, 7th Infantry, at your service." He bowed. "My friends call me Johnny. If you are headed for the fort, please allow me to give you a tour."

As they began to walk the last quarter mile to Fort Smith, Sarah and Morgan introduced themselves. Lieutenant Hill told them he was recently assigned to the fort after graduating from West Point. "I'm from New York City, and although this is pretty country, I do feel like this is the wilderness, yet your wagon train is obviously going even further west. Where are you headed?"

"We've come from Henderson County, Tennessee, and we're headed to Texas, actually to Dallas on the Trinity River. We even have 'Gone to

Dallas' painted on our wagon, thanks to Morgan." Sara slipped her hand into Morgan's.

"Texas . . . hmmm, what's in Dallas?"

"Opportunity. There's cheap land in Texas and the state is growing. Sara and I plan to open a general-merchandise store in Dallas. We believe we can build a business, raise a family, and enjoy a good life there." He squeezed her hand.

"We have to travel through Indian Territory first. Have you been there?" Sara asked.

Lieutenant Hill shook his head. "Just on the edge. No need to worry," he said, picking up on the bit of concern in Sara's voice. "The path you'll travel goes primarily through the Choctaw Nation. I suspect they live much like you will in Dallas."

"What do you mean?" Morgan sounded confused.

"The Choctaws are what the government calls a civilized tribe. They've mostly adopted white man's ways. They build cabins, farm, have schools. In fact, from what I hear, many make a living selling goods and services to people traveling through to Texas and further west. The same with the Chickasaws."

"Before the Indian removal, we had Chickasaws in Tennessee," Morgan paused, "before I was born."

"You'll certainly see Choctaws and Chickasaws on your trip. You'll also touch the edge of the Cherokee Nation as you leave Fort Smith. Young Cherokee bucks will follow you for a while wanting to trade. They'll show up in costume asking to trade. Seems like it's a game to them. That's fine, but they are notorious livestock thieves. They lurk along the Texas Road, all the way to the Red River, stealing horses. Best to guard your horses and milk cows."

"What about oxen?"

"Don't seem to have much use for them. Ah, here we are."

In front of them was a high, vine-covered stone wall with a gate. In front of the gate stood an armed sentinel. Sara watched as he snapped to attention, saluted Lieutenant Hill, and said, "Good afternoon, sir."

The Lieutenant saluted in return. "These are my guests."

"Very good, Sir, " The guard opened the gate and stepped aside. Walking in, Sara saw that the entire fort was enclosed with a twelve foot wall with porthole openings about every four feet. The grounds were green and lovely. A broad, gravel drive encompassed a parade ground centered with a flagstaff flying the American flag. Lieutenant Hill pointed out the barracks and the two-story brick officers' quarters. Sara could see soldiers lounging on the immense porches. Hill went on to identify the other buildings: quartermaster's store, enlisted men's barracks, powder magazine, and near the gate they had entered, the guardhouse.

Morgan spotted a cannon and asked about it. "We use it morning and night to salute the raising and lowering of the flag. Our band plays martial music then as well. Too bad you weren't here last night, we had a concert on the green."

"That would have been nice. I've never been in a fort before. I didn't expect it to be so lovely," Sara said.

"Lovely and lonely. The only excitement, if you can call it that, is the small town of Van Buren, across the river. I'm hoping my next assignment will be a larger, more active post."

Tour over, Morgan and Sara thanked Lieutenant Hill. As they were leaving, Morgan turned to extend an invitation, "If you ever come to Dallas, look us up. Remember, the name's Darnell.

The next day a group of the settlers—mostly men—planned to cross the river to Van Buren to explore the small town. Instead, Sara wanted to take advantage of a day off the road to air out the bedding and reorganize the jumble of things in the wagon; however, Morgan was eager to join the group. Telling him goodbye, Sara added, "No gambling, right?"

"I promise."

At the end of the day, Sara looked around the wagon in satisfaction. Bedding was completely dry and neatly folded. Pantry items were sorted and easily accessible. Other items were organized for the remainder of the trip. She thought it would have been nice to visit Van Buren, but this was time well spent. *It'll make the rest of the trip easier.* Seeing that the sky was taking on the pinks and dark blues of sunset, she started the cooking fire for supper. As she gathered the ingredients for camp bread, she heard the crowd returning from the day's last Van Buren ferry. At first she didn't see Morgan. Finally, as the others had made their way to their wagons, she saw Morgan trailing behind with the Johnson twins. *Oh no! Not those two bad eggs.*

The Johnson twins hurried by as Morgan stumbled, tangle footed, up to her. "Hello, sweetheart, how ya doin'?"

Sara wrinkled her nose at the smell of whiskey and cheap perfume and frowned. "I'm doing fine." The tone of her voice was brittle. "The question is what have you been doing?"

"Having a drink with my Johnson . . . good companions, Norman and Horse . . . no, Hor-us." He stumbled and fell. "Ouch! Hard ground."

Sara leaned down and looked into his face. "And just who else have you been carrying on with? You stink of perfume."

"Lucy with the light blonde hair," he sang and smiled a stupid smile. He noticed the fire. "What's for supper?"

"Not a blessed thing." Sara stood up straight and walked away, tears in her eyes. She sat on a stone overlooking the river, in sight of the wagon circle. She watched as the sky changed from blue to indigo to star-lit black. Sara rubbed her forehead. I've married a man who drinks, gambles, and goes with other women. *What can I do?* Hours later she returned to their wagon to find the fire out and Morgan wrapped in a quilt, asleep on the ground. She slept in the wagon.

When she woke the next morning, Morgan was gone. Sara didn't bother with breakfast. *He can fend for himself.* When she saw him coming back leading the oxen, she left to walk around the wagon circle. As she passed the Butler wagon, Cecilia looked up from packing away their breakfast dishes. Sara stopped to say hello. "Are you all right this morning?" Cecilia's eyebrows were raised and there was concern in Cecilia's voice.

"Yes . . . no . . . I'm not sure. I suppose everyone is talking about Morgan."

"I'm sure there is some gossip, but it'll die down quickly, there's too much else for everyone to focus on. We're headed for Indian Territory today and that's already the main topic of conversation. Why not walk with me today? No need to talk if you don't feel like it."

"Thank you, I'd like that."

Sara and Cecilia spent the morning walking beside the Butler wagon and admiring the verdant, rolling valley and occasional small mountains.

As they left Arkansas and crossed the border into Indian Territory, Cecilia told Sara that Grady Burnam, the youngest of the lawyers following the wagons on horseback, had begun to pay attention to the Butler daughter who had just turned seventeen. "Be sure he doesn't drink and gamble," was Sara's only comment. Sara shared the Butler's nooner of bread, cheese, and boiled eggs and enjoyed the banter between the family's children, their parents, and Cecilia. It reminded Sara of her own family in Tennessee. "I miss them," she told Cecilia and wondered what Papa and Momma would say about Morgan.

After the wagons circled for the night, Sara returned to her wagon. Morgan was finishing releasing the teams from the wagon. "I was worried about you, where did you go?"

"I was walking with Cecilia." She started to climb into the wagon.

Morgan took her by the arm and turned her to face him. "Sara, what happened last night?"

Sara jerked her arm out of his hand and folded her arms across her chest. "That's the question I should be asking you. You came home drunk again and smelling of cheap perfume. What am I supposed to think?"

"I'm sorry, I just planned on a couple of drinks, but we were all laughing and having fun and I guess I just kept drinking. The girl was just a barroom hussy."

"You mean Lucy with the light blonde hair?" She hurled the words at him with a voice full of hurt and anger.

He was silent.

"I have to fix supper." She pushed past him and into the wagon to gather supper's ingredients.

When she came out, he was gone with the oxen. Supper was another very quiet meal.

After cleaning up, Sara pulled the tent out of the wagon and began to put it up. "Here, I can do that." Sara let him, prepared for bed, and crawled into the tent early. She was asleep and unaware when Morgan joined her.

The next morning before the bell called the wagons to fall in line, Morgan patted on the wagon seat beside him. "We need to talk, come sit with me." Sara climbed onto the seat beside him.

"Are you still angry?"

"Yes, . . . but mostly I'm confused. It's like there are two of you. The Morgan who is good, loving, and considerate. He's the Morgan I love. Then there's the Morgan who gambles, who leaves, and stumbles home so drunk he passes out. And this last time, you came home smelling of another woman. That's not the man I love. I don't even like that man."

Morgan hung his head. "With your help, I think I can control the gambling, like I promised, but the pull of drink is strong. It may not be available this very moment, but it is still calling me. And when I drink, I can't seem to stop."

"Do you really want to stop drinking?"

"I do. Sara, I don't want to lose you."

"Well, let's get to Dallas and then we'll figure something out, all right?"

"A fresh start. A sober, fresh start in a new place."

"Yes," she said softly. "A sober, fresh start." *I only hope it will work.*

Walking beside the wagon, Sara heard a scream from one of the wagons behind her. Joining several others who were nearby, she ran to see what had happened. Mrs. Radcliff lay crushed and bloodied under her wagon. The woman lay face down with one arm under her body, the other thrust forward as if she had tried to break her fall. The dusty trail around her was dark with blood. *Oh no, what on earth happened?*

"I think the wheel got her," Aaron Davis had knelt beside Sara. He felt for a pulse and shook his head. "She's gone." He pointed at the rear wheel next to her. "Looks like her long skirt got caught on the wheel, and as the wheel turned it pulled her underneath and crushed her. By the time the wagon stopped, it was too late. Awful." He looked up at Albert Radcliff, who had run up beside him, "I'm so sorry."

Radcliff let out a shriek, fell to his knees, and began to rock back and forth, moaning his wife's name. By now the Radcliff's young children were gathering. The oldest cried out, "Momma," and began to cry. *They don't need to see this.* Sara picked up the youngest and herded the three others back to her wagon where she tried to keep them occupied with stories and fed them supper. A red-eyed Albert Radcliff came for them at sunset, still too upset to speak coherently, and took them back to his wagon.

Eleanor Radcliff's body had been placed on a board, covered, and taken around to the other side of the circle. The next morning, Sara joined the Captain's wife, Eliza Pollard, and Effie Butler in preparing the body for burial. They washed her, dressed her in a clean calico dress, braided her long red hair, and twisted the braids into buns over her ears.

"Just yesterday she asked me for my rabbit-stew recipe. Today she's gone. She'll never get to make it." Eliza Pollard sighed and slipped her comb back into her pocket.

Effie Butler straightened the collar of Eleanor Radcliff's calico dress. "She loved to sing. I could hear her in the evenin' as she made supper. I think 'Nelly Bly' must have been her favorite song. Had a pretty singin' voice. I know I'll miss hearin' it from across the circle."

Sara looked back and forth between the two ladies. "What will happen with the children? How can Mr. Radcliff manage?"

Eliza Pollard said, "During the day we ladies will take care of the children. At night they'll go back to their papa. Chances are Mr. Radcliff will marry again once we get to Texas. This time perhaps less for love and more for necessity."

"A necessity bride?"

"Seems that's the way of the world, Sara. In the meantime," Effie Butler said, "we need to take turns making meals for Radcliff and his children. I can talk to the other women about that."

"I want to help," Sara said.

Effie Butler smiled at Sara. "With child care and food both needed, it will likely take all us women."

Sara sighed. "You know, I feel badly. I didn't even know her first name until now . . . ."

Effie Butler shook her head, "I didn't either."

They buried Eleanor Radcliff, with her Bible, on a grassy slope beside a grove of trees. Mr. Radcliff knelt by the grave with his arms around his children. Another wooden cross was planted to the sound of "Rock of Ages." Sara felt bad for calling Mrs. Radcliff a chatterbox, even though she had just said it to herself. *She was a sweet woman. I need to be more charitable, less critical.* That night, sitting under a canopy of stars, Sara prayed for the Radcliff family and the safe arrival in Dallas of the remaining travelers.

Before setting out from Tennessee, Morgan and Sara knew that the trail to Texas would take them through Indian Territory. A merchant selling them supplies had said, "Once you're in Indian Territory, chances are you'll be visited by Indians, especially the Cherokee, who want to trade. Best to have somethin' to trade." Lieutenant Hill had echoed this when they met him at Fort Smith. Sure enough, they were startled one morning when the wagon line ahead of them came to a sudden stop. Young Daniel Pollard came running down the line. "Dozens of Indians ahead, Pa says to stay calm. Most likely want to trade, like we heard."

Sara felt her heart pounding in her chest. *Dozens of Indians?* She forced herself to take a few deep breaths and unclench her fists. Morgan saw her fear. "It's okay, honey. You heard what Daniel said, they'll just want to trade . . . like the couple with the berries."

"Somehow this feels different. I guess because there are so many."

In a few moments, they heard Captain Pollard call for the wagons to circle. After the wagons pulled into place, the men stood by their wagons. "Stay calm and no brandishing of weapons," Pollard called out. Most of the women disappeared into their wagons. Sara stood by Morgan.

"Get in the wagon, honey, where you'll be safe."

"No, I'm not about to miss this."

Everything went quiet as the Indians approached. Sara could hear the soft thud of their unshod horses' hooves as they rode closer and closer to the circled wagons. A light wind swirled the dust around the horses' feet as they came forward. The only other sound was a murder of crows cawing in the trees. Out of the corner of her eye, Sara saw Captain Pollard step outside the circle to face the approaching Indians. One of the Indians rode forward to engage Pollard. He dismounted, and Sara heard him say, "Trade," as he gestured toward the wagons and pointed back to the waiting Indians.

Pollard nodded and said, "Yes, trade." Sara exhaled without realizing she had been holding her breath.

As the remaining Indians started toward the wagons, Pollard and the Indian walked into the circle. The Indian wore a blue US Army coat with no buttons over a bare chest partially covered with what Sara thought might be a breastplate. Made of rows of small, tubular bones strung together horizontally, the garment extended from his shoulder blades almost to his waist. His legs were clad in deerskin pants with decorative beadwork along the outer side seam. Ornate beadwork also covered his moccasins. He wore three feathers in his long, braided hair, which Sara thought looked greased. His skin was the color of oak, and his silver earrings dangled at least four inches and swung as he looked around the circle. He turned and motioned the rest of the Indians forward. A dozen or more scattered to the various wagons.

A short Indian, dressed in a fringed buckskin shirt and breeches, approached Morgan at the front of the wagon. Hearing a noise, Sara looked back to see another Indian rummaging through things in the back of their wagon. She turned and ran to the rear of the wagon to face a big man with braids down to the middle of his chest. He was wearing a torn frock coat, derby hat, and loincloth. He had a different but not unpleasant smell. *Cinnamon . . . He smells like cinnamon.* Embarrassed by his partial nakedness, Sara was speechless for a moment.

Meanwhile the Indian had pulled a hand mirror out of an open box. He waved it at Sara, then held a large, cloth sack of what looked like blueberries out to her. "Trade?"

Sara's momma had given her the mirror for her sixteenth birthday. Sara shook her head vigorously and reached for the mirror. "No, something else."

He frowned. "Trade!" he said more forcefully, holding the mirror out of her reach. Tucking the mirror under one arm, he took a berry out of the bag, ate it, and pushed the sack at Sara, indicating she should taste.

Ignoring the berries, Sara looked for something else to barter with. Holding up one of Morgan's shirts, she offered, "Trade?"

The Indian shook his head and began looking at himself in the mirror.

Reaching into a small box which had been tucked into a back corner, Sara pulled out a large, pleated paper fan. She unfolded it, revealing colorful painted flowers. She fluttered it back and forth, generating a bit of breeze. Then she held it in front of her face, peering over the top. She definitely had his attention. Folding it back up, she dangled it in front of him. "Trade?"

"Trade," he agreed, setting the mirror down. He then handed the sack of berries to Sara. He turned, opened the fan, and walked away fanning himself. Sara tasted the berries. *Mmm, sweet. We'll have cobbler tonight.*

Sara returned to the front of the wagon just as Morgan had concluded his trade. "A package of tobacco for these deerskin moccasins. I think they'll fit you, honey."

Morgan was right. Soft and colorful, the beaded moccasins were a perfect fit. Sara was touched that Morgan had bartered for something for her instead of for himself. *He can be so thoughtful.* Sara hooked her arm around his waist and looked up at him, "Thank you."

A few days later, a second visit by a group of Indians started much the same but ended differently. Trading was underway when old man Thornton, the grandpa of the Thornton family, flipped his false teeth out of his mouth and into his hand. As Sara watched, the young brave, who had been offering him a buffalo bone necklace as his barter item, took one look at the teeth, shrieked, and ran for his horse. Eager to expand the joke, old man Thornton then began to hold the teeth, clicking them open and closed as he walked among the Indians. It only took a few moments for this to cause minor hysteria among the Indians, who mounted their ponies and dashed away in a cloud of dust. At the end of the day, an older Indian appeared, asking to see the "didanawidgi." Sara was in the group that gathered to hear his conversation with Captain Pollard. It took a while for Pollard to explain that old man Thornton was not a medicine man and the false teeth were not magic, just an invention of white men for those who had lost their teeth. Old man Thornton made the rounds of all the wagons that night reliving the incident and announcing that it was the high point of his life.

Early the following morning, the oxen were yoked and harnessed when Sara heard, "Gertie's gone. Anybody seen our cow?" Matthew Foy was standing in the circle as others harnessed their oxen. "We'd already milked her and tied her rope to the wagon. Next time we looked, she'd disappeared, along with her rope. Thought it was tied pretty securely to the wagon. Possible she just wandered off, but I kinda doubt it."

John Henry and Captain Pollard had been standing to one side of the circle talking. Pollard looked at John Henry, "Suppose it could be Cherokee livestock thieves?"

John Henry nodded. "I'll get a couple of other fellows on horseback and we'll ride back down the trail a ways, circle around where we've been camped. Then we can catch up with the wagon train on the road. If she wandered off, chances are good we'll find her. If not, it may have been the Cherokee. Pretty brazen to take her with people all around."

"Appreciate it, John Henry," Foy sighed, "Gertie's a good cow. Hate like the devil to lose her."

A few hours later, John Henry and the two lawyers, Adam Davis and Grady Burnam, caught up with the wagon train during the nooner. Sara joined the crowd that gathered to hear any news. John Henry looked glum. "No sign of the cow, but we did find tracks—one unshod pony and a cow headed north. Tracked 'em for a while, but by this time, they're long gone."

That night Sara lay in the tent remembering how kind the Foys had been to share their milk with the children each morning and how much laughter and high spirits had accompanied the bartering for butter and buttermilk. *Maybe we could all chip in and replace Gertie!* Before Sara fell asleep, she resolved to talk to Captain Pollard about taking up a collection. *There are enough of us that no one would have to donate much.* Sara fell asleep with plans dancing around in her head.

First thing the following day, Sara found Captain Pollard. Her plan came spilling out in a rush of words. "I think we should all chip in and buy a new cow for the Foys. They've given free milk to the children for the whole trip. They've provided valuable butter and buttermilk for cooking. I want to take up a collection. Can we find out which Choctaw farms sell milk cows? And—"

"Whoa, whoa, slow down. You're talkin' faster than greased lightning. You want the train to fork up enough cash to buy a new cow for the Foys?"

"Yes, I'll talk to all the ladies about it, and they can convince their husbands to donate. Do you know how much a milk cow costs?"

"Haven't bought a milk cow in years. If I had to guess, I'd say between twelve and fifteen dollars. I'll ask Thornton, he's a farmer. Likely know. A cow for the Foys . . . nice idea, Sara."

During the nooner stop, Pollard found Sara. "Farmer Thornton says twelve to fifteen dollars would likely buy a good cow, although Choctaw sellers might charge a premium. May not have much competition."

That evening Sara went around the circle talking to the women as they cooked their supper. "You know, Gertie the cow is gone. The Foy brothers have given free milk to the children for the whole trip. And they've been the source of our milk and butter for cooking. With Gertie gone, so's the butter and half their milk. Don't know about you, but I hate the thought of cooking without it."

At this point, most all the women agreed that meals would suffer.

"I believe we can buy a new milk cow from the Choctaws for twelve to fifteen dollars and surprise the Foys with it. If everyone chipped in a dollar and thirty cents, we should have enough money. Captain Pollard and the Butlers have already contributed, and Morgan and I have too. Even John Henry and Aaron Davis have each added a dollar and thirty cents."

Her closing line was designed to give the women leverage with their husbands. "Remind your husband that without that second cow hot buttered biscuits and cakes will be a thing of the past."

When Sara sensed a hesitation, she said, "Providing a new cow to Genesis, Exodus, and Leviticus seems the Christian thing to do, don't you agree?" The humor and biblical reference seemed to work. By the end of the next day, she had fourteen dollars and thirty cents. Only the Johnson brothers said no.

Sara showed Morgan the money she had collected for the cow purchase. "If we have to, we can bite the bullet and throw in an extra seventy cents to make fifteen dollars, can't we?"

"I can tell you are bound and determined to do this," Morgan said, "so if we need to, we can."

Sara smiled up at him, "Yes, I guess I am bound and determined."

On the fourth day out of Fort Smith, they turned south and began to see clearings with small patches of cultivated land and neat log cabins nestled among shade trees. John Henry and Aaron Davis agreed to ride ahead to farmhouses along the road to ask about cows for sale. The following day they came back to the train saying they had found a Choctaw farmer with milk cows to sell. John Henry had a suggestion. "What do you think about telling the Foys about the gift of the cow and letting them choose one from the farmer?"

Sara thought about it for a moment. "It would still be a surprise, wouldn't it? They will know a good cow when they see one and be able to negotiate a fair price. Makes sense."

"Tomorrow the wagons should pass the farm that has cows to sell. In the morning I'll borrow a second horse and take one of the Foys to choose a cow. Then we can catch up with the wagons on the trail."

The wagons had stopped for their hour-long nooner the next day when John Henry and Matthew Foy rode in. Foy was leading a tawny-colored cow with a white ring around her black nose. He rode around the circle introducing the new cow and saying thank you. "Her name is 'Choctaw' and she will have free milk for all of you for the rest of the trip."

That evening all three Foys came to Sara to say thank you. "She's a beautiful Jersey cow, can't imagine how she made her way to Indian Territory," Mark Foy told Sara.

"We are so pleased to have her," Luke Foy added. "To thank you for the campaign to replace Gertie, we brought you a pound of butter."

Sara thanked them for their generous gift, and as they walked away, Morgan said, "A nice reward for a good deed." Sara nodded as she tucked the butter into her salt can.

The next day Sara made the rounds, returning twenty-one cents to each donor, explaining, "Matthew Foy bought the cow for twelve dollars, so here is the unused money from your part. Thank you for chipping in."

Farmer Tanner's wife was not happy. "Husband says Foy paid too much. Shouldn't'a paid more than ten dollars for that cow. Been cheated. Weren't happy having to give money, anyhow. But you came all prissy and high-falutin', asking for 'a contribution'." The woman had twisted her face into an ugly frown.

Sara felt her temper rising. Reaching for the change in the pocket of her calico dress, she counted out a dollar and thirty cents. She took the woman by the wrist, turned her hand palm up, poured the change into her hand, and said, "Good afternoon," and walked away. Mrs. Tanner was left sputtering, "Well I never . . ." and scowling with her black button eyes.

She should be glad I bit my tongue and didn't say what I wanted to say. Probably made an enemy of Mrs. Tanner.

That evening John Henry and Aaron Davis joined them around the campfire after supper. While Sara finished brewing another pot of coffee, Morgan questioned the men about the Choctaw farm where the Foys bought their new cow. "What was it like?"

Sara added a bit of cold water to the coffeepot to settle the grounds. After a minute, Aaron Davis held out his cup while Sara poured. "Prosperous-lookin' little farm. Nice cabin sheltered in a copse of live oaks. Small fields of corn and hay, vegetable garden, couple of work horses, chickens pecking about, two hogs in a pen, and about a dozen cows."

Morgan waved the coffeepot away. "No thanks, honey. I'm plumb up to my eyebrows in coffee. What about the Indians?"

"Seemed like good people. Polite. Spoke English. Dressed like us," Aaron looked down at his dusty clothes, "only cleaner. Hospitable, invited us in and offered coffee. Cabin was neat as a pin."

"She had been weaving," John Henry joined the conversation, "and was eager to show us the loom and spinning wheel her husband had made for her. Cleverly made too."

"I wouldn't have a clue about making a loom or spinning wheel." Morgan stirred sugar into his coffee.

"I visited with the wife while Foy made his purchase. She said their son was at the Spencer Academy, a Choctaw school for young men, and her husband is a member of the Choctaw Nation Legislature. I could tell she was right proud of both of 'em."

Sara took a sip of her coffee, "Maybe people are more the same than we think."

Before the sun was fully up, the morning scramble began. Morgan hurried to gather the oxen and Sara took down the tent, folded the bed makings, and put everything back in place in the wagon. It was her day to take care of two of the motherless Radcliff children. Sara had just started the morning cook fire when Albert Radcliff delivered his two oldest girls, waved his thanks, and went to collect his oxen. Polly, age six, and Prudence, age five, ran to Sara's side. "Good morning, Miss Sara."

Sara gave each of the small, freckle-faced redheads a hug. *These are such sweet girls.*

"Good morning, girls. Want to play Huckle Buckle Beanstalk while I cook breakfast?"

"Yes please! Can I hide the key first?" Polly shouted. "Prudence started first last time."

Sara agreed and handed Polly a large key. "Prudence, come sit by me while I make coffee. Cover your eyes while Polly hides the key." As Sara worked, Prudence covered her eyes, and together they began to count out loud to sixty.

"Fifty-nine, sixty! I bet I can find the key really fast." Prudence jumped to her feet and began to search. Several minutes passed before she looked under the skillet sitting on the ground beside the fire. "Huckle buckle beanstalk! I found it. My turn to hide the key." The play continued for several rounds while Sara baked biscuits. Morgan returned and, after hitching the oxen, was talked into trying to find the hidden key. Morgan took his time to find it, including reaching on the top of his head and asking, "Is it on my head?" This question made Polly roll her eyes. Finally he located it resting atop one of the wagon wheels. He cried out, "Higgledy-piggledy buttered beans! I found it!"

This sent the girls into gales of laughter. "That's not what you say, silly." Prudence made a face at him.

"Hoppity scotchity cornstalk?"

"No! You must say huckle buckle beanstalk." Polly pronounced each word carefully for Morgan's benefit.

"Well then, huckle buckle beanstalk."

Sara looked up from the skillet. "Huckle buckle beanstalk! Breakfast is ready. Come get your biscuits and eggs." Sara had just announced that they all belonged to the clean-plate club, when Mark Foy came around with milk for the children. The girls grabbed their tin cups and ran to meet him.

"They love it that you'll play with them, Morgan."

"I have to admit that I enjoy it. Reminds me of when I was a kid. It's so sad that they've lost their momma. Radcliff is already talking about the necessity of finding a new wife. Says he can't manage by himself."

"I suspect that's true. The two younger children are ages four and two. Hopefully he'll find a good woman who'll have lots of love for an instant family." *A wife of necessity* . . .

Sara and the Radcliff girls walked beside the wagon that morning. When the girls tired of gathering kindling, Sara taught them to play I spy. At midday the wagons stopped for nooner, and Albert Radcliff joined them for cold corn muffins and canned, stewed tomatoes. The girls bubbled with excitement telling him about their day so far. "We played Huckle Buckle Beanstalk, but Mr. Morgan said higgledy-piggledy buttered beans instead."

"And at breakfast Miss Sara said we were members of the clean-plate club."

Radcliff smiled at his girl. "A couple more bites of tomatoes and you'll be clean-plate-club members now too. Papa has to go back to our wagon. You girls be good, and I'll see you tonight." Hugs were shared. Shortly, the wagons moved forward.

The game for the afternoon was rock-paper-scissors. When they heard Captain Pollard's cowbell, a tie between Prudence and Polly was declared. After the wagons were circled and livestock dealt with, Sara walked the girls back to their wagon. Prudence hugged Sara around the waist. "It's fun to visit you. Can we play games again next time?"

"We sure can. Have you ever played pine-cone toss?" Both girls shook their heads. "I'll teach you how next time. Be good and I'll see you then."

Back at their wagon, Sara looked at Morgan. "I really enjoy those two, but I'm worn out from keeping up with them. So many women have four or more. I guess juggling it all comes with practice."

"Let's hope we have a chance to try." Morgan tried a lascivious look, complete with wiggling eyebrows.

The face sent Sara into giggles. "Oh, Morgan, I hope so too."

A few days later, they found themselves in an undulating land dotted with small mountains and sharp-edged, rocky outcroppings. The wagons passed through shadowy, small ravines and splashed across shallow creeks. Finally the landscape opened onto a grassy savannah. Sara could see islands of oak trees scattered in the distance, but the primary feature of the landscape was miles and miles of blowing grass. It followed the breeze in rippling waves of gold and brown, much as Sara imagined ocean waves must look. The air felt drier and had an almost nutty smell.

As they traveled, Morgan commented on deep, narrow paths worn in the grass, sometimes two or three side by side. "Game trails, I guess."

Looking across the open landscape, rising dust caught Sara's attention. The cloud swept toward them. As it got closer, it turned, and Sara saw a large herd of horses moving at a brisk trot. "Look! Those must be the wild mustangs we've heard about. They're smaller than our horses in Tennessee . . . they look maybe fourteen or fifteen hands high, but see how stocky their legs are. Oh, look at the foals." The stallion in the lead stopped, briefly sniffed the air, tossed his head with a snort. The herd turned and galloped away, manes flying. "They look so wild and free." *And beautiful.*

That night around the campfire, when asked, John Henry told Morgan the paths he'd seen were buffalo traces, paths where the large bison herds traveled. "Not so many here now. They've moved mostly west of the cross timbers."

In the morning, walking alongside Morgan as he led the oxen, Sara waved her arms to encompass the vast landscape around them. "This is beautiful. It's a mosaic. Look, thick patches of small trees woven with flowering vines. They're scattered all through this wide-open prairie of waving grass. And look at the creek, it flows from one small pond to another, making a sparking chain in the sunshine."

"Enjoy the view now. In a few more days we'll enter the cross timbers. We'll be travelin' through nothin' but dense forest again."

"We've already traveled through lots of woods."

"Most of what we've seen so far has been pine forest. Accordin' to Washington Irving, there's nothing quite like the density of the cross timbers hardwood forests."

"Washington Irving? As in 'The Legend of Sleepy Hollow'?"

"Yep. He traveled through here in '32 with a superintendent of Indian resettlement. Wrote a book about it. I ordered a copy when I knew we'd be crossin' Indian Territory. Irving wrote that wanderin' through the cross timbers was like strugglin' through a forest of cast iron. Course, they didn't have a road to follow. Irving's book's packed somewhere in the wagon. I'll dig it out later, if you like."

"Yes, please. I remember Captain Pollard saying we'd be traveling through the cast-iron forest. Puzzled me at the time, now I understand the name." Early that afternoon the wagons circled, and the men went in pursuit of the white-tailed deer and elk they'd been seeing all day. Later, roasting a venison tender-loin for supper, Sara looked up and was startled to see a red wolf watching her from several yards away. She banged her metal spoon on an iron pot of beans heating on the coals of the fire. The wolf continued to watch her. Finally it turned and trotted away into the trees. "I'm sure he was attracted by the scent of cooking meat," she told Morgan as they ate. "Still, it was a bit unsettling." After supper Morgan found Irving's book, *A Tour on the Prairies*, and gave it to Sara. That night, under a blazing full moon, hoot owls serenaded them.

Two days later they were deep in the cross timbers of Indian Territory. "Irving's cast-iron-forest description was a good one," Sara told Morgan as she spooned left-over venison stew over the cornbread on his plate. "I've never seen trees like these. I think there are oak, elm, and maybe hickory, but they're small, twisted, and so close together that the canopies are inter-woven, almost like baskets."

"Uh huh, I spotted some hackberry trees as well. Can you imagine going through this without a road? Even our narrow trail with stumps is a challenge. The Arkansas forest was much more open than this. Not only are the trees dense, the understory is thick with briars, tangled vines, and small shrubs. That's why we had trouble tonight findin' a place to camp. Hardly any clearings."

"Yes, but it's beautiful in its own way. It's like traveling through a roll-ing, green tunnel. The vines with the red-orange, trumpet-shaped flowers are everywhere. We passed a plum thicket today, but we're too early for ripe plums."

"Too bad. Fresh plums would have been good. We'll be in and out of this green tunnel, as you call it, most of the way to Dallas. John Henry says that to the west of Dallas is cross timbers and to the east is blackland prairie. Guess we'll see it for ourselves in a few days."

Sara sighed. "We're almost there. I can hardly wait. In the meantime, listen to the woodpeckers."

Are they hammering a welcome or a warning?

The sound of Captain Pollard's cowbell drew the travelers to the center of the circle the following morning. "If my calculations are right, we'll be in Boggy Depot before the end of the day. It's a major Choctaw town with a store, so we'll spend the night there."

"How many more days to Dallas?" someone shouted.

"I figure we'll be on the road another week or so. Depends on how busy the ferry crossing the Red River is."

That morning the wagons moved out of the cross timbers and back into the savannah, a mixture of tree islands and open prairie. It was midday when the road widened, and Sara could see Boggy Depot. *Glad to see a town. It's certainly prettier than its name.* Nestled in the savannah, Boggy Depot was surrounded by grassland, with a scattering of trees. *It's bigger than I expected.* Lining the road were dozens of structures, varying from neat log cabins to simple two-story, wood-plank houses with barns and other outbuildings. Many houses had rail fences. The road into town split, forming an irregularly shaped town green, centered by a well. The road then came back together, passing a church, a store, other businesses, and more homes. Cultivated fields dotted the outskirts.

Finding a stretch of untilled prairie, they circled the wagons, tended to the livestock, and walked to town. Sara made a beeline for the mercantile store. It was surprisingly large and well stocked. A woman with pitch-black hair and high cheekbones, who Sara assumed was a Choctaw, was behind the counter. "Welcome to Boggy Depot. Let me know if you need help finding anything."

Sara thanked her and walked the aisles, looking at the merchandise and gathering what she needed. As she went, she noted things she and Morgan might consider stocking. *Wonder if we can get Louisiana brown sugar and shelled Indian corn?* Most of the other travelers had gone when Sara took her basket to the counter. "You have a wonderful store."

"Oh?" The woman looked up. "Thank you. No one has ever commented on it before."

"It's well stocked, organized, clean as can be, and you have some interesting items." The woman was silent but attentive, which encouraged Sara to go on. "My husband and I plan to open a store like yours in Dallas."

"Well, do tell!" The storekeeper's smile was broad. "Storekeeping is good business. I wish you luck. If your customers are like ours, be sure to stock lots of tobacco, bacon, and buffalo tongues—if you can get 'em." Sara thanked her for the advice, paid her bill, and as she stepped onto the covered porch, the storekeeper shouted after her, "Be sure to stock bottles of Mexican Mustang Liniment, we can't keep it on the shelves." Sara turned, smiled, and waved her thanks while mentally making a note to add Mexican Mustang Liniment to her list.

That evening after supper, Captain Pollard told the travelers that he'd been advised in Boggy Depot to go to Nail's Bridge to cross the Blue River. "Nail's Bridge is supposed to be the best crossing point. We'll aim to cross the Blue day after tomorrow. From there we go to Colbert's crossing, ferry across the Red River, and we're in Texas. Then four or five more days to Dallas!"

As they went back to their wagons, Sara saw another wagon train coming to a stop not far away. She was surprised at how many wagons there were. Later in the evening, Captain Pollard stopped by to report that the other train was headed for Oregon. "Their captain tells me they'll head to Fort Washita tomorrow and then continue west. I don't envy them the trip, it's long and hard. They have desert and mountains to cross. Thank heavens we don't have to compete with them at the ferry crossings. It takes a long time for fifty wagons to cross."

Captain Pollard was right about timing. They arrived at the Blue River and Nail's Crossing a day and a half after leaving Boggy Depot. The crossing consisted of a house, barn, store, and smokehouse, as well as the bridge. Sara took a deep breath. The smell of smoked meat coming from the smokehouse filled the air. Mr. Nail walked down the wagon line. "Before you cross the bridge, I got a side of beef nicely smoked, if anyone's interested. Costs six cents a pound." Sara and several others joined Nail in the store as he weighed and wrapped thick slices of the still-hot meat in brown paper for each of them.

Sara handed Morgan the package of meat as she climbed onto the wagon seat beside him. Once seated she looked over to see that he had already torn into the package and was greedily eating a slice with his fingers. "I'd forgotten how good freshly smoked beef tastes. Want a bite?" He offered a large chunk to Sara. She took a bite, and the moist, smoky meat made her mouth water.

"Oh my gosh, it's good! I'm sorry I didn't buy two pounds. This may not last until supper." It didn't. Tolls were paid, and the eight wagons, livestock, and horsemen quickly rattled across the long, wooden suspension bridge.

After a few hours, they left the Post Oak Savannah and re-entered the dense, green tunnel of the cross timbers. "I think we've moved into Chickasaw territory now. Apparently the Choctaw were allowed to rent some of the Choctaw Nation land to the Chickasaw. A small piece of it curves around between Nail's Bridge and the river. Colbert's ferry is on Chickasaw land."

That afternoon Sara was starting her cooking fire when Mrs. Tanner walked past. Sara looked up from lighting her kindling and the woman snickered. "Bet you don't know where your husband is or what he's doing."

"What?"

Mrs. Tanner pursed her mouth and made kissing sounds, then walked away looking self satisfied.

Sara sighed. *I'm sure she's just trying to aggravate me.* Still, the comment haunted Sara all night. *Was she trying to tell me something?*

The next day she told Cecilia what had happened. "You are wise to ignore it, Sara. She makes no bones about not liking you. Probably just trying to upset you for no real reason. The woman is a mean gossip." *Cecilia is most likely right.* Sara pushed her questioning thoughts aside.

At the end of the next day, they left the cross timbers and entered the flood plain along the Red River. They camped in sight of Colbert's Ferry and watched as a large wagon train was ferried across, wagon by wagon. "Must have been just ahead of us this whole time," Morgan said. "People are flowin' into Texas."

After supper Morgan and Sara joined several others walking down to see the Red River. It was a curving snake of water—wide, shallow, and rust colored. Sara said, "It's easy to see how it got its name. It's red with mud. Not the prettiest river we've had to cross."

"No," Morgan said, "but it's the last one we have to cross. We'll step off the ferry in Texas, honey."

The next morning they were awake early and formed a line to be ferried across. As they waited their turn, Sara watched wagons and oxen loaded on the large, wooden raft with slat sides. To keep the raft from floating downstream, it was roped to trees on either embankment. Colbert's sturdy slaves pushed the raft across the water with large poles.

"How much are the tolls?" Sara was counting out the toll money for Morgan.

"Each ox team is a dollar and twenty-five cents. We have four teams, so that's five bucks. Wagon is included in that. Then it's two bits for each of us. That's five dollars and fifty cents total."

"So . . . it's about what most of the others we've used have charged. Ferries must be good businesses."

"Yep. Captain Pollard says he heard in Boggy Depot that the Colbert Ferry carries between twenty-five and two hundred wagons every day. That sure is a good business. John Henry told me that Jonathan Colbert, who owns the ferry, is a Chickasaw citizen. He's done well. He also has a five-hundred-acre plantation, a sawmill, gristmill, cotton gin, and enough slaves to operate them all."

"Enterprising man."

It was their turn, and they were waved forward. Morgan jumped off the wagon seat where they'd been waiting and led the wagon onto the raft. The gate was closed behind them. Sara climbed off the wagon seat and stood beside Morgan. The river was slow flowing, and the trip across was smooth. As the raft returned to the other side, Morgan led the teams away from the embankment and a few paces to the road. "We're finally in Texas! We've come a long way, but we're almost there, honey." He picked her up and spun around. "Almost home to Dallas!"

Home to Dallas, I like the sound of that.

When the final wagons and livestock had crossed the river, the wagon train and its excited travelers angled southwest and joined the Preston Road to Dallas. Morgan turned to Sara on the wagon seat, "We can see the cross timbers to the east, but we've entered the edge of the blackland prairie we keep hearing about. Captain Pollard says we should reach the town of Denison today and camp on the outskirts." The mood of the travelers was high that evening. The sound of laughter and even a fiddle echoed around the circle after supper. Morgan had finished setting up their tent while Sara cleared away supper dishes. "I'm going to visit with the men for a while. I'll be back soon." With that and a wave, he was gone.

Sara's shoulders slumped. She was disappointed to be spending the first evening in Texas without him. *Have to find my own company.* Retying her sash and tucking her stray hair back into her bonnet, Sara made her way around the circle to say hello to the Radcliff children and to visit with Cecelia and her sister, Effie.

The Radcliff girls ran to her. "We're in Texas now," Polly said.

"We're going to live in a log cabin," Prudence was jumping up and down.

"Yes, it's exciting. We'll all have new homes in Dallas. Ah, I think your papa is signaling me that it's your bedtime."

"It is. Tell Miss Sara good night. Come on, girls." Albert Radcliff had his youngest in his arms, his four-year-old by the hand, and a frazzled expression on his face. "Time for bed, everyone."

He's a good father, but I suspect he will be relieved when he finds his new, necessary wife.

At the Butler wagon, Sara found Cecelia and Effie with their heads close together talking. Effie looked up. "Sara, we were just talking about you. We need to tell you something that you may not want to hear."

"Oh? What?"

"Gossipy Mrs. Tanner is at it again. She is spreading the rumor that Morgan is carrying on with the Flannigans' oldest daughter."

"No, not Morgan . . . besides, she can't be more than fourteen or fifteen—"

"Wait, Sara," Cecelia said. "We gave it no credence until today when we heard Mrs. Flannigan fussing at her daughter about it, and the girl admitted it. We were just talking about whether or not to tell you and had decided that you should know, rather than being caught off guard by Mrs. Tanner. I'm so sorry."

Sara steadied herself, leaning on the side of the wagon to keep from falling. *Dizzy . . . I'm going to be sick.* She covered her mouth with her hands. *Morgan, you're not the man I married.*

"Here, sit." Effie guided Sara to a large, wooden chest beside the wagon. Cecilia handed her a cup of water.

Sara waved the cup away. "He gambles . . . drinks . . . he . . . he cheats on me." She could hardly get the words out. "He's not who I thought he was." *I've made a terrible mistake.* Tears were streaming down her face. She wiped her nose with the back of her hand. Cecilia handed her a hankie. "What do I do?" she said through her tears. Effie and Cecilia were silent for a long time while Sara sobbed with bent shoulders and her head on her knees.

"Only you can decide that, Sara," Effie said.

Sara blew her nose and stood up. Her face was flushed, and her eyes were red. Her nose was still running. She sniffed. "Well . . . I'm glad you told me."

Cecilia wrapped her arms around Sara. "When or if you want to talk about it, I'm here." Sara relaxed gratefully into the hug.

Pulling away, she stood up straight. "Thank you both for being here for me, but I have to go back to the wagon now. I need to think." Walking back was a blur. She returned to an empty wagon. She could feel the anger bubbling up in her chest, and the hurt changed to fury. *Darn you, Morgan. Was marrying me just a ticket to Texas? Did you guess my papa would help pay for the trip? Do you even love me?* She let out a sob.

"Honey, what's wrong?"

Sara turned to find Morgan standing behind her. She raised her arm and slapped him across the face.

He stumbled back. Sara couldn't read his expression. *Surprise mixed with anger?* He rubbed his cheek. "What was that for?"

Sara could smell the whiskey on his breath. "You have to ask, when you've been fooling around with the Flannigan girl? That's bad enough. But good grief! She's what, fourteen, fifteen?"

Morgan smiled and tried to put his arms around her.

"Don't touch me!" Sara spun away from him.

"It didn't mean anything, sweetheart. Felt sorry for her. She told me she'd never been kissed."

"That's a lame excuse if I ever heard one. Morgan, married men don't go around kissing fourteen-year-old girls, or other women for that matter."

"Oh, honey—"

Sara cut him off, "Here." She thrust a quilt from the tent into his hands. "Get out. Go sleep with the bachelors at the back of the wagon train. I can't look at you tonight."

"Tomorrow you'll remember you're the one I love, Sara."

"Will I? I doubt it. Go."

Clutching the quilt, Morgan walked away.

Sara was suddenly exhausted. *I don't have the energy to do anything but crawl into the wagon.* She settled into the quilts alone with just one question in her mind. *What do I do?* She fell asleep with no answer.

It was still dark when Sara woke to shouts and the sound of running feet. "It's Darnell!" she heard someone shout. *Morgan? What now?* Sara roused herself and crawled out of the wagon. As she stood, John Henry came running. "Sara, Morgan's been snake bit."

"Snake bit?"

"He showed up last night at bedtime and said he wanted to spend the first night in Texas under the stars. Took off his boots and rolled up in his quilt. This morning he got up, started to pull on his boot without shaking it out, and there was a rattler in it. Danged thing struck and got him twice before slinking off into the grass. Come on." He grabbed her by the hand, and they ran to the bachelor's camp.

Morgan was sitting on the ground screaming, "Somebody do something!" Aaron Davis had slit Morgan's pant leg, and Sara could see two sets of angry, red puncture marks on Morgan's calf.

"Somebody do something!" Morgan shouted again. His face was flushed and his eyes wide.

An argument was going on about how to treat the snakebites. Several men had gathered and were huddled beside Morgan. They were arguing.

"Gotta put gun powder on the bite and set it alight. That'll burn the venom right on out."

"No, I've heard to cut out as much wound as we can and pour ammonia on it."

"Lots of whiskey will kill the venom. Give him plenty to drink and pour some on the wound."

Sara looked at John Henry. "What do we do?"

"I've seen all that done and more. He's been struck at least twice, and the bites look deep. I'm sorry, Sara, I don't know."

Oh, Morgan, if only I hadn't gotten mad and sent you away. Forgive me.

"Give me the whiskey treatment," Morgan shouted, with his hand outstretched. Someone handed him a partial bottle and he began to guzzle it. Sara watched as the liquor drizzled down his chin and onto his shirt. Morgan stopped to pour some on his leg, then went back to drinking. The bottle quickly emptied, and Morgan tossed it away. "Another one." He doused the wound again and began alternately drinking and dousing his leg. The second bottle empty, he dropped it and sat woozily, rocking back and forth, crying. "I'm gonna die. I know I'm gonna die." Sara took his hand. He looked up at her with watery eyes. "So sorry, Sara, so sorry."

"Oh, Morgan . . ." Sara was crying too. Before she could finish her sentence, his eyes rolled back in his head and he toppled to one side, unconscious. Sara could see the area around the bites beginning to swell.

"There's not much else we can do," Captain Pollard said. "Most likely there's a doctor in Denison. Heading there will be better than just waiting here. Might give him a chance. Sara?"

"Yes, let's get him to a doctor."

The men carried him to the wagon. Sara tried to make him comfortable on a pile of quilts while the men hitched the oxen. "I'll take the wagon to Denison for you," John Henry said.

Cecilia and Effie came to offer condolences and ask if Sara wanted company.

"Thank you, but I want to be alone with him."

Sara's thoughts were in turmoil. Cradling him in her arms, she wiped his damp, feverish forehead with her handkerchief, and whispered, "Morgan, please don't die. What would I do without you?" Sara rocked him in her arms as they traveled. His breathing became labored, and streaks of red developed on his leg.

He never regained consciousness. They arrived in the small settlement of Denison with his corpse. Sara was a nineteen-year-old widow.

They circled the wagons in Denison. Captain Pollard came to the back of the wagon and poked his head in. "He's gone," Sara said. Tears ran silently down her cheeks. "Can we stay here long enough to bury him in a cemetery? I couldn't stand to bury him by the side of the road."

"I'm so sorry, Sara," Pollard said. "I'll find the undertaker. See what I can do."

The oxen dealt with, John Henry came to the back of the wagon and looked in. "Pollard told me, Sara. I'm so sorry."

Sara's tears were hot on her cheeks. "My anger caused his death, John Henry. I hated some of what he did, but I did love him. Why did he have to go and get snake bit?"

"Wasn't your fault, Sara. I've learned that life is unpredictable and full of unanswerable questions. We just have to go forward the best we can."

A short time later, Pollard returned. "Denison doesn't have a town cemetery, but the undertaker is related to the William Lankford family, and they have a family cemetery. They are good people and have agreed to let us bury Morgan there. Would you like to do that?"

Unable to speak, Sara nodded her head.

Cecilia and Effie helped prepare the body for burial. Sara stroked Morgan's cheek. "He looks like a Greek god. I've wondered lately if that's why I fell in love with him so quickly." She began to cry. "I sent him away, so it's my fault he's dead, but I also feel some relief, and that makes me feel even guiltier. I shouldn't even admit that, should I?"

Effie raised one eyebrow and spoke in a slow, firm voice, "Sara, don't even think that. You are not to blame. The snake killed him. Not you. If anything is to blame, it's the way Morgan chose to live his life."

Cecilia squeezed Sara's hand. "Effie is right, Sara, this was not your fault, so don't feel guilty. As for feeling relief, it's only human. You were facing a life with a heavy drinker who gambled unwisely and chased other women. Honestly, that was nothing to look forward to."

With tears in her eyes, Sara looked at Cecilia and nodded. She knew that was true. "It's just hard to sort out my feelings right now."

Late that afternoon Morgan was buried in a pine box in the Lankford's cemetery, next to a large oak tree. The travelers stood around the open grave in the late spring sunshine and sang, "Softly now the light of day fades upon my sight away. . . ." The young Flannigan girl let out a wail and fell to her knees as the casket was placed in the ground. Sara ignored her. She threw the first handful of dirt and heard the thud as it hit the plain pine box. At the end of the service, she stood graveside until the casket was covered.

Sara thanked Mr. Lankford for allowing the burial in his family's cemetery. As the funeral goers returned to their wagons and prepared to move on the next morning, Sara paid the undertaker, giving him additional money for a stone, along with Morgan's birth and death dates. "Will you also have 'Gone to Dallas' chiseled on the stone, please?"

He nodded. "Sorry for your loss."

Captain Pollard and John Henry walked Sara back to the wagons. "How are you holdin' up?" John Henry's brow was furrowed. "Young Miss Flannigan's performance just now will give that biddy Mrs. Tanner more fuel for gossip. Just ignore it, Sara."

Pollard said, "John Henry's right. Most on the train are disgusted with Mrs. Tanner and give little credence to what she says. Keep your chin high and stare her down. Chances are she's a coward if you stand up to her."

"Captain Pollard's givin' you good advice, Sara."

All evening travelers came to Sara's wagon to offer condolences and food. As it grew dark, Cecilia said, "Would you like me to stay with you tonight, or would you rather be alone?"

"Alone, I think. I need some quiet time to grieve."

Sara sat by her dying fire and watched the coals slowly turn to ashes. *It's as if there were two Morgans.* She thought about the sweet, thoughtful Morgan who was affectionate and made her laugh. The Morgan who was willing to share her dream of a store. *He's the man I fell in love with. He's the Morgan I grieve for.* She resolved to forget the other Morgan, the one who drank, gambled, and chased other women. *I'll just remember the Morgan I loved.*

The next morning John Henry tied his horse and mule to Sara's wagon and harnessed the oxen. "We have about four more days on the road, least I can do is help you get to Dallas safely."

"Thank you, John Henry."

"I'm truly sorry about Morgan, Sara. How are you doin'?"

"I'm sad and I'm struggling with some guilt. We quarreled, and I made him leave our wagon. If I hadn't done that, he'd be alive."

"Figured you two had a fight. Way I look at it, Morgan made some bad decisions. If anything led to his death, it was those choices. You were a mighty fine wife, Sara . . . a better wife than he was a husband. Remember that if you start feelin' guilty. May sound harsh, but it's true. Set the guilt aside and remember the good times."

That night Sara, the list maker, wrote down the positive memories she had of Morgan. *He danced every dance with me at the party on the night we met. Wouldn't let anyone cut in.* A tear splashed on her notepad. *How we laughed as he put wiggly worms on my hook when we fished in the horse farm pond. He was more squeamish than I was.* She smiled as she thought about baking the mosquito-and-apple pie. *Wonder if he ate two pieces just to make me feel better about the mosquitoes in the crust?* She remembered when he courted her. *He brought Momma flowers on my birthday to tell her thank you for having me. What fun we had riding and jumping fences. When my hat blew off as we rode the first day at the horse farm he retrieved it and kissed me for the first time. This is the only Morgan I'll grieve for and remember.*

As the small outpost of Denison disappeared behind them, the wagons rolled toward Dallas across the grass-covered Grand Prairie, a small island prairie surrounded to the east, west, and south by the gnarly, stunted oak trees of the cross timbers. Sara watched as the rising sun caught the yellow blossoms of Indian grass and the purple of blazing star and wild indigo flowers. At one point off to the west, she could see the charred remains left by a prairie fire. The smell of smoke lingered in the air. *It's a new day and I have to learn to face it alone.*

As they walked, John Henry said, "This is a small version of blackland prairie. What's on the other side of the trees to the east of this is the big blackland prairie. It'll be good cattle-grazing country, plenty of grass and wide-open spaces." John Henry guided the oxen to avoid a mudhole full of the sticky, black gumbo created by the mix of rain and black soil. "Buffalo used to roam all this grassland in numbers too big to count. It was a sight to see. Not nearly so many here now, they mostly roam further to the west, millions of 'em. Make mighty fine eatin'. Especially the tongue."

"My momma sometimes cooks beef tongue. I like it." Sara realized she hadn't eaten the day before and she was hungry. "Speaking of food, I have some cornbread and a bit of the wild honey from the honey tree Michael Butler found. Want some?"

John Henry nodded. "I'd be much obliged."

At the end of the day, the road had crossed the small Grand Prairie and reached the edge of the cross timbers. They camped there overnight and then again entered the dark, rolling, green tunnel of trees and vines the next morning.

Although John Henry was driving Sara's wagon, and despite their age difference, they were each conscious of propriety and concerned about potential wagging tongues. To protect her reputation, Sara had asked Cecilia if she'd be willing to spend the evenings and nights with her. She'd said, "Of course."

John Henry said goodbye following each day's drive and joined the other bachelors at the end of the wagon line for supper and the night's sleep. Cecilia came across the wagon circle in time to help with supper, eat with Sara, and stay the night. At the end of the third day in Texas, Sara realized John Henry had assumed the role of surrogate uncle. "Thank you for helping me, John Henry."

John Henry smiled. "Happy to do it, Sara, having someone to watch over gives me a purpose, something I've lacked since my family died."

Listening to the chorus of wolves at sunset on the third night in Texas, Sara was especially glad to have Cecilia's company. As they gathered wood for the campfire and then prepared a pot of squirrel stew, Sara said, "Cecilia, may I ask you an impertinent question?"

Cecilia grinned. "Only if you don't mind an impertinent answer."

Hoping not to hurt her friend's feelings Sara asked, "Why have you never married?"

Cecilia's reply was serious. "I was very much in love once and engaged to be married. Johnny, my intended, drowned a week before our wedding when a ferry boat overturned in the river."

Sara gasped. "That's so sad!"

"To make it worse, there was gossip. Another girl, who had set her cap for Johnny, spread the rumor that he regretted asking me to marry him and had drowned himself. I knew it wasn't true, but it was hurtful. I learned then that when untrue or unkind things are said you have to ignore them as best you can."

"That can be hard to do."

"Yes, but dwelling on the hurtful things can make you bitter."

"You never found anyone else you loved?"

"I had other opportunities to marry, but I made up my mind to never settle for someone I didn't love as much as I had loved my Johnny. No one ever measured up. I went on to teach school, and I guess I spent my love on my nieces, nephews, and students. I have no regrets about not settling."

That night, wrapped in her blanket, just before drifting off to sleep, Sara thought about what Cecilia had said about not settling. *If I marry again, I won't settle for someone I don't love. And I will choose very, very carefully.*

At the end of the fifth day in Texas, they stopped early, circled the wagons, and camped a few miles outside of Dallas. Cecilia told Sara the travelers planned to celebrate the end of the long trip with venison roasted over the campfire and a party. "Captain Pollard plans to play his fiddle, Mark Foy has unpacked his concertina, and John Henry says he'll accompany on his harmonica. Do you want to come?"

"You go on. I'd rather stay here at the wagon tonight. I'll be fine."

Sara could hear music and laughter from the party as she began to consider what to do. *I'll be in Dallas tomorrow. Alone.* She wondered if she should return to Tennessee and give up her dream of a store. Could she even start a store by herself? Fail, and she'd be alone with no money. *Destitute women don't have many choices in the West. Guess I could be someone's wife of necessity. No,* she told herself, *I want to live my dream.* As she settled in for the night and closed her eyes, she thought, *Sara Darnell, storekeeper. That's who I'll be in Dallas.*

Dallas?
"This ain't no town!"

Sara could sense the excitement of the group of settlers who led their wagons down the Preston Road and into Dallas the next morning. But as they got closer, it was obvious from the muttering Sara could hear that their jubilation had turned to dismay. Dallas was not what the travelers had expected. Sara looked at the dusty, potholed trails forming a square around a squat, two-story brick building set in a scattering of trees. *Maybe a courthouse?* The structures on the square were mostly low, rough log cabins hunkered down in the brown earth. *There are more vacant lots than buildings.* Some of the buildings had business signs, others appeared to be homes. A two-story log hotel with stables, a couple of two-story brick buildings, and a two-story log boardinghouse—according to the sign swinging in the wind— rose above the simpler cabins and were the dominant structures. There were numerous log cabins and sheds randomly scattered away from the square. A network of dusty, winding foot paths connected them to each other and to the square. Hens and a couple of ragged roosters pecked at the dry ground, and two hogs were rooting at the edge of someone's small garden plot. Clothes hung haphazardly on a rickety looking clothesline. There were a couple of horses tied in front of the courthouse and only half a dozen people in sight on porches or on the streets of the square. A lone wagon sat in front of one of the cabins. A mongrel dog was asleep in the shade it cast. Sara could hear distressed conversation from the wagons around her. Hearing the ruckus, a few people began to come out of the scattered structures. Soon a tall, black-haired, deeply-tanned man in a suit and derby hat came into the street and shouted, "Welcome to Dallas! Please come forward so you can hear me and I can greet you." Sara's first impression was that he had the look and sound of someone in authority. *Wonder who he is?*

Sara and the other travelers gathered around him as he shook hands and welcomed them. "I'm Alexander Cockrell and I offer the land here."

Ah, the man in charge.

The Johnson twins stepped out of the group. Horace shouted, "This ain't Dallas. The Peters Colony man promised Dallas was a real town."

"Dallas is a real town, young man. We are the county seat. We've got a courthouse, a church, some schools, a hotel. Almost 450 people." He gestured toward the square. "There's a general store, a sawmill, a weekly newspaper. I've even built a new wooden toll bridge across the Trinity River." Cockrell smiled. "Settlers here have great prospects."

Horace frowned. "Don't look like it."

"On the contrary, Dallas is growing. A large group of two hundred settlers has come from France, Switzerland, and Belgium to establish a colony on the limestone cliff just across the river." He pointed to a bluff in the near distance. "They believe there is no better opportunity in Texas than that offered by Dallas."

John Henry looked at Sara, wiggled his eyebrows, and grinned. "Sure sounds like a land promoter. This is his one chance to make a sale before folks move on down the road."

Cecilia's brother-in-law stepped forward. "My name is Michael Butler. I heard John Neely Bryan was the man to see about lots."

"Yes sir, he was. I bought his interests in the land and the ferry and have been responsible for the Dallas land grants ever since 1853."

"But what about the Peters' Colony? Isn't that what this is?" shouted Norman Johnson.

"It was the Peters' Colony. Not anymore," Cockrell said. "Peters' investment group received the Texas land grant for this colony and promoted it. Mr. Bryan, not knowing it belonged to them, developed it and granted lots and acreage. Ultimately, Peters' company gave up the colony for land in West Texas, and Dallas became Bryan's. I purchased the rights to it from him in 1852. I assure you that your homestead claims will be legal in the state of Texas."

"How large are the homesteads here?" someone shouted.

"A single man receives 320 acres, 640 acres for a couple. It's mighty fine land." Cockrell gestured toward the Dallas citizens who had come out of buildings and begun to gather. "Why don't you talk to some of these folks? They seem real curious to visit with you. I'm sure they'll be happy to answer questions."

Cockrell pointed at a two-story brick building on one corner of the square. "That's the corner of Commerce and Jefferson Streets. I'll be in my office in the brick building there, if you have more questions. I'm ready to help you select your new homesteads. Come on in when you're ready." He smiled a toothy grin. "Welcome to Dallas."

Farmer Thornton stepped forward. "I'm ready to talk, Mr. Cockrell." The two men walked toward Cockrell's office together.

As others stood deciding what to do, Sara noticed three women standing in front of one of the log structures. Walking over she introduced herself. "Hello, I'm Mrs. Darnell from near Rome in Henderson County, Tennessee. I regret to say that I'm newly widowed. I lost my husband to a rattlesnake bite the morning after we crossed the Red River. I need some womanly advice."

At the end of the day, Sara's traveling companions had split into two groups. The Pollards and the Butlers, along with the Thorntons, the Fishers, and the Fowlers, decided to stay in Dallas, as did John Henry and the lawyer Aaron Davis. The Johnson twins, the Tanners, the Flannigans, lawyer Grady Burnam, the three Foy brothers (with their cows), and the newly widowed

Mr. Radcliff, with his four children, chose to move on down the Preston Road toward Waco, Austin, and San Antonio.

"What will you do?" John Henry asked Sara. "Are you sure you don't want me to help you find safe transportation back to Tennessee to your family?"

"Thank you, but no. Morgan and I wanted to make a life here and I want to stay."

"It won't be easy for a young woman alone."

"I know, but I have a plan." Toward the end of the day, it was finally Sara's turn to meet with Alexander Cockrell. She stepped into the brick building and saw an open door to the left of the staircase. She took a deep breath, whispered to herself. "I can do this" and stepped into the doorway.

"Come in, please." Cockrell was sitting at a round table at one end of the room. A few papers were spread across the table. There were two desks facing each other in the center of the room. Several bookcases and cabinets with drawers lined the walls. He pulled the papers into a stack and motioned for Sara to take the chair across from him.

"How can I help you?" he asked.

"Mr. Cockrell, I'm Mrs. Sara Darnell from Henderson County, Tennessee. My husband, Morgan Darnell, died from a rattlesnake bite our first day in Texas. So, I am newly widowed."

"Oh my! That's terrible. I'm sorry for your loss."

Sara nodded her thanks. "Despite this, I've made the decision to stay in Dallas. I plan to open a general store and I have a proposition for you."

"All right, young woman, what's your proposition?"

"Although I no longer have a husband, I'd like to claim land as a widow."

"That may be possible—"

Sarah held up her hand to stop Cockrell. "The money I have arrived with is enough to rent a building and start a general mercantile store, but I don't have the money now to pay the surveying, registration, and other fees for a land grant."

"If you don't have the funds . . ." His voice trailed off.

"I don't *yet* have the funds," Sara said. "I'm simply asking you to hold a 320-acre grant for me for three years. In the meantime, I'll live in Hattie Brown's Boardinghouse and run my store. After three years, I should be able to pay for my land grant. If I can't pay in three years, you may grant the land to someone else."

Alexander Cockrell looked across the table at Sara. "Mrs. Darnell, why should I agree to this?" Cockrell focused his piercing, dark eyes on hers. "Forgive me, but you seem too young to have ever run a store."

Sara didn't blink. "Looks can be deceiving, Mr. Cockrell. My father has a horse farm in Henderson County, Tennessee. I have no brothers and am the eldest child, so I was often called upon to help Papa in his business. I can keep books. I understand how to manage inventories of supplies and can even direct employees. I am nineteen, not afraid to work hard, and confident that these skills will help me run a profitable store. The only risk you bear, Mr. Cockrell, is holding one of many unclaimed lots for a short period. I'd guess that you don't have high expectations of granting all the lots in three years."

Cockrell nodded. "Most likely, it will take longer."

"Dallas will benefit from a second store that will offer basic supplies and provide things that ladies tell me are missing from the existing store. The ladies I spoke with today complained that the current store meets the needs of the men but ignores the women. The women have difficulty getting acceptable calico, sewing notions, home goods, things for their children, and other than the most basic supplies. They also confirmed that if I order them, a freight service can bring these needed things in from Shreveport. My store will be a fine addition, especially for the ladies of the community. I suspect your wife would agree. How about you?"

Cockrell burst into hearty laughter. "I declare! I believe you'd win a debate with our best Texas politicians. How can I say no? The Texas Constitution does allow women to own property. As a widow, I'm going to consider you qualified for a grant. Let's look at the map and see which 320 acres capture your fancy, Mrs. Darnell."

Sara chose 320 acres of blackland prairie on the eastern edge of the town plat. "When the time comes, can I change the location based on what else might be available?"

"I have marked the acreage with your name. That will serve to hold a grant for you. If you wish to change when you make your payment, you can. I'll have a letter drawn up tomorrow with the details of our agreement. By the way," Cockrell grinned, "the freight company you mentioned is mine.

We ship freight between Shreveport, Jefferson, and Houston. We can sure handle your merchandise needs. Welcome to Dallas, Mrs. Darnell." They sealed the bargain with a handshake.

Leaving the square, Sara saw John Henry. "Have you met with Cockrell? she asked.

"Sure have. Chose 320 acres on the northeastern edge of the colony. It's good grassland and the East Fork of the Trinity runs through it. My cattle will have plenty of water and grazing and ample roaming room."

He grinned until his eyes crinkled and shook his head when Sara told him about her meeting with Cockrell. "Sounds like your plan is well underway."

"It is. Morgan and I'd been told that a freight company delivered merchandise to Dallas from Shreveport. Turns out to be Mr. Cockrell's freight company. I am making a list of merchandise to order for Sara's Complete Merchandising Emporium. Do you like the sound of that name?"

John Henry raised one eyebrow. "Yes, but remember sign painters charge by the letter."

It had been a long, exciting day, and John Henry left to find a room at The Crutchfield House Hotel, a two-story building on the edge of the square, just across from the courthouse. Sara made her way to Mrs. Brown's boardinghouse, across the square, where she arranged for a room and two meals a day—breakfast and supper. Mrs. Brown was a tall, slender woman with lush, brown hair pulled into a knot on top of her head. A few loose strands escaping the knot softened her look. Sara guessed she was in her forties. Mrs. Brown set down the book she was carrying to give Sara a tour of the house. As she gestured for Sara to follow her upstairs, Sara noticed that she had long, expressive fingers.

The log boardinghouse was a two-story structure with wood-plank floors. There were three upstairs bedrooms, the smallest of which Sara chose, since it was a single. It had a small bed, a three-drawer dresser large enough for a washbowl and pitcher on top, a water pail, chamber pot, and a couple of wall hooks for clothes. *I'll need more wall hooks.* There was also a small looking glass, a wooden chest, a braided bedside rug of blue and white, and a lockable door. Downstairs was one room with a fireplace, a woodstove for heating, a pine table with four chairs, and, in the corner, three small, unmatched chairs with dubious upholstery. Another mixed-color braided rug covered the floor by the chairs. A rain barrel sat at the side of the house near the kitchen, which was in its own small log structure and contained an iron cooking stove. A rough lean-to shed served as a washroom for clothes and linens and for bathing. The privy, or outhouse, stood away from the house a bit. Based on the structures Sara had seen so far, the boardinghouse was one of the nicer buildings in town.

Mrs. Brown cleared her throat as they finished the tour. "Breakfast is at six. Supper is at five thirty. Miss either meal and the cold food will be left on the table for an hour. Curfew is at ten, and guests are only allowed for one hour in the evening and only downstairs. Understand?"

"Yes, ma'am." Sara felt the need to salute the woman.

Over supper, Mrs. Brown told Sara, "My husband was one of more than four hundred men killed by a Mexican firing squad in the Goliad massacre in 1836, at the start of the Texas Revolution. My son was just three. He and I lived in Galveston for years. Then, in 1848, I sold the donation land grant the state had given me as a widow of Goliad. I didn't want to farm, so I came to Dallas and built the boardinghouse. My son lives and works in Galveston."

"How far away is Galveston?"

Mrs. Brown thought for a moment. "Probably four hundred miles as the crow flies. Farther by road."

Sara's eyes widened. "Texas is big."

That night after Sara climbed into bed and pulled the quilt up to her chin, she said a brief prayer, then began a mental list of what she needed to do the next day. Explore the town. Find a vacant building for her store and negotiate with the owner. She should sell the oxen and wagon, probably to a farmer. The oxen should command good money, which she truly needed. She wanted to finish her list of merchandise and arrange an order that freighters could fill in Shreveport and deliver to Dallas. In the dark, a bit of doubt crept in. *Can I really build a business alone?* Her eyelids fluttered as she thought about the tasks ahead, and she drifted off to sleep to spend the first night in her new home. She dreamed of riding across Tennessee's bluegrass fields with Morgan and racing to jump the fences. When she woke, the dream was clear in her mind and she felt sad. Moments later, the dream and the feeling had melted away.

The next morning, after a cold-water sponge bath, Sara took her only black dress out of her trunk. Hurrying to dress, she pulled on her cotton chemise, stepped into her drawers, pulled up her knee-high stockings, and secured them with garters. Next she stepped into her shoes and then pulled on her split-front corset, pulling the laces tight. Deciding a hoop was not necessary, she added one crinoline underskirt, ankle-length pantalettes and tied a small cloth pocket around her waist, aligning it with where she knew there would be a small slit in her dress. Hurrying, she slipped on the high-necked dress, adding a clean white cotton collar and matching cuffs. Grabbing her bonnet and gloves, she lifted the dress's full skirt, and ran downstairs. Mrs. Brown had hot coffee and corn cakes with honey ready and waiting. As she ate, Sara asked, "Are there any empty buildings on the square that might be suitable for a store?"

Mrs. Brown thought for a moment. "Well, we had two druggists for a while, only needed one, so the second moved on. His place was the log building next door to Webster's Saddlery on Commerce Street. It's on the opposite side of the square from old man Crutchfield's hotel. You might take a look at it."

With the last bite of corn cake gone and Mrs. Brown saying she didn't need help with the dishes, Sara tied on her bonnet, pulled on her gloves, and was out the door in a flash. A rainstorm had blown through the night before and what had been a dusty tangle of paths weaving between buildings had become a sea of mud, dotted with puddles and tufts of brown grass. Wishing for taller boots, Sara lifted her skirts out of the mud and began to explore. *I want to see the Trinity River.*

Following the directions to the river, which Mrs. Brown had given her the night before, she walked across the muddy road to the courthouse on the corner of Houston and Commerce Streets. Trying to avoid the biggest puddles, she then turned and walked two short blocks down Commerce to the Cockrell Bridge on the small bluff at the edge of the Trinity. The toll keeper's cabin was on the riverbank beside the bridge. A clean-shaven black man in a boxy, homespun jacket and pants was lounging in a chair in front of the wooden tollgate. He turned to Sara and stood, removing his wide-brimmed, flat-topped straw hat. "Wanna cross, ma'am?"

"No, I've just arrived and wanted to see the Trinity River and the toll bridge."

He grinned. "Fine bridge, ain't it? Used to be jus, a place to ford the river. Indians and buffalo crossed here for who knows how long."

"I didn't expect a covered bridge. It really is impressive. It's like a long, open-ended wooden box across the water."

"Yes 'em. Took a buncha boards. Massa Cockrell started a steam-powered sawmill jus' to build it. Mill's noisy as hell a-poppin', but it sure can cut de lumber. I worked on buildin' the cedar crib pilings, filled 'em with rocks. . . . Lawdy, lawdy, they be there forever."

"How long is it?"

"She's 620 feet, one side to the other. And look there." He pointed. Sarah saw a planked causeway across the river bottom. "Gov'ment said we done had to build that too. And the house 'cross the street . . ." Sarah turned to see a two-story, white-washed house. "That be the Cockrell's"

"Massa Cockrell trusts me to collect de tolls. Built this house for me." He pointed toward the log cabin. "He tole me, Berry Derrit, you be in charge dis bridge." Sara heard the pride in his voice.

Sara thanked toll-taker Derrit for the information and walked away, following the bank of the river. It was a narrow, deep channel. John Henry had told her, "The Trinity's a sweet-water river 'cause it doesn't flow through any salt." *Might not be salty, but sure looks muddy.* The flow was slow, placid. She remembered Captain Pollard saying that the area was called "Three Forks" because the Clear, West, and Elm forks of the river came together just above Dallas. Looking across the water, Sara saw that the far bank was thick with trees. *More of the cast-iron forest, I suppose.* Although, through the trees, she could see the Preston Road going south and the beginnings of a few smaller trails meandering in other directions. The cross timbers cast-iron forest dominated the landscape to the west. The one exception was a limestone bluff rising out of the trees to the southwest, climbing about 250 feet in height and ending just before reaching the river.

The sun was hot. It had burned the clouds away, leaving the air muggy without a cooling breeze. Sarah took a deep breath. *The humid air smells . . . well, I'm not quite sure how it smells, . . . just pleasantly green, I guess. If you can call a smell green.*

Turning away from the Trinity, she walked back toward the square. As she'd seen yesterday, random cabins serving as homes or businesses were lightly sprinkled on four sides of the courthouse. *It's hardly a solid square.* A scattering of other structures could be seen off the square. A web of footpaths connected them to the square and to each other.

It didn't take long to identify the property of the long-gone druggist. *Looks as if it's been vacant for a while.* The covered porch was littered and dirty, the front door was hanging on one wooden hinge. But it seemed solidly constructed and the logs were well chinked. Sara knocked and, hearing no answer, stepped in past a large spiderweb. In the main room, there were dusty floor-to-ceiling shelves along the walls, a set of shelves through the middle of the room, and a paper-littered counter in front. Hinged, wooden shutters covered a small window. There was an iron stove for heating in one corner. Sara guessed the building was about thirty feet square. The back had been divided into two small rooms with a back door in between. *It's perfect!*

"And who are you?" A booming voice echoed in the empty room, startling Sara. She wheeled around to see a huge man in a black workman's apron standing in the doorway. Several sharp tools protruded from his apron's large front pocket. He had a serious expression that wrinkled his brow above a broad nose that appeared to have been broken in the past. His dark, straight hair was parted on the side and combed at an angle across his forehead. He ducked down to enter the door.

Sara gulped. Trying to sound as businesslike as possible, she said, "I'm Mrs. Darnell. Mrs. Brown at the boardinghouse told me this building might be for rent. It's vacant and the door was half open, so I stepped in to see if it might be suitable for my purposes."

"And just what might your purposes be?" the giant asked in his rumbling voice, fixing his prominent, round eyes on hers.

"I wish to establish a general-merchandise store. Do you know if this building is available?"

The giant was looking a bit less threatening. "I do know, and it is. I'm Ira Webster. The saddle shop next door is mine." He gestured to indicate which side. "My cousin opened a drugstore here a year and a half ago but has moved on to Jefferson. I suspect that he'd be pleased to rent it if you can come to agreeable terms. There's a law office across the way." He gestured toward what Sara knew was Jefferson Street. "The lawyer there, Mr. Clements, represents my cousin in matters concerning his properties in Dallas. Just look for his sign. Speak with him and tell him Ira Webster sent you."

"Thank you, Mr. Webster. I hope that our businesses will soon be neighbors."

As she left the building, Sara turned to see a woman in a faded calico dress and matching bonnet picking her way across the muddy swamp of the street. As the woman approached, she smiled and extended her gloved hand to Sara. "Welcome to Dallas. I'm Mrs. John Neely Bryan. My husband is away right now, but I wanted to meet you. Happy to have more women settlers. We women are still a small group here."

Mrs. Bryan was in her thirties, pale and fine-boned with walnut-brown hair and brown eyes. Sara was touched by the woman's warm greeting. "I'm Mrs. Darnell, a new widow from Tennessee. I'm looking forward to being part of the community. In fact, I hope to open a general-merchandise store."

As they talked, Mrs. Bryan pointed to a log cabin with a covered breeze-way connecting two rooms. "We live over there. You can see that Dallas is still very primitive, but we're making progress. When John and I first married, we lived in a tent made from the sailcloth that had covered John's wagon. Then John built us a single-room cabin. Now our two-room log cabin feels downright luxurious." She laughed. "One gets used to the conditions. Hope you'll like it here. Good luck with your store." She walked away, avoiding a large hog wallowing in a deep mudhole in the middle of the swampy street.

Sara crossed the square and located the single-room log cabin which was Lawyer Clement's office. The lawyer looked up and peered over his glasses as Sara stepped in. Clements sat behind a small desk and was almost hidden by a large, untidy stack of books, papers, and old newspapers. Sitting on the edge of the desk were three tin cups filled with various levels of what looked like coffee. Sara was struck by how thin the lawyer was. He had sparse, white hair that floated around his head as he moved, mutton-chop whiskers, and a bushy, white mustache, both almost lost in the wrinkles in his face. His suit was old fashioned, yet it seemed appropriate for he was not a young man.

"What can I do for you, young lady?"

"I am Mrs. Sara Darnell. Ira Webster sent me. I'm interested in renting the vacant pharmacy building next door to his saddlery shop. He says you manage it for the owner."

Clements gestured for her to sit down. She carefully lifted a stack of papers off the chair across from Clements. "Just stack 'em on the floor." As she did, several pencils rolled out of the stack and under the desk. She sat.

"Why does a little slip of a girl like you need a building?" His voice was thin—Just like him, Sara thought—and nasal.

"I plan to open a general-merchandise store."

"Humph, wouldn've pegged you as a businesswoman."

"Well, I am. Is the building for rent?"

"Yes, if the rent is right and you're willin' to sign a lease."

"What rent are you asking?"

"Six dollars a month for a six-month lease with three-months' deposit.

"Seems high for a small place like Dallas. Demand for space can't be too great since the building looks like it's been vacant for quite a while. I'll pay four dollars a month, but I'll give you a twelve-month lease, starting in two weeks, with a deposit of two months' rent."

Clements looked at her over the top of thick glasses. "Humph . . . Fair enough. Come back tomorrow afternoon with the deposit, and I'll have the paperwork ready to sign." Clements slowly shifted in his chair, stretched, and reached under the desk to chase his errant pencils as Sara nearly danced out the door.

Next on Sara's list was a visit to the existing general store. The sign read "West's Store" and hung on a single-story, log building located two doors down from Clements' office. It was catty-corner across the square from the building she had just rented. She adjusted her bonnet and stepped from the covered porch into the store. It too had shelving covering the walls and a single shelf down the center. There was a boy stocking shelves but no sign of the proprietor. Sara could see immediately that the store was, as the Dallas ladies has told her, a male-oriented store. Hammers, saws, axes, files, and other tools covered one wall. A glass-fronted counter displayed guns, and a countertop display case was full of tobacco products. Stacks of folded clothing for men, blankets, buckets, tin cups, and pierced-tin lanterns competed for space in the center shelving. The back door was open, and outside she could see piles of oxen yokes, plows, and big seed bags. The second wall had canned goods, coffee, castor oil, flour, cornmeal, and other food staples. Sara finally found two bolts of calico, a few sewing notions, a small stack of queensware dishes, and some cooking pots Sara understood why the ladies of Dallas were complaining. The store had very little for them other than basic pantry supplies. *There's certainly room for another store catering to women's needs.*

Leaving West's Store, Sara walked back to the river and sat on a large rock in the dappled shade of a live oak tree. She sat with her pad and pencil, enjoying the soft sounds of the mockingbirds and river frogs as she refined her list of merchandise to order for the store. *Let's see, the list of food, fabric, and sewing products looks good, with the addition of more flour. Wonder if I can afford to add three darning eggs, two buttonhole cutters, maybe two earthenware foot warmers, and three sugar nippers?* She chewed on her pencil and slowly added to her list. An hour later, Sara smoothed her skirt and made her way to Mr. Cockrell's office.

A loud "Come in" answered her knock on the door.

As she opened the door, Cockrell rose from behind his desk. "Mrs. Darnell, what can I do for you?"

"If you have a moment, I'd like information on ordering merchandise from Shreveport for my store."

"Happy to oblige. Sit down, please."

As Sara sat, she saw that, in contrast to Lawyer Clements' office, the Cockrell office was neat as a pin. Files were lined up on the desk, pencils rested in a cup, and a threaded-screw candlestand stood on one corner of the desk. The candles were burned down almost to nubs. *Work goes on here into the evening.*

Cockrell cleared his throat, and Sara realized she was staring at the desk. She quickly shifted her attention to him.

"Ordering is a pretty simple process. The merchandise wholesaler sends me current product and price lists. You can create your order from that. We have a freight load comin' in tomorrow from Shreveport, and the freighter will carry your order request and your 50 percent deposit back with him. The next scheduled freighter will deliver, and I will accept the final payment plus the freight costs. Takes about six weeks overall."

Cockrell reached in his desk drawer for the current product list. "That what you'd like to do?"

"Yes, please." Sara took the product and price lists. "May I take these and bring them back later with my order?"

"That's fine. Freight should arrive midday tomorrow. Deadline for your order would be first thing the next mornin'. Freight costs are on the price sheet too."

Thanking Cockrell, Sara left to review the product list and calculate the cost of what she hoped to order.

As she walked back to the boardinghouse at the end of the day, she thought about the Morgan she had fallen in love with. *You'd have enjoyed today, Morgan. I'm sorry we can't do this together. But I'm determined to start a store you'd have been proud of.*

After supper Sara took the time to write to her family.

> *Dear Momma and Papa,*
>
> *I hope this finds both of you, Grandma, and my sisters all well. I have wished for you all during the last several months. I hope you received the letters I sent from Little Rock and Fort Smith.*
>
> *I have arrived safely in Dallas, but I have terrible news. On our first day in Texas, Morgan was struck by a rattlesnake and died. I buried him*

in the small settlement of Denison. There is no town cemetery, so he is in the William Lankford family cemetery on the edge of Denison. I paid for a tombstone with his name and "Gone to Texas" carved on it along with his birth and death dates. At least he got to cross the Red River and step on Texas soil.

A letter is enclosed for Morgan's parents. Do you think you could find a way to send it to his family? I know they live somewhere near Nashville, but I don't have an address. Papa, maybe you know someone who knows them? Thank you for trying.

I made many friends on the trail and they watched over me the rest of the way to Dallas. Papa, you'll be glad to know that a tough former Texas Ranger drove the ox teams for me, and Momma, a respectable former schoolteacher became my companion.

The village of Dallas is much smaller than I expected, just a series of log structures scattered randomly in a rough square. Mr. Cockrell, the promoter, says it has fewer than five hundred people. The streets are just dusty, dirt paths. When it rains, I know I'll wish for tall boots.

My plan is to stay in Dallas and follow my dream of starting a store. I have also chosen a 320-acre homestead which Mr. Cockrell will hold for me for three years. I hope to be able to pay the proper fees for it then.

There are a few farms scattered nearby. Papa, if you were here I suspect you'd ask about the farmers' crops. The land here is virgin blackland prairie and has never been plowed. I'm told by locals that horses are not strong enough to pull the plows. Instead, the first plowing takes five yokes of oxen to bust the sod (as the process is called). Most farmers are trying corn or cotton and at least one farmer has planted wheat. The ground is fertile, and some planting is done by dibbling, which I understand is making a hole with a stick and dropping a seed in. As a result, crops are small.

Mustang horses run wild here. They are smaller than our Tennessee horses. You would enjoy seeing them.

The citizens I've met—including Margaret Bryan, the wife of the founder of Dallas— have been friendly. I have a private room in a boardinghouse run by Mrs. Brown. I am her only guest right now, but she tells me that she gets occasional travelers and sometimes the freighters hauling goods between the small communities will also have a passenger who will stop overnight. Mrs. Brown puts on a stern, somewhat serious face but at heart seems like a good woman. Her house rules are very strict, which is good. She keeps a rifle in the main room and I suspect she knows how to use it if necessary. No need to worry. I am in a safe, comfortable place.

I have contracted for an existing building for my store and hope to have my merchandise order delivered by ox cart from Shreveport within a month or so. The outside of the new store is rough with unhewn logs, but the inside walls are square and smooth. There is a puncheon floor. This was a new term for me, but it means the floor is made with split logs, smooth side up. The floor is a bit splintery but superior to the packed dirt floors of many cabins here. There are shelves from floor to ceiling, a long front counter, and two small storerooms at the back. The chimney is made of mud-covered sticks. I have a wide porch which the clapboard roof also covers. There is a small outhouse out back. Previously the building was a drugstore. It measures about thirty feet on each side. It is on the town square and I believe it is perfect for my store.

Mail arrives every two weeks or so, depending on road conditions. It comes by mule from the town of Bonham. We don't really have a post office, so the mail comes to one of the businesses and is placed in a cotton bag on the wall. The bag has a pocket for each letter in the alphabet, so one just looks for the correct pocket to check the mail. Please do write to me. Mrs. Sara Darnell, Dallas, Texas, should be a sufficient address. I'll be watching for your letters in the pocket marked D.

The light is fading, so I'll say goodbye for now. I miss Morgan, but as you can see, I am doing just fine. Don't worry about me. Know that you are missed.

Your loving daughter,
Sara

Early the next morning, Sara dropped her merchandise order off at Cockrell's office. No one was there yet, so she slipped it under the door and walked to The Crutchfield House Hotel to post her letter in the outgoing-mail bag. The hotel was an L-shaped, two-story building built of logs. It had a covered porch in front and a livery stable out back. There was a small reception area on the ground floor, and as she entered, she could see an ornate bar and a dining room behind it. John Henry had told her that the kitchen was ruled by a French chef. They had both shaken their heads, wondering how a French chef came to be in Dallas.

"Can I help you?" The young clerk at the reception desk was sitting on a high stool behind the counter. "Need a room?" His voice cracked and deepened from a high pitch to a lower one. He blushed.

"No, I just came to mail a letter. But I'd like to know more about the hotel."

The boy sat up straight. His blond hair was shaggy, and his homespun suit was too big for his thin frame. "This is the biggest hotel in Dallas. You can see our bar and dining room." He pointed behind him. "We have sleeping rooms on both floors and a couple of small meetin' or eatin' rooms on this floor, near the dining room. Even have a livery stable behind the hotel for guests' horses."

Sara counted a dozen room keys hanging on wall hooks behind the desk. The clerk saw her looking at the keys. "I check people in and out. I take care of the post-office services too." The clerk pointed at the mailbags on the wall opposite the reception desk. "Just drop your letter in the outgoing bag. It's on the left. If you need stamps, I can sell you some. Mailman from Bonham won't be here for another week. Your letter will go out then." Sara held the already-stamped letter up for him to see, thanked him, and dropped it in the outgoing bag, on the wall next to the large incoming-mail bag, with its alphabetical pockets.

Next she made another visit to Lawyer Clements. She stuck her head in the door and saw him behind his still-cluttered desk. "Back again? You're early, but I happen to have your lease ready to sign."

Sara sat down and noticed a fourth cup of coffee in line on the edge of his desk. This cup was full and steaming. Clements handed Sara the lease. After reviewing it, Sara said, "The lease looks fine, but I have a question."

"What's your question?"

Sara held up the copy of the lease. "I am ready to sign this and I have the deposit for you now. Would you allow me to begin cleaning the building and preparing for my inventory delivery? I know we said the lease will start in two weeks but access starting today would be very helpful." As she spoke, she opened her bag, pulled out silver coins, stacked them in front of Clements, and smiled. "Would that be all right?"

Clements studied her with squinting eyes. "How old are you?"

"Nineteen."

"You're not a lawyer are you? Or planning to study law?"

"Oh my, no. Why do you ask?" Sara was holding the unsigned lease.

"Because I wouldn't want to go against you in court. Yes, you may start your cleaning today. Just a reminder, the door doesn't have a lock, so you'll want to get a padlock. Beginning on month three, just come by monthly with your rent on the first business day of the month."

"I will." Sara signed the lease and handed it to the lawyer. "Thank you, Mr. Clements."

Clements grunted and went back to his current cup of coffee as Sara slipped out the door.

Access granted, Sara began preparing the store. Wearing her oldest calico dress with one of Morgan's shirts over it, like a smock, she started by collecting the trash and empty boxes that littered both the inside and the porch, then swept the porch clean. She carried the trash to Ira Webster's trash pile behind the saddlery. He had volunteered to burn it with his trash. Then, armed with a broom, rags, and two buckets of soapy hot water, Sara went to work cleaning the inside of the store. After sweeping the floors, she dusted and scrubbed everything with soapy water. Taking the buckets of soapy water to the porch, she dumped them on the already swept porch floor and broomed the water away. *With these dusty streets, the porch won't stay clean long, but it can at least start clean.* Tired, but happy with what she had accomplished, she slept well that night.

The next day she returned to the store with more soapy water and a stack of scalded corn husks. Hattie had explained that women who were lucky enough to have puncheon floors scrubbed them with scalded corn husks. "The husks pick up the dirt and the splinters," she had told Sara. After several hours on her hands and knees, Sara agreed the corn-husk treatment worked. The floors looked clean and were splinter free. The dirty, splinter-filled corn husks were added to Ira Webster's trash pile. As Sara dumped the husks, Ira Webster came out the back door of his saddlery with a cardboard box of trash. "I'm a mess, Mr. Webster." Sara gestured at her unusual combination of clothing, which was also wet and dirty in spots.

Webster laughed.

"I've seen you looking cleaner. How's the store comin'?"

"The dirt is all on me, I have a splinter in one knee, but the store is clean as a whistle. Tomorrow I can start stocking the merchandise Morgan and I brought from Tennessee. By the way, thank you for replacing the front-door hinges. I can latch and padlock the door now."

"Glad to help. It will be good to have an active business beside mine, rather than a vacant building."

"Let's hope I can make a success of the store, so you don't have a vacant building as a neighbor anytime soon."

"Well, all I can tell you is that when my wife, Marilyn, heard about your store, she told me it was high time somebody opened a business with women's needs in mind."

Sara smiled. "I hope she's one of many women who feel that way."

The next day John Henry came in the door of the store as Sara was unpacking beeswax candles and packages of vegetable seeds. In his hands was a straight-backed wooden chair. "Thought this might come in handy."

"Yes, thank you. I've been standing all day unpacking things and being able to sit behind the counter to work will be a great relief."

John Henry set the chair down behind the counter. It wobbled. He repositioned it on the floor. It continued to rest on just three legs. After both he and Sara had made several repositioning attempts to set the chair straight, Sara began to laugh. "The problem seems to be that the floor planks aren't level. We used to have a three-legged stool in our barn, guess this will just be a three-legged chair. In any case, I am happy to have it. Thank you. By the way, any word on your cattle?"

"No, but I didn't really expect any yet. My partner and the cow chasers will move the herd slowly so the cattle don't lose too much weight along the way. They'll send a rider ahead to alert me as they get closer. I've been spending my time starting to build a bunkhouse and a corral for any mustangs we can catch and break." He suddenly looked serious. His brow furrowed and his eyebrows lowered. "I wanted to talk to you about buying your wagon and oxen."

"Of course I'll be happy to sell you the wagon and teams. You have been such a help, John Henry, I feel guilty charging you much of anything."

"I want to pay a fair price, Sara."

"How about 60 percent of what we paid new? I can show you the receipts. The wagon needs some minor repairs but is in good condition, considering. I suspect there are a great many oxen on the market since our wagon train came to town. More sellers than buyers, most likely. I'd throw in the yokes and reins as well for the same price."

"If you're sure, I'd be foolish not to say yes."

"Then we have a deal. The wagon is behind the boardinghouse. I should have it unpacked by tomorrow night. You could pick it up the next day. The oxen are in Ira Webster's corral. It's behind his livery stable. I'll let him know I've sold the oxen to you."

After reviewing the original purchase receipts, John Henry paid Sara and left to visit Cockrell's sawmill before it closed for the day.

Pocketing the hammered silver dollars from the sale to John Henry, Sara realized the payment was more than enough to pay for her first merchandise order. *Sara's Merchandise Emporium is off to a good start.*

As Sara was folding up her list of the inventory they had brought with them, a red-faced, stocky man with droopy eyelids burst through the door. "You!" he said, pointing a fat finger at her.

"I beg your pardon?" Sara frowned. *Who is this?*

"So you are the person who foolishly wants to open another store," he was almost shouting.

Sara attempted to smother her rising temper and speak calmly. "I gather you are Mr. West, proprietor of the existing store."

"I can tell you that you'll fail miserably. Miserably! One store is quite enough, so you must move on, go somewhere else, leave!" West's face was getting redder and redder and he waved his short arms wildly.

I won't let him intimidate me.

Sara took two steps forward with her hands on her hips, forcing Mr. West to step back. "I can tell you that there *is* room for another store." She took a deep breath and spoke firmly. "I have reviewed your merchandise and, although it is of sufficient quality, it's primarily basic foodstuff, hardware, limited housewares, tools, guns, lead and powder—things which the men of the community need. I, on the other hand, I plan to appeal more to the ladies. They tell me things for them are sadly lacking." Sara smiled and her tone became friendlier. "I think there is room for us both to run profitable operations. As Dallas grows, our stores can complement each other and grow as well." *Maybe he'll be reasonable.*

"Don't be so confident that you can succeed, a young woman can't run a proper store!" And with that, Mr. West stormed out of the store, slamming the door shut with a bang. *It's hard to reason with someone so angry.*

Sara collapsed weakly on her three-legged chair. Her hands were shaking and she felt tears forming. *No, I am not going to let him make me cry!* It was several minutes before she felt calm enough to lock up and go to supper. Before leaving she peeked out to be sure Mr. West was not in sight and then hurried back to Mrs. Brown's boardinghouse.

The next day was off to a better start. Moments after Sara arrived at the store to begin unpacking and pricing her goods, Cecilia Stewart knocked on the door. "Mrs. Brown at the boardinghouse said I'd find you here." Sara, smiling with delight, gave her a big hug. Cecilia was eager to hear how the store was progressing. As Sara gave her a tour of the store, she shared with Cecilia what had happened with Mr. West.

Cecilia frowned. "After hearing how angry he was, I'd be concerned about him, Sara. He sounds overly emotional and very threatened by the idea of your store."

"I am concerned. In fact, I have decided to delay my opening a few days until my full inventory comes in from Shreveport. Then I'll have things that the ladies here told me they can't get from Mr. Red-Faced West. If he sees our stock is different maybe he'll calm down. He certainly doesn't seem to believe in friendly competition. He makes me more determined than ever. Enough about Mr. West," Sara waved her hand as if shooing a fly. "How are you, Effie, and the rest of the Butlers?"

"Just fine. We are camping in our wagon but are more than ready to have a cabin to move into. I guess I should just be glad we're not still in the mud and muck of the Arkansas swamps!"

"When do you think you'll have your cabin?"

"Hopefully soon. My brother-in-law, two other men from the trip, and Captain Pollard have decided to do house-raisings. They're working on the Pollard cabin now. Once it's finished, we're next. We women are keeping them fed and encouraged. Mostly we're nagging them in hopes of speeding up the process. Once the house-raisings are done, the men will combine ox teams and bust the sod."

They were interrupted by a loud cry from outside. "Here come the Frenchies!"

"It must be some of the European settlers from across the river. Let's go see." Cecilia led as the two stepped out onto the store's porch and into the dirt street. Cecilia was right. A dozen people were ambling along, peering at the town with interest. Sara admired the women's colorful cotton dresses with poufed sleeves. These were topped by long, decorative bib aprons, white and starched. Many of the men wore smocks or decorative vests over blousy, white shirts, and knee-length breeches with long socks. A few wore suits and two sported red berets. Several in the group wore wooden shoes. *Interesting clothes. They certainly do look foreign.*

"*Bonjour, comment allez-vous?*" Cecilia asked the group, with a smile.

Sara looked at her in surprise. There was a sudden rush of French words coming from the visitors as they gathered around Cecilia. "*Excusez-moi, mon francais est rouille,*" Cecilia said. There was another rush of French words. Cecilia turned to Sara with a look of distress. "My French is so rusty, I should never have started this."

"Please allow me to introduce myself and to assist." A young man bowed to the two ladies.

"Edouard Charles Beaulieu at your service." He spread is arms in a wide gesture to include the others in his group. "My friends and I are from La Réunion, across the river. They are the newest arrivals to our community."

As he began to introduce his companions, along with their professions, Sara heard potter, tailor, pastry cook, banker, musician, but her attention wandered to Beaulieu. He certainly didn't look like a settler. She guessed he was about six inches taller than she. His skin was pale and a bit sunburned. His hair was dark walnut. Roughly parted in the middle, it curled softly around his head, just brushing his white collar. As he spoke, his thick, dark eyebrows danced above large, dark brown eyes. A neatly trimmed, short beard and mustache made him look a bit older than he probably was. A thin scar rose from his short beard toward his ear. His perfectly fitted black suit and his fashionable leather boots made Sara think that if he simply added a cape and top hat he'd be dressed for the opera. It had gone quiet, and Sara realized she had everyone's attention. "I am pleased to meet you all. I am Mrs. Darnell, also a new arrival."

After a few brief exchanges, Edouard Charles Beaulieu wished them a good morning, bowed again, and the group continued their procession.

"How did you learn French, Cecilia?" Sara asked, as they stepped back into the store.

"When I was a child, we had a French Canadian neighbor in Pennsylvania. When Mother died, our father hired her to look after us while he worked at the bank. She taught me French. I taught it to young ladies in my classes for a while, but it's been years since I've used it. Would you like to hear what I learned yesterday about La Réunion?"

Sara nodded.

"Yesterday I met Mrs. Cockrell, who seems very nice. I was curious about La Réunion, and she showed me an article about the colony in the *Dallas Herald*. The first group of colonists arrived about a year ahead of us. They are French, Swiss, and Belgian. Apparently the community is based on the ideas of some dead French socialist. Named Fourier, I think."

"Socialist?"

"Yes, it's a utopian agricultural cooperative. It seems the idea is that they share the work and the results equally. They're trying to grow grapes, other fruit, and grains. Mrs. Cockrell said they've bought five hundred cattle and some pigs and sheep."

Sara thought for a moment. "The people we met looked prosperous, but were any of them introduced as farmers?"

Cecilia shook her head. "No, there wasn't a farmer in the group we met. According to Mrs. Cockrell, there are just two experienced farmers in the entire colony. She told me her husband is concerned that, unlike our side of the river, the two thousand acres the community's agents bought on the limestone cliff are not really suitable for farming."

"Yet they've left their homes and come to Texas to farm." Sara shook her head in disbelief.

"According to the paper, it must have been an awful trip. They sailed for two months from Belgium to New Orleans. Took another ship to Galveston, then travelled to Houston, expecting a short voyage up the Trinity River to their new colony."

"But the Trinity isn't navigable."

"You might travel the Trinity up this far in a canoe—if you could carry it part of the way—but a real boat is out of the question because of all of the giant, tangled knots of trees and brush floating in the river."

"So how did they get here?" Sara asked.

"They walked the 250 miles to Dallas . . . many wearing wooden shoes. They hired ox carts and drivers to transport their belongings. It took almost a month to get here. Can you imagine?"

"I certainly can't imagine making that walk in wooden shoes. I hope their odds of success are higher than they sound," said Sara.

And I hope my odds of success are higher than Mr. West seems to believe.

That afternoon, Sara was shelving boxes when—thud! The box slipped out of her hand, fell from where she was standing on the third rung of the red stepladder, and landed on the floor. With the sound, her mind flashed back to the thudding sound of the first shovels full of dirt landing on Morgan's coffin. Tears formed in her eyes.

"Sara? Sara?" John Henry was holding the fallen box up to her.

Brushing the tears away, Sara said, "Sorry, John Henry, I was lost in thought."

"Dadgummit! Craziest thing I've ever seen. Stocking a store with empty boxes."

Sara shook away the thought of Morgan's grave, repositioned the box, and climbed down off the red stepladder, smoothing her skirt and reaching up to replace a hairpin that had fallen out of the light-brown braid curled into a bun at the back of her neck. "In another week, when the freight wagon arrives from Shreveport, I can open the store and begin replacing the empty boxes on the top shelf with more supplies. I hope to be fully stocked in a few months. In the meantime, the store will look more fully stocked than it is."

"Well, before you open, I'd best get to Cedar Springs to the Gold and Johnson Distillery and buy a barrel of whiskey for you. Every successful establishment here—except the church—has a tapped barrel and a gourd cup in the back for men customers. It will be my contribution to your success."

Sara smiled up at John Henry. "Thank you." She was grateful to John Henry. "I had no idea that liquor was a secret to success in the West."

"I'll head out now. Told Ira Webster I'd come today to pick up the oxen you sold me. Better hook 'em up and go get the wagon. It's empty, right?"

"Yes. It's ready for you. Thanks again."

Not long after Sara's Gone to Texas wagon train had arrived, North Texas had a freak storm. It was late May, but what the Texans call a "blue norther" blew arctic winds across the prairie. The temperature plummeted. That morning Sara woke shivering in the unexpected cold. Gathering her quilt around herself, she tiptoed across the cold boardinghouse floor to her water pitcher and washbowl. Ice crystals had formed around the edges of the water in the pitcher. Pouring the icy water into the bowl, she splashed it on her face and quickly dried it with her towel. She stepped out of her nightgown, pulled on her underwear, petticoat, and dress. Looking out the window, she saw a thin layer of snow in front of the boardinghouse and snow still falling. "Can you believe snow in May?" Sara exclaimed to Mrs. Brown as she came down the stairs to breakfast. "Is this usual?"

"No, I've never heard of snow this late in the year, but you can bet it will be gone tomorrow or the next day and it will be warm again. Texas weather is unpredictable. Although this is more unpredictable than usual." Mrs. Brown was right, but walking to the store, Sara saw that the children of the village, and a few adults, were taking full advantage of the sticky, white stuff while it lasted. Much work went into rolling up enough snow for a few snowballs. Children were playing on the courthouse grounds and making one small and somewhat muddy snowman, complete with a top hat and carrot nose. Sara shivered and pulled her cape tighter.

The next day, there was nothing left but a mud puddle and a hat. Sara saw a hog eating the carrot. The *Dallas Herald* reported that residents who had already planted vegetables lost them to the cold, snowy weather. This included the farmers of the La Réunion colony. Fortunately it was early enough in the season that most replanted for a slightly later harvest.

The baker from La Réunion, Gaspard Serrurier, left the utopian socialist colony and moved across the river to Dallas. "He'll be a guest at the boardinghouse until he can find space for a bakery and a residence," Mrs. Brown told Sara.

The first morning at breakfast, Mrs. Brown and Sara had difficulty pronouncing his name, so he suggested, "Call me Mr. Baker." He was a heavyset young man with very curly, sandy hair framing his face. His arms were extremely well muscled. *From kneading dough?* Sara and Mrs. Brown agreed that the word "jolly" described him well. He was so eager to learn English that he followed Mrs. Brown around asking the English words for things.

After a day or two of this, he came into the kitchen while Mrs. Brown was preparing dinner. She gestured to a pile of carrots she had started to chop. "Carrots," she said and handed him the knife. "Chop." He nodded and went to work, mumbling, "Carrots, chop." Soon he was a fixture in the kitchen, cooking with her, and expanding his vocabulary. When Mrs. Brown told Sara about this, she said, "I enjoy having him in the kitchen. Tomorrow he wants to bake bread. I'll sure miss him when he leaves for his bakery and new home."

The next morning Sara and Mrs. Brown were eating breakfast when Mr. Baker came downstairs carrying a large, rectangular, wooden bowl with deep, outward-slanting sides. He screwed threaded legs onto the bowl, bringing it to tabletop height. *"Boîte à pâte,"* he said, smiling.

Mrs. Brown nodded. "Dough box," she said. "Excellent, today we make bread?"

"Oui, bread today." He turned, went back upstairs, and came down again with a giant bag of flour.

Sara finished her coffee, grinned at Mrs. Brown, and said, "Good luck."

Sara stood in the small office of the *Dallas Herald,* but there was no one in sight. "Hello," she called. Suddenly a face popped out from behind a screen in the back of the room. The face's most noticeable feature was a smear of black ink from chin to one ear. The rest of the man came from behind the screen, looked at Sara, and said, "The young widow starting the store."

"Yes, I'm Mrs. Darnell. You must be Mr. Latimer."

"J. W. Swindells, Latimer's partner, since 1851."

Sara smothered a giggle. It seemed Mr. Swindells spoke in headlines. She guessed that was appropriate for a newspaper man. "I need your assistance, Mr. Swindells. I wish to place an advertisement, but I've never done so. Can you please guide me?"

"Four sizes, two typefaces to choose from, all priced accordingly." *Another headline!*

Swindells wiped inky hands on his typesetter's apron and handed Sara a sheet illustrating sample ads of varying sizes and showing two typefaces.

"Does Mr. West often advertise with you?" Sara noticed the ink smear had now progressed to the end of Mr. Swindells' long nose.

Swindells considered his answer and rubbed his nose, further smearing the ink. "West advertises when he has sales."

"Any sales coming up?" Sara asked.

"We are holding a sale ad for Mr. West with instructions to run it imme-diately when your store is set to open." This long answer seemed to exhaust Mr. Swindells and he abruptly sat down at the desk, took off his horned rim glasses, and rubbed his eyes with his inky fingers.

Having gained the information she was seeking, Sara thanked Mr. Swindells and told him she would be back to place her ad.

"Deadline is three days before publication," a very inky Swindells said, still speaking in headlines.

Sara returned to the boardinghouse to gather the last few items of merchan-dise she had unpacked from the wagon and left in her room. She could hear laughter coming from the kitchen, the separate, small building a few yards from the house itself. The door was open, and she peeked in to see Mr. Baker nearly up to his elbows kneading dough in the dough box. Mrs. Brown saw Sara. "Come on in, Mr. Baker is teaching me to make French bread."

Looking at the amount of dough in the dough box, Sara said, "A lot of French bread."

"I'm not sure how many loaves we're making, but we started with thir-ty-two cups of flour. Mr. Baker says we can keep two loaves and the rest is for The Crutchfield House Hotel."

Mr. Baker looked up from his kneading. "Chef there is French, will buy my bread."

"You can sample our work tonight at supper. Real French bread," Mrs. Brown said.

"Sounds good. See you then. I'm headed back to the store to stock the last few things we brought from Tennessee."

At the end of the day, Sara had done all she could to prepare the store until her merchandise shipment arrived from Shreveport. Walking back to the boardinghouse, the sun was warm and the shade of the live oak, pecan, and cottonwood trees by the creek that flowed behind the boardinghouse looked inviting. Stepping into the shade of the trees, Sara felt the temperature drop. The glare of the early summer sun was replaced by dappled light, and she could hear the faint bubbling of the creek's flow. Looking down into the water flowing over the rocky creek bed, she felt the tension in her shoulders relax.

As she walked she had a moment of doubt about staying in Texas. *Should she have gone home to Tennessee? Will I fail miserably like Mr. West predicts?* Sara straightened her shoulders. *No! I can do this. I will do this.*

At supper that night, she took her first bite of Mr. Baker's long, thin, crusty loaf of French bread. It was delicious. "We only have two loaves?" Sara asked, slathering her last bite with more butter.

"That's right," Mrs. Brown said. "If we want more, we'll have to eat at Crutchfield's."

Mr. Baker was beaming. "Crutchfield's is—how you say?—first customer!"

The next day was Sunday, and Sara pressed her one black dress and attended services at Dallas' small log church, which was nestled in the trees a short walk from town. The sound of the familiar hymns reminded her of home and brought her comfort. As she sat in the rustic pew, she was struck by the construction of the church. Many of the horizontal logs in the walls were unusually short. At the end of the service, Sara was welcomed by numerous members of the non-denominational congregation. A dozen people sur-rounded Sara with a flurry of welcomes and introductions. *I'll never remember all these names, but I appreciate the friendliness.* She looked at the women in decorative straw hats, rather than bonnets; the men in frock coats or broad-cloth suits, white shirts with ties, and derby hats. *Everyone is dressed in their Sunday best. They look like a church congregation back home in Tennessee.*

When she commented on the unusual construction of the building and asked about the history of the church, she was met with laughter. "You could call this our King Solomon church," the farmer who had led the singing and praying told her. "The church was built a few miles south of Dallas in 1846. By 1850 our congregation had split into two groups—one that wanted the church moved to Dallas and one that preferred it to be west of the Trinity. The solution was to split the existing building in half and share the resulting logs to build both a Dallas church and another church west of the river.

"I see," Sara laughed. "You split the church building just like King Solomon suggested splitting the baby between two quarreling mothers."

"Exactly! Only in this case, the splitting actually occurred. It worked well."

Walking home, Sarah smiled to herself at the parallel. *Can I convince Mr. West we can split the business and both be successful?*

The next morning Sara heard the rumble of a heavy wagon and opened the store door to see a cloud of dust and two teams of oxen pulling a wagon to a stop behind her store and the saddlery. A dirty, thin-necked man, with a rough, acne-bubbled face and a gun on his hip, climbed out of the high-wheeled wagon, along with his equally dirty young helper, and shouted, "Goods for Mr. Ira Webster and Mrs. Sara Darnell!"

Webster came out of the saddle shop and Sara joined him beside the wagon. "Webster's boxes come off first, then Mrs. Darnell's. Once that's done, we need directions to the Adams ranch outside of town, then we need directions to whiskey. We've worked up a mighty thirst." The freighter looked at Sara. "You Mrs. Darnell?"

"I am."

'Well ain't you a pretty little thing?" He smirked and looked Sara up and down. His lecherous look made her very uncomfortable.

Sara narrowed her eyes. "When you've delivered Mr. Webster's boxes, please knock on my door, and I'll show you where to put my boxes and the large coffee grinder."

About an hour later the freighters knocked on the door with the store's delivery. Sara had the freighters stack most everything in one of the back storerooms and pile the remainder behind the counter. The two-wheel, hand-operated, red cast-iron coffee grinder took pride of place on one side of the counter. Sara investigated it with delight. Standing almost eighteen inches tall, with a twelve-inch-wide wheel on each side and a wooden coffee-catching drawer, it exceeded her expectations. *It's beautiful!*

As soon as the freighters were gone, Sara could contain herself no longer. She began to spin around with her arms extended. *Oh, Morgan! It's going to be a wonderful store. I just wish you could see it.*

Sara worked the rest of the day opening boxes, sorting and pricing merchandise, and deciding how and where to display it. She lined canned goods with their colorful salmon, tomato, peach, plum, and jelly labels at eye level in the store's center aisle. A barrel of coffee beans, with a scoop, sat on the floor near the coffee grinder. A scale stood conveniently on the other end of the counter. There was a large roll of brown wrapping paper behind the counter, and John Henry had helped her hang a very large roll of twine from the ceiling. A piece of twine trailed down from the roll so Sara could reach it. Tobacco tins and cigar boxes, with their fancy designs, were stacked on a shelf behind the counter with various medicinal products and bars of brightly boxed bar soap. There was a neat pile of large bags of flour and bags of one-pound cones of sugar on the floor at the end of the center aisle. Queensware and ironstone dishes and cutlery were arranged on one shelf. Cooking pots and kitchen knives were nearby. Stacked on shelves along the back wall, Sara had bolts of patterned calico, red flannel, and denim. She had taken sample strips of the fabrics and strung them like bright, tiny flags from the ceiling. All kinds of needles, colored thread, and other sewing notions were neatly stacked with packages of paper sewing patterns. Bonnets and aprons hung from special wooden racks. Jars of spices were displayed with a price list: cinnamon or cloves, eighty-seven cents a pound; mace, seven dollars a pound; nutmeg, three dollars a pound. One-pound bags of Dwight's Saleratus and boxes of pearl ash for leavening occupied another shelf. A basket of vegetable-seed packets stood beside boxes of beeswax candles. Boxes of washing soap, borax, and thumb bluing were displayed together. After stocking more items, Sara began work on a master price list to post on the wall and on the countertop. Another copy would go in the counter drawer for her reference.

The time flew by and the light shifted its angle, reminding Sara that it was time for supper. She checked the back-door latch, then closed and secured the window shutters. Gathering up her things and preparing to leave the darkened store, she was startled by the opening of the front door. The dirty, middle-aged freighter stepped in, closing the door behind him. He stood looming in the entrance, staring at her.

Sara felt a flash of fear. *There's nowhere to run.*

He took several steps toward her. "Heard you was a widow woman. I'm Jesse. Thought you'd like to take a walk with me," he leered, leaning into her face. He reeked of stale sweat, whiskey, tobacco, and oxen. *I have to get rid of him. How?*

"Thank you for the delivery, but no. Good night," Sara spoke firmly. *Leave, please leave!*

He grabbed her by the arm, pushing her against the counter. "You can call me Jesse and we're going to have a real good time." He continued to hold her arm and leaned his weight against her, beginning to unbutton the top of her dress.

"Stop, no!" Sara struggled, then screamed and screamed again.

A dirty hand covered her mouth. "Now you just hush, honey. Ain't nobody going to hear you and I'd hate to have to hit you." Tears began to streak down Sara's cheeks. With his other hand, Jesse began to pull up Sara's skirt. Sara squeezed her eyes shut. Suddenly Jesse's fumbling stopped.

"Let go of the lady."

John Henry! Sara opened her eyes as Jesse stood up straight and slowly raised his hands in the air.

"Didn't mean her no harm," said Jesse.

"I got a Colt revolver pointed at your back that says you did," John Henry said, his voice a full octave deeper than usual. "I'm here to see that no harm comes to her." John Henry spoke softly, but with a deep rumble, as he slipped Jesse's gun out of its holster. "Now you are going to leave and not come back. You may pick up your gun from Mr. Cockrell tomorrow morning, and you'll not do freight runs to Dallas ever again. If you do, you'll answer to me. Consider yourself lucky that I didn't shoot you on the spot. I was afraid it would distress the lady. Now get out." John Henry spun Jesse around and gave him a swift kick out the door. "Run, before I change my mind and shoot you anyway."

Jesse ran.

Thank heavens!

"Sara, are you all right?" John Henry asked.

Tears flowed down Sara's cheeks. "I am. He just . . . it was . . . I was so frightened. You came just in time. How did you know?" Sara could hardly form the sentences.

John Henry slipped an arm around Sara's shoulders. "When my delivery came, we discovered one of the boxes was yours, and I thought I'd drop it off if you were still here. I knew Webster would still be open at the saddle shop. If you were already gone, I figured I could leave it with him."

At that moment, Ira Webster stepped in. "I thought I heard a scream, everything okay?"

Sara began, "That vile freighter was here and—"

"He gave Sara quite a scare," John Henry said. "I walked in just in time, took his gun, and sent him on his way with a warning to never come back to Dallas. Hopefully Cockrell has contracts with other freighters. We don't need his kind here."

"I didn't much like him either. Well, glad you're all right, Mrs. Darnell. Good night." Webster headed back to the saddle shop.

"Looks like you've been unpacking. Are you happy with your order?"

Sara wasn't ready to change topics. "John Henry, I think I should keep Morgan's gun in the drawer of the counter here. I think I'd feel safer."

"Only if you know how to use it safely. Have you ever fired a pistol?"

"Yes, and a rifle too. I'd sometimes hunt with Papa. I'm a good shot. Once we had a mountain lion after one of our horses in the paddock. Papa was gone, so I shot it with a long gun."

"One day soon, why don't we go out on the prairie, and you can practice with Morgan's gun and then decide if you want to keep it here. In the meantime, I'm going to walk you to the boardinghouse. I don't believe you have anything to worry about from that Jesse character, but I do want to hear if you are happy with your new merchandise."

Back at the boardinghouse, before leaving, John Henry told Mrs. Brown a brief version of what had happened. Sara's landlady put her arm around Sara and led her to the kitchen. "Land sakes, child! Let's get you fed and off to bed early tonight. You've had quite a shock." Dinner was ready and Mrs. Brown pulled a hot dish from the cookstove. "Our redheaded neighbor, Ellie Duffield, gave me some dewberries this morning and I added some green mustang grapes for a cobbler. A bit of supper and dish of cobbler will make you feel better."

Sara was learning that Mrs. Brown's answer to most any problem was food. The cobbler was delicious.

The next morning Sara had just shooed a neighbor's chickens away from the door of the store and was putting her key in the padlock when Ira Webster ran up to her. "Mrs. Darnell, that freighter was found shot dead in his wagon just outside of town this morning. Seems he was drinking in the back of West's store last night and telling people that John Henry had threatened him over you. The marshal just arrested John Henry for murder. Of course, John Henry denies he shot the man."

"If he says he didn't, then he didn't," Sara said firmly. "Where's the marshal now?"

"Most likely he's still at West's store, talking to West."

"Thanks for letting me know." Sara spun on her heel, tightened the ties on her bonnet, and headed for West's store with fire in her eyes. *John Henry arrested! He would not have shot that man.*

Sara charged into West's store and found West and Marshal Moore leaning on the counter, talking. She interrupted. "What's this about John Henry Adams being under arrest?"

"Well, well," said West. "Looks like your ex-Texas Ranger got a bit jealous about you carrying on with the freighter and murdered him."

Sara slapped him in the face. West's eyes widened and his mouth flew open. Before he could speak, Sara said, "How dare you! That awful, dirty scoundrel came into my store last night and tried to take advantage of me. Wicked man! Thank heavens John Henry came along and stopped him when he did. He took that man's gun and warned him to never come back. And for your information," she said, poking West square in the middle of his chest, "John Henry is like an uncle to me since my husband died. A true friend. And for you to imply otherwise is downright despicable. Someone else shot that man, and I'll go to my grave saying that!"

West rubbed his cheek. He turned to the marshal. "Did you see what she did to me?"

Before the marshal could answer, Sara looked at West and quietly said, "And if you ever slur my reputation again, I'll slap you again but harder. You are saying these things because you are unhappy to have competition for your store, aren't you? Well, you are not going to make me close my shop."

"Whoa now," the marshal looked at Sara. "John Henry could have gone after him and shot him, especially since the freighter didn't have his gun."

"Nonsense," Sara countered, stepping back and shifting her look to the marshal. "If he had been going to shoot him, he could have done it rescuing me. There would have been no question then that it was in my defense. Besides, he would never shoot an unarmed man."

"Well then who did it?" the marshal asked. "We don't have any other likely suspects. The dead man was a stranger here, who else had a reason to kill him?"

This marshal is too lazy to investigate.

"I don't know," Sara admitted, "but if you aren't willing to investigate, I intend to find out who did it myself." Sara turned to West. "And don't you *dare* spread false gossip about me." She left in a swirl of skirt and crinolines and slammed the door.

Sara ran to the two-story, log jail located off the square. The door was locked. There was one small window with bars. She shouted John Henry's name. In a moment, his face appeared behind the bars. "Sara? What are—?"

"John Henry, I know you didn't kill that freighter—"

"No, I didn't. I told the sheriff that I left you at the boardinghouse, had dinner at Crutchfield's, and rode home. He's stuck on the idea that I killed the man. Not much I can do to prove him wrong from in here."

"I'd break you out if I could. I want you to know that I believe you and I'm going to find out who did kill the freighter."

"Now Sara, don't do anything to put yourself at risk."

"Don't worry, John Henry. I can take care of myself, and I'll discover the killer and get you out of that jail." With that, she turned and went straight to the office where she had met with Mr. Cockrell and knocked on the door.

It was Mrs. Cockrell who opened the door. "Oh, you're Mrs. Darnell, aren't you? Alexander has told me about you, and I've looked forward to meeting you. Please come in. Alexander is across visiting La Réunion this morning. I was just making a cup of tea. Would you like to join me?"

As much as Sara wanted to blurt out the reason she was there, she reluctantly remembered her manners. "I'd like that very much, Mrs. Cockrell." Sara watched as Mrs. Cockrell finished making tea and poured two cups. Sarah Cockrell was a slender woman with shiny, mahogany-colored hair parted in the middle, pulled back, and turned under into a bun at the nape of her neck. Heavy brows arched above deep-set gray eyes. She wore a white cotton blouse with long, full sleeves and a rounded collar. Her skirt was black cotton embroidered with white flowers and very full. A solid black sash was tied in a bow at the front of her waist. *She looks as fashionable as if she's stepped out of* Godey's Lady's Book.

Once the ladies were settled at the office's round table with their tea, Mrs. Cockrell said, "Please call me Sarah. I understand you are Sara too."

After they compared the spellings of their names, Sara said, "Mrs. Cockrell . . . uh . . . Sarah, I have an urgent problem that I hope Mr. Cockrell might be able to help me with. My friend John Henry Adams has been accused of murdering a freighter who tried unsuccessfully to molest me last night. Fortunately, John Henry rescued me, took the man's gun, and sent him on his way, telling him to never come back to Dallas. This morning the freighter was found shot dead in his wagon outside of town. The marshal has arrested John Henry for murder and has him locked in the town's log jail. I don't believe he did it."

"Tried to molest you? That's terrible. I'm so sorry that happened to you, are you all right?" Mrs. Cockrell frowned, looking genuinely concerned.

"I'm fine, just distressed about John Henry's arrest. He has been such a good friend to me. He's like an uncle who watches over me. I'm grateful to him and want to help him by finding out who did kill the man." Sara sighed. "I thought one place to start would be finding out more about the freighter. I know he contracts with your freight company."

"I help Alexander with scheduling the freight runs. Which freighter was it?"

"I don't know his last name, but his first name was Jesse, and he delivered a combined wagonload for the saddle shop, my store, and John Henry's ranch yesterday."

Mrs. Cockrell opened the drawer of the desk and pulled out an account book. After flipping through several pages, she looked up and said, "Jesse Parker did yesterday's deliveries. His helper was Seth Boswell. Looks like yesterday was the second time we used Jesse Parker. He made a delivery for us last month. Albert Hudson has a farm a few miles out of town, just west of the Preston Road. He ordered cotton seed, a new rifle, some farming tools, and household goods from Shreveport, which were delivered last month. I suppose you could talk with him to see what he might know about the freighter."

Sara thanked Mrs. Cockrell, who wished her luck in her investigation. *Just like her husband, Mrs. Cockrell radiates confidence.*

Sara left feeling she had two clues—the farmer Albert Hudson and Seth Boswell, the young assistant freighter. The marshal had made no mention of Boswell today or any intent to find and question him or other customers Jesse may have interacted with. Sara wondered where Boswell had gone.

After acquiring a thin gelding from Ira Webster, whose saddle shop also served as a livery stable, Sara got directions to the Hudson farm, about three miles outside of Dallas proper. It was a windy day as Sara started out, and the prairie grass was golden and swaying in the wind. It was hot and the Texas heat rose in waves from the ground. The air smelled dusty. Sara had heard Mrs. Brown bemoaning the fact that this summer had brought a drought to the Three Forks.

Sara could see the evidence all around her. The ground was dry and cracked and what few crops she saw looked parched. After a while, Sara spotted a dry creek bed and followed it about half a mile before seeing a small, cultivated field with what she guessed were cotton plants, struggling to survive in the dry earth. Beyond the field was a double log cabin. Connecting the two rooms was a roof-covered hallway, open on both ends. There was an old hound resting in the dirt-floored hall, which was littered with harnesses, tools, and a wooden plow. Sara guided her horse to a stop in front of the house.

A woman was hanging wash on a line strung between two poles planted in the dusty ground. A small child in a sagging diaper and stained shirt played in the dry dirt beside her. "Saw you a comin'," the woman remarked. She had on homespun dress that might have once been blue. The hem was stained brown from the dirt and one sleeve was torn. Her bonnet was faded, the ties grimy with dirt. Sara saw that she had her hand in a soiled apron pocket and suspected that the pocket contained a pistol. This frontier woman was obviously cautious and prepared. "Don't get much company out here. What's you doin' out here alone?"

Sara dismounted. The woman continued to look at her with curiosity. Her hand was still in her pocket.

"I've ridden here from Dallas, Mrs. Hudson. My name is Mrs. Darnell. Cockrell Freight delivered goods to you last month, and I have a question about the freighter who made the delivery."

The hand remained in her pocket. "My husband is in the house, guess you better come in."

Mrs. Hudson pushed the door open, and Sara stepped into the dirt-floored cabin ahead of Mrs. Hudson, who had scooped up the child and was holding him or her on her hip. If anything, it was hotter inside than out. Sara's eyes gradually adjusted from the bright sunlight to the darker room. Mr. Hudson was sitting at a small table. He was a big, burly man with long, stringy hair and a scowling face that had obviously not been shaved for several days. He had a heavy bandage on his arm and was finishing a bowl of what looked like cornmeal mush. His hands were filthy.

Mrs. Hudson set the child down. "Lady here come from Dallas to ask questions about our delivery from Cockrell's last month."

Hudson looked up without making eye contact. His eyes were beady. "What business is that of yours?"

"The freighter who made the delivery was found murdered this morning. My friend has been arrested for killing him. I know he didn't do it, and I am trying to find out more about the freighter to help find out who might have really killed him," Sara said.

"Ain't got nothing to say about him." Hudson was gruff and stood up abruptly, knocking over the bench he had been sitting on. "Guess you might as well head on back to Dallas." He moved toward Sara.

She stepped back. Mrs. Hudson opened the cabin door, further indicating that Sara should leave. Sara hesitated a moment. "How did you hurt your arm?"

Mr. Hudson flinched and shouted, "I said git out!" Sara hurried out and quickly mounted her horse. The Hudsons were still standing in the doorway until Sara could no longer see the cabin. Sara was thoughtful on her ride back to Dallas. *That was certainly an unfriendly reception. I don't know what the bandage means, but it might be significant. Hudson wouldn't talk about the freighter. Why not?* Sara had to wonder if Hudson was involved, and if so, how?

As she rode back into town, Sara saw the marshal had driven the freighter's ox wagon into Dallas and suspected the burlap-wrapped object in the open wagon parked by the courthouse was Jesse's body. She shivered. Taking a man's life was a hateful thing. She knew John Henry had killed in war and in his duty as a Texas Ranger, but she refused to believe he would shoot an unarmed man.

Sara knew she needed to talk to Jesse's assistant, Seth Boswell. Where was he, and how could she find him? Her sleep that night was restless.

The next day, working in the store with the door open to offer some relief from the heat, Sara heard screaming and stepped onto the porch to see her neighbor from several doors down, Miss Ellie Duffield, chasing a young man out of her yard and swatting at him with her broom. "Stay away from my garden!" she was screaming. Sara knew that Miss Ellie Duffield had set up a school in her cabin and taught the small children of the settlers who valued book learning.

The vegetable thief was clutching a handful of carrots by their green tops. He ran behind the buildings and disappeared into the woods by the creek.

Miss Duffield approached Sara. "That's the second time my garden has been raided in two days. Yesterday someone stole several bunches of radishes. Probably the same person."

"Did you recognize him?"

"Didn't get much of a look at him, but don't think I know him. Would love to visit, Mrs. Darnell, but I have squirrel stew on the stove and need to tend to it." With that, she hurried away.

Could it be Seth stealing the food? Sara padlocked the store, retied her bonnet, and followed the thief into the woods.

As she stepped under the trees and into their shade, the temperature dropped. Where could the thief have gone? Sara could hear the sound of water flowing in the nearby creek. She knew there were no buildings to hide in in these woods. *Step outside this little wooded area and you're in open prairie. If I were hiding, what would I do? Maybe build a shelter to hide in?*

Sara began to walk through the trees along the creek, looking on both sides. It wasn't long before she spotted a row of branches leaning against the trunk of a large, fallen tree. Looking closely, she realized the branches formed a small, tunnel-shaped shelter. One opening was closed with tree branches and leaves, the other end open. She peered inside. *There's the thief.* Seeing her, he tried to scramble out of the blocked end of the shelter. Sara reached in and grabbed him by the ankles and pulled.

"Ouch! The branches are scratching me. I'll come out."

The thief backed out of the small shelter on his hands and knees. Afraid he would run, Sara grabbed his feet and held on to his ankles. He turned his head to see her. "Miz Darnell?"

"Yes. You're Seth, aren't you?

Seth shook his head. "Yes'm, Seth Boswell."

"Why are you hiding out here?" *Good grief! He looks about twelve.*

"Didn't know what else to do. Jesse's dead. I ain't got no money. Marshal's got the wagon. Don't have no way back to Shreveport. Ain't eaten nothin' since breakfast yesterday. Didn't think that woman would miss the danged carrots, but she went crazy."

Sara said, "You're safe for now, Seth. Come on, we'll go back to my store. I'll find something for you to eat, and we'll figure out what to do next."

Once inside, Sara had Seth sit at the counter. She picked up the cloth bag she had packed her lunch in and began to set its contents on the counter. "Tell you what, Seth, I'll share my lunch with you if you'll answer some questions for me." Seth eyed the cheese, bread, and small dish of leftover fruit cobbler with interest. "You may have all the cobbler as well as some of the bread and cheese." At the mention of the cobbler, the young man's face lit up.

"Yes, ma'am!"

"Two nights ago, after you made your deliveries, Jesse was drinking at West's store?"

Seth looked sheepish. "Yes'm," he muttered through a mouthful of bread.

"I assume you were with him?" Another nod from Seth. "Tell me what happened afterward."

Seth took a bite of the cheese and sighed deeply. Sara wasn't sure if he was sighing at the question or just enjoying the cheese.

"Well, Jesse was pretty drunk when we left West's. I helped him back to where we'd left the wagon. We'd stopped and staked the oxen by the river so's they could graze and reach the water. We was just startin' to bed down for the night when some feller come riding up."

Seth's story came out in a rush of words. "Before he even climbed off his horse, he started shouting that Jesse had stole' his best horse. It's true that we took a horse back when we was here before. Jesse tol' me he'd bought it from the farmer we'd delivered goods to. This angry feller—it was the same farmer—said he knew Jesse had stole' the horse 'cause another man tol' him that he'd saw Jesse ridin' it."

Seth paused to cram a bit more cheese into his mouth.

"What happened next?"

"Jesse got real mad and started saying the farmer couldn't accuse him of being a horse thief. The farmer jumped off his horse and started runnin' at Jessie. Now, Jesse didn't have no gun in his holster, so he pulled his Bowie knife out of his boot. Called it his 'Arkansas toothpick.' I knowed it was plenty sharp. The farmer was waving his gun, and Jesse cut him pretty bad. The farmer shot him, called him a damned horse thief again. Sorry to cuss, Miz Darnell, but that's what he said. Then the farmer got back on his horse and rode away."

"So the man who shot Jesse was the farmer you delivered goods to on your last trip?" Sara wanted to be sure.

"Yes, I 'membered him because he pitched a fit that an iron skillet his wife wanted wasn't in the first order we delivered. It weren't in stock last month, but we gave it to his wife this trip. Didn't much like that farmer, but him killin' Jesse was self-defense." Seth started on the cobbler.

I knew John Henry wasn't guilty! Now, with Seth's help, I can prove it.

"Will you tell all this to the marshal?" Sara asked. "Then I'm sure Mr. Cockrell can arrange for someone to drive you and the wagon back to Shreveport."

"This cobbler sure is good." Seth stopped and looked at the crumbs on the counter. "Dang, I've eaten all your lunch."

Sara smiled. "Don't worry, Seth. I'd give you another lunch if I had one. When you finish the cobbler, let's go talk to Mr. Cockrell and then to the marshal."

The Cockrells were both in the office when Sara and Seth knocked on the door. After Seth told Mr. Cockrell what he had seen, and Sara shared details of her visit to the Hudson farm, including the fact that Hudson had a bandaged arm, Cockrell told Seth he could arrange transportation for him back to Shreveport, but first Seth would need to tell his story to Marshal Moore.

The marshal would then determine if Seth would need to stay for the trial of the farmer, Albert Hudson. Cockrell and Seth left to visit with the marshal.

"That was good detective work," Mrs. Cockrell told Sara.

"I'm not sure Seth would have told me the story if I hadn't had the berry cobbler to offer him." They laughed together, and Mrs. Cockrell said, "You've been a good friend to Mr. Adams. You may well have saved his life. Murder is a hanging offense."

"Do you think Farmer Hudson will hang?"

Mrs. Cockrell shook her head. "Probably not. Most likely, Jesse's killing was self-defense. The marshal will look at the facts you've gathered. Probably won't even be a trial. John Henry should be released from jail before the day is over."

Sarah Cockrell's prediction was correct. Later in the afternoon, John Henry appeared at the door to Sara's store. Apart from being unshaven, he looked none the worse for wear. "Sara, the marshal told me what you did. Thank you for believing in me and working to find the real killer." There was a catch in John Henry's throat. "The marshal was just willin' to assume I was guilty, and Hudson was trying to hide what had happened. If not for you, the truth might never have come to light, and I might have swung from a rope."

"My goodness, that would not have been the appropriate end for a Texas Ranger. Besides, I enjoyed playing detective."

"Well, I certainly have benefited from the result. Thank you. Mrs. Brown will be expecting you for supper about now, and I'm headed back to my camp at the ranch. It will be good to get back to my own bedroll—the cot in the jail was darned uncomfortable."

"Any word on your herd?"

"Yes, a traveler coming north on the Preston Road came to the ranch early yesterday to tell me he passed them. My partner asked him to deliver the message that they expect to be here early next month. They've stopped in Central Texas, along the Brazos River, to fatten up the cattle." John Henry's face lit up. "Can't be soon enough. By the time they get here, it will be about time to drive the five-year-old steers to Shreveport. I'll join the drive from here to there. Then my partner and our men will take the steers on to New Orleans to sell, while I bring back the remuda—those are the extra horses from the cattle drive. I'm hoping the mature beeves will bring at least twenty dollars a head. Next year we may do a drive to Kansas, but this year, timing will be right for sale in New Orleans."

"That's good news. In the meantime, be sure to come to town and buy the *Dallas Herald*," reminded Sara "My advertisement will run in next week's issue, and my opening will follow on Saturday." She raised her eyebrows in question. "Will you come?"

"Wouldn't miss it, Sara. You can count on me to be here! And thank you. You most likely saved my life."

A few days later, Cecilia showed up at the store. "Sorry I haven't been by sooner. Our cabin is finally finished, and I've been helping Effie and her girls unpack the wagon. Effie has plenty of hands at work organizing things inside, so thought I'd see if you need help getting ready for your opening."

"You are a godsend. There is so much to be done," Sara sighed.

"Give me some tasks and I'll get to work." Cecilia took her bonnet off and reached for the extra apron Sara was offering. As she tied it around her waist, Cecilia asked, "Any more issues with Mr. West?"

"Haven't seen or heard from him lately. I expect his next move will be an advertisement this week. Don't know what his sale ad will say. Wish I did.

"At any rate, let me tell you what I have planned. Since Mr. West's store mostly meets the needs of the men of Dallas, my ad will appeal to the ladies. After all, they buy the food, household goods, and things for themselves and their children. Women here can't afford many extras, but if I offer something free along with the staples they can afford, I'm hoping they will be attracted to my grand opening and discover that I carry things that they need and want."

"I think that makes sense. What would you offer free?"

"Have you noticed that most of the women in the community, and even some of the ladies I've seen from La Réunion, are still wearing the bonnets and straw hats they must have worn on the trail? And worn is the right word. Most are pretty bedraggled."

Cecilia laughed. "Bedraggled is the right word for mine."

"Well, I've ordered two dozen colorful new cloth bonnets and two dozen straw hats for the store opening. Since women here get very little news about fashion, I thought they'd be excited to know about the Dolly Varden hat-and-dress craze that was sweeping Tennessee when I left."

"Oh, that was just starting in Kentucky as we were leaving for Texas!" Cecilia said. "It was based on the character in one of Charles Dickens' books, right?"

"Exactly. So, let me show you the advertisement I'm planning to run in the *Herald* for the store opening. I'd like your reaction to it." She handed Cecilia a sheet of paper.

Cecilia read aloud:

GRAND OPENING!
SARA'S MERCHANDISE EMPORIUM
Brand New Calico Bonnets
Fashionable Dolly Varden Straw Hats
Take your pick FREE if you spend just fifty cents
Spend fifty-five cents and add artificial cherries
and the ribbon of your choice.
Until supplies last, so come early.

Dolly Varden hats are the new fashion rage!
Inspired by Charles Dickens's character Dolly Varden,
from the book "Barnaby Rudge." Dolly was the locksmith's daughter . . .
"A pretty, laughing girl; dimpled and fresh, and healthful—
the very impersonation of good-humor and blooming beauty."
Dolly Varden dress patterns, yardage of bright calico and chintz,
sewing notions, even lace available and affordable.
Plus all the staples you need: flour, sugar, salt, pepper,
beans, coffee, rice, corn oil and more, all at FAIR prices.
Store will open at 7:00 a.m.
Mrs. Sara Darnell, Proprietor

Cecilia read the advertisement and looked up with a smile. "Poor Mr. West. The ladies will be lining up to shop at your store. Don't change a word. This advertisement will work."

"I hope you're right. Since you've offered to help, here's your first task. Your penmanship is much better than mine. Would you please copy the advertisement onto a large card that I can prop up on the counter?" Taking the advertisement, large card, and pen Sara offered, Cecilia went to work. Soon she handed Sara the finished card.

"Oh, I love the straw hat you drew on the card. This is perfect. Thank you. Now, please help me arrange a display of the hats and bonnets."

At the end of the afternoon, Sara and Cecilia took off their aprons and Sara declared the store ready for the opening. "Could not have accomplished so much today without you, Cecilia. Come and choose a bonnet and a hat plus the ribbon and berry trim you want. It's small thanks for all you've done."

A few minutes later, Cecilia left with her chosen hat and bonnet in hand, promising to be back to help with the store's grand opening, and Sara went to the *Herald* to place her advertisement. Later that week the newspaper came out and when Sara compared her ad with West's ad for a sale on a few small items, she smiled.

The morning of the grand opening of Sara's Merchandising Emporium, Sara was up early. She dressed carefully, putting on her crinolines followed by her best dress—the black, high-necked dress with the detachable white collar and cuffs and the full skirt. Bowing to practicality. she opted for one petticoat and no hoop. Over breakfast, she reminded Mrs. Brown to be sure and come to the store's opening

"You can count on me to be there. I saw the advertisement and I need a new bonnet."

When Sara arrived at the store at six thirty, she found a line of women had already formed on the porch. "Give me just two minutes and I'll open early for you." After putting on her apron and taking a quick look at the hat display, she opened the door and invited her first customers inside.

It wasn't long before the store was busy with curious women. Sara listened to the excited conversations.

"Just look at all the bolts of different calico prints."

"Yes, and there's chintz too. Look at all the different spools of thread."

"And she even has sewing-thread caddies!"

"Ribbons, look at all the colored ribbons."

"Oh my! Here's lace."

"Plums! Can't remember when we last had canned plums."

"Did you see the stockings and the Dolly Varden dress patterns?"

"How about the bonnets! I want the blue floral, which one do you want?"

"Look at the Dolly Varden straw hats, can you believe we can have one free? I'll be wearing mine to church on Sunday."

Women began to line up with their purchases. The wife of John Neely Bryan, Dallas' founder, was first in line. Sara glanced at the items Margaret Bryan had set on the counter. "Good, you found the Dolly Varden dress patterns."

"Yes, I really like the gathered overskirt on the dress. Can't wait to make it."

"Margaret, I can tell at a glance that these items more than meet the minimum purchase for a hat or bonnet. Go choose which one you want while I total this and wrap it for you. Miss Cecilia Stewart is back there to help. Get a yard of ribbon and some cherries too. Cecilia will wrap the hat trimmings for you. "

The morning is starting well. Sara hoped the sales continued.

Mrs. Thornton, the farmer's wife, who had been on the wagon train with Sara, brought her purchases to Sara. "I was discouraged when I visited West's store, but this store has the things I need. I'm so glad you've opened." A number of other ladies made similar comments.

Sarah Cockrell came to the counter with a basketful of purchases. On top were two Dolly Varden dress patterns. She stacked the items from her basket onto the counter. "Sara, your store is such a nice addition to Dallas. Look at how many things I found. Cecilia Stewart helped me with a Dolly Varden straw hat and ribbons." Paying for her purchases, she laughed. "With my new hat, I feel more fashionable already."

The next woman in line placed her items on the counter along with a slightly ragged bonnet. "Can you wrap my old bonnet with my other pack-ages? I want to wear my new one home."

Sarah laughed. "I'll be happy to."

The next customer put a basket of four dozen eggs on the counter. "Will you barter for these?"

"How much credit would you like?"

"Enough for a hat plus berries and ribbon."

"I'll give you fifteen cents credit plus the hat and trimmings."

"Done! Thank you."

Sara reached behind the counter for a new supply of brown wrapping paper and looked up to find Mrs. Brown standing there with numerous items, from stockings to a fat ball of twine. "I had no idea you'd have such a good selection of so many things. I want all this, plus four ounces of hard candy. I'll take a dozen of those eggs too."

Sara asked, "Was there anything you wanted that you didn't find?"

Mrs. Brown thought for a moment and said, "Do you think you could get any books?"

"Hmm . . . I don't have much extra shelf space, but I might be able to special order if you have an idea about the titles or kinds of books you'd like."

"Maybe something by Charles Dickens?" Mrs. Brown said.

"Books are a good idea, Mrs. Brown. Let me see what I can find out from the wholesaler."

"Thank you, Sara. I think it's high time you called me Hattie instead of Mrs. Brown."

"I'd like that, Hattie. Thank you."

The flow of customers continued all day. Lots of merchandise crossed the counter and flowed out the door. By five o'clock, the bonnets were gone and only one straw hat remained.

Ellie Duffield dashed into the store at four minutes past five o'clock. "Sara, do you still have Dolly Varden straw hats left? Please tell me you do!"

"Just one. Go shop and I'll hold it for you."

John Henry poked his head in the door as Ellie was leaving with her hat and purchases. "I watched outside for a while. Looked like you had a steady stream of ladies. Are you happy with your grand opening?"

"It was even better than I had hoped."

Cecilia came from the back of the store. "Hello, John Henry, if you've come for a bonnet, we've given them all away." She grinned at him.

He chuckled. "Just here to see how the store opening went. Sara tells me it went well."

Cecilia nodded. "Went well is an understatement. It didn't slow down all day. I'd say it was a huge success, thanks to Sara's creativity with the hat-and and-bonnet giveaway. Women loved it."

"Glad to hear it. Congratulations on a good first day, ladies." He turned to Sara. "May it be the first of many good days for the store." The sound of Crutchfield's dinner bell echoed across the square. "I'm off to Crutchfield's for dinner. Grouse on the menu tonight." He wiggled his eyebrows and headed out the door.

"Sweet man," Cecilia said, smiling.

The final four ladies were too late for hats or bonnets. Sara promised the disappointed women that she would order more. She took their names so they could collect their choice the following month when her shipment arrived.

At five forty-five, tired but happy, Sara and Cecilia closed the store. "Thank you for helping, Cecilia. There was no way I could have handled the counter, measured the ribbon and yardage, and answered all the questions by myself."

" I enjoyed myself and met so many women. Judging by the response, I'd say women like your store."

"Thank heavens! You know, we actually had more customers than I'd hoped for."

"One of the women told me Mr. West was standing in the street glaring at your store."

"Well, silly man, he's just going to have to get used to the competition."

"Unless you need me for anything, I'm headed home to kick off my shoes and relax."

"No, go rest. I plan to do the same." Sara gave her a thank-you hug.

After Cecilia left, Sara sat in the three-legged chair to tally the opening-day sales. She'd sold about 30 percent more than she'd expected. Taking a chance on the hats had paid off. There was money now for the next reorder of inventory. Hopefully today's customers would spread the word about the store. *I need to think of something to attract customers next week.* Sara yawned. *But now I need to go to supper and then to bed.*

Back at the boardinghouse, Sara pulled off her shoes and wiggled her toes. She smiled. *I wonder if Hattie will care if I come to the supper table in my stocking feet.*

Dear Momma and Papa,

I hope you, Grandma, and my sisters are enjoying the summer and that it is cooler in Henderson County than it is in Dallas. My goodness it gets hot here.

Sara's Merchandise Emporium is open as of yesterday. How do you like the name?

There was already a line when I arrived at the store at 6:30 a.m. on opening day. Women here can't afford many extras, but by offering a free straw hat or bonnet with a minimum purchase, first-day sales were very good. The wholesaler gave me a good price on the hats, so the day was profitable. I am encouraged.

Mrs. Brown baked a fresh peach shortcake for supper last night with peaches from the nearby community of Farmers Branch. Farmers there grow lots of fresh produce, including peaches. Apparently the settlement used to be called Mustang Branch, because of all the wild horses in the area, until farmers there began to produce so many fruits and vegetables that they changed the name. Anyway, I'm hoping to find a small but steady supply of Farmers Branch fruits and vegetables for the store.

I don't have much new to report. I've been so busy working on getting the store open that I haven't done much else. Although, Momma, I am going to church, as I promised you I would.

I'll write more news in two weeks. Please do write me. So far there have been no letters in the D pocket of the letter bag. I am told it takes quite a while for mail to get to us here.

My love to you, Grandma, and both my sisters. I miss you all.

Your loving daughter,

Sara

On week number two, Sara's ad in the *Herald* announced a tea party at her store. Every customer who made a purchase was invited to enjoy a free cup of tea made with the clear, artesian spring water from the limestone cliffs across the Trinity at La Réunion. The Trinity River water, easily available in Dallas, was notoriously muddy. There were several springs around Dallas; however, the water from the artesian wells on the limestone cliffs bubbled to the surface clean and clear.

Early in the week, Sara hired Daniel Pollard to bring a large barrel of the spring water across from the other side of the river. The day of the tea party, Sara arrived at the store early in the morning to prepare. Daniel Pollard had made a small table from sawhorses and planks, then positioned it in a back corner of the store. Sara covered this "tea table" with a tablecloth she'd brought from Tennessee and arranged her china teapot and Grandmother's nine china cups on the table. Beside them she placed a canister of tea. After filling a small ironstone bowl with sugar and a pitcher with cream, she placed them on the table along with a number of spoons. At one end of the table, she placed the slop basin, a bowl where tea drinkers could dump used tea leaves and cold tea from their cups. As a final touch, she added a small vase of wildflowers gathered the previous day and a glass jar of gumdrops with some small tongs.

Her kettle of hot water was ready on the store's stove. The water barrel sat just outside the door. A bucket of soapy wash water and one of clean rinse water waited in one of the two storerooms. As she stepped back to admire the table, she heard Cecilia and Ellie Duffield's voices. Ellie and Cecilia had volunteered to pour the tea and wash the cups. Sara said, "Come in, I'm in the back."

"Oh, how pretty the table looks," Ellie said, as she and Cecilia came around the center shelf.

"Thank you, and thanks again for volunteering to be my hostesses."

"We're ready. Just tell us exactly what you want us to do," Cecilia said.

"Each lady who makes a purchase will be given a card with the words 'Invitation to Tea.' They'll bring you the card and trade it for a cup of tea."

"Do we save the Invitation-to-Tea cards?" Ellie asked.

"I only have a dozen invitations, so when that many accumulate, I'll come pick them up to reuse. Or, if you're not busy, run them up to me at the counter. Once you have the card, just make the tea. Use the tea leaves from the canister on the table here, pour the water, then add any sugar and cream they request. I thought a gumdrop on each cup might be nice too. They may take the cup and browse or stand and visit. Help me watch that no cups walk out the door."

Cecilia did a quick scan of the table. "Nine cups?"

'Right. When the cup is finished, just dump the remains in the slop bowl. The cup-washing buckets are in the storeroom. There's hot water on the stove and the barrel to refill it is just outside the back door. The stove's hot, so water for tea should reheat quickly."

"Simple enough," Cecilia said.

Margaret Bryan was first to arrive. She was wearing the straw hat Sara had given her the previous week. "Sara, I've been looking forward to this ever since I saw your tea-party advertisement. Imagine, a tea party in Dallas! For my purchase, I need two ounces of cinnamon and some crackers. I promised my children I'd return with treats, so I also want a pound of penny candy— an even mix of rock candy, stick candy, and horehound."

Sara weighed the requested items. She tore a piece of brown paper and folded it around the cinnamon, tying the small package with string cut from the roll dangling from the ceiling, then did the same with the crackers Margaret had taken from the cracker barrel. "How would you like your candy wrapped? Since you're staying for tea, how about I wrap it in paper and tie the package like the cinnamon, rather than rolling the paper into an open cornucopia that might spill?"

Margaret Bryan said, "Good idea, please do." She paid Sara, tucked the packages into her basket, and took her invitation to the tea table.

By this time, a line of ladies had formed. "Just bring me your purchases and I'll give you your invitation to tea," Sara said. Several women left the line to shop. Eliza Pollard was next. "Eliza, it's so nice to see you. Cecilia told me that your cabin is finally finished. You and Captain Pollard must be so glad."

"We are. We've finally unpacked the wagon and it's time to restock my pantry. Just getting a few things today 'cause I knew you'd be busy with the tea party, but I'll be back with a long list tomorrow." Sara ground and wrapped two pounds of coffee and added the four cans of fruit and the bottle of castor oil Eliza wanted, put them in her basket, and gave her the tea invitation. Eliza paid her in hammered Mexican dollars.

In less than two hours, Sara had used all twelve invitations and walked back to the tea table to retrieve them. A group of women were clustered around the tea table talking and laughing.

A gray-haired woman with a dried-apple face and red, watery eyes turned to her. Sara recognized her from church. *Mrs. Cook, I think?* The woman's teacup was rattling in palsied hands. "Sara, I never knew a store could be so much fun! Sara's tea party should be an annual event. I'm visiting over tea with friends I haven't seen in months."

Margaret Bryan said, "And what a treat to have tea in pretty china cups."

Sara lingered, talking for a few moments, then excused herself to go back to the counter. "More customers waiting for me." Customers continued to stream in all day.

At one point in the day, Sara looked up to see Mr. West peering into the door with a frown on his face. When he realized he'd been seen, he scuttled away.

By six o'clock, Ellie, Cecilia, and Sara had folded the tablecloth and washed, dried, and put away the last of the china and utensils. "The tea party was a roaring success," Ellie said, "but I can't wait to take my shoes off."

Cecilia looked down at her own feet. "Barefooted sounds really good right now. By the way, the gumdrops were really popular, Sara. Several women commented they hadn't had a gumdrop in years. I realized I hadn't either. Took me back to my childhood. The red ones were the most requested."

Sara thanked Cecilia and Ellie for all their help and gave each of them a hug and a canister of tea. After locking up, she sat in the three-legged chair and tallied her sales for the day. She was pleased. Her total sales were almost as high as on opening day, but today's profits were higher because there wasn't the expense of the giveaway hats. *Sara's Merchandise Emporium is off to a good start.*

And so it went. As summer progressed, Sara's creative approach wooed the ladies of Dallas and the surrounding area to her store. The men continued to buy their gunpowder, lead, tools, and other items from West and visited his back room for a gourd of whiskey, but by the end of the summer, Sara had captured much of the ladies' trade.

Summer had welcomed a host of wildflowers to the prairie around Dallas. Taking a prairie walk one Sunday afternoon, Sara looked at the bright purple blooms scattered across the landscape. The store could certainly use a bit of color. She walked back to the store and found a small shovel and two buckets. Back on the prairie, she dug up purple coneflowers and replanted them in her buckets. As she worked, she stopped and let the soil run through her fingers. *Farmers say this is some of the richest soil in the country. Hope it works in my flower buckets.*

The buckets were heavy. It took a separate trip to carry each one to the store's porch. Sara put one on each side of the door and watered them. She stepped back to admire them. *Pretty. I hope they'll grow.*

Two mornings later, Sara arrived at the store and found the plants shredded, soil dumped all over the porch, and the buckets overturned. *Why on earth would someone do this?* She collected her broom from the storeroom and swept it up, muttering the entire time.

A week later, Sara found horse manure splashed all over her front door and dripping onto the store's porch. *I bet nasty Mr. West did this. I just know it!* One more case of vandalism and she'd either confront West or go to the marshal. *I refuse to put up with this!* She walked around to the back door and gathered a pile of brown paper, mop, broom, and a work apron from the store. She heated a large pot of hot water and filled a bucket with hot, soapy water. Carrying all this to the porch, she realized the process of cleaning up the mess would ruin her shoes. She took them off, along with her stockings, and put on her apron, trying to tuck her skirts up. She gritted her teeth and stepped onto the manure-splattered porch, feeling the squish of muck between her toes. The feeling sent shivers down her back. *Ugh! Don't think about it, just work fast.*

Stacking several layers of brown paper in front of the door, she took a big stick and scraped what she could onto the paper. *The stench is awful.* She folded the paper and carefully carried it around back to the trash pile to be burned later that day. Next she took the bucket of hot, soapy water and carefully poured the water on the door, watching dirty residue drip. She refilled the bucket from the rain barrel and added some hot water. After pouring water on the door several times, she took a scrub brush and brushed the logs with soapy water. When all evidence of the manure was gone, she wiped the logs down with a dry cloth. *Now I have to deal with the porch.*

She started by sweeping as much as possible into a soggy pile. Sweeping as much as she could onto a thin board, she carefully carried it behind the store and into the woods, where she buried it, board and all, being sure to pile extra dirt on it. After refilling her bucket, she took a mop and washed the porch floor, refilling her bucket when needed, and rinsing her mop several times. When the water in the bucket remained clean, she soaped her mop and the dirty broom and rinsed them well. Finally, comfortable that no odor was left in the mop or bucket, she put them beside the back door to dry. She then took a small shovel and turned the dirty soil around the porch. Hours after beginning the cleanup, Sara washed her feet, hands, and arms well, and went back to the boardinghouse to clean up a bit more and change clothes. By midafternoon, she opened the store. *Hopefully, the people I had to turn away as I worked will be back to buy.*

A few mornings later, Sara came in much earlier than usual, latching the door from the inside as she did when she was alone in the store after hours. She was sorting goods in the storeroom when she heard rattling noises at the front door. "Who's there?" she called. No answer, but she heard the sounds of retreating feet. Waiting a few minutes and listening to be sure there was no sound of activity, she opened the door to find no one in sight but evidence of damage to the lock. Sara was uneasy and went to Marshal Moore's office at the jail to report all three incidents. He looked at Sara and shook his head. "You don't have any evidence. Haven't seen anybody. Say you think it might be Mr. West." He made a grunting sound. "Probably just kids. Let me know if you have some real clues."

Sara looked at his almost smirking face in disgust. "Some lawman you are. If I could vote, I'd vote against you." She wheeled around and stormed out, leaving the door open. *If he wants it closed, he can do it himself.*

Fairly quickly Sara realized that the demands of storekeeping made it difficult to handle the domestic task of laundry. Washing clothing once a week, even for one person, was more than a full day's work. Prewash soaking, preparing hot water, washing, bleaching, starching, and ironing spilled over into two days. Knowing that the town's many single men didn't do their own washing, Sara sought out a laundress. Mrs. Mizell, who lived several blocks from the town square, was recommended as a dependable washerwoman. Sara found Mrs. Mizell outside her cabin, surrounded by the tools of her trade. There were laundry tubs lined up on a washing bench for easy access to the clothes soaking inside. Sara recognized an ash hopper where lye was made from ashes, then mixed with animal fat to make soap. And there was the laundress herself, stirring a steaming copper pot of water and laundry with a large, wooden washing paddle. Behind her was a clothesline strung between poles. Clean clothes held by line pegs flapped in the breeze. Other clothing was draped on drying racks.

Sara introduced herself and asked Mrs. Mizell if she would be willing to take on additional weekly laundry for one person and how much she charged.

"You the new storekeeper?" Mrs. Mizell stepped away from the heat of the fire under the boiler pot and wiped the sweat from her round face with a towel she had around her neck. She smelled of dried sweat and soap.

"I am."

"If I do your laundry and ironin', would you be willing to barter?"

"I'd be happy to barter. You'd prefer that to cash money?"

"I would. Mr. Mizell takes any cash money I collect. If I could barter, I could trade for some things for myself."

Hmm . . . seems there are advantages to being independent that I'd not considered before.

Sara nodded at Mrs. Mizell. "I'll set up an account for you, give you a credit equal to the amount you bill me for laundry, and you can spend your credits whenever you like."

The two agreed to a barter amount for each pound of wash. "As for ironing, we'll agree on a price by item when you bring in your laundry," Mrs. Mizell said.

"Fair enough," Sara said, smiling at the arrangement.

Ellie Duffield showed up at the store one Saturday afternoon as Margaret Bryan was leaving. Watching her go, Ellie said, "She's very brave, just ignores the gossip about her husband, John Neely Bryan. You know he's the founder of Dallas, right?"

"Yes, but Margaret told me he's gone right now."

"Gone? I guess so." Sara could tell Ellie was winding up to share the latest gossip.

"It's a huge scandal. Last year, Bryan believed that another local man, who'd had a bit too much to drink, was paying unwanted attention to Margaret. Bryan shot him."

Sara hadn't expected that. "He shot him?"

"Yep. In fact, he thought he'd killed him. So he fled across the Trinity. As rumor has it, Bryan somehow contacted his lawyer, who followed him with business documents requiring his signature. His lawyer told him the man wasn't dead."

"Did Bryan come back then?"

"No. Maybe he didn't believe it or was afraid the man's wound would still prove to be fatal, because he hasn't been heard from since. There's new talk about it and new speculation about where he might be. Poor Margaret. I am hopeful that the gossip will soon stop, for her sake, and that her husband will return."

"So he's been gone for a year, and she's not heard from him?"

"That's what I understand."

"How sad for her." *She doesn't know where he is, or how he is, or if he'll come home. The uncertainty would be terrible.*

"He left in '49 for the California gold rush, but came back after a year. Hopefully he'll come back this time too." Ellie shrugged her shoulders and held up her empty basket. "Anyway, I came to shop. I need bacon, butter, and where are the cotton stockings?"

"Follow me," Sara led the way to the shelf with stockings, still thinking about the missing John Neely Bryan.

The *Dallas Herald* published an article about weather which Sara read with interest.

> *"North Texas has several seasons. These seasons don't necessarily coincide with other parts of the country. Winter usually eases in at the beginning of*

January and lasts through February. Some years it barely freezes, and other years winter is notable for ice storms, occasional balmy days, and frigid blue northers which blow in from Canada. Spring sneaks in by early March, bringing April rain. By May the prairies are in bloom. The hot season is June through August, when the temperature is guaranteed to make man and beast pretty miserable and mosquitoes happy. September is Indian summer, when kids and grown men and women are tempted to play hooky from whatever tasks might keep them indoors. October usually starts as a continuation of Indian summer, but by its final week, leaves are turning, pumpkin pies are showing up after supper, and sweaters and jackets are pulled out of trunks where they've been stored. November and December can't make up their minds about what season they belong to. Days vacillate between shirtsleeve weather and pile-on-the-coats days. Texans like to say, 'If you don't like the weather, wait five minutes or go down the road five miles.' This applies to most any of Texas's seasons except the hot season. You can count on June through August to be hot or hotter."

It wasn't long before Sara had a second taste of strange Texas weather. The thunderclap seemed to reverberate inside Sara's small bedroom. With the second large clap echoing in her ears and the bright flash of lightning illuminating the room, she jumped to her feet and ran to the window, expecting to have to close the shutters against a deluge of rain. *This summer's drought must be ending.* Not a drop of rain was falling. The thunder and lightning continued, and Sara watched through the window as the dry storm—alive with rolling thunder and giant bolts of lightning—rolled through town and across the prairie. In the morning Hattie told Sara and Mr. Baker that they had witnessed what was called "dry lightning." "It's best not to be outside when a dry-lightning storm strikes," Hattie said

"Well it was certainly fierce, water or no water." Sara said. Mr. Baker shook his head and simply said, *"Mon Dieu!"*

Unpacking her most recent merchandise order, Sara found a small package with a note from her wholesaler attached. "Mrs. Darnell," it read, "I received

your request for novels by Charles Dickens. My firm does not have a relationship with a publisher other than for schoolbooks; however, the enclosed book is one which came by accident some time ago with an order of *McGuffey's Readers*. It is not by Charles Dickens, but by another British author, a woman no less! Perhaps your customer will enjoy it." Sarah opened the package to find a book titled *Wuthering Heights* by Emily Brontë. Sara rewrapped the book and took it home at the end of the day. Opening it over supper, Hattie said, "Oh, Sara, thank you. I can't wait to read it! Books are so hard to come by in Dallas that I've nearly worn the words off the ones I have, they've been read so many times. A new one is better than gold. And this one is written by a woman!" As soon as the dishes were done, Hattie's nose was in the new book.

One afternoon in late summer, the store was quiet. Outdoors the sun was sneaking in and out of fair-weather, white clouds and a subtle breeze was dancing through the trees, making the leaves whisper summer secrets. Sara moved her three-legged chair outside on the front porch. Almost dozing, Sara was snapped awake by a loud rumbling and shouts of "Here comes a herd!" Sure enough, coming through the main street in a cloud of rising dust, which made Sara sneeze, were several riders and a large mass of cattle. *There must be at least four hundred.* The riders were working to keep the cattle close together and moving at a controlled speed. As the first rider rode by Sara, he tipped his hat and gave her a brilliant smile. As the herd passed, Sara stood to watch and realized that this was probably John Henry's long-awaited herd. Sure enough, she spotted his T-Lazy-R brand. She remembered he'd said it was T for Texas and R for Ranger.

As the last of the herd passed, a big bull bolted from the ranks. Several more followed and suddenly there was a mini stampede. Horrified, Sara saw that several tons of moving beast were headed for a little boy in a blue shirt standing at the very edge of the road. Startled, the boy began to run but stumbled. Without thinking, Sara jumped from the porch and hurled herself toward him, pushing him out of the path of the running animals and landing flat on her stomach on the ground. She tried to rise and made it to her knees but one of the huge, moving animals slammed against her as she knelt, leaving her bruised and her one black dress in shreds.

As the cattle moved on, followed by the cow chasers' extra horses, Captain Pollard's son Daniel ran to help. "Are you hurt, Mrs. Darnell? You jumped right in the middle of those cattle! That was mighty brave." When Sara was able to rise, the little boy was nowhere in sight.

"Did you see the little boy? Is he all right?"

"Yep. He's fine, his momma scooped him up and took off with him." Daniel insisted on walking Sara back to the store to be sure she was all right. She closed the store early and limped back to the boardinghouse where she warmed water over the cookstove, poured it into the large hip tub in the washing shed, and stepped in to soak her sore body. Back in her room, in addition to bruises and badly skinned knees, she discovered she had a black eye.

The next day as Sara approached her store, she saw Mr. West waiting at her door. Sara muttered to herself, "Oh no, I don't have the energy to deal with him today." As she got closer, she saw that West was clutching a pile of black fabric which he held out to her. "I'm sorry, Mr. West, I don't understand." Looking at him questioningly, Sara realized he had tears in his eyes.

"Mrs. Darnell, people told me what you did yesterday." His voice was quavering. "The boy you pushed out of the way of the cattle, at great risk to yourself, I understand, was my six-year-old son, Reuben. I'm sure you saved his life."

"I'm just glad he wasn't hurt." *Mr. West's son!*

"Reuben walked away with only a scraped chin and skinned knees, thanks to you. I was told your black dress was ruined. Here is enough black silk to make a new dress. My wife, Lois, is a fine seamstress. If you'll choose a pattern, she'll be happy to make a dress for you. It's the least we can do."

"That's very generous, Mr. West. Thank you." Sara took the offered silk. "I'm glad your son was not seriously injured."

Mr. West stood up straighter and began what sounded very much like a prepared speech. "Mrs. Darnell, I owe you an apology. When I realized you were going to open a store, I don't know what came over me. I worked so hard to build my business. I was afraid of losing it. I am also ashamed. The petty vandalism you suffered was because of me. I apologize. You'll never have to worry about it again. You were right. There is sufficient business for both stores. From now on, you can count on me to be a friendly competitor. Bring your pattern and the silk back to me when you are ready, and Lois will get to work on your dress."

Sara smiled at West. "Apology accepted and I'll be delighted to accept Mrs. West's offer to make a dress for me. Please thank her. I look forward to meeting her soon."

Mr. West said goodbye and hurried across the street to his store.

My goodness, the world does work in mysterious ways. And I do need a new black dress.

Two days later, John Henry appeared at the store. Dusty and unshaven, he was moving slower than usual, but had a big smile on his face.

"Your herd finally came," Sara said excitedly. "What a lot of cattle! I saw them pass through town."

"I understand you did more than just see them," John Henry said, eyeing Sara's fading black eye. "You ready to be a cow chaser?" His eyes crinkled beneath shaggy eyebrows as he grinned.

"I think I'll stick to shopkeeping. How many cattle did you bring in?"

"Our T-Lazy-R brand is on 427 cattle. Whit and the boys road branded our cattle before bringing them north. A couple of dozen strays joined our herd along the way. They have a mix of brands."

"Who is Whit?"

"Whit Wainwright is my partner. He came in with the herd. You'll meet him soon. His dad was my best friend before he died. We served together as Texas Rangers. I've known Whit since he was this tall." John Henry held his hand at about three feet above the floor. "He's grown into a fine man like his dad. He'll apply for his 320 acres next to mine and we'll operate the ranch together 50-50. He came into town with me today but headed straight to Webster's Saddlery for some new spurs and cow-chaser supplies for Jellie and Zollie Wensel, our cowcatchers."

"You mentioned strays with different brands, what do you do with them?"

"I guess you could say there's an informal law of the range." John Henry shrugged his shoulders. "The strays are mixed with ours, so, when we round up the steers to sell, we gather the odd brands and sell them as well. The money for the sale of the strays is generally deposited with the county treasurer, along with information about their brands."

"What does he do with it?"

"Once a year, cowmen will send their representatives around to the various counties and collect the money for the sale of cattle bearing their brands. When we brand calves, they get the same brand as their mother, so over time, a cowman can end up with steers scattered across lots of counties. I suspect we lost a few cattle as our herd crossed the state. Each county issues numbers to the ranches operating in their county to help identify them. The T-Lazy-R is ranch number two in Dallas County."

"When will you take your cattle to market?"

"Whit and the boys brought the cattle up pretty slow so they could graze as they traveled, and the boys could brand the spring calves born along the way. A couple of weeks on our grass here to fatten them up and we'll gather the mature steers, those about five years old, drive them to Shreveport, and barge them to New Orleans."

"Barge them to New Orleans?" Sara wasn't sure she'd heard right. "You can transport a whole herd of cattle by barge?"

"Yep. We might make more money with a cattle drive to Missouri, but longhorns carry a tick-borne disease called Texas fever. Doesn't bother longhorns, but it can be deadly to other kinds of cattle. The farmers in Missouri are turnin' back Texas herds for fear their cattle will be infected. This year our herd is small, 'bout 150 five-year-old steers, and we figure we might get as much as thirty or forty dollars a head in New Orleans. Next year, when we have a new batch of five-year-olds, we'll consider a cattle drive to Kansas or Missouri if they've opened up to Texas beef, otherwise, we'll head to Shreveport again and barge 'em to New Orleans."

"I know about the horse business, thanks to my papa, but I had no idea how the cattle business works." Movement at the front door caught Sara's eye. Sticking across the doorway was a blue-denim leg with a boot. The leg began to move, rattling the shiny spur decorating the heel of the boot. "Hey, John Henry, how do you like my new spurs?"

John Henry laughed. "Get in here, Whit, and meet Sara."

Whit Wainwright took off his black cowboy hat as he stepped into the store. "So you're the Mrs. Darnell I've heard John Henry speak about? Pleased to meet you."

"And I'm happy to finally meet John Henry's partner." Sara took in the young cowboy. He was several inches taller than Sara, slim waisted and broad shouldered. Tanned from the trail, except for a white band of skin around his forehead where his hat had rested, he wore a three-button shirt neatly tucked in under a fringed suede jacket. There was a red neckerchief around his neck. His blond hair was past his collar and a bit tangled. Like John Henry, he wore a Colt revolver.

"I hear one of our steers gave you that black eye." His voice was slow and had what Sara was beginning to recognize as a Texas twang. "Sure sorry, ma'am."

Sara thought he sounded more amused than sorry. She couldn't think of a retort, so she just looked at him. This seemed to embarrass him. He flushed and began twisting his wide-brimmed hat in his big hands.

"I'm headin' back to the saddle shop to look at some rope. I'll be there, John Henry, when you're ready to head back. Nice to make your acquaintance, Mrs. Darnell." With a nod, he was quickly gone.

John Henry gave Sara a quizzical look. "What did you think of Whit?"

"Too soon to know" was Sara's noncommittal answer.

"Bonjour, Madame."

Sara looked up from the ledger she'd been working on to see Mr. Edouard Charles Beaulieu step into the store. He was as well turned out as when Sara and Cecilia had first met him with the group from La Réunion, but this time he wore a ruffled shirt and a scarf, rather than a tie. "Mr. Beaulieu, how can I help you?" Sara asked, standing and closing her ledger.

"I have come with an invitation. La Réunion wishes to host the people of Dallas at a grand *soirée* with piano music and dancing. It will be held in two weeks on Sunday evening in our communal dining building and all are invited. One of your Dallas citizens has told me that this would be a desecration of the Sabbath. I have explained that in Europe we work six days a week and have only Sunday for recreation and rest. We wish for you all to join us. Mr. Cockrell has promised he will not charge tolls on his bridge that evening."

'Your invitation is lovely and I'm sure many of our citizens will join you. As a widow for less than a year, I'm not sure I should attend. It may not be seemly."

"*Au contraire*, social rules give way to practicality on the frontier. You should come and enjoy the festivities. I should very much like to see you there." Beaulieu gave her a beaming smile. "*Au revoir*, dear lady."

Word of the grand soirée spread like wildfire, and the small community bubbled with excitement. Women flocked into the store to buy dress patterns and bright calico yardage, new ribbons, or whatever frippery they could afford. Sara enjoyed listening to the chatter as women shopped:

"I told my husband that we most certainly will attend."

"My sweetheart asked to escort me to the soirée. I need new ribbons to match my dress."

"We're taking the dancing lessons the French dance master is offering at the Art Saloon."

"A soirée, isn't it exciting! I'm making a new dress to wear. Do you have white lace?"

In the midst of the excitement, Cecilia and Sara's neighbor, Ellie Duffield, were talking with Sara at the store's counter, as customers came to pay for their purchases. Sara said, "Morgan's been dead less than a year, I don't think I should attend a party."

"Of course you should go," Ellie said. "Sara, you work so hard, no one will think less of you for going to the grand soirée. You always act like a lady. You've been the image of propriety—it won't hurt your reputation one bit to attend."

Sara looked to Cecilia for support. "I agree with Ellie, you should go, Sara. In fact, why don't we three attend together?"

And so it was decided that Sara would attend. She hoped Mrs. West would finish her black dress in time. *If I'm going, I need to wear widow's weeds.*

Hattie Brown asked if she might accompany the ladies. "I wouldn't miss the grand soirée for the world. I used to love parties when I was a girl."

Mrs. Brown took her skirt in hand and did a few dance steps. Sara grinned. She was seeing a new side of her stern landlady. *Is the gruffness just a facade for her boarders?*

Mrs. West delivered Sara's new black-silk dress in ample time for the party. Sara was delighted with it. The bodice featured a high V-neck formed by small pleats running from each shoulder to the center of the dropped waist. The sleeves were long and poufed but fitted at the wrist. The separate skirt was tightly gathered and very full.

Dressing for the soirée, Sara added a hoop with an under and over petticoats. She then slipped into the two-piece dress and added a black lace collar and the strand of pearls her momma had given her for her wedding. She parted her hair in the middle and pulled each side into a soft drape or pad over her ears. Taking the ends of the long hair, she twisted the two sides together, winding it into a knot which she pinned at the back of her head and covered with a bit of black lace. Wishing she had new shoes to wear, she cleaned her everyday pair and tried to buff them to a bit of a shine. *They'll have to do.*

As she came down the boardinghouse stairs, Hattie looked up and said, "Your new dress is lovely, Sara. Are you happy with it?"

"I am pleased as punch." At the bottom of the stairs, Sara spun around. "Look at how much yardage Mrs. West put in this skirt."

Ira Webster and his wife, Marilyn, had offered to provide a ride to and from La Réunion. In midafternoon the four ladies climbed into the Webster's wagon and joined the caravan of excited guests going the three miles across the Trinity to the grand soirée.

As they approached the small village of La Réunion, Sara expressed her surprise at how many structures there were. Buildings were a combination of stone and wood and were neatly arranged in rows. The dirt streets were straight and there were winding walking paths between buildings. Several people were walking toward the dining hall where the party was being held. In and among the scattered trees were several large garden plots and corrals for a few horses. Ira Webster told her that the colony's promoter, Victor Considérant, had organized construction before the first group of colonists arrived. Webster pointed out the two-story cottage for Considérant, a laundry, chicken house, forge, common house for some settlers, and a large communal dining hall. Sara saw that a few small houses were finished and additional cottages were under construction.

Inside the large dining hall, tables and chairs had been placed along the walls, leaving the center clear for dancing. *Plank floors! That will certainly make dancing easier.* Punch bowls and cups covered several tables, and the piano was already playing a merry tune. Some of the Texans joined in with their fiddles as the grand soirée began.

Sara guessed there were seventy-five or eighty people crowded into the room and spilling outside the door, where many men were standing and talking, yet there was still some room for dancing. *This building is larger than anything in Dallas.*

La Réunion colonists were dressed more formally than on the day she and Cecilia had seen them on the street. The men wore black tailcoats and neck scarves while the ladies in their silk party gowns were more fashionably dressed than the Dallas women, most of whom wore colorful calico dresses. *La Réunion colonists certainly look affluent.*

Sara, Cecilia, Hattie, and Ellie found chairs while Marilyn Webster pulled her somewhat reluctant husband onto the dance floor. Sara noted that Ira Webster was light on his feet for such a big man. The musicians, led by the piano, began a waltz as dancers from both colonies took to the floor. Edouard Charles Beaulieu, as beautifully dressed as Sara had come to expect, had a brief consultation with the pianist, and the music changed to allow eight members of La Réunion to demonstrate an elegant quadrille. Sara watched closely as four couples formed a square; *les dames* and *les cavaliers* bowed to acknowledge each other as the music began and then performed a series of intricate figures composed of dance steps moving forward, backward, and sideways with a frequent exchange of partners. *Very elegant and nicely done.*

After this, the fiddles struck up a vigorous polka. *Not so elegant but much livelier.*

As the polka came to a breathless stop, Considérant and Cockrell stepped forward, shook hands, greeted the group, and invited everyone to have a good time at the first grand soirée for the two villages. *Considérant is an imposing-looking man.* His almost-black hair, brushed neatly back from a receding hairline, was long enough to cover his ears. The most striking feature of his face was a long full mustache, the sides of which hung down well below his chin. He wore a double-breasted suit coat over checked trousers. *That mustache must be his trademark.*

Maxime Guillot, owner of a Dallas carriage and wagon-making company, was introduced as a French immigrant who had volunteered to serve as the event's translator when needed. In contrast to Considérant, Guillot had short, black hair and full lips that protruded out of a black mustache. He wore an embroidered vest under a frock coat enhancing an overall impression of neatness. *"Dapper" is the word that comes to mind for Guillot.*

"Good evening, ladies." A clean-shaven John Henry appeared out of the crowd. Sara thought he looked distinguished in his black suit, white shirt, and string tie. He turned to Cecilia. "Miss Stewart, would you like to dance?"

As they joined the fast-moving polka dancers, Ellie looked at Sara and wiggled her forehead, making her eyebrows and her wire-framed glasses bounce. "How about that? Don't they make a nice couple?"

Before Sara could answer, a young man in a dark brown Prince Albert suit stood before her with an offer to dance. It took her a second to recognize John Henry's partner, Whit Wainwright. His blond hair had been trimmed and he was clean shaven. Sara recognized the untanned band of skin on his forehead, which was usually protected from the sun by his hat. *He certainly cleans up nicely.* Whit took her small hand in his large one and led her to the dance floor just as the music shifted from the polka back to a more-staid waltz. Whit was a surprisingly good dancer. Sara flashed back to waltzing with Morgan at their wedding party and how that happiness had been shattered. She stumbled. Whit caught her. "I'm sorry," he said, "my fault."

"No," Sara said, "the fault was mine. The dance brought back a painful, very emotional memory. I apologize but I need to sit down."

"Of course." Whit led her back to her chair and went to get her a glass of artesian spring water.

Ellie was dancing with a short, muscular fellow with a square jaw, broad neck, and good boots. He had introduced himself as La Réunion's carpenter. Hattie was across the room laughing and chatting with a group of Dallas women. John Henry and Cecilia were still on the dance floor.

Whit returned with Sara's water and sat beside her. He seemed to understand the source of Sara's emotion. "John Henry told me about your husband, I'm sorry for your loss. You are very brave to have stayed in Dallas and opened your store without him."

"Brave or foolish, I'm not sure which. The shop was Morgan's and my dream, and I was determined to make it happen. I've been very fortunate so far that the store is doing well. Speaking of doing well, you dance very nicely."

Whit laughed. "You mean for a cow chaser."

"No—" Sara said.

"No, seriously," he went on, "my mother insisted that I learn to dance when I was growing up. She said I'd never find a proper young lady if I couldn't dance. I was surprised to find I enjoy it."

"Hey, Whit." Sara looked up to see two young men. She did a double take—they were identical.

"Hello ma'am, I'm Zollie Wensel. "

The other chimed in, "I'm Jellie Wensel."

"Yes, we're twins," they chorused. Obviously the two had their introduction routine down pat. They were a matched pair of small, young men with large eyes, short noses, flat ears, and generous mouths. Altogether a more attractive combination than she would have expected from the individual features. She realized they even dressed alike—white shirts, three-button black vests, and black, homespun trousers. *Ahh, their neckerchiefs are different patterns. . . . But, tied the same—point in front, knot in back.*

Pulled out of her thoughts by Whit's voice, Sara realized Whit was telling her something. "The Wensels are the top cow chasers at the T-Lazy-R ranch. Boys, please meet Mrs. Darnell of Dallas."

The brothers made a face at Whit. "Actually we are the only cow chasers, considering that John Henry and Whit here are the range bosses," Zollie pointed out. *Or was it Jellie?* Sara wasn't sure.

"Pleased to meet you, ma'am," the two said in concert.

"Happy to meet the two of you."

"See you back at the ranch, Whit." The two short, stocky men turned and headed for the punch bowl. Sara noticed they were equally bowlegged.

Sarah and Whit sat and talked while the party activity hummed around them. "John Henry told me he's known you most of your life, Whit. And that your dad was his best friend."

"Yep. Grew up near Gonzales. That's where we had our farm, 'til Dad joined up with the rangers in the mid-1830s. 'Bout the same time John Henry joined. Two of 'em were close as peas in a pod. Saw a whole lot of John Henry when I was growin' up. After Dad died, we moved to Austin where my mother's brother and his family lived. As a kid, I worked in my uncle Paul's butcher shop."

"So you started as a butcher. How did you become a cowman?"

"Didn't much like butcherin'. When I was sixteen, decided I'd rather gather cattle than butcher 'em. Went to work as a cow chaser on the Sam Burton ranch."

"Where's that?"

"Big ranch down on the Brazos River outside of Waco. Spent the last five years chasin' and gatherin' longhorns down around San Antonio and drivin' 'em up to Burton's Ranch. When they were ready to sell, we'd do a cow hunt, gather 'em, and drive 'em up the Shawnee Trail to Baxter Springs, Kansas."

"You like the cow chaser's life?"

"Yep, sleepin' under the stars, beef stew on the fire, the sounds of the herd. When John Henry gave me a chance to operate a ranch as his partner, I jumped at it. Can't imagine a better life."

Sara decided John Henry had found a good partner. Whit Wainwright seemed to appreciate the opportunity John Henry had given him. *I suspect he's honest and hardworking too.*

As the night grew late, lanterns were lit, empty punch bowls collected, and partygoers headed for home, everyone agreeing the grand soirée had indeed been a grand success.

Riding back home in the wagon, Sara saw that a smiling Ellie hummed continuously and Cecilia had a lot to say about John Henry. "Didn't John Henry look handsome tonight? He's a much better dancer than I'd have ever guessed."

Sara and Hattie were the first to be dropped off. They thanked the Websters for the ride and said good night. Hattie nearly danced into the house. Sara took a chance and teased her, "I think Aaron Davis is quite taken with you. You remember Davis was one of the two lawyers who had traveled by horse with my wagon train? Nice man, Hattie."

"He's a charming man and very smart," Hattie replied. "Do you really think he liked me?"

"He spent most of the evening with you, I think that's evidence that he does. Hattie gave Sara a sly smile. "And John Henry's partner spent most of the evening with you."

"Well," said Sara, "Whit is interesting to talk to. He knows a lot about Texas, and he shared his cattle drive adventures with me. We have John Henry's friendship in common, that's all."

"Speaking of John Henry, did you notice that Cecilia talked about little else on the way back to Dallas? And Ellie and Gerard Favre . . . he's a carpenter, right? They nearly wore out the dance floor."

"Oh, Hattie, you are a born matchmaker, aren't you?"

Hattie looked pensive. "Perhaps."

Dear Momma and Papa,

Your letter arrived today. I was so excited to find it in the D pocket of the cotton bag. I was hungry for news of you all and glad to know you received my first two letters, although it certainly took a long time for their delivery. Watch for two more from me that are already in the mail.

I was sad to read that Mila had a bout of influenza, but happy to know she is fully recovered. Please tell Haley she certainly can have my back copies of Godey's Lady's Book. *After all, what are sisters for but to pass along important things? I miss my sisters!*

After the grand soirée, which I wrote about in my last letter, Dallas citizens debated about how to return the favor with an event for the people of La Réunion. Since Dallas doesn't have a building big enough for an indoor event, it was finally decided to host an early-fall picnic, horse race, and a shooting competition. There were to be two different races, each with from four to six riders. The race would be on a straightaway on the prairie, just outside of town. The shooting targets would be whiskey bottles on sticks placed at various distances. Although it's fall, the weather has remained nice, and the chosen day luckily turned out to be ideal for the event. This time the traffic on the bridge was from La Réunion to Dallas.

The necessary number of horse-race contestants was found, including one from La Réunion. Zollie and Jellie Wensel, the two cow hunters from the T-Lazy-R, entered the first race, along with Mr. Ira Webster, owner of the saddlery shop, and Mr. Aaron Davis, the lawyer. It was quite exciting and a bit dusty. It was a very close race and Mr. Davis won by a nose. My landlady was quite excited, as she and Mr. Davis have become friendly. Turns out he is an accomplished horseman from Kentucky.

Contestants in the second race included a man from La Réunion. I don't recall his name. Also, Whit Wainwright (John Henry's partner), young Daniel Pollard, and two local farmers. The farmers on their wagon horses quickly fell behind, and Whit Wainwright was in the lead most of the way. He fell back at the finish line, and young Daniel Pollard crossed the line first. You have never seen such an excited young man. Daniel has announced that he wants to be a jockey. He is still growing, and I am afraid he will outgrow this dream within two years. There is evidence that he will be a large man like his father. Nonetheless, he happily has bragging rights as the winner. I am convinced Whit let him win. When I teased him about it, he simply said, "Winning the race was important to Daniel." Whit is a good man.

After the race, it was time for the picnic. There were vegetables, canned by the ladies in the summer, along with cornbread. Zollie and Jellie Wensel roasted a cow—they called it "barbecue." The cow was John Henry's contribution to the event. Prairie chickens were also on the menu.

Of course, there were buttermilk pies. Momma, the piece I had was not nearly as good as yours. When the plates were clean, the ladies visited while the men adjourned to the shooting competition. Whit, Ira Webster, and Mr. Beaulieu were declared the winners. I was told that the men were surprised by Mr. Beaulieu's marksmanship. Apparently his cryptic explanation was that in Paris one must be prepared for duels. What a character he is.

The T-Lazy-R steers are on the road to Shreveport, then on to New Orleans by barge. Yes, barge! After selling the cattle in New Orleans, Whit, Zollie, and Jellie will buy new horses and head to South Texas to gather more wild longhorn steers to bring back to the T-Lazy-R. John Henry will ride back from Shreveport with their original horses. Whit tells me that this is the tail end of this year's cattle market, but they are optimistic that they can get a good price. Cecilia blushingly told me that John Henry stole a quick kiss when he told her goodbye. I have high hopes for the two of them!

Mr. West has advised me to be frugal and to limit my orders of perishables as winter arrives since business may decline then. Given what has happened with the weather, people will have even less than usual to spend. Mr. West has proven to be a friendly competitor, as he promised.

La Réunion has suffered greatly this summer, and there is much unhappiness over the glowing descriptions of the opportunity that brought the Europeans here. They feel they have been misled. One man, Mr. Baker, has already left La Réunion and come the three miles from across the river to settle in Dallas. He is currently at the boardinghouse and building a cabin that will serve as his home and bakeshop. Since many of us sampled his pastries at the grand party, we eagerly anticipate the opening of his bakery. Mr. Baker is an interesting addition to the boardinghouse. He speaks a bit of English and is learning quickly, but we were perplexed yesterday when he asked for butter for his morning coffee. He actually wanted cream.

I continue to be happy at Hattie's boardinghouse. We have become friends and have good conversations and much laughter while washing the supper dishes and in the evenings. Her stern manner hides a jolly soul.

I enjoy the job of storekeeper. As time passes, I am meeting most of the settlers in the area of the Three Forks and also learning what merchandise sells. Please tell Grandma that her gift of an early inheritance has made all the difference in my ability to be successful. Papa, the sale of the wagon and eight oxen has provided me with important savings and should sustain me through the winter.

I am happy and healthy, although I miss Morgan and all of you.

Your loving daughter,

Sara

P.S. Momma, I know you worry about me, and I appreciate your reminder that as a widow I must act with total propriety. I try. Rules are different here due to the circumstances of life. Often I have to walk in town without an escort. Most women do the same. As a businesswoman, I meet with lawyers and some salesmen. I do so in the store or offices during business hours. I am conscious of my reputation and remember the lessons about being a lady that you and Grandma taught me and reinforced by example.

"Bonjour, Madame Darnell." Busy with another customer, Sara looked up to see Edouard Charles Beaulieu, as elegantly dressed as usual. Sara smiled and nodded at him. When her customer had completed her purchase and left, Sara greeted him, "Good morning, Mr. Beaulieu. How may I help you?"

"I have made a decision about which I wish to inform you, Madame. I am following my friend the baker and leaving La Réunion for Dallas."

"I don't know your profession, Mr. Beaulieu. What will you do here?"

"I am a dance master." Beaulieu bowed. "In Paris I taught the young ladies and gentlemen to dance. From me they learned the cotillion, the quadrille, and other dances. There is no business for me at La Réunion, and I don't wish to be a farmer. I am hopeful that there will be more opportunity in Dallas. Victor Considérant, the promotor of our colony, has just fled to San Antonio. I don't have high hopes for the colony's successful continuation, so I am leaving."

"Mr. Considérant is gone?" Sara's eyes widened with shock.

"He packed his bags yesterday and he left. New settlers are still arriving, but he has deserted the colony. I didn't find out until he was gone. Had I known he was such a coward I'd have challenged him to a duel."

Sara's eyes blinked in surprise, and she blurted out, "With swords or pistols?" Embarrassed, her cheeks reddened.

Beaulieu seemed to think her question reasonable. "With pistols, Madame. I prefer pistols."

Is the scar on his cheek from a sword duel?

The dance master bid Sara good day and stepped out the door as a gust of wind blew fall leaves inside.

Sara closed a few minutes early and crossed the street to the shoemakers. It was definitely time for a new pair of shoes. Recently arrived in Dallas, shoemaker Felix Newberry had come with illustrations of popular shoe designs for ladies and gentlemen. After perusing the illustrated options, Sara choose practical, low-heeled boots rising above her ankles. The short boots had front lacing and a side gusset of elastic, which Mr. Newberry informed her was a new invention of an American, Mr. Charles Goodyear. The elastic gusset would make the shoes easy to slip on and off, he told her. Sara was talked into adding tassels at the top.

When Sara got back to the boardinghouse, she found Ellie Duffield in excited conversation with Hattie. "Sara, I was just telling Hattie that the postmaster told me that Mr. Cockrell received a letter from John Neely Bryan earlier this year."

Sara chuckled. Ellie was a gossip but a good-natured one. She liked to be the first to hear the news and was eager to share it.

"Now we know he's alive and the return address was the Creek Nation."

"That's in Indian Territory, right?" Sara asked.

Ellie shrugged and pushed her wire-frame glasses back on the bridge of her freckled nose.

"Yes, north of the Choctaw Nation, up by the Cherokee's land, Sara," Hattie said. "The Muscogee Creek Indians used to be in the southeastern part of the US. During the Indian removal, the government moved them into Indian Territory."

Ellie frowned. "Okay . . . but why would John Neely Bryan go there, Hattie?"

"From what I've been told, when he was young, he had cholera. Doctors told him to live an outdoor life with the Indians. Stayed with the Cherokee for four years. He knows Indian ways and speaks several Indian languages. If he believes he is being pursued for murder, guess it makes sense for him to hide in Indian Territory."

"Speaking of Indians, can you guess the name of Mayor Pryor's youngest daughter?" Ellie asked. Hattie and Sara shook their heads. "Pocahontas Pryor," Ellie told them.

"You're right," Hattie said, "I'd never have guessed."

Sara chimed in, "Jellie, Zollie, Pocahontas . . . names in the West are certainly interesting."

As Sara slipped under the covers that night, she thought about what an exciting day it had been—from news that Considérant had fled, to new shoes, and news of Bryan hiding in Indian Territory. She had no idea that the next day would bring excitement of a different kind.

The next day was a fall day with dark thunderclouds threatening rain. The loud rumble of wagons brought Sara from the back of the storeroom to the store's front door. The street was clogged with a dozen open wagons. Men in buckskin were piling out of the wagons and dismounting horses, soon filling the street. Two groups quickly formed, one going into West's store and the other crossing to Sara's. "Howdy, ma'am. We need a mighty lot of provisions. We're headed west for buffalo." The speaker was a buckskin clad man with a furry hat and bad teeth that alternated between yellow and brown. He held several empty burlap bags in one hairy fist. His fingers were stained tobacco brown.

"I'm well stocked," Sara said. "What do you need?"

The man held up two large, empty bags. "This bag filled with beans, this one full of coffee." He pointed to two more empty bags. "Flour and cornmeal in these. We also need salt, saleratus, molasses, and honey. Also tobacco, cod-liver oil, cigars, some penny candy, and a few bars of lye soap. If you got bacon and jerked venison, we'll take what you got. How about iron skillets, got any? Oh, also need two big iron pots and six bottles of Mexican Mustang Liniment."

"I can provide all that." Sara supervised as the hunters filled the bags and helped them find other provisions which they might need. Tallying the sale, Sarah realized she had made more money with this one sale than she usually did in a month. As they carried their bags and piles of provisions out, the leader said, "Thank you, ma'm. Let's load all this in the wagons and head for the grog shop, boys." There were hoots of agreement.

The noisy sounds of loud laughter and carousing from the grog house echoed down the street for hours. As Sara was on the porch locking up, the rowdy group began stumbling back to their horses and wagons. As one group passed Sara, she could hear drunken arguing. "You damn cheat! You was dealing from the bottom. I know you was. I want my money back." Sara couldn't hear the mumbled reply. Suddenly she saw the first man pull his revolver and fire. Sara felt a blow and fell to the ground. She was only half-conscious of hearing someone shout, "Get Doc Adams! Mrs. Darnell's been shot and I think she's hurt bad!"

Sara opened her eyes and looked around, her vision blurry.

"She's come to," Doc Adams said. "Sara, you've been shot. Don't think anything vital has been hit, and the bullet passed through your arm." Having no chloroform, the doctor asked for whiskey. A bottle of it was found and poured over the wound and into Sara, who lapsed into semiconsciousness. Sara slipped in and out of consciousness as he was bandaging her left arm. She opened her eyes and groggily said, "Hello, Doc Adams, I didn't vote for you."

Doc Adams chuckled, "Well, I've never run for election. If I only doctored patients who would be willing to vote for me, I'd most likely have a small medical practice. You have me confused with Doc Pryor, the mayor." Before the doctor had finished his comment, Sara had slipped back into the black hole of unconsciousness.

Sara woke early in the morning, before the town roosters crowed. Opening her eyes, she saw Hattie sitting near the bed in a rocking chair. "Hattie, what are you doing sitting there?" Sara moved to push herself into a sitting position and cried out in pain. "What on earth? My arm . . . a bandage . . . what?" She rubbed her forehead. "And I have a terrible headache."

"You were shot yesterday by—"

"Shot!?" Sara tried to sit up, but pain shot though her arm.

"Yep, accidentally shot by some fool buffalo hunter who'd had too much to drink and was waving his revolver around, firing bullets helter-skelter. You were unlucky enough to catch one."

"Buffalo hunters?" Sarah asked.

"Apparently they came to stock up on supplies from both your store and Mr. West's before continuing west after the buffalo herds. Don't you remember?"

Sara shook her head. "But I do know that my arm and my head both hurt."

When Doc Adams arrived, Hattie told him that Sara didn't remember the events of the day before and that she was sick at her stomach and complaining of a headache. After examining Sara, Doc Adams announced that the pistol wound looked as good as could be expected. On the other hand when she fell, the blow to her head was severe enough that he thought she had rattled her brain. "You need to stay in bed for several days and sleep as much as you can," he told her.

"I have a store to run," Sara told him.

"You can miss a few days now or a great many days later if you don't give yourself enough time to recover, Mrs. Darnell. I believe you to be a sensible woman, so please rest now." He looked so serious that Sara decided she had best follow his instructions.

When he left, Hattie said, "I forgot to tell you that, while he was patching you up, you woke up and told him you didn't vote for him."

Sara wasn't sure whether to laugh or be horrified. "I really must have given my head a whack if I said that."

Sara slept most of the day. When she woke, Hattie told her that a parade of visitors had knocked on the door to ask how Mrs. Darnell was recovering. "Mr. West's wife came by to let you know that when they heard what happened, Mr. West crossed the street and closed and padlocked the door to secure your store. Said they wanted you to know so you wouldn't worry."

Sara was grateful to Mr. West. *A nice thing for him to do.* She knew he was right. She would have worried about the store being unlocked, and was glad she kept the key in her pocket. Later that afternoon, Hattie came upstairs with a flowery get-well note Edouard Charles Beaulieu had delivered for Sara. *He's such a nice man and very French.*

The following day, Sara found that her arm was still painful and pretty useless; however, she was feeling better. She was also increasingly cranky at having to stay in bed. *I really need to be at the store. I can't afford to lose business.* "One more day," Doc Adams had told her. "Then we'll talk about maybe letting you get up. Understand that you'll have to take it easy for a couple of weeks."

Recognizing that she would have difficulty stocking the store and assisting customers while one handed, she sent word to the Pollards to ask if she could hire sixteen-year-old Daniel to assist her in the store once she was allowed by Doc Adams to return. The answer was yes.

Doc Adams' answer was yes, as well, when Sara asked the following day to be allowed to get out of bed. "Don't let her overdo it," was his admonition to Hattie.

"I'll do my best," was her response, "but this young lady has a mind of her own."

Sure enough, two days later Sara was at the store with her new assistant, Daniel Pollard. She still didn't remember the day of the shooting. Hattie had told her the buffalo hunters had purchased supplies, and Sara found her cashbox held the equivalent of a full month's worth of sales. While Sara sat on the three-legged chair and gave directions, Daniel stocked the shelves with stockings, Bibles, tableware, and other items from the storeroom. "I saw we had a bunch of boxes of different kinds of canned goods in the storeroom. I restacked them by type. It'll make taking inventory easier. Hope that's all right?"

"That's a good idea."

"Also, I noticed that the heavy cooking pots are on a shelf that some customers have trouble reaching. Can I move 'em down a shelf and put the boxes of candles on the higher shelf? They're lighter. Be easier to take off the shelf."

"Good thinking, please do it." *Hmm . . . Daniel is not only energetic, he's full of ideas. I'll see how he works out. Maybe, if he's interested, I could afford him as a full-time assistant.*

A short time later, the store door opened and John Henry stepped in. "I leave town with my longhorns and you go and let some buffalo hunter throw lead at you."

Sara looked up from her ledger and grinned. "I don't remember a thing about it, but I have a bullet hole in my arm to prove it. What's your news? Did you get your cattle on the barges to New Orleans? That's a sight I'd like to have seen."

"Yep, we drove the longhorns to Shreveport without problems. Put the steers in stock pens on the Cross Bayou 'til we could load 'em onto the rough cattle boats. Then shipped 'em down the Red River. Whit and the Wensel boys should be in New Orleans now, negotiatin' with cattle buyers."

"Then what?"

"They'll head to San Antonio, hire three or four more cow chasers, gather more cattle from near the Mexican border, and drive 'em up to the ranch, along with more mustangs. Figure it'll be at least a couple or three months 'fore I see 'em again. Hope to have more ranch buildings done by the time they're back."

"So, you've finished the bunkhouse and the barn?"

"Yep, I plan to start on the ranch house next. I just rode in from Shreveport and am plumb tuckered out and tired of my own campfire cookin'. I wanted to come to town to say hello to you and Cecilia. Thought I'd have supper at old man Crutchfield's hotel. Understand the twenty-five-cent bill of fare tonight is quail on toast, the quail having been shot by Crutchfield himself."

"Sounds good. I'm sure Cecilia was pleased to see you back safely, I sure am."

"I was glad to see her as well. Sara, Cecilia is a fine woman." Sara could have sworn that under his tan John Henry was blushing. "I hear Crutchfield ringing the bell for supper now, guess I'd better go while there is a seat still open. Take care of that arm." With that, he was out the door. Cecilia had said nothing about the relationship with John Henry, but Sara hoped it was progressing.

Another relationship which was progressing was between Sara's landlady, Hattie Brown, and lawyer Aaron Davis. One evening at supper, Hattie had casually asked Sara what she thought of Aaron Davis. "You were on the same wagon train, weren't you?"

"That's right, he and John Henry were two of the single men who followed the wagons on horseback. I like Aaron. On the road he didn't hesitate to jump in when help was needed. He's smart. I know John Henry has great respect for him. I remember you danced with Aaron most all evening at La Réunion's soirée."

"Yes, and I met with him today for some legal work regarding some land I own. I asked about a book on his desk. Turns out he's a reader too. We talked about books for about thirty minutes and then got off on other topics. Must've talked for an hour and a half. Really enjoyed talking to him. He invited me to dinner with him at Crutchfield's on Sunday."

"I hope you said yes."

"I did. Feels strange though. I haven't gone anywhere with a man in decades."

"Well," Sara said, "I guess it's about time you did."

★ 1857 ★

Lions, Tigers, and a Cotton-broker

Sara's first winter in Dallas saw temperatures plummet and gale winds blow. Those few settlers who had been in the Three Forks area since the 1830s said they had experienced nothing like it before. Soldiers who were traveling down the Preston Road from Indian Territory to Austin told Mr. West that the Indians were saying the winter was unprecedented, although, West told Sara, he doubted it was described exactly in those words.

The Trinity River froze so solidly that Dallas citizens dressed in their warmest clothes and flocked to the river with anything that would slide on the ice. Sleds were improvised and the Trinity became a winter playground. The wind was sharp and smelled of wood smoke from the town's heating stoves and fireplaces.

Sara, still nursing her gunshot wound and bundled up in several layers of warm clothes and wrapped in her cape, was standing at the edge of the ice with Sarah Cockrell, watching seven-year-old Aurelia, the oldest Cockrell child, skate. Edouard Charles Beaulieu skidded up to them, pulling an improvised sled with a rope. "Would you like a ride, ladies?"

Sara and Sarah looked at the flat, wooden-slat surface mounted on the narrow edge of boards, which had been sanded smooth. "Did you make this?" Sarah Cockrell asked. "It's actually quite clever."

"No, my carpenter friend, Gerard Favre, made it for me this morning. It works well. I can pull it as I run, and it slides smoothly. The faster I run, the easier it is to pull. Which of you would like to try it first? I'll pull."

"Thank you, but I'll just enjoy watching," Sarah Cockrell said.

"Then you must let me pull you, Mrs. Darnell," Beaulieu bowed as he spoke. Sara declined as well, using her still-tender wound as an excuse.

Beaulieu trudged off pulling his sled and had soon talked one of Farmer Thornton's daughters into accepting a ride. True to his word, the faster Beaulieu ran, the faster the sled slid along the ice, accompanied by the delighted shrieks of the young Thornton girl. When Beaulieu slowed to avoid a collision with two children and a sliding rocking chair, the sled kept coming and only his fancy footwork kept the sled from crashing into him. He dropped the rope and the sled banged into the edge of the riverbank. The girl jumped out and disappeared into the crowd of revelers. Sarah Cockrell laughed and said, "My, but we made a wise decision."

Sara's concern about business slowing in the winter proved to be groundless. Dallas was close to several major Red River crossings. Buffalo hunting was increasing as the government put a bounty on buffalo in an attempt to control the Indians and as the market for buffalo tongue and buffalo hides grew. Both Sara's store and West's store prospered as buffalo hunters crossed the river and stopped for supplies before turning further west. Despite the added costs of an assistant and investing in more inventory, Sara's savings grew and was safely locked away in the bottom of her trunk in her room at the boardinghouse.

One afternoon the door to the store opened and Sara looked up as two bearded, long-haired, buckskin clad men with buffalo-skin coats, tall boots, and long guns over their shoulders stepped in. The older, heavily bearded one spoke. "Mrs. Darnell, we came through here for supplies a few months back on our way to shoot buffalo. Comin' back through Dallas, we just now heard that before we left last time Applegate here shot you when he was drunk and waving his six-shooter around. Brought him in here to apologize. Apple, tell the lady you're sorry."

Apple pushed an armful of buffalo hides at Sara. He was a lanky young man with a scraggly, brown beard and a sweet face. "I was liquored up, ma'am. Sure sorry I shot you. Glad you appear to be recoverin'. Brought you two buffalo hides. Hope you won't hold no grudge."

Sara tried to keep a straight face. "You are forgiven, Mr. Applegate. Thank you for the apology and for the hides. Just promise you'll keep your gun in your holster when you are in Dallas."

"Yes, ma'am." Apple quickly escaped out the door.

His partner nodded at Sara. "Thank you, ma'am. We'll head back here for supplies for our next hunt." He stepped out, leaving Sara holding two huge buffalo hides. She ran her hands through the soft fur. *That was certainly a surprise. These will be wonderfully warm winter blankets.*

In addition to being on the wagon-train road going deeper into Texas, Dallas was a stopping point on numerous stagecoach routes. A mail route between Dallas and Ft. Belnap made two trips a week. Dallas was on the northbound route from San Antonio through New Braunfels, Austin, and Waco. A tri-weekly stage served Dallas and Palestine. Another route serving Dallas went south from Clarksville to Waco. These routes connected with others leaving the state to the east and west. Travelers shopped during the breaks when the stages stopped for fresh horses. Sara began to carry items that she learned travelers asked for, including ready-to-eat food items, fresh handkerchiefs, and small cushions to sit on.

When Sara heard the stage trumpet blasts, alerting the town that the stage was rolling into the square, she would prop the store door open and prepare for business. After a while she got to know several of the drivers or "brother whips," as they were called, and they would direct passengers toward her store. Both Ira Webster's livery stable and Crutchfield Hotel's stables expanded to serve as hostlers to the stages, caring for the tired teams of horses and providing fresh ones.

Hattie Brown's Boardinghouse had more frequent guests since passengers would often stay over to transfer to another stage route to reach their destination. Hattie was kept busy doing laundry, preparing rooms, and cooking meals.

The arrival of the stages had caused the town aldermen, concerned about the condition of the streets, to activate a provision in the town's incorporation document. This provision gave the board of aldermen control over the public square and streets and allowed them to require all free male citizens between the ages of eighteen and forty-five—and the few male slaves in town—to work on the city's streets for at least five days each year. Such work kept the dirt streets relatively passable, but the stages still bumped into town over potholes and across wagon ruts. Rainy weather continued to create mudholes and giant puddles. Most tree stumps had been removed from the streets, not always the case on the roads connecting towns. Periodically, Sara would spot several men, shovels and rakes in hand, working to reduce the size of a pothole or attempting to level out a rut. Without that work, Sara could only imagine how bad the town streets would be.

One damp afternoon, Sara spotted Doc Pryor working with a couple of other men on a particularly deep pothole, shovel in hand. Red-faced, with his neck tightly wrapped in a scarf, and his nose running, Sara could tell he had a cold. "Should you be out in this weather, Doc Pryor?"

"Don't worry, Mrs. Darnell, my doctoring business is slow, I'm just hoping to share my cold and create some new patients." He laughed as his helpers scattered to other potholes. "That's better. There were too many shovels for this one pothole."

Sara and Daniel were taking inventory when they were disturbed by the commotion of clattering wagon wheels and shouting. Opening the door, they were engulfed in a cloud of dust blowing from a moving line of ox-drawn wagons. "Keep goin' and we'll circle by the river, nearer the bridge." The voice carried from the lead wagon. After the last wagon and trailing livestock rumbled by, Daniel said, "We're likely to have customers from the wagons later today."

Just before closing time, Sara and Daniel were each helping customers when a heavyset woman in a lace-trimmed bonnet and brightly colored shawl bustled in followed by a teenaged black girl in a faded calico dress. The woman thrust a basket into the girl's hands. "Here, Hanna, take this and fill it with the provisions we need and hurry."

A panicky look came over the girl's face. "Miz Mildred, I . . . I don't rightly know what we need." The woman's hand flashed out, slapping Hanna in the face and leaving a handprint.

Sara covered her gasp.

"Well for Pete's sake," the woman said, "don't you have a brain in that frizzy black head?"

"I'm sorry, didn't know we'd be shoppin' today, Miz Mildred."

"What is it you do know, girl? How to be lazy and good for nothin'?" Miz Mildred was shouting now and raising her hand for another slap.

Sara stepped forward. "Please lower your voice and refrain from slapping this young woman."

The hand dropped. "How dare you? I can shout at my slave and slap her all I wish. She belongs to me."

"Well, this store belongs to me and you'll please leave. Your behavior is appalling, and I won't tolerate it in my store. Daniel, please open the door for Miz Mildred."

"Well I never!" Miz Mildred glared at Sara and marched out the door, after grabbing Hanna by the collar of her dress and dragging her along. The young woman looked over her shoulder and smiled at Sara.

"My goodness, Sara." Effie Butler had been standing by the coffee grinder, watching the encounter. "What a nasty woman. I hope their wagon train is moving on to somewhere else."

"Me too. I just hope she doesn't take her anger at me out on that poor young woman. I know the argument is that we need slavery in the South to support the cotton business, but it just doesn't seem right. Imagine being treated like that."

"The circus is coming to town!" Daniel burst into the store one spring morning, waving a copy of the *Herald* newspaper. "It says right here that Edrid's Great Circus and Menagerie is coming to Dallas next week. There will be lions, tigers, hyenas, and other wild beasts. Can you believe it? Right here in Dallas?" It was all Daniel could talk about that day. In fact, the circus and menagerie provided positive conversation and anticipation for the entire town.

The very next day, an advance agent of the circus rode into town on his horse, blowing his bugle to gather a crowd. He handed out promotional bills to those who had gathered at the sound of his horn. Stepping into Sara's store, he said, "Let me post a promotional broadside at your entrance, and I'll give you two free passes to Edrid's Circus. You'll see amazing things and fierce beasts."

Sara laughed. "We certainly don't want to miss the fierce beasts. Post your broadside." He handed her two tickets, and Sara passed one to Daniel, who was all but jumping up and down. According to the broadside, the circus would be in town for two days only. The promotional piece promised, "In addition to the exotic, wild beasts, Dandy John and his trick ponies, acrobats, lion tamers, and clowns will thrill and amaze you. All performing under the Big Top circus tent. Seats will be available for ladies and children. Music provided by the famous Menagerie Band. Hours for the two days: 10:00 a.m. to 4:00 p.m. and 6:00 p.m. to 9:00 p.m. Tickets twenty-five cents."

"How on earth do you think the circus got here?" Sara asked Ira Webster, as they were both reading the circus broadsides while posting them outside their businesses.

"That's exactly what I asked the circus agent," Webster replied. "He told me they came up the stagecoach road to Austin after successful performances in Galveston and Houston. They performed in Austin, then followed the Preston Road to Waco, where he said they received glowing reviews." Webster laughed. "Guess the agent couldn't resist adding a bit of promotion to his answer."

Sara said, "I suppose that makes him good at his job."

"Anyway, from Waco they followed the road north to Dallas. After leaving here, he told me, they plan to head to Shreveport on the freighters' road and then float down the Red River on barges to New Orleans. Said they've slogged through a lot of mud. With the spring rains, I reckon the roads must be mostly mud and potholes."

The day of the circus, Dallas woke early to find a white-faced, red-nosed clown in a baggy, striped costume performing in front of the courthouse.

He made silly faces and performed somersaults, flips, and handstands to the cheers of the crowd. When a large-enough crowd had collected around him, he added silly jokes. "Why did the lion spit out the clown? Because he tasted funny." The crowd groaned. "What do you call a stinky elephant? A smelly-phant." More groans and laughter.

Clutching a roll from Mr. Baker's shop, Sara had stopped to join in the fun. Spotting Mrs. John Neely Bryan in the crowd, she waved and walked over. "Good morning, Margaret." She gestured toward the clown. "This certainly adds excitement to the day, doesn't it?"

"It does."

Reminding everyone that the show would start at ten o'clock that morning, the clown made several silly efforts to mount his horse, the last of which left him sitting on it backwards. He rode away waving the horse's tail and shouting, "See you at ten!"

Watching the clown leave, Margaret Bryan said, "If the circus is as entertaining as its clown, it'll be well worth attending. My children and I could use some cheering up. I know you're a widow and will understand that it can be lonely without a husband."

Sara nodded. *I do know how it feels to be lonely. I miss my family and Morgan . . . at least the man he was when we first met.*

"John has been gone more than a year and a half. Mr. Cockrell received another letter from him, this time from the gold mines of California. The letter says John is mining in hopes of making enough money to return to me and the family. I'm heartsick for my four children. Will they ever know their father loves 'em? Not sure why I'm tellin' you this, Sara. Please don't share this with anyone."

"I won't. I feel lonely sometimes too," Sara said as they parted. "If you ever want to talk, or just need company, you can usually find me in the shop." As Sara reached out and squeezed Margaret Bryan's hand she felt tears forming in her own eyes. *Oh, Morgan, I am lonely, but your betrayal makes me afraid I might choose wrong again.*

Wiping her eyes and turning away from the square, Sara hurried to open the store. She had promised Daniel he could have the day off to attend the circus. They had agreed Sara would mind the store today, then she would attend the performance the next morning while he covered the store. Sara had thought about closing but decided to stay open, believing the circus would draw people from outside town who would be likely shoppers before and after the big event.

The next morning, Sara, Ellie, and Ellie's beau, carpenter Gerard Favre, stopped at the store on the way to the circus. Daniel was still so excited about all he had seen that he was hardly coherent. "Wait 'til you see the animals! Fierce . . . . and the man put his head in its mouth, and it ate raw meat. But I never saw the egress . . . ."

The three laughed after leaving the store. Gerard, whose English was quickly improving, asked, "Was he speaking English? I only understood a few words."

Ellie said, "I think he was telling us something about a lion tamer putting his head in a lion's mouth. And then something about raw meat. Could that be?"

"Let's just hope the head in the mouth didn't result in the raw meat." Sara raised her eyebrows. "If it did, there may not be much of a wild-beast show this afternoon. I think he also said he never did see the egress."

"I don't know about an egress, but did you hear that this circus may be getting an elephant?" As usual, Ellie was eager to share the news she'd heard.

They arrived at an open area on the edge of town to find a line of people already waiting to enter. In front of them was a large, wooden screen painted with snarling lions, exotic cats, and other wild animals. This served as both barricade and entrance. Once they reached the front of the line, their tickets were collected by the clown Sara had watched earlier. They then stepped through the doorway in the screen and into a dusty field with a large, canvas tent. Curving in a semicircle in front of the tent were the circus's wild beasts in their caged wagons. The air had a musky smell of animal dung. Sara read the descriptive signs out loud. "African Lion – the King of Beasts, Man-Eating Asian Tiger, Ethiopian Bone-Eating Hyenas."

Ellie said, "I had no idea lions were so big, but somehow the hyenas are even more frightening."

"I think it's the snarling and slobbering that makes them so scary," Sara said. "Plus, I think their cage smells the worst."

After Sara and her friends had made the rounds, peering into the cages along with a growing crowd, the circus' ringmaster walked out of the tent in his top hat and tails. He had gray hair, a receding chin, and a booming voice. "Ladies, gentlemen, and children, prepare to be amazed as the fierce Asian tiger is fed ten, yes ten, pounds of raw meat. See how quickly this massive, meat-eating monster gobbles his food and imagine how quickly he could eat you, young man. Yes, you!" He pointed at a boy of about six who was getting a bit too close to the cage. The ringmaster snapped his fingers. "Gone before you know it!" The boy's eyes widened, and he scurried several steps back to his mother. "Here comes our tiger tamer now. Please step back, everyone." Sara quickly took three steps back.

The tiger tamer, a slim man wearing tight pants and a fringed shirt, came out of the tent with a bucket of red meat and a long-handled fork. Plunging the fork into the bucket, he speared a large, bloody chunk of meat. A shiver went down Sara's spine. The caged tiger leapt from the bale of hay on which he'd been resting and began snarling and reaching a paw through the cage's bars. Ellie let out a shriek. The crowd stepped farther back. Teasing the animal with the meat, the trainer waved the fork just out of reach. The cat went mad, snarling and reaching through the bars of the cage. *Daniel was right about fierce animals!* The hyenas in the next cage began to howl and dash about with foaming mouths. Sara's eyes shifted to the bloody piece of meat on the end of the fork. Finally, the trainer deftly dropped it through the bars and into the cage. The tiger was on it in a flash and it was gone. The trainer repeated this nine more times. Each time the tiger devoured the food almost before it hit the floor of the cage. *Amazing. Imagine them in the wild.* The hyenas were still howling as the last morsel disappeared behind the frightening teeth of the tiger. Sara looked at the door of the tiger's cage to be sure it was padlocked.

"The thrills are just beginning," promised the ringmaster. "Place your attention on our mighty lion, the King of Beasts, straight from the African continent on the other side of the world. You've seen how fierce tigers are— imagine the force and fury inside this wild creature. Don't let his beauty fool you. He is ferocious. Our world-famous lion tamer is among the bravest men on Earth. Why do I say that? Because he is about to put his head inside this beast's mouth." *So this is what Daniel was trying to tell us.* "Yes, you heard me right. I'm going to ask you to be totally still and silent, so we don't startle the beast. Not long ago we had a man who thought he'd shout at the most

dramatic moment. If you wonder where we get our raw meat . . . well . . ."
What a gruesome thought.

At this point the bare-chested lion tamer arrived in spangled tights. His chest was covered with colorful tattoos. He posed for the crowd, showing off the animals inked on his chest. "I think he might be the tiger tamer with a new mustache and a sharp pole," Sara whispered to Ellie.

The man stepped onto a short stair at the end of the wagon, opened the door to the cage, and stepped in, leading with the sharp pole. The lion roared. Children began to cry. Mothers shushed them. Slowly the trainer moved toward the roaring lion. Sara realized she was holding her breath. The trainer raised the pole to the lion's mouth and gently pushed it open. The lion's teeth were huge, and Sara gasped with the rest of the crowd. Sara saw Ellie grab Gerard's hand. The trainer continued to tease the lion's mouth open with the pole as he slowly stepped forward. The crowd was silent. When the opening was large enough, the trainer slipped his head inside the lion's mouth, paused to a long count of three, and removed it. He backed out of the cage with the pole pointed at the lion, closed the door, and bowed. The crowd cheered and applauded. Sara joined the applause. Ellie said, "We've already gotten our money's worth."

The excitement continued. They stepped into the tent where a small set of bleachers had been set up for ladies and children. Ellie and Sara took seats, and Gerard stood nearby with the other men. Dandy John, a small man in a blue leotard, stood on prancing horses and did various and sundry tricks. "Amazing," Gerard said when Dandy John swung down and extended himself along the side of the horse as it trotted. "That's what John Henry told me the Comanches do." Sara said, "They actually shoot their arrows from that position." The clowns made Ellie, Gerard, and Sara laugh until they cried. They held their breaths, watching the daredevil acrobats build human towers and somersault through the air.

As they left the tent, Ellie pointed. "Look at the spun sugar candy."

Sara turned to see a man standing by a large copper pan over a fire. On a small table beside him were small, delicate balls and coils made of golden strands of spun sugar. As they watched he dipped a wooden-handled fork—made with multiple long wire prongs—into the pan of melted sugar. Quickly he lifted the dripping tool and waved it back and forth across two horizontal, wooden rods that were parallel and positioned about a foot above the table. The falling sugar created long, golden strands hanging from the rods. Before the strands could fully cool, the man gathered them gently into his hand and shaped the strands into a loose ball. Next he took a spoon and dripped the syrupy sugar, making rings around a small rolling pin. Sliding the cooling rings off the rolling pin, he held up a golden spiral.

"It's beautiful," Ellie sighed.

"It looks like spun gold." Sara said.

"It's sugar?" Gerard asked. "You can eat it?"

"You can." Ellie grinned. "It's delicious."

They each asked for a ball of the candy which the candymaker wrapped in paper cones for them.

Sara leaned over her cone and took a deep breath. *It smells so sweet.* She bit into the sweet strands, and came up with a mouthful and a chin covered with sticky candy. *I feel like a kid.* She looked at Ellie, who was feeding Gerard with her fingers.

"I've never had this before," Gerard said."

"Do you like it?" Ellie asked.

"I may have to eat two balls to decide," Gerard said with a grin. "Sticky, but nice."

Several times they saw someone walk through the crowd with a sign that said, "Egress this way" or "Follow me to the Egress." The third time they spotted such a sign, Gerard slapped himself in the forehead. "I get it. In Latin 'egress' means the exit." When they were ready to leave, they followed the man with the sign to a roped off area behind the tent, and the three tired friends "egressed," as Sara put it, and left Edrid's Great Circus and Menagerie through an archway in a wooden screen.

"I had such a good time," Ellie said.

Gerard agreed. "I liked the lion tamer best."

"I liked it all," Sara said.

Outside the roped area they saw a man arguing with a circus employee. "I didn't wanna leave. I simply followed the sign thinkin' I'd see another wild beast, an egress. No! You can't charge me twenty-five cents to go back in!"

"What a terrible trick," said Ellie. Wonder how many people end up paying a second twenty-five cents?"

"Guess it goes to show that not every business is honest," Sara said.

When Sara returned to the store in time to see how sales had done for the day, she told Daniel, "The circus was wonderful. You were right, the wild beasts were frightening. I'd only seen them in books before. You're not thinking of running away with the circus when it leaves, are you?"

"No, ma'am." He was emphatic. "I talked to one of the circus kids. He told me they ought to rename it the Mud and Muck Circus. They travel the dirt roads. Comin' up here they slogged through foot-deep mud and were lucky to make six or eight miles a day. They don't get paid a salary, just a share in what the circus takes in at every stop."

"I understand the mud part, what about the muck?" Sara asked.

"One of the circus kid's jobs is mucking out the cages. He told me as soon as they get back to civilization, he is heading home. He said farming is better than circus life. Join the circus? No thanks, I like my life here just fine."

Sara breathed a sigh of relief.

That night Hattie told Sara that Aaron had taken her to the circus for the late afternoon performance. "We had such fun. He bought me spun sugar candy and we agreed we liked the lion tamer the most." Sara smiled to see Hattie so excited.

Early one afternoon, Sara heard pounding hoofs, and the entire store began to vibrate. She and Daniel ran to the door in time to see the first few steers as they barreled down the street past the courthouse. "Doggone! This is a big herd," Daniel hollered over the sound of the bellowing herd. "I bet it belongs to Mr. Adams."

Sure enough, through the dust Sara could see one of the cow-chaser Wensel twins—*Jellie?*—acting as lead rider and steering the herd from near the front of the mass of beeves. It seemed to take a very long time for the herd to pass the store. She had not seen Whit Wainwright and assumed he was working as a swing or flank rider along the opposite side in an attempt to keep the mass together. She had spotted two other cow chasers she didn't recognize riding swing and flank on the store side of the herd. The other Wensel twin twin— *Zollie?*—was riding drag at the back to keep cattle from straying and to nudge the slower calves along. Sara was pleased that she remembered the positions Whit had told her, when they talked at the soirée, and what each position was responsible for.

Steers dominated the herd, and Sara was again amazed at the immense size of the animals. Whit had explained that a four- to eight-year-old steer could weigh as much as eight hundred pounds, and at age ten one could weigh as much as eighteen hundred pounds. Sara thought John Henry and Whit would be pleased with this herd—a great many large bulls and lots of calves for the future. Come August, after they fatten over the summer, there will be many more steers to sell than last year. *My goodness, I'm beginning to think like a rancher.*

Two days after the T-Lazy-R herd came through, Sara heard the blast of the stage horn, and a dusty stagecoach limped into town with a damaged wheel. Sara propped her door open with a rock in hopes of attracting customers while the stage was in town. Looking up, she saw Whit Wainwright step down from inside and turn to place his hands on the tiny waist of a young blonde woman and swing her gently out of the stage. As the girl turned, Sara saw a heart-shaped face with large round eyes, and a deeply dimpled chin. Sara heard her exclaim, "So this is Dallas, darlin'? I can't wait to see our ranch."

Our ranch? Whit married? Sara was surprised to feel a sudden wave of disappointment. Heat rose in her face and tears formed in her eyes. Quickly stepping back into the store, she hurried past Daniel and into one of the storerooms, closing the door behind her and leaning against it. She had been nurturing expectations that in the future she and Whit might evolve into being more than friends. Once she had composed herself, she left the storeroom.

"Oh, here she is," she heard Daniel say as he, Whit, and the girl came around the end of a shelf.

"Hello, Mrs. Darnell," Whit began. "I want you to meet my new bride, Emmeline Strickland Wainwright. Emmeline, this is Mrs. Darnell, the shopkeeper from Tennessee, who was on the same wagon train as John Henry."

Emmeline Wainwright smiled at Sara with a sparkle in her aquamarine eyes, took Sara's hand, and said, "What Whit didn't tell me was how pretty you are. It is my pleasure to meet you. I hope we will be good friends. Please call me Emmeline." With that, she turned in a circle, looking at the store. "Whit told me about your store and how you've created it all yourself. I'm so impressed and eager to shop here."

"I'd be pleased to have you as a customer, and I'm sure we will be friends." Sara tried to smile back at Mrs. Wainwright. "And both of you, please call me Sara."

"I assume the herd has come in?" Whit asked.

"Two days ago. It looked about double the size of last year's herd." Sara was happy to have a new topic.

"Yes, this year's herd is a bit more than twice the size of last year's. Thought we'd get here ahead of the herd, but one of the wheels on our stagecoach broke while we were fording the Brazos. We were able to push the stage out of the river but had to stop until the driver could fix it well enough to make the final miles to Dallas. Once it was fixed, had to smear tar on the spindles for lubrication. Lost a lot of time." Whit suddenly seemed to realize that he was dry, but still somewhat mud crusted. "Oh shoot! I'm trailing dried mud on your floor. I'll step out."

"Don't worry, Daniel was planning to sweep in a bit. Besides, you're not likely to be the only passenger tracking in mud."

Emmeline turned to Sara. "Actually, the delay was a nice break from the bumpy stage. Riding in a stage is almost like having the hiccups." She laughed. "But the Brazos is a beautiful river, and the countryside was covered with red-orange wildflowers with yellow tips on the petals. We have them at home too. We call them fire wheels. One of the other passengers told me you folks up here call them Indian blankets."

"Yes, aren't they pretty? They fill the prairies here." Sara turned to look at Whit. "How did you two meet?"

Whit beamed. "We met down south of San Antonio on our way to gather cattle. Just before we started our hunt, we stopped at her father's ranch to ask if he knew any experienced cow chasers lookin' for work. He did and offered us his hospitality while he sent word out that we were hiring. I got to know Emmeline then. Guess it was love at first sight for me."

Love at first sight. I felt that way about Morgan. "That's romantic . . ."

"It was. For the next two months, I spent as much time as I could on the Strickland Ranch. Hired an extra hand to help gather cows so I could be around Emmeline more. When our cattle count was almost high enough, I proposed. We married as soon as we had a full herd. Emmeline was the prettiest bride you ever did see."

"Whit was the handsomest groom," Emmeline said, taking Whit's arm and smiling up at him.

Emmeline may be charming, but right now, I don't like her one bit.

"We're headed for the hotel and will be there 'til John Henry can send one of the men with a buckboard to pick us up, plus all of Emmeline's possessions." He glanced out at the many packages coming off the stage.

Sara turned to see the growing pile of parcels. "Let me ask Daniel to help you carry things to the hotel. Nice to meet you, Emmeline, and best wishes. Congratulations, Whit."

"Much appreciated," Whit said. Emmeline echoed her thanks as they departed arm in arm. Daniel followed.

Sara rolled her shoulders and rubbed her neck, trying to clear her head. As she stood quietly, a realization dawned. Despite all her new friendships, she missed the kind of closeness she had shared at first with Morgan. She felt a growing sense of loneliness. And she had really liked Whit.

As summer arrived, more of the La Réunion settlers left the utopian colony and moved to Dallas. As customers shopped in the store, they chatted with each other and Sara about the latest arrivals from across the river. "The butcher from La Réunion has a cart selling fresh meat. He was in front of the courthouse this morning," a customer told Sara.

Sara walked to the courthouse midday and found the butcher and his cart by following the sound of a small bell he was ringing. The butcher wore a white apron over a blousy shirt with breeches, cuffed at the knees, long striped socks and wooden shoes. He was a small man with fat cheeks and a lilting French accent. "I have fresh beef steaks, venison roasts, and prairie chickens today. What would you like?" The meat was hanging from a T-shaped bar mounted on his wheeled cart. Sara chose a large prairie chicken and dropped it off with Hattie on her way back to the store. "Lovely," Hattie said. "It's a nice fat one and we'll have it for supper."

Freshly brewed beer arrived in the form of a brewery started by an "escapee" from La Réunion. At least that's how the Belgian characterized himself. Not being a drinker, Sara didn't visit the brewery, but John Henry reported that the beer was "outstanding, and the brewery is an asset to the community."

A milliner opened a small shop with custom-made hats. Sara began seeing the hatmaker's creations at church on Sunday. They were stylish and often large creations with bird feathers, bows, and artificial flowers. Sara admired the hats as ladies entered and left church but was careful to select a seat behind a child or small man so that she could see.

Edouard Charles Beaulieu, Dance Master, was offering dance classes, with some success, and assisting fellow Frenchman Adolph Gouhenant in marketing his Art Saloon photographic studio. The photographic studio had become a center for the town's social and cultural activity. People gathered there for conversation, dances, art shows, photographic sessions, and meetings of all kinds. Gouhenant's reputation as a portrait photographer and his charismatic personality also drew travelers to the studio. His daguerreotype photographs were increasingly popular with locals and visitors alike. Edouard Charles Beaulieu talked Sara into having her photographic portrait made with Gouhenant's daguerreotype camera. "You can send it to your family back home," was how he finally convinced her.

Sara arrived at the Art Saloon wearing a new dress and her short boots with tassels. She had splurged on the dress, finding a local seamstress to make it for her. It was pale-gold cotton with a delicate pattern of small, burgundy-colored leaves. High-necked, it had small, round buttons from the neckline to the waist. The full skirt was pleated and her waist was cinched to a mere seventeen inches.

Looking at the boxy camera, Sara asked, "How does it work?"

"It's a long process," Gouhenant told her. "Are you really interested?"

"Yes. It seems like magic to capture an image so perfectly."

"I take a silver-plated copper plate, clean and polish it, place it in a closed box over iodine until it turns a yellow-rose color. The plate then goes into a light-blocking box, which I slide into the camera. When I remove the camera lens, the plate is exposed to light and the image is captured and then carefully developed using more chemicals."

"Oh, my," Sara said.

"You see," he smiled, "science, not magic."

Sara selected a half-plate-size image, four and a quarter inches by five and one half inches.

"You must be perfectly still for five minutes or more if we are to capture a good image," Gouhenant said. "Move, and it will be blurred." He positioned Sara sitting in a chair. "I have a head clamp on a stand which I am going to place behind the chair. I'll hide the clamp under your hair. This will hold your head still." Soon Sara was locked in place.

Gouhenant worked for a moment with the daguerreotype camera, then said, "I'm taking off the lens cap. Remember, be perfectly still."

It seemed like an eternity had passed when Gouhenant finally said, "You can move now. Give me a few days and I'll have your photograph ready. I believe it will be lovely."

Three days later, Gouhenant came by the store with Sara's photograph. "I hope you like it. I think it turned out well. I'd like to make a copy to display in the Art Saloon as a sample image. May I?"

"I do like it, thank you. Of course you may display a copy as a sample." *How strange to hold an image of myself in my hand. I look so serious.* In the picture, Sara sat in a chair facing forward. Her elbow rested on one of the chair's high arms, her hand under her chin. Her other hand rested gracefully in her lap. Her skirt flared out around her with one tasseled boot peeking out from the dress's hem. Sara's expression was unsmiling but relaxed. Her eyes looked directly into the camera.

Daniel looked over Sara's shoulder at the portrait. "It looks just like you, Sara. It's like magic, isn't it?"

Sara grinned at Gouhenant, then turned to Daniel. "Not magic, Daniel. It's science."

Ellie and Sara were walking in the shade along the river on a Sunday afternoon, watching the slow-moving water and trying to escape the summer heat. Ellie was fanning herself with a paper fan. "Did you read in the *Dallas Herald* this week that, because of all the new stagecoach and wagon-train activity, Mr. Cockrell has decided to build a new, three-story brick hotel on the courthouse square?"

"Yes, I saw the article." Sara guessed Ellie would have ferreted out details somehow. She loved being the first to know.

"I've heard it is going to be quite luxurious," Ellie said. "The lot is over-sized and the three-story hotel will cover the entire lot. It's even going to have a ballroom. I can't wait to see it! It will be even more impressive than his two-story, brick office building on the southeastern corner of the square and about twice the size of the courthouse."

Another sign Dallas is growing. Hope my business and savings will grow as well.

That night at supper, Aaron Davis and Ellie Duffield were both guests. When Hattie brought dessert to the table, Aaron stood and said, "I wish to announce that I have asked Hattie to be my wife, and she has said yes."

"Oh, Hattie, how wonderful," Sara stood to hug her.

"Wait," Ellie said, taking the pie from Hattie's hands. "Now you can hug. We don't want to dump the engagement pie on the future groom." She laughed, set the pie on the table, and said, "My turn to hug you, Hattie."

Hugs shared, Hattie began to slice the pie. Sara said, "Have you set a date?"

"Sometime this winter," Aaron said. "I've told Hattie the sooner the better, but she says we're at the mercy of the circuit preacher."

Sara was thrilled for Hattie and Aaron but wondered what their marriage would mean to the boardinghouse. *Will Hattie close it? Will I have to move?*

Sara was working on the account books at the counter, and Daniel was unpacking a box of Webster's *Blue Back Spellers* and McGuffey Readers, which Ellie had ordered for her students, when a loud humming sound filled the air, and the store grew noticeably darker inside. Daniel and Sara looked at each other in confusion. Daniel opened the door, stepped onto the store's covered porch and into the street. Sara followed. Looking up, neither was sure what they were seeing. In the near distance, a huge black mass swept across the sun, darkening the sky. The humming sound grew like rolling thunder. As they watched, portions of the dark cloud would swoop down to the ground. As the dark threat hovered above them, Daniel cried, "Flying bugs!?"

"Locusts!" Sara watched as some of the locusts landed on laundry hanging on the clothesline of a nearby house. A woman ran out of the house and threw a blanket over part of her garden, then began frantically waving her apron at the seething mass of insects, all to no avail. Sara and Daniel watched in shock as the locusts finally rose as one, leaving the laundry line bare and the blanket and garden gone. All around them everything green had been devoured. Swatting the random locusts that had landed on them and crushing others still on the ground, they hurried back inside, slamming the door. Daniel shook his head. "Never seen nothin' like it."

"Now we know why the Bible calls it a plague of locusts."

In just minutes, the damage to the farmers' crops, which had just started to grow, was total. Most replanted and hoped the shorter growing season would provide an adequate harvest.

On a Sunday afternoon, Whit and Emmeline, along with John Henry and Cecilia, arrived at the boardinghouse with a fifth horse. Cecilia waved excitedly and called out to Sara, "Put on something you can ride in and hurry. A herd of buffalo has been spotted west of town. John Henry tells me it's a sight not to be missed."

Sara was shocked to see Emmeline riding astride in a divided skirt rather than riding sidesaddle. Emmeline saw Sara's surprise. "Sara, we only have two sidesaddles. Besides, I grew up riding like this on my family's ranch. Only way I could keep up with my brothers."

Within five minutes, Sara was mounted sidesaddle on a frisky cow pony, and each paid their thirty-five-cent toll for one person and one horse to toll-collector Berry Derrit, and headed across the Trinity bridge and up the limestone escarpment. They could already hear the roaring of the bison herd. Soon the five riders could look down across a wide expanse of Grand Prairie between the east and west cross timbers. Sara gasped. Stretching from the base of the escarpment, across the Grand Prairie toward the eastern cross timbers tree line, was a massive, seething, endless herd of buffalo. Even on her horse, she could feel the vibration of the earth. The air was heavy with dust and the musky smell of the animals. A cloud of steam was rising from the sea of the colossal beasts. Carefully, the five picked their way partially down the side of the escarpment for a better view. Sara could see immense hump-backed, bearded bulls with long, shaggy, brown coats and fat, curved horns.

"I hear there's millions of bison fillin' the country from Canada down to Mexico, prob' tens of millions," Whit said, hollering above the roar of the bellowing animals. "Indians sure rely on 'em . . . buffalo. Been at the center of Indian culture forever, I guess. The herds migrate and arrive here in North Texas in the summer to graze."

I've never seen anything like this. What must millions of them look like?

"Don't often come quite this far east on the prairie anymore though. Probably looking for more grass after the locusts came through. I tell you, back East, people sure do like those buffalo robes and coats, here in the West too. Sara can tell us all about demand for dried buffalo tongue. She sells 'em in her store."

"Why is just the tongue desirable? Is the remaining meat not good?" Cecilia shouted, forehead furrowed.

"Bison meat is mighty good, leaner than beef," Whit said, "but most hunters just leave it to have more room to carry back the hides and tongues. Awful waste."

"They must be five or six feet tall at the withers," Cecilia shouted to John Henry.

He nodded and shouted back, "Yes, and the fully grown ones are ten to twelve feet long, plus a tail that adds a foot or more." Their shouting was almost lost in the bellowing of the herd.

As she studied the herd, Sara realized that many of the buffalos seemed to be divided into separate groups of bulls and groups of females with their offspring. She watched as one bull seemed to be herding a female, while another bull bellowed and tried to approach her. 'What is going on there?" Sara shouted and pointed.

John Henry answered, "Summer's mating time. The tending or herding bull is trying to block the female's view of the challenging bull, which is bellowing to get the lady's attention. In this case, it doesn't look like it worked. The challenger has moved on."

Emmeline pointed out several buffalo that were wallowing in muddy, shallow depressions. A shot rang out, but the group didn't see a buffalo fall. Then another shot brought down a massive bull. Sara expected to see the herd stampede. But even the bulls closest to the grounded one continued to graze without distraction. Another couple of shots, another fallen buffalo. Still no reaction from the herd.

"They don't panic and run like cattle, so they are easy to kill. Look there," said John Henry. He pointed down the cliff, and they spotted a hunter in a tall, soft-sided top hat just as he fired again. "After a while, the smell of the carnage may make them uneasy enough to run."

They continued to watch for a bit and then turned their horses back to town. Sara appreciated being included with the two couples, but she still felt like a tagalong.

Dear Momma and Papa,

It is hard to believe that Grandma has passed. I wish I could have been at her funeral. As long as I can remember, she was a powerful force in my life. I'll wear the beautiful hair mourning brooch you sent and remember her with love. Like Morgan, she has left a hole in my heart. I am sure she is in heaven.

Summer was difficult this year. The locusts and a severe drought have caused farmers' crops to suffer. Daniel commented yesterday that his Pa told him it was so dry that the bushes were following the dogs around. That's a fair description of this past summer. Most families grow several bushels of corn for their own use, and when the corn crop fails, the food supply is short. We are not close to the markets for crops, and the high cost of transportation to market makes our farmers' harvests too expensive, compared to the competition. I'm told the transportation rate is twenty cents per ton, per mile, which is not only unaffordable, it makes most harvests here unprofitable.

Farmers raise a few cows, hogs, some feed to sustain the livestock, a few bales of cotton, and some corn, and try to live as cheaply as possible. There is some talk that cotton does well in our soil, and if the transportation issue can be solved, cotton may be the profitable crop of the future for our farmers. There is hope for a railroad or making the Trinity navigable from the Gulf of Mexico to Dallas. Either would solve the problem, but so far it is only talk.

As I mentioned in my last letter, with the addition of buffalo hunters and stage passengers, my business continues to do well, but it hurts me to see our own farmers suffering. I have begun to offer some credit to farm families I know well and believe will make good on their debt when they can. I am very careful doing this as I can't afford to put my own business at risk. I continue to save what I can toward paying the fees for the 320 acres of land Mr. Cockrell is holding for me.

I need to find new lodging soon since Hattie Brown and her suitor, the lawyer Aaron Davis, have just become betrothed. The wedding is set for later in the year. The boardinghouse will then become their home. Mr. Davis has been living in a bachelor cabin off the square. I am very happy for them, but uncertain where I might find lodging that I'll enjoy as much as Hattie's boardinghouse.

The other boarder, Mr. Baker, has completed his bakery and will soon be living above it. He can converse fairly well now in basic English, although the occasional mistake can be quite funny. Hattie and I tried not to laugh yesterday when he called Hattie's beef stew with potatoes "beet stew with tomatoes." When he leaves I'll miss him as well as the delicious crescent-shaped pastries he often bakes for us on Saturdays, when we can provide enough flour and butter. He calls the pastries "croissants." Hopefully he will sell them in his shop.

I am expecting another shipment of merchandise this week, and Daniel and I'll be busy restocking shelves and recording all the arriving goods. Our stock has been low this summer since there are generally no freight deliveries in July and August. The hot weather makes it too difficult to water the freight wagon's oxen. I'm learning to stock up in the spring. I've become quite the experienced storekeeper but would be lost without Daniel's help.

He is a cheerful spirit, learns quickly, and we laugh and work well together. Customers like him as well.

The stagecoaches carry mail now, and our letters should travel faster to each other. The drivers or brother whips, as they are called, tell me they can make five to eight miles each hour. I commented to Ellie the other day that the stagecoach horses had the most beautiful tails. She laughed until she had the hiccups and then managed to tell me, through her continuing giggles, that false hair was added to make their tails more impressive. "Some horsewoman you are for not figuring that out," she told me. With the blowing of the whip's stage trumpet announcing the coach's arrival, the bravado of the whips, and the fancy horse tails, the stagecoach provides lots of drama. It is always interesting to see what kinds of passengers clamber out. Hopefully, some will be my customers.

Speaking of stagecoach passengers, Whit Wainwright and his new bride, Emmeline, arrived by stage from South Texas recently. She seems very nice. Daniel told me he thought she was "chipper as a jaybird." Translated, that means cheerful. Daniel is a wealth of Western sayings.

My wound is healing nicely, according to Doc Adams. Daniel tells me that he has a cousin who was shot and can now predict the weather based on aches around his wound. Time will tell whether or not my wound will be a useful predictor of the weather. At any rate, I wish you sunny skies and enough rain to keep the grass high for the horses.

I'll end this letter and send all of you my love.

Your storekeeper daughter,

Sara

P.S. I'm enclosing a daguerreotype photograph of me taken by Adolph Gouhenant, Dallas' photographer from France. I think it makes me look too serious.

One early summer afternoon after church, Sara was walking in a wooded area around a nearby creek when she was startled to see a young man sprawled on his stomach in the grass. Thinking at first that he might be injured, she said, "Sir, are you hurt?"

"Shh," he said. Sara squatted down beside him and realized he was peering through a magnifying glass at a big beetle. "It's an entomological species I've never seen before." Carefully he lifted the bug on a flat, wooden stick and quickly slid it into a collection case, which he snapped closed. Rising awkwardly to his feet and brushing bits of grass off his prominent brow, the tall, thin man introduced himself with a soft French accent. "I am Julien Reverchon, a naturalist. My father and I have an orchard and farm outside of town."

Sara introduced herself, and together they walked back toward town. "What will you do with the insect you just found?"

"Research it. I believe there are plant and insect species here that are new to science."

"We have insects here that haven't been identified?"

"I'm sure of it. So, I collect and research the insects I find . . . the ones I've not seen in Europe. If they are not identifiable, I hope to record them as new species. I have already collected many interesting insects and plant specimens, which I have mounted. When Father doesn't need me on the farm, I wander the forest and prairie in search of new samples. There's a whole world of insects. Most people never pay attention to it."

Interesting man . . . collects bugs . . . hmm . . . "My friend, Miss Ellie Duffield, has a school for young children. She might be interested in having you bring some of your collection to show her class. I think the children would be fascinated."

Reverchon stopped in his tracks. "Share my samples with children? Yes . . . perhaps they would like to go on a collecting expedition with me?"

"An insect collection expedition? What an interesting idea for Ellie's class. I'll ask her." The pair arrived on the edge of town. Reverchon said goodbye and wandered toward the river with his collection boxes to look for more samples.

The next day was Sunday, and Sara saw Ellie at work in her garden. Ellie looked up and waved. "I am overrun with carrots, would you take some to Hattie?"

"Happy to." Sara joined Ellie at the carrot patch as Ellie pulled a few more of the orange roots out of the ground and added them to her pile.

Sara said, "I met someone interesting yesterday and thought of you."

Ellie stood up and dusted off her hands. "Of me, why?"

"Well, he's a young man who collects and studies insects, and that gave me an idea for your school. He has mounted insect samples which your students would probably find interesting. He seemed willing to bring some of his bugs to your class."

"Hmm . . . It might be an interesting diversion for my class. Especially if he could provide names for the bugs and share information about them." Ellie began to clean the dust off her glasses, wiping them on her apron.

"I'm sure he can. He also suggested taking the students on an insect-collecting expedition."

Ellie laughed. "The children could most likely lead the collecting expedition. They spend so much time outside that they're familiar with a great many bugs and plants. They'd probably enjoy helping him find more samples."

"I'll watch for him and make introductions, if you're interested."

"Please do." Ellie handed Sara a pile of carrots. "Tell Hattie there are more where these came from. If I eat many more, I'll turn orange."

Sure enough, about a week later introductions were made, and the two new acquaintances began to plan an outing for Ellie's class to go on an insect-and-plant-collecting expedition along the river with Mr. Reverchon.

Hattie and Aaron's wedding was only a month away, and Sara had been searching but hadn't found a new place to live. She had approached the lawyer representing her store's landlord to ask if he had additional property available for rent, but he didn't. She had not found an existing building for rent and didn't have time or money to build. Walking from the store to Ellie's house late one afternoon, she saw a lawyer she had done some business with carrying boxes out of a two-story, brick building on the square. "Why, Mrs. Darnell, I'm pleased to see you. I am moving to Austin to join the firm of a classmate of mine. I'll no longer be practicing law in Dallas." Sara wished him good luck.

She started to continue walking, but instead, turned on her heel and asked, "Do you know if this building is available?"

"I believe so, I was the only tenant. My office was downstairs, and I lived upstairs. The owner is Edwin Wells, his office is several doors down from The Crutchfield House Hotel. I'll have moved out by the end of today." Sara resolved to pay Mr. Wells a visit the very next day.

Sara found Mr. Wells in his log-cabin office just off the square. The room was lined with bookcases, which overflowed with books and piles of folders. Mr. Wells was a round, little man with a bulbous, red-veined nose and the rosiest cheeks Sara had ever seen. He sat on the very edge of his chair and leaned forward with his elbows on his desk. "If you are interested in the building, you need to know it's all or nothing. You must rent it all. Can't have just one story. Must have both." The man talked in quick, sharp bursts with a New Englander's accent.

"May I see the building?"

"You may. It's not locked. Should be empty. Take a look, let me know if you're interested."

The two-story, brick building was larger than Sara had first realized. *It must be about thirty feet square . . . about the size of my store.* The downstairs was one large room with plank floors. There were two parlor stoves for heating the room and two large glass windows on either side of the front door. Sara realized it would take lots of new shelving to make the room workable as a store, and a storeroom would need to be carved from some of the space.

The upstairs door could only be accessed by an outdoor staircase running halfway along the side of the building. Climbing the stair and entering the second story, Sara stepped into a large room with doors to two smaller, adjoining rooms. *This is more space than I really need, but it would be nice.* The floors upstairs were plank, and there was a cast-iron cooking stove. The cookstove would be one less thing to buy. *That's good.*

Sarah returned to Wells's office. As she entered, he looked up from his paperwork. "What do you think? Do you want it?"

"Perhaps. You won't consider renting just the top floor?"

"Nope. It's all or nothing."

"What rent do you want?"

"Eight dollars a month, two months in advance. No less than a year's lease."

"I'll give it some thought," Sara said. "Thank you, Mr. Wells."

All the way back to the store, she was considering if her store could be moved to the ground floor while she lived upstairs. The biggest negative was her current store lease. She was committed for four more months, and she liked like her current location. *What are my options?* She hardly slept that night for trying to decide what to do. She was still undecided by noon the next day.

Leaving Daniel in charge of the store, she decided to visit Sarah Cockrell and seek advice. Sarah Cockrell was in her office and invited Sara to sit a spell and visit.

"I'm in a bit of a pickle," Sara told her. "I need to be out of the boardinghouse in three weeks. There is almost nothing to rent, and I don't want to move to the hotel."

"You've found nothing suitable?"

"I've found one place I like, but it's two story and the owner will only rent the whole building. It would be perfect for a downstairs store and an upstairs home, but I still have four months left on my store lease. While I like the new building, the timing for moving the store is wrong, and moving would cost more than I can afford. I respect your business sense. Would you help me think of some options?"

"I'd be happy to help, Sara. I have a meeting in a few minutes. How about coming back at the end of the day, and I'll have had a bit of time to think about your problem? You'll probably have some new thoughts by then too."

At the end of the day, as she walked down the street to see Mrs. Cockrell, Sara was still uncertain about how to proceed. Sarah Cockrell opened her office door and said, "Come in and have a cup of artesian spring water with me." When the water had been poured and a little honey added, Sarah Cockrell said, "Well, I have two ideas. The first idea is to open a second shop in the new location, keeping your existing store where it is. I don't mean open the same kind of store—something different, something that you believe Dallas has a need for."

Sara started to speak, but Mrs. Cockrell held up her hands in a stopping gesture. "Wait before you comment, let me tell you the other idea. Keep your existing store where it is. Rent the new space, both floors, just as the landlord asks. Move your home upstairs. Then rent the downstairs to another business. Since it's becoming difficult to find business space now in Dallas, you should be able to rent the downstairs for more than half of what you negotiate for the total building. You'll just need to be sure that your new lease doesn't forbid you from renting the bottom floor to someone else."

"I like both ideas," Sara said. "I'm not sure I'm ready for a second store just yet or even what kind of store a second one might be, but someday I do want to expand. Right now my money needs to go into savings so I can pay you the fees for my 320 acres. That bill is coming up this summer."

"How about the other option . . . renting the bottom floor?" Sarah Cockrell asked.

"I like the idea of renting out the ground floor." Sara was thoughtful. "I hadn't thought of that since I won't own the building. I should go to a lawyer, shouldn't I? He could draw up the rental agreement so there is no language that would keep me from renting half the building."

"That's smart," Sarah Cockrell said. "Having agreements drawn up by your lawyer is almost always to your advantage. Show up with a signed lease in hand—if it is fair your landlord will usually be happy to sign on the spot."

Sara continued to think through the idea. "I'll want to ask my landlord for at least a two– or three-year lease, won't I? Then I can offer the renter of the first floor the same time period. One year would be too short. My landlord will also want the security of a longer lease from me."

"And you said I had a good business mind!" Sarah Cockrell laughed. "Sara, you are becoming quite the businesswoman yourself."

"Thank you so much for your help. I'd never have had that idea by myself." The two ladies parted, Sara's head buzzing with thoughts about moving and becoming a landlord.

That evening Sara and Hattie were chatting about Hattie's upcoming wedding as they cleaned up after supper. Hattie was up to her elbows in soap suds, and Sara was drying dishes when there was a knock on the door. Sara tossed the dish towel over her arm and answered the door.

"Surprise, Momma! Uh, oh, I beg your pardon, I'm lookin' for Mrs. Brown." The young man looked around as if to assure himself he was at the right door. Hattie heard his voice and ran to the door with soap suds flying. She was now hugging him and crying. "Benjamin, I didn't expect you until the day before the wedding." She stepped back. "Let me look at you. You look wonderful, more and more like your papa every day. I've missed you, son."

"I've missed you, too, Momma." More hugs ensued. Sara studied Hattie's son. He was clean shaven, and his hair touched his collar in back. He was slim but neither too short nor very tall. He stood very straight, and his movements were quick and precise. She wasn't sure why, but an expression her papa had used about one of his Tennessee walking horses flashed into her mind: *wiry, fiery, and energetic.*

Taking Benjamin by the arm, Hattie turned him toward Sara. "Benjamin, this is Mrs. Darnell, my friend and boarder. Sara, this is my son, Benjamin, who lives in Galveston."

Sara extended her hand to Benjamin, who shook it gently. "I'm delighted to finally meet you. My mother tells me in her letters that she has enjoyed having you as a boarder."

"I'm happy to meet you. Your momma has told me a bit about you— she's quite proud of you, you know."

Formalities completed, Sara found a reason to excuse herself and go upstairs so the duo could visit. As she lit her small oil lamp and climbed the stairs, she heard Hattie say, "I'm eager for you to meet Aaron. I'm so glad you could come this far ahead of the wedding. We can have a nice, long visit."

Long after Sara had gone to bed, she woke to hear an upstairs bedroom door close quietly.

Hattie and her son had talked long into the night. *Homecomings are happy things.* Feeling a little homesick for her own family, she rolled over and dreamed of running horses.

The next morning Sara dressed and was downstairs a bit early. Hattie was humming as she put iron-skillet biscuits on the table. Benjamin Brown came into the room yawning. "Good morning, Momma," he nodded at Sara. "Mrs. Darnell."

Sara observed Mr. Benjamin Brown as he ate his breakfast. He had on a matching coat, and trousers, and a white shirt with a clean, high standing collar tied with a large bow tie. He looked very comfortable in a suit, but somehow Sara suspected he'd been equally comfortable in the denim pants and long-sleeved, cotton shirt he'd arrived in the night before. As she studied his face with its high forehead and nicely shaped nose, Benjamin raised his gold-flecked brown eyes from his biscuit and caught her stare. Sara smiled. "Pass the berry jam, please."

Finishing her breakfast, Sara reminded Hattie that she would meet her at Mrs. West's home for the fitting of the wedding dress at 5 o'clock. She told Hattie and her son goodbye and was off to see Aaron Davis, her lawyer and Hattie's betrothed, about drawing up two leases for the new building as quickly as possible. The first lease she would take to the building owner for his signature. The second lease would be for her tenant to sign. Given the number of newcomers to Dallas and the lack of business space, she was hopeful she could find a tenant. Aaron quickly understood the leases Sara wanted. "Clever idea, Sara. Hattie closing the boardinghouse has forced you to find a new home, but you seem to have found a good solution."

"I'm actually excited about it, Aaron. What's more, I'm so pleased for you and Hattie. You both deserve a lot of happiness. I'm meeting Hattie in a few minutes for the fitting of her dress, so I'd best be off. Thank you for your help." With that, Sara was out the door.

At 5 o'clock on the dot, Sara met Hattie at Lois West's. Sara had offered Hattie the dress she had worn for her own marriage to Morgan. When she had lifted the white, satin dress with its tight bodice and dome skirt out of her trunk, Hattie had sighed, "It's so lovely." Once on, supported with a hoop and worn with petticoats over lace-trimmed pantaloons, it was truly beautiful. Lois West announced that with just a few simple alterations and some lace around the bottom, it would be a perfect fit for Hattie.

On the way back to the boardinghouse, Hattie said, "The investors in the company Benjamin works for in Galveston believe that Dallas is an up-and-coming town, and they want my Benjamin to move here and open a cotton-factoring operation for them. He'll be back home."

"I know you're excited about having him back in Dallas."

"I sure am. He'll scout out a location while he's here for the wedding, go back to Galveston to confer with the investors, then be back to do what's necessary to move to Dallas and get the new business up and running."

"What exactly does a cotton factor do?"

"Cotton factors are primarily brokers. They advance money on farmers' crops, sell the cotton for the farmers, negotiate the sales contracts, and provide other services. Some companies, like Benjamin's, also provide financial services. If you want more details, you'll have to ask Benjamin to explain."

"That's interesting. I think I will."

The next day Sara took the lease Aaron had drawn up for the two-story building on the square to its owner, Edwin Wells. He seemed surprised and pleased that she had come with a prepared lease in hand. Mr. Wells agreed to the conditions, which included a three-year term, and eagerly signed it at what Sara considered a reasonable rent.

That night at supper, Hattie said, "Despite all we talked about last night, son, I never asked how your stagecoach trip was."

"Fast. We charged along day and night, stopping only for fresh horses and the occasional change of driver. It's good that it's fast because the interior conditions are cramped at best. There were only two of us on each seat. My riding partner was a very large woman with a knitting bag the size of a big dog. Across from the two of us was a thin schoolteacher traveling to Shreveport and a beefy man who took up two-thirds of the seat. To everyone else's discomfort, he persisted in filling the coach with billowing smoke from his cheap cigars."

"Eww! Were they with you the entire trip?" Hattie asked.

"Sure were. The knitter beside me fussed at the cigar smoker nonstop." Benjamin began to speak in a falsetto voice, "Sir, please stop smoking those foul cigars. Your smoke is most offensive."

"The smoker kept puffing and said, 'Madame, not any more offensive than the constant click, click, clicking of your knitting needles.' They bickered for hundreds of miles. He blew smoke, she threw her knitting bag on his feet. He lit a second cigar—that was two at once. She began to count stitches out loud as she clicked."

"Did you ask them to stop?" Sara asked.

"The teacher and I both did. The two of them just glared and continued. About midway, the schoolteacher leaned over to me and quietly said, 'What do you think would happen if we simply pushed them out? Justifiable homicide?'

"When we finally pulled into Waco, I suggested that perhaps one of them might want to wait for the next stage to Dallas so they wouldn't have to continue their squabble. The man took quick offense and made a gruff sound deep in his throat. 'Separate? Certainly not, sir. We're married!' He turned to the knitter and said, 'Let's go find refreshment, my dear.' They walked away hand in hand. Never been more surprised." Benjamin grinned.

Both ladies laughed. Sara said, "Who would have guessed?" *He's funny.* She admired the twinkle in his eye and how he could turn a situation of annoyance into one of amusement.

After supper, as she and Benjamin helped clear the table, Sara told Hattie she had found a place to live. As Sara was explaining where the building was on the square, Hattie said, "I think I know which building you mean, but isn't it two stories?" Sara explained that her plan was to live upstairs and that her lease was written to allow her to rent out the bottom floor.

Benjamin asked about the size of the building, its construction, and what Sara thought the rent might be. After hearing the answers, he said, "I might be interested for my company. Could I visit it in the next day or so?"

Sara nodded. "Of course. When you are ready to look at it, tell me and I'll give you the key. Hattie was telling me that your new business is cotton factoring. We had cotton factors in Tennessee, but since Papa had a horse farm rather than a cotton plantation, I never gave them much thought. What exactly is it that do you do?" Breakfast dishes cleared, Sara and Benjamin sat at the table again to continue the conversation.

"Well, there is a lot involved and I get pretty enthusiastic about it, so stop me if I'm telling you more than you want to know. First, it's important to know that most Southern cotton is exported to England where the spinning mills are located. Once the cotton is picked, ginned to remove the seeds, and packed into bales, it has to be transported to a port where it can be shipped to England and delivered to the mills that have ordered it."

"The cotton goes all the way to England?"

"Yep. Most of it. The cotton is paid for on delivery in England. The money then travels back to the farmer. So, there is a long time between the picking of the crop and payment. Farmers need cash or credit to start a new crop. They really can't wait until the payment for their previous crop comes from English mills. Can you imagine the problems that delay would cause? Are you with me so far?"

"I am."

"Good. The time gap between needing the money and receiving it is where cotton factors, like me, provide help. We advance an up-front, discounted payment to the farmers. We will negotiate sales contracts with the mills, store the cotton bales until they can be shipped, and ship the cotton to the English mills, where our representatives will collect the proceeds of the sale. In other words, factors assume the risks associated with the crops. We also can order the seeds, farming supplies, and merchandise farmers need, in return for a commission on the purchase. That's what the term 'commission merchants' means. We also make loans to cotton farmers."

"Your momma says your firm offers financial services too."

"Yes. Now this gets a bit complicated. You really interested?"

"Yes, I'm curious."

"As you know, we do not have a national paper currency in the US. To make things worse, Texas has outlawed state banks. No banks, no issuing of banknotes. This makes buying and selling anything a bit complicated. I'm sure you've discovered this in your own business."

Sara nodded. "Yes, people bring in banknotes issued by banks all over the country and want to use them in Texas. Some of these bills are worth face value, some aren't worth anything. I have to figure out which is which. It gets confusing."

"You're right, paper money gets very confusing. It's the strength of the issuing bank and how far away it is that creates the differences in value."

"If only everyone understood that! Some people want to argue about what out-of-state money is worth. Fortunately, merchants like me have a banknote-reporter list showing various banknotes and their discounted values. There are a variety of silver and gold coins, including Mexican pesos and hammered silver dollars. Establishing the values of various coins is made a little easier by a regularly published list of foreign coins and what they are worth. It would sure be helpful if everyone paid in gold or silver, but they don't."

"You've clearly defined the problem, Mrs. Darnell. To deal with all this, my company, R. and D. G. Mills, has come up with a creative approach. We don't issue our own money, that would be illegal in Texas. Instead, we have gathered large amounts of worthless paper money issued by a wildcat bank in Louisiana. Mills, my company, endorses these worthless bills and guarantees them. These dollars circulate as good currency. People call these bills 'Mills' Money' and every bill is worth full-face value because Mills' Money is backed by gold."

"But isn't that the same as issuing currency?"

"Nope. The Texas Supreme Court says we are reissuing and guaranteeing existing currency and it is legal."

"So . . . if I understand . . . you make loans to cotton farmers in Mills' Money. You order merchandise for farmers, taking a commission on the transaction. You buy farmers' cotton at a discount, in advance of the crop. Or you sell their cotton, after harvest, for a commission. Then you store the cotton until you can ship it to England, where the cotton mills buy it. Are all these transactions done in Mills' Money?"

"Yes, you catch on fast. Soon we will have quite a lot of Mills' Money circulating in Dallas. All guaranteed to be full value. People can bring their gold, silver, or other hard currency to us to exchange for Mills' Money. In addition, we'll have demand accounts. We will set up an account for a person, and that person can deposit funds in our safe. These account holders can access their funds on demand."

Sara was getting the idea. "So . . . merchants like me can do transactions in Mills' Money and know it is guaranteed at face value. My goodness, if you can make that happen, you'll be a hero in Dallas."

"It works well in Galveston and New Orleans. The owners of the company believe Dallas will soon be an important inland cotton market, so my job is to make it work here. I've leased a local warehouse for storage, and North Texas cotton will be shipped to our representative in New Orleans for transport to Manchester, England, where our Mills representative will finalize sales."

"I had no idea factoring involved so many things."

Two days later, Benjamin looked at the building Sara had leased, came by the store, and said, "It is by far the best option I have seen, Mrs. Darnell. I'll take it." Sara gave him the lease to sign.

As he added his signature, he said, "Who knew my new business would have a landlady—and a smart one to boot." Sara blushed at the compliment.

Always eager to be the first to share news, Ellie knocked on the boarding-house door on a Sunday afternoon. After joining Sara and Hattie inside, she announced that the town's new log jail was now open. "Sheriff Henderson and Marshal Moore are giving tours, and I've just come from there. The new jail is still made of logs, but it is bigger and has more than one cell. I guess we are better prepared for drunks stumbling in from the saloons outside of town in Boggy Bayou or the men who bet illegally on Sunday-night dog fights near the square."

Hattie frowned. "How do you even know about those things, Ellie?"

"We ladies know, we are just not supposed to talk about such scandalous things."

Sara was thoughtful. "Even so, there doesn't seem to be much trouble here. Why do we have both a marshal and a sheriff?"

Ellie settled her wire-frame glasses more securely onto her freckled nose. "People in the county elect a county sheriff. Since Dallas is the county seat, the county sheriff is located here. Towns appoint marshals. So we end up with two lawmen—and the sheriff has a deputy. I suppose we should feel pretty safe."

"Only if they do their jobs," Sara said.

★ 1858 ★

Death and a Wicked River

With her four small children in tow, John Neely Bryan's wife, Margaret, came into Sara's store one morning in January to purchase supplies. As she paid for her purchases, she said, "Finally got a letter from John . . . . he's still in California searchin' for gold. Told me he's workin' hard but strugglin'. Says he'll be home as soon as he can find enough gold to pay his way. I am disheartened, Sara. No tellin' when the children and I'll see him again."

Sara didn't know how to comfort her. "Perhaps his luck will change. We can only pray that he'll return to you and your children soon." *Poor Margaret. Managing with four small children and no husband can't be easy. I may be alone, but I have no reason to complain.*

Hattie Brown and Aaron Davis' winter wedding was held at Gouhenant's Art Saloon. When Sara arrived, she found the large room had been transformed from photographic studio into a perfect wedding setting. Chairs had been set up for the guests, leaving an aisle for the bride to walk down. The front of the room had two tables covered with arrangements of the wildflowers Sarah and Ellie had picked. In the back of the room, another set of tables was decorated with vines and wild grapes and each held a cake—an apple-sauce wedding cake and a groom's pound cake—both provided by Mr. Baker.

Soon friends and neighbors crowded the room.

"I'm nervous," Hattie said as Sara helped her into the altered wedding dress and adjusted her veil.

"You look lovely and there's nothing to be nervous about."

"I'm a middle-aged woman who hasn't had a husband for decades. I just hope Aaron won't be disappointed."

"Oh, for Pete's sake, Hattie. It's obvious he loves you and you love him. Listen, the violinist from La Réunion is starting the music." Sara handed Hattie her wildflower bridal bouquet. "Let's find Benjamin and get you down the aisle to Aaron."

Hattie took a deep breath. "I'm ready."

Benjamin walked his mother down the aisle to a smiling Aaron Davis. A whiskered circuit minister in a wrinkled frock coat performed the ceremony. Sara and Mr. Baker stood up for the couple.

After the ceremony, chairs were cleared so there could be dancing. Two fiddlers joined the violinist. The gentlemen tapped into a whiskey barrel in another room. Although ladies didn't admit to drinking, Sara observed that some of the ladies were livelier as the party progressed. When it was over, not one crumb of Mr. Baker's cakes was left. Aaron declared it a wonderful event. As the final guests departed, Gouhenant set up his camera and prepared to make the wedding portrait. Sara congratulated the groom, hugged the bride, and returned to her new home over the soon-to-be cotton-brokerage office. She still had no furniture, so she slept on a pile of quilts and buffalo robes on the empty room's floor.

Chatting with Sara, while making purchases at the store, and hearing that Sara had moved into her new home but didn't even have a mattress, Eliza Pollard said, "Sara, I met a farmer's wife who makes Louisiana mattresses. Paul and I have one and it is the best you can imagine."

"Louisiana mattress?"

"I suppose it's how they make them in Louisiana. It sounds strange, but the result is wonderful. Spanish moss is scalded, buried until it starts to deteriorate, then dug up, boiled, and rinsed. After it dries, it's picked clean and packed into a mattress bag—I think it's called a 'bed box'—made of cotton ticking and topped with a thick layer of carded wool. Most comfortable mattress we've ever had. If you want, I can direct you to the woman who makes them."

"I do need a mattress."

Later that week, Daniel borrowed his Pa's wagon, and the two of them bundled up for the wagon ride to the mattress maker. The winter temperature was brisk, but the sun was bright, and Sara was grateful that the North Texas wind wasn't blowing. The farmer's cabin was set in the prairie, about two miles past the edge of town, amid small fields fallow for the winter. The young farm wife who opened the cabin door introduced herself as Mrs. Doucet. "Are you here to see the mattresses?"

Sara nodded. "Yes, please. Your accent is lovely, Mrs. Doucet. Have you moved here from La Réunion?"

"Oh no, my husband and I are Acadian—or Cajun, as some people call us. She dusted off her hands and said, "Excuse me, I've been working with my sleeves rolled up." As she spoke, she folded them back down and buttoned them at her wrists. "Our families were French Canadians who came to Louisiana almost one hundred years ago. The moss mattresses are part of the culture we've developed since then. I learned to make them from my mawmaw—my grandmother." Grabbing a red-flannel cape from a hook by the door, she said, "Come, let me show you." She led the way to a large, wood-plank structure, more barn than shed. In front of the building was a giant iron pot on the cold remains of a fire. Drying racks held long strands of moss. As they approached, Sara shifted her look to the side to see the young woman more closely. She had pretty, arching eyebrows over large eyes and a slightly pursed mouth that looked like it could be stubborn. As she opened the building's door, Sara noticed her hands were chapped. The shed was still cold from the night air, and it took a moment for their eyes to adjust to the dim light. Sara saw baskets and baskets of moss on the puncheon floor. Tangles of moss hung like webs from all the beams, as if a giant spider lay in wait on the ceiling. Leading them to a pile of mattresses in the corner, Mrs.

Doucet said, "These are finished." With Daniel's help, she pulled the top one off the stack and onto the floor. "Try it out, if you like."

Carefully arranging her skirts, Sara lay down on the mattress. "I wasn't sure what to expect, but this is very comfortable. Will the moss bunch up and be lumpy over time?"

"No, it shouldn't. It might pack down a bit, but just give it a good shake. The mattress you're on is big enough for a double bed."

The women haggled, just long enough to say that they had, but came to quick agreement on price.

While Daniel loaded the mattress, Sara asked, "What brought you across the border to Texas?"

"The opportunity for our own land in the blackland prairie. We believe there is opportunity here. My husband convinced me to move when he told me I could get moss from East Texas and still make my mattresses. I hope you'll enjoy yours."

"I'm grateful to have it. Thank you."

As Sara and Daniel made their way back to town, Sara thought, *What fun it will be to write home about my mattress made of moss.*

Edouard Charles Beaulieu, upon learning Sara needed furniture for her new home, suggested she visit La Réunion. "Several families are returning to Europe and will not be taking all their furniture. I'll be happy to make introductions. I believe that you would be pleased with the furnishings and the prices."

Daniel borrowed his father's wagon and team. He and Beaulieu accompanied Sarah on her furniture search. Their first stop was a stone-and-log cottage where Beaulieu introduced Sara to Mr. and Mrs. Archambeau. "The colony is not what we expected," the young husband said, "so we wish to return home to France. It would cost too much to take our furniture. We would be pleased to sell it instead of abandoning it."

How sad to come all this way and be so disappointed. Poor Mrs. Archambeau is wiping tears on her apron.

"Your furniture is lovely," Sara said as they led her through the two-room cottage. Sara chose a large, rectangular, trestle table, six ladder-back chairs with cane seats, and a navy-velvet-upholstered settee.

A price was agreed upon. *I'm probably paying more than I should, but I don't have the heart to take advantage of their situation.*

As she was paying for the furniture, Sara noticed a book on a chest. Glancing at it, she saw that it was *Bleak House* by Charles Dickens. "Is the book in English?" Sara asked.

"Yes. We bought it thinking it would help us with our English. But we no longer need it."

"Is it for sale?"

"If you wish to have it, it is yours with our compliments," Mr. Archambeau said.

"That's very generous, thank you."

The Archambeaus thanked Sara for the furniture purchases.

"I wish you safe travels home," she said.

As they left, Beaulieu said, "You paid more than you needed to."

"Probably, but the little extra will be helpful to them."

Eyes narrowed, Beaulieu studied Sara for a moment, nodded, and said, "Yes."

The second stop was an apartment in the communal building where Sara met the Durands, an older couple returning to Belgium.

"We wish to sell furniture," Mr. Durand told Sara. "All is for sale. Let us show you."

He led her through the small apartment, proudly telling her the history of each piece. *This breaks my heart. Every item is like family to them.* Sara thought how hard it must be to leave their furniture behind and wished she were rich enough to pay to send it all home with them. *At least I can give them something for a few pieces.*

"Could I please buy your bed? The carved headboard and footboard are beautiful. Also the small, five-drawer chest with the brass hardware." Sara pointed at the small, needlepoint carpet. "And the rug and the china cabinet." Mr. Durant turned to Beaulieu. "*L'armoire de porcelaine?*"

Beaulieu said, "*Oui.*"

Prices were agreed upon, Sara knowing she had again paid a little too much. *I'll have to be frugal for a while, but it was worth it to see their smiles.*

As Daniel and Beaulieu loaded the furniture in the wagon, Beaulieu smiled at Sara and said "Madame, you have a soft heart."

Sara crossed the bridge back to Dallas with a wagon full of furniture. Daniel and Beaulieu helped her move everything upstairs and place it where she wanted it. With her furniture moved in, Sara hurried to the store and wrapped the Charles Dickens book in brown paper, tied it with a string, and took it to the boardinghouse. Hattie opened the door when Sara knocked. "Something for you," Sara said with a smile.

"For me?"

"A small thank-you for my former landlady."

Hattie pulled the string and tore the wrapping. Her eyes widened. "Oh, Sara! *Bleak House*, by Dickens!" She held the book in her left hand and stroked the cover with her right. "I can't wait to read it. I can't imagine how you found it. Thank you."

"You're welcome. I hope it's a good one. I'm in the process of settling into my new space so can't stay to visit this afternoon, but I'll see you in the next few days and tell you about my La Réunion furniture."

"Maybe you can come for supper soon?"

"I'd like that."

That night in her newly furnished home, Sara opened her hope chest from Tennessee. She unpacked the special things she had collected, beginning as a young girl and up until her marriage. Embroidered bed and table linens, her grandmother's china cups and teapot, silver cutlery, a cut-glass vase—things for a bride to make a house a home. Wrapped in paper at the bottom of the trunk was the embroidered nightgown Sara had worn on her wedding night. *What would our lives be like if Morgan hadn't died? I'll never know.*

Shortly after moving in, Sara invited Ellie to come and see her new home above the cotton-factor's office. "It's wonderful," Ellie told Sara. Fingering the china teapot on the trestle table, she said, "You are so lucky to have things from your home in Tennessee. I wish I had something from my parents." Sara had never talked to Ellie about where she had grown up or about her family history. Before Sara could ask, Ellie began in a whisper, "My pa, ma, brother Willie, baby Elizabeth, and I lived in Bastrop down on the Colorado River. One morning in July of '37, Ma was frying corn pone in a skillet. I remember listening to the grease sizzling as she dropped the cornmeal batter into the pan. Elizabeth was on the floor, playing with two old sewing spools, and I was sitting beside her, just daydreaming and watching the dust motes float in the air. Strange what I remember. I was only four years old. Pa and Willie were nearby in the field, hoeing weeds. I could hear their laughter.

"There was a sound like thunder, but it didn't stop. I remember Ma screaming. She knew the Comanches were coming and the thunder was the sound of their horses. Ma opened the back door, pushed me out, and told me to run hide in the woods. I did."

"Where did you hide?"

"I crawled into a hole under a log. Neighbor found me there the next day. I never saw my family again. A nearby farm family took me in. Told me my family members were all dead except for Willie. He was eleven. They must have taken him. If he's still alive, he's probably a redheaded Indian brave. That's what happens, you know. They capture the young boys and adopt them into the tribe. They say the boys take to Indian life and don't want to be rescued." Ellie's voice cracked and she was silent.

"Oh Ellie, I had no idea, I'm so sorry." The story gave Sara chills.

"The neighbor who took me in had been a schoolmarm. She educated me, and when I grew older, I helped her teach children in the area. Four years ago, I sold my parents' land and moved to Dallas. Opened my little school."

"Why Dallas?"

"I'm told the last Indian raid resulting in deaths around here was in 1844 on Rowlett Creek. I believe we are safe here. The line of military forts protects us. Dallas is hundreds of miles east of the Comanche raiding area, and there is a treaty of sorts with tribes in Indian Territory. I know I was lucky, but I wish for my family. Thunder still frightens me."

Sara put her arms around Ellie and held her as she cried.

Later in the week, talking over dinner, Sara told Hattie what Ellie had shared with her about the Comanche raid. Hattie sighed and shook her head.

"Unfortunately Ellie's story is a common one for those living west of the Brazos River and west of the line of government forts. If you haven't already heard the tale of Josiah Wilbarger, you most likely will. Back in the '30s, Wilbarger and five others came under Indian attack near Austin. Wilbarger was scalped while still conscious and left for dead. He survived and lived for eleven years with his skull exposed. People called him 'the man who would not die.'"

"Goodness! I didn't know you could survive being scalped. Ellie says she thinks we are safe from attack here in Dallas. What do you think?"

"She's right. We haven't had deadly raids in northeast Texas in more than ten years. People on the west side of the Brazos River are not so fortunate. Comanches still raid and terrorize that area."

"I have seen reports about raids way west of us in the *Dallas Herald*."

"Many people are concerned that raids will increase since the US government has made big cuts in the number of troops in the forts. The soldiers don't often pursue the Indian raiders either. That's why Texans are complaining that the US government isn't doing enough to protect us."

That night Sara slept restlessly and dreamed of a redheaded Indian brave with a frightening, painted face. In her dream, he stepped out of the trees, looked at her, laughed, and raised his tomahawk. The dream woke her early and she was happy to see the sunrise.

Later in the week, Sara joined Hattie and Aaron at the former boardinghouse for supper. Afterwards she and Hattie sat downstairs in the boardinghouse's upholstered chairs while Aaron did some work sitting at the table. Hattie was knitting a scarf, and Sara was reading the week's issue of the *Dallas Herald* out loud. "This is interesting," she pointed to an article in the paper. "Remember when we read that the government brought camels and five handlers to Texas, on the possibility that camels would be better than mules for hauling supplies between our military posts?"

"Yep. I don't think I told you, but my cousin in San Antonio says the camels are at Camp Val Verde. The military uses 'em to carry supplies back and forth to San Antonio. She says the camels draw a crowd when they come into town."

"I'll bet. Well, today's *Herald* article says that a few months back, as a military test, a surveyor named Beale—accompanied by an infantry escort—successfully led a group of twenty-five camels, two camel drovers, and numerous mules more than twelve hundred miles from Texas to California."

"And what was the result?" Hattie asked, looking up from her knitting.

"Mr. Beale says, to his surprise, the camels were superior to the mules. In fact, many of the mules died. The expedition's camels were left in California, the remaining forty-five camels are still in Texas at Camp Val Verde."

Hattie looked up from her knitting. "Camels superior to mules? That may be so, but my cousin in San Antonio says camels are nasty beasts that smell terrible. I think I might prefer mules, as stubborn as they might be."

"Guess it might depend on whether or not you need to cross the desert."

"You have a point."

On an early spring day, Daniel came out of the storeroom mopping his face with a cloth. "Summer hasn't quite started and it's already hot as the dickens."

Sara looked at him seriously. "Where is 'the dickens?'"

Daniel frowned. "What?"

"Where is 'the dickens'?" Sara asked again. "When it is really cold, you say it's cold as the dickens. When the rain is pouring, it's raining like the dickens. In the summer, it's hot as the dickens, and in the fall, it's windy as the dickens. Where is this dickens? I don't ever want to go there."

Daniel realized he was being teased. He thought for a minute. "Well I guess you're already there 'cause every time I say 'as the dickens', we're right here in Dallas."

Sara thew up her hands in surrender and laughed. "I guess I can't argue with that reasoning."

A breathless Cecilia rushed into the store one late morning in April. "There's going to be a duel!"

Sara dropped the pincushions she'd been unpacking. "A duel? But who . . .?"

"Marshal Moore accused Alexander Cockrell of breaking some sort of town rule. Words were exchanged, and the marshal challenged Cockrell to a duel. They are beside the courthouse and both have double-barreled shotguns and revolvers. Is John Henry in town? Maybe he could stop them."

"Haven't seen him," Sara said. Cecilia grabbed Sara's hand and they joined the rush of people to the courthouse. They arrived just in time to see the two men facing off for a duel. Before anyone could act to stop it, there was a burst of shots and Cockrell fell. He lay faceup in a growing pool of blood.

Doc Pryor came running out of the courthouse. "I saw it all." He thrust his top hat and cane into Sara's hands and leaned over Cockrell whose breathing was labored, red foam coming out of his mouth. Cockrell's midsection was bleeding badly, and the dirt around him was growing dark with his blood. After a moment, Doc Pryor said, "He's been gut shot and has multiple wounds. We can't move him. I'm sorry. What a terrible waste."

Sarah Cockrell came running around the corner of the building screaming, "Alexander!" Seeing Cockrell on the ground, his clothing red with blood and the puddle of blood spreading around him, she turned to Moore, shouting, "What have you done, you vile man?" Screaming and sobbing, she began beating him on the chest with her fists. Cecilia slipped her arms around Sarah Cockrell and pulled her gently away from Moore. Sarah fell to her knees beside her unconscious husband and wept.

"It was all fair and square, Mrs. Cockrell," Marshal Moore said. He picked his hat up off the ground, smoothed his mustache, and walked away. Within the hour, Cockrell was dead.

Doc Pryor gestured to two men nearby. "Let's get Mr. Cockrell's body home."

Sara gently pulled Mrs. Cockrell to her feet. "Time to take him home," she said softly.

A stretcher was collected from Doc Pryor's office and Cockrell was placed on it. Sara and Cecilia supported the weeping Mrs. Cockrell on the three-block walk to the Cockrell house by the river.

Word of the shooting had spread fast, and several of the Cockrells' slaves rushed out of the house. Tears were flowing down Mrs. Cockrell's housekeeper's face, but she took charge. "Carry him into the kitchen and put him on the big table, so's we can clean him up." She gestured to another woman. "Hetty, cover the table with lots of sheets and make sure the children don't see him like this. Miz Cockrell, you come with me." She nodded her thanks to Cecilia and Sara. "I'll put her to bed now."

Ellie was already at the store when Cecilia and Sara returned. "I heard about Mr. Cockrell. What a shame. All over a couple of hundred dollars."

"He was killed over money?" Cecilia asked.

"Yes. Marshal Moore borrowed two hundred dollars from Cockrell, then refused to pay him back. Finally, Cockrell took him to court to make him pay. Court ordered the marshal to pay, but he still wouldn't. He carried a grudge over the lawsuit and picked a fight with Cockrell. At least that's the story that's going around."

"That's terrible," Sara said. "Mr. Cockrell was a good man. I don't like anything about Marshal Moore."

The next morning Sara stopped by the Cockrell house to check on Mrs. Cockrell. Sally, her housekeeper, opened the door. "She's up this mornin' with her children. She'll be receivin' company this afternoon. Do come back."

Leaving Daniel with the store, Sara returned to the Cockrell house that afternoon. Several women were leaving as Sara arrived. The housekeeper took her into the living room. Sara waited several minutes, worrying about what to say to offer comfort. Sarah Cockrell stepped into the room, her eyes puffy and the circles under her eyes dark. Sara stood. "I am so sorry for your loss, Sarah." She began to cry. "I don't know what else to say, the words seem useless."

"Your being here says enough, Sara. Thank you. I never imagined anything like this. I loved him." She took a deep breath. "Thought we'd grow old together. My task now is to keep his legacy alive and be sure his children remember him for the fine man he was."

She is so strong.

"Will you do something for me?" Sarah Cockrell asked.

"Of course."

"Will you ask Adolph Gouhenant to come tomorrow morning before the funeral to make Alexander's death portrait? It would give me great comfort to have his photograph."

"I'll talk to him on my way back to the store."

The next day Adolph Gouhenant took his daguerreotype camera to the Cockrell home and made Cockrell's portrait in his coffin. "He was a fine-looking man, even in death," Gouhenant told Sara later.

Cockrell's funeral was attended by almost every adult in Dallas. Others came into town to attend. He had been a fair and honest man and was well respected by the citizens of the town he had been so instrumental in building.

Following the funeral, Sarah Cockrell shed no more public tears. It was reported in the *Dallas Herald* that she promised to work to ensure her husband's legacy. She would assume responsibility for her husband's business ventures and initiate new projects: The toll bridge would continue under the operation of the black slave named Berry Derrit. The brickworks and steam-powered circular sawmill would continue producing. The lumberyard would remain in successful operation, as would the freight business. She also promised to complete the new hotel her husband had begun.

The marshal, represented by four lawyers, was not convicted.

Sarah Cockrell pursued the debt Marshal Moore had owed her husband. The court forced him to pay it. She told Sara that it provided no consolation.

A few weeks later, Sara was invited to Sarah Cockrell's office for tea. When Sara arrived, Mrs. Cockrell was concluding a meeting with two men who were challenging the terms of a contract they had signed with the Cockrell lumber company. "Do come in, Sara, we're almost through here."

"We're not happy with the contract terms," one man said forcefully.

"Yet you agreed to them before and signed the contract," Mrs. Cockrell said in a calm, matter-of-fact voice.

"Well things have changed," the other man said.

"I understand things have changed." Mrs. Cockrell paused and looked at each of them, holding her gaze for several seconds. "My husband is dead, and you thought you'd see if the widow would agree to better terms for you, to her disadvantage. Please understand that I will not."

The first man began to bluster. "Well, well . . ."

"Well," Mrs. Cockrell said, "if you can show me how we would both benefit from a change in price and terms, I'll be happy to meet to discuss it. Until then, good day, gentlemen." She rose from her chair. Mrs. Cockrell's young, male assistant appeared from nowhere with their hats and ushered them out.

"Oh my, that was impressive," Sara said. "I hope I can learn to negotiate and manage while remaining a perfect lady like you do, Sarah."

"I'm guided by just a few rules: Work quietly behind the scenes—there are some in town who resent a successful woman. Smile, speak softly, don't be afraid to say no, and never back down. Be an iron fist in a velvet glove. And keep a pistol in your drawer, just in case." Sara thought of Morgan's pistol in the drawer at the store. It was insurance she hoped she'd never have to use, but knowing it was there gave her peace of mind.

Sara and Daniel were restocking shelves toward the back of the store when Sara heard, "Miss Sara, Miss Sara!"

Before she could reach the front of the store, two small girls were hugging her around the waist. Sara looked down. "Polly . . . Prudence? Oh my! It is you. How you two have grown."

Polly said, "Yes, I'm nine."

"I just turned eight," said Prudence. "Remember when we played Huckle Buckle Beanstalk, Sara?"

"I do." *And Morgan made them laugh with "higgledy-piggledy buttered beans. That was Morgan at his best.*

"We had fun with you, Miss Sara," Polly said.

Sara looked around, but not seeing their papa, she asked, "Where did you come from? Why are you in Dallas?"

"We're movin' to Jefferson with Papa and our new momma." Sara looked up from the girls as a smiling woman joined them. She extended her hand to Sara. "Hello, I'm Louisa Radcliff. The girls were so excited when they heard that you were here, they ran ahead of me. Albert is having a wagon wheel repaired. So the girls and I came to say hello." The new Mrs. Radcliff was a large woman with a big nose and an infectious smile. Sara warmed to her immediately.

"I am happy to meet you and so pleased to see the girls," Sara said. "They told me you are moving to Jefferson?"

"Yes, I'm from Jefferson. I was visiting my sister in Waco when I met Albert. He courted me for two months and we were married last week. We're moving to Jefferson. My father has a blacksmith shop there. While he does shoe horses and oxen, mostly his work is making and repairing farm equipment, making kitchen utensils, and working on hardware for wagons, carts, and even door and shutter hinges. If you remember, Albert is a blacksmith, so he will join my father in business."

"Guess what?" Prudence said. "In our new house, we are going to have our own bedroom, with ruffled curtains."

"And grandparents!" said Polly.

Louisa Radcliff laughed. "I think my hardest job as a momma may be keeping my parents from spoiling the girls rotten."

Prudence grabbed Polly's hand. "We want to see the store." Sara nodded and the girls were off to explore.

Albert Radcliff, accompanied by his two small boys, walked into the store. "Mrs. Darnell, I see you've met Louisa." He curled him arm around his new wife's waist and she looked up at him and smiled.

"Albert, I was just telling Mrs. Darnell how excited Polly and Prudence have been about seeing her."

Albert Radcliff looked at Sara and said, "Thanks to you, they have good memories of the wagon train, despite hard times. Thank you."

"I have good memories of time spent with them. They are sweet children."

"They are," said Louisa Radcliff. She looked back at Albert. "I am five-times blessed."

Polly and Prudence ran back to them, pulling a laughing Daniel by the hands. "This is Daniel, he works with Miss Sara," said Prudence, "but he has never played Huckle Buckle Beanstalk!"

"You'll have to teach him," Polly said.

"And I'll have to take this rowdy bunch to the hotel and feed them, so we can leave as soon as the wheel is ready," Albert Radcliff said.

"I have thought about you often," Sara said. "I'm glad to know you are doing well. Mr. and Mrs. Radcliff, congratulations and best wishes on your marriage." She turned to Polly and Prudence. "You lucky girls be sweet and come see me again sometime."

The six Radcliffs left, walking toward Crutchfield's. The girls turned and blew kisses to Sara.

I wonder if someday I might have sweet children like those two. I hope so.

There had been three days of intense rain and the Trinity had turned into a roaring water monster, when a crowd of men ran past the store toward the river, shouting, "Cockrell's toll bridge has collapsed!" As they passed, Daniel asked if he could follow. Sara sent him on his way with instructions to hurry back and report what had happened. He was back shortly to tell her that the entire western section of the wooden bridge over the river had fallen, due to the rushing floodwater, and the bridge was unusable. As far as anyone knew, there were no injuries. Sara rushed to the river to see the damage. She was amazed to see the normally quietly flowing Trinity had overflowed its banks and was a tumultuous rush of turbulent, foaming water uprooting trees and spinning them through the swift water as it raged. As Daniel had reported, half of the wooden bridge had totally collapsed into the roaring water. Trees, brush, and a dead cow had already piled against the remaining half of the bridge, which looked ready to follow the first. *This doesn't look like it can be repaired.*

The toll master, Berry Derrit, was standing on the riverbank, wringing his hands and moaning. "Wicked river! You took my bridge."

Sarah Cockrell joined Sara on the riverbank. "Came to see the damage for myself."

"This is terrible," Sara said. "As if you didn't have enough to worry about without this."

"It was bound to happen, Sara. It was a rustic, wooden bridge. The Trinity is notorious for flooding. When it does, the river turns from placid to ferocious. I had hoped Alexander's wooden bridge would last until an iron bridge could be built. It didn't, so in the meantime, we'll have to get along with a ferryboat." She noticed Berry Derrit standing on the shore, still wringing his hands. "Looks like I need to comfort my toll master. See you soon, Sara."

She doesn't waste energy on what can't be changed.

Hattie was working in her small vegetable garden behind the boardinghouse when Sara left the store one summer afternoon. Fenced with brush to keep critters out, the garden contained cabbages, beets, turnips, and potatoes, all planted among corn to provide shade and hold moisture. Hattie was harvesting some of her crop, and Sara offered to help. Hattie had already made several mounds of earth in an open space within the brush fence. She and Sara laid the root vegetables on the mounds, covered them with corn husks, then buried everything under a thick layer of soil. Hattie added more soil to the final mound and dusted off her hands. "Sure would be nice to have a root cellar. I figure this is the next best thing. The brush fence should keep wandering hogs from rooting up the vegetables."

Sara raised an eyebrow. "Root cellar, root vegetables, and rooting hogs! I think there is a pun in there somewhere."

Hattie smiled. "A pun in the garden is fine, but not a pig in the garden. Stay for supper, why don't you?" Gathering up some turnips and potatoes they had set aside to add to the night's stew, the ladies headed for the kitchen. Peeling the potatoes beside Hattie, Sara realized Dallas had truly become home.

Hearing someone walk into the store, Sara put down the sewing notion box she'd been unpacking and stepped to the front of the store. Standing in the door was a short, stocky man in a very wide-brimmed hat. He was backlit by the bright sunshine outside so it took a moment for Sara to recognize him. "Señor Barros, I am pleased to see you. Your wife told me you've been ill."

"Si, Señora Darnell. I am now recovered and I have come to retrieve my good name."

"Retrieve your good name? I don't understand?"

"Growing up I learned that when you have a debt the person who holds your debt also holds your good name. While I was ill and could not farm or make my clay pots, you gave my wife credit in your store. I am in debt to you, so you hold my good name. I have come to pay my bill."

Sara knew that Señor Barros had received a Spanish land grant before Texas became a republic. He was one of very few hispanics in Dallas county. Señor Barros had a reputation in Dallas as both an excellent potter and a solid citizen. She had extended credit to his wife when he was ill, trusting that it would be repaid. "Let me pull my account book and see how much is due."

"I believe it to be $7.25. We have kept a careful tally," Señor Barros said.

Sara lifted her account book from the counter drawer and quickly flipped through the pages until she found the one she wanted. "Yes, $7.25 exactly," she said looking up with a smile.

Señor Barros carefully counted out the amount due in small silver coins. He placed them on the counter. "I also wish to thank you for bartering for some of my clay pots."

Sara smiled. "The pots have been popular. If you have more pots to barter, I'd be pleased to work out a more permanent arrangement."

Señor Barros nodded. "I would like to do so. May I bring you pots to choose from, and we can agree on a barter amount?"

"Please do," Sara said. "I'm glad you are healthy again."

Señor Barros thanked Sara, and as he turned and left she reflected on his comment that someone holding a debt also holds the debtor's good name. *If I ever have children I'll teach them that.*

★ 1859 ★

The Madame and the Ballgown

The Cockrell's three-story St. Nicholas Hotel dominated the square long before its completion. As final touches were being made to its interior, the manager announced a grand-opening ball. Three months ahead of the opening announcement, Mrs. Cockrell had told Sara what she was planning but had sworn her to secrecy. "Sara, the ladies of the town will need ball gowns, and I thought you'd need time to order the fabrics, lace, cage-crinoline hoops, and other items dressmakers will need to make the gowns in time for the opening ball."

"Oh my!" Sara's eyes lit up. "A ball is a grand way to open the hotel. Ladies of the town will be delighted. And it will mean a lot of business for my store, for dressmakers, and for other shops in town. I'll do my best to order what Dallas' ladies will need. Thank you for letting me know in advance."

The formal announcement of the big event came two days after Sara received her special shipment. Ladies poured into the shop to make their selections. Whit's wife, Emmeline, was standing with fabric from two different bolts of silk draped over her shoulders. "Which one, Sara, the sky blue or the pale lemon yellow?" Sara considered the two colors for a moment and said, "The sky blue would be lovely on you. Look at the rolls of ribbons too. There is a matching blue in the ribbon box."

"How many yards do you have left of this fabric?" another customer asked.

"Do you have lace in any color other than white?"

"Is there embroidery thread in pale green?"

"Do you have fabric for crinoline petticoats and pantaloons?"

"How much do you want for this?"

There had been such a flurry of activity in the store that Sara had gone home exhausted at the end of the day ever since the grand ball had been announced. She had not had time to give a thought to what she would wear, or if she could even go without an escort. She doubted that would be proper.

Gradually details leaked out about the event. Ellie kept Sara up to date. There would be an orchestra led by a noted violinist. People were coming from as far away as Houston. Military officers billeted in Fort Worth were being invited. As more information was revealed, grand-ball fever just intensified. Dressmakers were busy and the boot-and-shoe store had a parade of people going in and out every day. Ladies were dragging husbands or beaus into the Art Saloon where Edouard Charles Beaulieu was teaching several group dancing lessons each day. "Grand balls are certainly good for business," Sara confided to Daniel after the first week of the rush.

Sara, busy unpacking the latest merchandise delivery, turned to set a fabric bolt on the counter and came face-to-face with Benjamin Brown. "Oh!" she said, dropping the bolt on the floor. Both leaned down to pick it up, cracked heads, and came up laughing. "Are you trying to knock some sense into me?" Benjamin said. He laughed. Before Sara could think of a quick retort, he continued, "If so, it worked. I am here to tell you that I'm headed to San Antonio to meet with one of the company's primary investors. I'll hurry back in time for the opening of the hotel. Would do me the honor of accompanying me to the grand-opening ball?"

Sara couldn't speak for a moment. She looked into Benjamin's twinkling eyes as he added, "Please do say yes."

"Yes," Sara said as she maintained eye contact, "absolutely, yes." Both burst into big smiles.

That night Sara lay in bed thinking about the ball. *I really like Benjamin. He's smart and fun and I am attracted to him. We'll see how I feel about him after the ball. I wonder if he drinks and gambles?* With that, she yawned and went to sleep.

Before Benjamin's invitation, Sara had assumed she would not be going to the grand-opening ball and had suggested Hattie wear the wedding dress to the event. They agreed that adding a short, floral cape or overskirt would transform the dress from wedding dress to ball gown very nicely. This left Sara with the issue of what to wear. She had nothing appropriate and no time to have a dress made. *What can I do?* She might have to decline Benjamin's invitation to attend for lack of a ballgown.

The next afternoon the stage arrived. As usual, Sara opened the store's door. Among the passengers was a very elegant strawberry blonde. As the whip helped her out of the stage, Sara thought she presented herself as a stylish, refined lady. She wore an apricot-silk dress with a white-lace collar, wide Pagoda sleeves, and white-lace undersleeves that puffed at the wrist. In the latest style, the bodice and skirt were two separate pieces. *Is she wearing makeup? My goodness.* Not wanting to be seen staring, Sara stepped away from the door and busied herself unpacking bottles of castor oil.

The woman stepped into the store, nodding in Sara's direction. Taking off her gloves, she wandered through the store, picking up a few small items. She lingered until the other customers were gone and the stage had left. It was time to close when she approached Sara and paid for her items in silver coins. "My name is Novella Adison," she said, extending her hand.

Sara took the extended hand. "I'm Mrs. Sara Darnell."

The woman looked closely at Sara. "You're obviously the proprietor of this store, Mrs. Darnell. I've come to Dallas to set up a business—may we talk privately and frankly?"

Sara's curiosity was aroused. "Of course." She sensed no threat from this woman, who projected an unusual amount of confidence with her direct words and assertive voice. Daniel had just left for the day. Sara closed the store.

"You may not wish to be seen with me, nor will you want it known we have spoken."

"Why is that?" Sara asked.

"Because the business I have come to establish is a brothel." Novella Adison watched Sara's expression. *A brothel!* Sara blinked and her chin dropped. "Oh!" was all she could say. Ellie had told her there were gambling houses and saloons south of the courthouse in Boggy Bayou, a rough area along the river. Sara was curious, but decent women were not supposed to go there or even know about it. That there might be brothels had not occurred to her.

"Would you prefer that I leave now?" the woman asked. Sara knew propriety would require that she say yes, but she was fiercely curious and there was something fascinating about this woman. *A madame! Yet—her speech, her clothes—I would have guessed she was a banker's wife.*

"No, let's talk," Sara said.

"You have a successful business and know Dallas. I need referrals to a banker and a lawyer who will work with me discreetly. I wouldn't say who had referred me, simply that I have heard that the banker and lawyer are reputable. I'd also like a bit of background regarding the influential business-people in the community. My brothels are run with very strict rules, both for my girls and our customers."

"Rules?"

"Gentlemen who frequent us must act like gentlemen toward the girls, and the girls are carefully selected. I have learned that a brief meeting with the main leaders in the community can help my business quietly fit in with little friction and fewer problems. Actually, having a well-run brothel will help prevent problem brothels from coming to town. And believe me, there are many problem brothels. Would you be willing to assist me in these two things—referrals and information?"

Sara studied Novella Adison for a moment. Sara wondered if she was Miss or Mrs. She had not used either title. "Ask your questions and I'll let you know if there is something I prefer not to answer."

"Fair enough. Can you refer me to a lawyer and a banker who might be willing to assist me?" Sara mentally ran through the list of lawyers she knew and finally settled on a fairly new arrival. Sharing the name with Novella Adison, she explained that she had selected him because he was new to Dallas and might not yet have many clients. He was also from New Orleans, already a large, cosmopolitan city; thus, Sara assumed, the lawyer might have a liberal point of view. Sara didn't say that she also thought the lawyer might be swayed by Novella's pretty face and cultured manner, something Sara wouldn't have associated with a brothel owner.

Novella Adison nodded and her smile grew as Sara explained why she'd selected the lawyer. "Very good reasoning. I shall approach him."

"The banker referral is a bit more challenging as Texas doesn't have banks. However, a Galveston firm that offers some financial services is planning on expanding to Dallas. I can give you the name of the gentleman who will be in charge here, but you must never say that I gave you the information." Novella Adison agreed and Sara gave her Benjamin Brown's name. "He will not be back in Dallas for a couple of weeks. With regard to influential businesspeople in town, the person with the most influence is a woman, Mrs. Sarah Cockrell."

"A woman?" Novella Adison raised an eyebrow in real surprise.

"Her husband, Alexander Cockrell, bought the rights to the Dallas colony from the previous owner, built a bridge across the Trinity, added a sawmill, and started other businesses. After he was killed, Mrs. Cockrell took over the business affairs and has continued to build and develop businesses. The hotel on the square is her venture. She is very smart, fair, and straightforward."

"She's influential?"

"Win her over and you have a powerful ally. If your argument doesn't convince her, it will be difficult for you, I suspect. The Art Saloon next door is run by a Frenchman, Adolph Gouhenant. He is well respected and very involved in the community. I don't know what his views might be." Sara went on to mention several other leading citizens, including a few she identified as most likely being against the idea of a brothel, regardless of how well it was run.

"Thank you, Mrs. Darnell. You have been most helpful, and I have already forgotten that we have even met. If I can ever do a favor for you, please let me know." A small smile quickly passed her lips.

Suddenly a thought flashed through Sara's mind. "There just might be something you can do for me." Sara explained her ball-gown dilemma.

"That's a problem I can easily solve. I had new dresses made before coming to Dallas." She looked closely at Sarah. "We are about the same height and size. With minor alterations, one of my new dresses should fit you well. You may wish to add a bit of lace to make the neckline a bit more discreet. A dress is a small price for the help you have given me today. I'm thinking of two dresses, neither has been worn. Would you prefer a soft-green silk or a pale-lavender satin? Each has a bell skirt, matching crinolines, and pantaloons."

"Thank you," Sara said. "I'd like to borrow the lavender one, please. You are very generous. I'll ask the dressmaker to alter the gown in a way that will allow the stitches to be removed so I can return the dress in original condition."

"Nonsense, please keep the dress as my thanks for your help. It will be delivered in a box tomorrow. If you see me again and value your reputation, it will be best to not speak."

Sarah unlatched the door so Novella Adison could slip out, carrying her small packages and appearing to be the store's last customer. She was joined by a short man in a frock coat and bowler hat who escorted her down the street. Sara noticed he limped.

Oh my, so much for propriety. What would Momma think?

The next morning, as promised, a box was delivered to Sara at the store. Opening it, Sara gasped, and a thrill ran down her spine. Packed on top was the berthe—the ball gown's wide, detachable collar, a V-necked confection of tiny, satin pleats, lace, and ribbon that would fit across the shoulders, cover the dress' neckline, and rest on the very top of the sleeves. Sara's first thought was that the berthe looked like a large piece of jewelry. Setting it gently aside, she lifted the gown from the brown paper it was wrapped in. *This is the most beautiful ball gown I've ever seen.* The color was the same lavender shade that sometimes crept into the Texas sunset. Resisting the temptation to try it on then and there, she reboxed it.

That evening at home, Sara lifted it again from the box and spread it on her bed. Slipping out of her everyday dress, she carefully pulled the ball gown over her head. The dress had a low-cut V-neck—a bit too low. The gathered, short sleeves were trimmed with ribbon and lace. A smooth, fitted bodice came to a point just below the waist. Whirling around, Sara could tell that the bell skirt was full enough to lay in soft folds when she added her hoop. The same pattern of satin pleats, lace, and ribbon that adorned the berthe also created a decorative stripe, which circled the bottom of the skirt, then swept upwards, creating a spiral around the skirt which ended in back at the waist. *Gorgeous.* Sara carefully tucked the dress back into the box.

The next morning, Sara took the dress to Mr. West's wife, Lois, for her expert alterations. Trying it on and seeing her reflection in the full-length mirror, Sara was delighted.

"This is simply beautiful," Lois said, "and the color suits you, Sara. But we do need to fix the neckline. A bit too revealing, wouldn't you say?"

"Can you alter it by adding more lace?"

"Easily! The new lace will blend with the lace on the collar. Problem solved." Lois smiled, pulled pins from her pincushion, and began to fold the bottom of the ball gown. "It's also a bit long, so I'll hem it to about here." She leaned back so Sara could see the pinned-up length in the mirror. "That measures three inches above the floor."

Sara nodded. "Perfect for dancing."

"Of course, you'll need pantalettes," the seamstress added.

"Matching ones came with the dress."

Later that day, Sara found hair ribbons in a darker shade of lavender in her store's ribbon supply and bought a pair of pale-gray, low-heeled satin slippers at the shoe store. She was ready for the St. Nicholas Hotel's Grand-Opening Ball.

The morning of the ball, Sara joined Hattie at the boardinghouse. Hattie had secured a large barrel of spring water the day before. A tin hip tub in the enclosed bath-and-laundry shed was partially filled with warm water, which the two had heated on the kitchen's iron cookstove and carefully carried inside. Sara bathed first, lathering with castile soap, then washing her hair with the soap and rinsing it with black tea splashed with a bit of vinegar to add shine. Finished, with her hair wrapped in a towel, Sara helped Hattie empty and refill the tub with more warm water. While Hattie bathed, Sara dressed, then sat outside in the sun and brushed her hair. When it was dry, she added a tiny bit of oil, brushing it in with one hundred strokes. Parting her hair in the middle, she braided both sides, looped the braids over her ears, and then pulled the ends back, securing them in a bun at the nape of her neck. When Hattie came out to dry her hair, Sara offered to empty and rinse the tub. Finishing that task, Sara thanked Hattie and gave her a hug before heading home to prepare for the ball.

That evening Benjamin called for Sara at her home above the cotton-factoring business. Hattie and Aaron, perfect chaperones, were with him. Upon seeing Sara come down the stairs, Benjamin's eyes lit up. "Sara, you look . . . beautiful," he said rather breathlessly.

"Thank you."

Hattie winked at Sara. She was wearing the cream-colored-silk wedding dress Sara had loaned her. To change the look, Lois West had made a silk-and-lace shawl collar in cream with pale-green trim and had added a pale-green sash, which tied in back. The shawl collar was held in place by a pinchback glass brooch.

"I've never seen you look lovelier, Hattie." Sara said.

Aaron nodded. "That's just what I told her."

Hattie smiled at her husband and son. "You fellows look mighty nice, as well."

Both men wore black frock coats over white shirts and colorful silk vests. Aaron's slim trousers were a subtle black-and-white check. Benjamin's were black. Their slim, black-silk neckties were looped in a bow with one end jauntily extended, adding a bit of style.

As they walked the short distance to the new hotel, Benjamin told the ladies that he and Aaron had spent the afternoon at the new barbershop for haircuts, shaves, and to use the bathhouse there. "The barber charges twenty-five cents for a fresh-water tub. Used water is only fifteen cents."

"I certainly hope you two chose fresh water," Hattie said.

"But, Momma, you told me to always be frugal," Benjamin chuckled.

Hattie laughed. "Frugal, but not foolish."

"Don't worry, dear," Aaron said. "I saw to it that Benjamin forked over the full twenty-five cents for fresh water."

Sara smiled. "I'm certainly glad, since I'll be the one dancing with him."

Arriving at the new hotel, Sara saw that all three stories of the imposing, new brick structure were aglow with whale-oil lamps. Joining the crowd of excited guests swarming into the lobby, they passed walls covered with tapestries and were quickly swept into the ballroom toward the rising sound of conversation and laughter. Sara glanced up at the large chandeliers that hung from the ceiling and cast dancing shadows on the walls. Sara knew they were lit with nondrip spermaceti candles. She had ordered them for Sarah Cockrell. *No wax dripping on ball gowns tonight.* More glowing light came from blown-glass whale-oil lamps held by decorative, metal wall brackets. *The room is beautiful. I feel as if I've left Dallas and stepped into a fairy tale.* The orchestra, seated on a raised platform along one wall, began to play a lilting waltz. A semicircular balcony with a balustrade already held a group of honored guests, some leaning over to wave at friends below. Scores of wildflower garlands, cedar boughs, and wreaths of green leaves added color and texture and filled the room with the scent of flowers. Chairs lined the walls, leaving the rest of the room open for standing and dancing.

Following a musical introduction, a bugle call signaled the grand march. Benjamin and Aaron guided Sara and Hattie into the line of guests that was forming for the parade around the room. Pairs of gowned ladies of all ages and men in evening dress or frock coats, worn over elaborately adorned waistcoats, began to circle around the ballroom. A few men in blue broadcloth military uniforms and their ladies also joined the line. As the guests paraded, Sara saw John Henry and Cecilia across the room, as well as Whit and Emmeline.

Looking for Sarah Cockrell, Sara saw her standing on the balcony, watching everything below. She wore a simple, lace-trimmed, black-velvet dress suitable for a recent widow. She had told Sara that she wished to remain in the background for the evening, allowing her hotel manager, a well-known captain in the Indian wars and former state lieutenant governor, to assume the role of host. Sara smiled and waved discreetly. Sarah Cockrell did the same. Looking up at Sarah Cockrell on the balcony, Sara suddenly understood that by bowing to convention, staying quietly behind the scenes, and drawing as little attention to herself as a businesswoman as possible, Sarah Cockrell was the most powerful person in Dallas.

Circling past Whit and Emmeline across the room, Sara admired what Emeline's dressmaker had done with the sky-blue silk yardage Emmeline had purchased at the store. The bell-shaped gown had an off-the-shoulder berthe of white lace. More white lace cascaded from blue ribbon bows stitched around the skirt. *Lovely.* Sara smiled at Whit's cravat of matching blue silk.

Cecilia and John Henry circled past them, smiling and whispering to each other. Cecilia's rose-colored gown, with a three-tiered skirt and three-quarter-length sleeves, was pure elegance. John Henry was freshly shaved and barbered. In his black frock coat with a red-tartan vest and narrow, black bow tie, he looked less like a rugged Texas Ranger and more like a prosperous cattleman.

When the grand march had circled the room twice, the music stopped, and the manager of the new hotel welcomed everyone, wished them a festive evening, and said, "Let the dancing begin." On cue, the band began to play a waltz. Sara was swept into Benjamin's arms and they whirled around the room. From the waltz, the band transitioned into a minuet and then a quadrille. Later in the evening, the polka, the Virginia reel, and the schottische were requested. Sara decided Edouard Charles Beaulieu's dance classes had worked. The dance floor was full of smiling men and women.

Taking a break after a breathless polka, Sara and Benjamin accepted punch from a tailcoat-clad waiter as Whit and Emmeline stepped off the dance floor. Moving through the crowd, the four came together. After handshakes, hugs, and compliments on attire, Whit said, "This ball is certainly a first for Dallas."

"I'm afraid the ball has fueled a conspiracy," Benjamin said.

Three heads snapped toward him. Emmeline frowned. "Conspiracy?"

"Yes, so much new business resulted from all these guests preparing for the ball that the barbers, dressmakers, jewelers, even the man from the shoe shop, are meeting right now and plotting ways to greatly increase the number of balls in Dallas." Benjamin laughed.

"I'll join in that conspiracy," Sara said and Emmeline nodded.

Whit looked at Benjamin and grinned. "These gals would probably join most any old group that promised them the chance to wear their ball gowns again."

"And they do look lovely." Benjamin slipped his hand into Sara's and squeezed.

Cecilia and John Henry joined them from the dance floor and John Henry gestured to the line of waiters standing by with punch trays. At the waiter's arrival, the men took fresh glasses for their ladies and themselves. "Cecilia, tell me about your shawl." Sara had never seen fabric in the deep-purple color before. The tasseled, purple shawl was tossed across Cecilia's shoulder and draped beautifully across her sweeping skirt.

"It's made with a new dye called mauveine," Cecilia said. "John Henry ordered it for me from New Orleans. Isn't it pretty?"

"Yes, and it is perfect with your rose-colored gown. Very fashionable." Sara turned to compliment John Henry on his red-tartan vest. Her mouth gaped open and her eyes widened. John Henry's eyebrows had been tamed! Gone were the wild brows that had given him such a distinctive look. His eyebrows now looked ordinary.

Seeing her expression, John Henry began to laugh. "The darn barber talked me into letting him trim my eyebrows to make me look more civilized. When he finished trimmin', they were still wild, just shorter. Cecilia put some mustache wax on 'em to calm 'em down. I can't wait until they grow back."

At that moment the orchestra struck up another waltz and John Henry broke away from the conversation. "Excuse us, we can't let a waltz go to waste." Laughing, he and Cecilia were swept away into the waltzing crowd.

"I wonder if John Henry has his gun tucked inside his frock coat," Sara whispered to Benjamin.

"Habits are hard to break," was Benjamin's reply. "I think we all feel safer with John Henry around. If he's armed, it's fine with me. By the way, where are Ellie and Gerard tonight? Have you seen them?"

"Ellie is sick. One of her students came to school with itchy, red eyes. All puffy, crusty, and watery. Afraid it might spread to other students, she sent him home. Now she has a terrible case of whatever it is. She made me promise to remember everything about the ball so I can tell her all about it. I feel so sorry for her. She's so disappointed."

"What awful timing. Ellie is so social, I suspect missing the ball makes her more miserable than her malady. You'll have to be Dr. Sara and give her a good, healthy dose of ballroom gossip."

"The perfect prescription. I've already memorized what all the ladies are wearing."

As the music shifted to a minuet, Benjamin pointed out Hattie and Aaron dancing. "I'm so glad Momma found Aaron. She's been so lonely for a such long time. I sometimes think that's the real reason she started the boardinghouse—for company. Momma deserves a fine man, and I think Aaron is just what she needs."

"They seem happy and well suited. I'm so pleased for them both."

As they circulated through the crowd, Sara introduced Benjamin as both the man whose Dallas cotton-factoring business would open soon and as Hattie Brown Davis' son. The news of a cotton brokerage for Dallas was well received, and by the end of the evening, Benjamin flexed the fingers of his right hand. "My hand is actually sore from all the handshaking I've done tonight. That last fellow shook my hand three different times after he heard I was bringing cotton brokerage to town. I guess that's a sign the time is right for the business."

It was the wee hours of the morning before the last of the punch was gone and the good-night waltz was announced. As the final music played, the orchestra leader sang the traditional closing song. "We will hang up the fiddle and the bow. You've danced all night till broad daylight. We will hang up the fiddle and the bow."

As the four tired but happy partygoers walked away from the hotel towards home, Benjamin leaned close to Sara. "Thank you for going with me. I had a wonderful time."

Sara looked up into his warm, brown eyes. "I had a wonderful time too." She slipped her arm into his for the walk home.

Tucked in for the night and reliving the ball in her mind, Sara realized how much she had enjoyed going with Benjamin. *He's awfully nice.* She drifted off to sleep.

The grand-opening ball behind them, Sara's focus returned to her store and Benjamin Brown's to completing the cotton factoring office and preparing to open for business. Ellie's beau, Gerard Favre, was engaged to reinforce the outside doors, finish out the downstairs office space with new plank floors, and add tellers' cages and two private offices. One of the offices would house the safe that had been ordered. Benjamin's company agreed to pay for these improvements. Sara had already employed Gerard to enclose the staircase to her level so that it was accessed by an outside door with a lock.

Downstairs, office desks and chairs had been ordered, along with locking, metal cash drawers for the tellers. Benjamin was most excited about the safe. He had accompanied Sara to church one Sunday and, on the walk back to the square, he told her all about it. "The safe is made by a new firm, Diebold and Bahmann of Cincinnati. Mr. Charles Diebold and I corresponded, and I placed the order for the safe as soon as the investors approved the purchase. The safe sounds like a beauty and I can't wait to see it."

He didn't have to wait long. A freight wagon pulled by two ox teams rolled up to the building a week later. Carpenter Favre had modified a sturdy cart to accept the heavy safe. The freighters loaded the safe and rolled it inside to its location. Even with the special cart, it took two strong men to put it into place in the niche Gerard had made in the wall.

After supper, an excited Benjamin invited his mother, Aaron, Ellie, Gerard, and Sara to the office to see the safe. The combination-lock safe was three and a half feet tall, two feet wide, and a bit more than two and a half feet deep. Inside were a smaller combination-lock safe, two locked key drawers, and an open area for money bags or other storage.

The outside was beautifully painted in a floral design that sparkled when it caught the light. "It's special jeweled paint," Benjamin explained. Even the inside was beautifully decorated. Gerard, Aaron, and Benjamin began a conversation about the construction. Soon terms like boiler-plate wrought iron, hardened steel, three hundred pounds, metal rods, and plaster-of-Paris fireproofing were being bandied about.

Meanwhile, the ladies' discussion had turned to other things. Hattie was showing off a pair of pearl earrings Aaron had given her as a wedding gift. The pearls were met with admiring compliments. Ellie was complaining about there being six other schools in Dallas, all competing for students. "Of course, some schools are for older children, but still, it is more difficult for me to attract and keep students. I'm considering reducing tuition."

Sara said, "Instead of reducing fees, can you think of things you might offer that the children and parents would find attractive, things that competing schools don't offer?"

"You mean like the plant-and-insect-collection expedition with Mr. Reverchon?" Ellie asked.

"Perhaps. How was that received?"

"I'm not sure who enjoyed it more. The children loved being the experts who knew where to find lots of interesting insects and plants. They were also pleased to learn the names of things. Mr. Reverchon explained that plants, insects, and animals have everyday names and formal, Latin ones too. During the day he found bugs and plants that he'd not seen before. He seems shy, but I think he enjoyed being the center of attention. He was very patient with the children. So everyone was happy. Two of my older boys are helping Reverchon mount the items they collected," Ellie paused, "I'd have to say it was a success."

"Maybe you could start to build a special science program around that. Adolph Gouhenant is always looking for ways to draw people into the Art Saloon. He might be willing to have an exhibition of the mounted insects that your class has collected. A couple of children could talk about their favorite insect. Mr. Reverchon would probably have ideas about how to make it interesting for parents and others. You'd probably draw a crowd. the *Herald* might even write a story about it."

"A hands-on science program with a few field trips," Ellie said. "It just might work. Thank you."

At this point the men had concluded their safe-construction conversation and agreed the new Diebold safe ought to keep valuables safe and criminals out.

Sara told the others good night and, as they left for the walk home, went upstairs to what she had begun to think of as her cozy retreat.

Sara was arranging bags of Dwight's Saleratus on the store's shelf when Benjamin burst in the door. "Take a break and come with me for just a few minutes." Benjamin grabbed her hand and pulled her out of the store. Sara hurried to keep up with him as they walked back to the cotton-factoring office. Once there, Benjamin looked at her. "It just went up, what do you think?" She was confused until he pointed up to where a new sign hung above the door. "R. and D. G. Mills" it read in large, capital letters of black and gold. Below, in smaller letters: "Cotton Factors and Commission Merchants."

"It's a beautiful sign. Now the word will spread that you are opening soon."

"That's what I'm counting on," Benjamin said with a big grin.

Once the business' interior was completed, Benjamin asked Sara to help him write an opening announcement for the *Dallas Herald* newspaper. Leaning over the office counter with paper and pencil, Sara suggested he might invite Dallas citizens to come in, meet him, and see how secure their money would be in the company's new Diebold safe. "Some of our citizens may not have had access to demand accounts before. If you can get them in the door to meet you and see the safe, they might be more comfortable depositing money." Benjamin liked the idea and, when interviewed by the *Dallas Herald*, he told Sara, he had made it a point to invite people in to view the safe during the two days before the company officially opened for business. The announcement drew a crowd curious about the safe.

Benjamin also placed an ad in the *Herald* under the headline "Cotton Factor and General Commission and Forwarding Merchant." The ad read: "Personal attention given to selling and shipping of cotton. Will sell on commission or advance on same. Orders for supplies promptly responded to when accompanied by cash. See Benjamin Brown, R. and D. G. Mills of Galveston. Located on the square in Dallas."

On the day of the brokerage's open house, Benjamin was still in the office when Sara came home from the store. He stepped outside and met her at the door to the stairs. "Guess what? The company has its first depositor. We don't officially open until tomorrow, but this customer insisted on making a very large deposit using gold. I can't tell you who, but with this one deposit, we are already ahead of my goal for month two. Thank you for your idea about inviting people to come in to see the safe. You are amazing, Sara."

Sara looked at Benjamin and realized how much she liked him and how comfortable she was with him. "I know you'll make this business a success." She told him good night and climbed to her cozy retreat, wondering if his big depositor was Novella Adison. The next day she exchanged assorted bank notes and silver for Mills' Money and deposited her funds in a new account.

Benjamin kept Sara up to date on the cotton brokerage's progress as a small but steady flow of depositors began. "You were right, Sara, many of the new customers have come from places where they had banked their money, others have come in proud to have funds to deposit for the first time. I try to treat each customer with courtesy, thank them for their trust, and welcome them as depositors."

"Are you able to make loans to the cotton growers yet?"

"Yes. Deposits are growing. That, plus the support of our investors, means I can start loans and advance purchases of cotton crops. The Dallas branch of the Mills company is off to a roaring start!"

Benjamin had asked to escort Sara to church one Sunday morning. As they walked, Sara asked Benjamin when and why he moved to Galveston.

"After my pa died at Goliad, during the Texas Revolution, we joined the Runaway Scrape."

"The Runaway Scrape? What was that?"

"Well, after the Goliad massacre and the fall of the Alamo, the Mexican Army was moving east, winning battles as they moved across Texas. Settlers panicked, left everything behind, and began to flee toward Louisiana. I was too young to remember, but it must have been terrible. Momma says thousands of women, children, and older folks, from as far west as the Colorado River, left everything behind and fled in wagons, on horseback, and on foot toward Louisiana. Most of the men were off fighting. Food was scarce. Fording the rivers was hard, due to flooding, and lots of people died along the way."

"It sounds awful." Sara could hardly imagine the confusion and chaos of thousands fleeing. "Did you and your momma get to the US?"

"No. Before Momma and I could cross into Louisiana, word came that Sam Houston's forces had defeated the Mexican Army at San Jacinto and Santa Anna had been captured. But when we got home, there wasn't much left of our homestead. The Mexican Army had even burned our crops. We packed up what little was left and moved to Galveston, where Momma had family."

"How did you end up in Dallas?"

"We stayed in Galveston until Momma decided to move us here and start a boardinghouse. She wanted me to have a college education, so when

I was old enough, she used money from selling some land to send me to Baylor University."

"Is that in Galveston?"

"No, Baylor is in the town of Independence in Washington County. Anyway, one of my school friends was the son of a rich businessman in Galveston. He took a liking to me, and when I left school, he hired me to work for him in his investment office. He invests in real estate and is an investor in several businesses in San Antonio and Galveston, including R. and D. G. Mills."

"So you went from his investment office to Mills?"

"Yes. When the Mills company was considering a branch office in Dallas, he asked me if I'd be interested in return for a salary and a share of profits. Down the road, there'd even be an opportunity for some ownership. You bet I was interested! As you know, for the past year I've worked to learn the factoring business and now, here I am. I just hope I can make a success of the business."

"It sounds like you're doing well so far."

"Yes, I think so."

"Oh!" Sara said, "I hear singing. We must be a bit late. Let's hurry and maybe we can slip into a back pew before the sermon starts." Benjamin grabbed her hand and they ran.

Daniel stood looking out of the store's open door. "It's raining like the dickens. Not many customers will show up today. Want me to unpack and stock the last two boxes that were delivered last week? Been too busy 'til today." Sara agreed that was a good way to spend the time and off he went to restock shelves.

Sara was about to close the door to shut out the wind that had arrived with the rain when she heard two stage horn blasts and watched the stage rattle past the front of the store. As it passed, she saw a woman hurrying from the protection of the courthouse. She was sheltered from the storm by a large umbrella, but as the woman shifted the umbrella's angle to block a wet gust of wind and rain, Sarah realized the woman was Novella Adison.

The stage had come to a full stop just a few yards from the store. There was only one passenger. The man that stepped out caused Sara to catch her breath. He had a short, neatly trimmed beard and mustache. His chiseled features revealed high cheekbones and a strong chin. He was deeply tanned. *Like a sculpture come to life.* Over his black, Prince Edward suit was a casually draped wool coat with a fur collar. Under his vest he wore a ruffled-front white shirt with a white cravat. He had on knee-high black boots, and Sara saw the flash of a gun low on his hip. He turned, saw her, and gave her a very direct, slow head-to-toe look that came back up and lingered on her face.

She felt a sudden rush of heat as goosebumps formed on her skin. This was quickly followed by a lightning flash of fear. This man radiated danger.

"Hello, darling." The man and Sara both turned to Novella Adison.

"I thought you'd never get here," Novella said. The man hooked his arm around Novella's waist, and they walked away, both sheltered by the umbrella. They were followed by the limping man in the bowler hat.

Late that afternoon Ellie dropped by the store after her classes to restock her flour and honey supplies. "I know we ladies are not supposed to even know there's a Boggy Bayou," she whispered, "much less what must go on there, but I just heard that today's stage brought a notorious gambler who shot a man in Mississippi and is on the run. A parent of one of my students recognized him."

"Really? What's his name?" Sara asked.

"Jack Black, but I was told that in the gambling houses they call him 'Devil Jack Black.'" Ellie shuddered.

Well, the madame and the gambler.

Sara was not sure where the idea came from, but talk turned to having a Dallas County fair. A planning committee was formed. When Ira Webster approached Sara about joining the committee, she thought of Sarah Cockrell's behind-the-scenes philosophy. Sara suggested Daniel could represent the store.

Daniel was pleased but hesitant. "I've never been on a committee. I wouldn't be sure what to do."

"Daniel, you're smart and you've made good suggestions and solved problems here at the store. If you like, we can discuss ideas for the fair before the first meeting."

After the first committee meeting, Daniel bounced back into the store full of enthusiasm. He was hardly in the door before reporting. "The Cockrell representative immediately volunteered use of empty land on the eastern edge of town for the fairgrounds, you know, at the intersection of Commerce Street and the Preston Road. There's also space there for a campground for those coming from outside of town. The sawmill manager agreed to donate sawdust to cover as much of the fairgrounds as possible to keep down the mud or dust, whichever it might be. The committee also voted to collect money from local merchants for canvas cloth, and Ira Webster agreed the saddle shop would make a tent for exhibits."

"So it was a good meeting?" Sara could guess his answer, based on his obvious excitement.

"Yep. We already decided on the categories for competition. We'll have a livestock competition with prizes for the biggest hog, prize bull, and strongest ox. Ladies can enter their best pies, cakes, and biscuits in baking competitions. We set up a subcommittee to choose judges from around the county for each competition.

"We'll meet again in a few days to agree on a list of exhibits and activities. Can we talk about some ideas before then?"

"We can."

As the county-fair planning meetings continued, Daniel came back with frequent reports. The committee agreed that exhibits for ladies would include needlework, carpets, quilts, and shawls. Plows and tools would be exhibited for the men. One exhibit table would hold the most unusual insects that Ellie's class had collected and Mr. Reverchon had mounted.

The list of activities kept growing. There would be music, a demonstration from the dance club established by Edouard Charles Beaulieu, and a Maypole. Gerard Fave had agreed to try to make a wooden merry-go-round for the children, who would also be offered pony rides. The big event on the first day would be a potluck picnic supper featuring a roast bison cooked by the T-Lazy-R Ranch cow chasers. Supper would be followed by demonstrations of roping and horsemanship featuring the ranch's Mexican vaqueros and cow chasers Jellie and Zollie. A jousting tournament would end the riding demonstrations.

Benjamin asked Sara to order two flagpoles, one large US flag, and a Texas flag of equal size, all paid for by the cotton brokerage. Adolph Gouhenant offered to make a large "Dallas County Fair" banner. With Sarah's permission, Daniel agreed the store would pay for two large poles to support the banner. Not to be outdone, Virgil West volunteered to provide the prize ribbons.

It was to be a four-day event. Spring dates were set, with alternate rain dates agreed upon.

Two days before the county fair opened, wagons full of families began to arrive. Others came on horseback, a few on mules. The camp area filled up and, by the first day of the fair, had spilled over to the very edge of town.

On opening day, Dallas woke to warm weather and a cloudless sky. At the appointed time, the Dallas mayor and five district commissioners stood by as district clerk Edward Browder cut the entrance ribbon. The politicians were almost trampled by the excited crowd.

Benjamin had asked Sara if he could escort her to the fair, and they stood back from the entrance watching as the crowd flooded the fairgrounds. "Where would you like to go first, assuming you are willing to risk life and limb in that crowd?"

"Let's go see Gerard's wooden merry-go-round. Ellie told me he was proud of how it turned out. We'll also be less likely to be trampled by children than excited adults." Sara was right; most of the children had not yet discovered the merry-go-round. Several small children were riding, with one small boy working hard to push.

"Climb on," Benjamin told Sara. "I'll push." Sara sat on the merry-go-round, tucking the skirt of her calico dress beneath her legs and holding her straw hat in her lap. Benjamin began to push. The children screamed in delight as they twirled round and round. Sara watched Benjamin's face and saw delight there as well. When she was too dizzy to continue, she shouted over the children's laughter, "Enough for me, my head is swimming!"

"Oh no," Benjamin laughed, "you're good for just a few more rounds." When he did stop, Sara stumbled off dizzily and fell into Benjamin's arms. Laughing, face-to-face, they both froze. Looking into each other's eyes, Sara thought for a moment that he was going to kiss her and realized that she wished he would. He shifted his hands to her waist, straightened her up, and held her briefly until she was steady on the ground. "Well," he said, "Gerard's merry-go-round certainly works."

Visiting the baking competition, they were pleased to see that Hattie's biscuits had won a blue ribbon and Mr. Baker had a blue as well for his mixed-berry cake.

They circled through the tool section of the tent, trying to guess what purpose a strange tool some farmer had invented might serve. They made a point to stop by the table with the insect display. Mr. Reverchon was there. "Ah, Mrs. Darnell, thank you for the introduction to Miss Duffield. These insects are the result of the collection expedition I made with her class. Most enjoyable and productive." Sara was pleased to see the sign on the table read "Insect Exhibit provided by Duffield School for ages six to twelve. Tuition $1.60, monthly. Goose-quill pens and schoolbooks provided. Quarterly science expeditions led by Mr. Julien Reverchon, naturalist." While Benjamin admired the bugs, Sara told Reverchon that Ellie Duffield believed the class had benefited from his expedition. They left Reverchon beaming with pleasure as several children, leading parents by the hand, converged on the table.

Moving outside to the livestock, they were amazed by the biggest hogs they'd ever seen and noted that the Thornton farm had won first place for the biggest hog. No surprise that the T-Lazy-R Ranch had won blue for its longhorn bull. The ox competition consisted of a sled upon which barrels of rocks were piled. An ox was hitched to the sled, and barrels were removed until the ox could pull the sled. The number of barrels removed was then counted and tallied. The fewer barrels removed, the better the score. Each ox had its turn. When all was said and done, the winners would be announced. The competition was still going strong when Sara and Benjamin tired of it and moved on.

As the afternoon progressed, children and young women from Edouard Charles Beaulieu's dance classes performed a dance around a flower-bedecked Maypole, with proud parents watching. The May dance was performed several times in the afternoon with different Beaulieu dance classes. Sara thought it was charming.

They visited briefly and shared comments about the exhibits with John Henry, Cecilia, Whit, and Emmeline. They waved at Ellie and Gerard, shouting at Gerard, "We love your merry-go-round!"

Making their way over to the picnic area, they found the Wensel twins busy with the bison barbecue. Sara and Benjamin had both wondered aloud how Jellie and Zollie could cook enough for this crowd and were surprised to see no spits with roasting buffalo. Benjamin frowned. "Are you not cooking a bison?"

"We had hoped to see how you cooked it," Sara said.

Zollie explained, "Heck . . . oh, sorry ma'm. We knew we couldn't cook enough today for all the folks, so we started early yesterday. We had already made two giant spits. That was the hardest part. One spit was for a small four-hundred-pound bison, another for an eight-hundred-pound steer. Figured we'd need all that meat."

"That's a lot of meat," Benjamin said.

"You'll be surprised how fast it goes. Anyways, under each spit we built two fires, with some space in between. Tried to line up the fires with the front and hindquarters of each animal. The tender center cooks without fire right below it. Just before they was done, we heaped wood coals between the two fires to finish off the center of the meat. The whole time it cooked, we mopped it again and again with a mixture of rendered beef fat, sugar, salt, and water. Jellie and I had mop duty."

Jellie said, "We did a lotta moppin'. Just before the meat was finished, we added a bottle of John Henry's good whiskey to the moppin' sauce. He says the alcohol burns away, just leaving a good flavor."

Benjamin grinned. "Take any nips of that good whiskey?"

Jellie looked a bit sheepish. "Uh . . . uh . . . only enough to make sure it was good."

Benjamin spotted several rows of large, metal buckets beside a cloth-covered table. "Is the meat in those buckets?"

Jellie said, "Yep, when the meat was done, we let it cool a bit, cut it off the bone, chopped it, and filled the buckets with it. Worked most of the night. Today we're adding a special sauce to the chopped meat, heating it, and serving it up."

Sara could smell the smoky aroma of meat cooking. "It certainly smells like something is roasting."

"Smells good, don't it? Mrs. Wainwright suggested we roast a couple of pigs here today so the smell of cooking would add atmosphere to the barbecue. Our vaqueros, Juan and Carlos, done this many times in Mexico, and we learned a lot from them. They were the chief cooks. Me and Zollie just did what we was told. Mrs. Wainwright stood by and translated when we needed her."

Benjamin inhaled deeply. "People can follow their noses to the food. It smells so good you may have a stampede of hungry fairgoers."

Jellie laughed. "Don't worry. We know how to handle stampedes."

Zollie jumped in to add, "Heck yeah, we'll round 'em up and line 'em up."

Zollie gave them samples of both meats. "The beef's my favorite, there's enough fat to make it real tasty." The bison was salty, a bit gamey, and delicious. The beef was tender and so moist they had to use Benjamin's handkerchief to wipe their chins. Like Zollie, they liked the beef best. Thanking both men and telling them they would be back for more at suppertime, they looked for a cool place to sit down.

There was a cluster of big, old oak trees at the edge of the fairground. The stately trees had large branches that curved to the ground, creating a sheltered room between the huge trunk and the branches' edges. Stepping between the low branches and into the shade, the two sat on the ground. Benjamin leaned over and drew Sara close to him.

Sara didn't resist as he tipped her chin up and gave her a long, lingering kiss. Sara melted into his arms. Pulling back, leaving Sara breathless, he said, "You have no idea how long I've wanted to do that." He kissed her again urgently, and she put her arms around him and kissed him back.

Suddenly a little kid burst between the branches, startling them. He put his finger to his lips. "Shhh," he hissed. "Hide-and-seek." Sara stifled a giggle. Benjamin grinned and whispered, "How romantic." Leaving the little boy to his hiding place, they slipped out hand in hand.

As they walked toward the picnic area, they saw Gerard and Ellie. "Your wooden merry-go-round works like a charm," Benjamin told Gerard. "How did you make it?"

"I used a . . . How do you say '*moyeu de roue*'?"

"Wheel hub?" Ellie suggested.

"Yes, wheel hub and big wagon wheel. Mounted the hub to a flat piece of metal the blacksmith made for me. Made a round, wooden platform and topped the wheel with it. Had the man who makes . . . how you say . . . uh, barrels add a metal hoop around the edge to make it strong. Used the axle to make the center pole. Buried a big rock, mounted the hub to it, and attached the platform. Added some wooden posts to hang on to and, *voilà*, *un manège*. The merry-go-round."

"I think I followed all that," Benjamin said. "At any rate, it is very clever."

"*Merci.*"

They filled their plates at the picnic with an assortment of potluck dishes, from carrot pickles to pecan pie. Sara couldn't tell you what she ate, and the truly amazing demonstration of rope tricks, calf roping, and even bronc riding by the T-Lazy-R Ranch's cow chasers was lost on her. For her the fair was successful for other reasons.

After the fair Hattie and Aaron walked with Benjamin to deliver Sara home safely. The older couple waited in the dirt street while Benjamin took her to the stairway door, leaned down, and gently kissed her. "Good night, sweet dreams," and he was gone.

Sarah climbed the stairs and paused before pulling out her key. *Benjamin's kiss took my breath away. But is it love?*

A few days after the fair John Henry, Whit, and Emmeline came into the store to stock up on supplies and visit. While the men began to gather supplies, Emmeline and Sara caught up on their respective news. "Whit and I are going to have a baby sometime this winter," Emmeline confided with a shy smile.

"That's wonderful." *A baby!* Sara was genuinely pleased for them. She had grown to like Emmeline, and Sara looked forward to her visits to the store.

"My father is sending my niñera to me from his ranch."

"Your 'niñera'?" Sara had no idea what a niñera might be.

"I'm sorry, niñera is Spanish for 'nanny'. She was with me from the time I was tiny. My mother died young and Niñera Maria was a mother to me. She is one of the family. It was hard to leave her. And now she will help me with my own baby. I am so eager to see her."

Whit and John Henry reported that their fourth herd of steers was already on its way to market with the Wensels and the three Mexican vaqueros recruited in San Antonio. "We've discovered that we need to learn some Spanish to ranch in Texas. Emmeline translates for us," Whit said proudly.

Whit and Emmeline walked out to the buckboard with their packages, but John Henry lingered. "Sara, I guess I am not too old or too hardened to fall in love. I want to propose to Cecilia. What do you think?"

Sara thought about Cecilia telling her she wouldn't settle for someone she didn't love as much as she had loved her fiancé. "I think she'd be foolish to say no."

"I've been expanding the ranch house in hopes she'll say yes. Do you think she'd be willing to marry an old ranger and be a ranch wife?" John Henry asked softly, with the nervous frown that crinkled his eyes.

"First of all, you are not that old or hardened. Cecilia has spent years helping at her sister and brother-in-law's farm, so I suspect life on a ranch can't be too different. Emmeline tells me there's a baby on the way and a nanny coming. Your household is certainly growing. A wonderful woman like Cecilia as a wife would round out your family nicely. Most important, you both deserve some happiness. Ask her. I'll pray for a ranch wedding soon."

John Henry took a deep breath, sighed, and quietly said, "Thank you."

Sara looked at her calendar. It had been three years since she'd arrived in Dallas, in the summer of 1856, and it was time to pay the fees for the 320 acres Alexander Cockrell had set aside for her, a promise Sarah Cockrell had pledged to honor.

Sara had saved enough money to pay the necessary surveying and recording fees and to build the required cabin on the land. She breathed a deep sigh. While it would reduce her savings, what remained—she hoped—would be adequate for her business. The store continued to be profitable. The rent from the ground floor of the two-story building that had become her home helped pay for her lease on the building. Barring some unexpected crisis, she could continue to save. She was already a depositor at Benjamin's company. Her money, she had decided, would be more secure in the safe than hidden in the store or at home.

Sarah Cockrell was pacing beside her desk, with a frown on her face, when Sara was led into her office.

"Is everything all right?" Sara asked. "Would you prefer I come back later?"

"Give me just a minute to calm down, Sara. I've just had disturbing news." Sarah Cockrell took a deep breath. "An absolutely wicked woman has come to Dallas. I don't know her intentions, but they will not be good. She is a notorious madame named Novella Adison who presents herself as a refined lady; however, she is anything but. Not only does she run gambling establishments and houses of ill repute, she blackmails her customers."

"Blackmails?" Sara's eyes widened.

"Yes. Her objective is to buy up as much real estate in a town as possible. She blackmails some people into selling and also overpays to buy the businesses of those she feels might have enough influence to hinder her."

How could I be so naive? I was taken in by her story of running an honest brothel and even gave her information and referrals. I'm too embarrassed to admit it to Sarah.

"With enough ownership, she and her partner, a gambler rightly named Devil Jack Black, end up running the town. He has already arrived here by stage. By the time they finish, the town is a hellhole of drinking, gambling, and prostitution. They invite in outlaws and other desperate men, so it becomes a haven for criminals. The good citizens must live in an environment of crime or flee. Honest businesses are driven out of town. They've done this already in a Kansas town."

"That's terrible. You believe they want to do that here?"

"Yes, but we can't let that happen. I'm not sure how to stop it, if that's their intent—and I believe it is. Apparently Novella Adison quickly worms her way into the good graces of a few businesspeople and, at first, they turn a blind eye to her illegal ventures. She has already established her first house of ill repute in Boggy Bayou. Heaven only knows what's next."

"Oh my!" Sara remembered the fearful reaction she had to Jack Black. So, the two of them work together. *Would there be a future price to pay for the gift of a ball gown?*

Confiding her concerns about Novella Adison and Devil Jack Black had calmed Sarah Cockrell. She smiled, shook her head, and said, "Enough about that. We have some pleasant business to take care of, don't we?"

The two women sat at Mrs. Cockrell's desk. Between them was Sara's stack of gold coins and a small pile of Mills' Money. Looking at the map, Sarah Cockrell pointed at a plot with Sara's name on it. "This is the land you chose three summers ago. There are other plots available, if you wish to make a change. Or you can choose two town lots of the equivalent value. Do you know what you want to do?"

"My thought was to locate my land adjacent to one or two of the farms planting cotton, then negotiate with the farmers to plant on my land and pay me a share of the profits. That way I have some revenue from my acreage, and I meet the land-grant requirement of having at least fifteen acres under cultivation. Or I could allow a settler with no land to settle on mine with a crop-sharing arrangement. The possibility of having town lots instead hadn't occurred to me. Those could also be revenue generating, I suppose." Sara bit her lip. "What's your opinion?"

"It depends upon your objectives. In the short term, I think the town lots might be to your advantage if you could afford to build on them. You could then lease them like you've done with the new cotton brokerage. Dallas is growing and the availability of empty, completed buildings is limited. The stream of money would be monthly rather than once a year. Also, you wouldn't have the risk of crop failure. You would incur up-front building expenses and it might take a while to pay those off, assuming you had to borrow the money to build."

"I couldn't build without going into debt, but I see how owning town lots might make sense."

"In the longer term, if you chose 320 acres very close to town, at some point your acreage most likely would become part of the town, and you could divide your land into many more town lots. The money you can afford to invest and the time you are willing to wait for profits are things to consider as you decide. If you want to think about it for a few days, that's fine."

Sara nodded. "I'd like a few days to think. This decision is a big financial one for me. I don't want to make it lightly."

Sarah Cockrell agreed that time to think about it was important. She began to scoop the gold coins and bank notes Sara had given her into a small drawstring bag. As Sarah Cockrell drew the drawstring tight, Sara asked, "Will you deposit your money with Benjamin Brown's new business?"

Sarah Cockrell looked up and smiled. "No, I have my own safe, but the fewer people that know that, the better."

"My lips are sealed," Sara promised.

That evening Sara visited Hattie and Aaron's house and asked Benjamin's advice about the choice of land. His comments were much like Sarah Cockrell's. Either choice could pay off. The issue to answer was her goals as a landowner? Only she could answer that.

Walking Sara home down the dark street to the bank building Benjamin told her that Gerard had expanded his cabin and made it a double. "Gerard has offered to rent one side to me for a reasonable amount. Think I'm going to accept the offer. Mom and Aaron would be happy for me to stay with them, but they need their privacy. Living there, I feel like I'm imposing on their new life together."

That night Sara focused her thoughts on making the decision between acreage or a town lot. Finally, she decided to choose the long-term alternative and select acreage that could be cultivated now with the possibility of becoming part of the town in the future. The decision made, she went to bed and dreamed of riding the merry-go-round with Benjamin. She slept with a smile on her face.

The next day Sara and Mrs. Cockrell poured over the map of the Dallas colony. Mrs. Cockrell had retained ownership of long swaths of land along the borders of the existing town. Sara chose a plot adjacent to the narrowest strip of Cockrell land. "As the town grows, this land should grow in value. For now, it should be prime cotton farmland. What do you think?"

"A good choice," Sarah Cockrell said.

A week later, a breathless Cecilia burst into the store. "I've run all the way, Sara. Just had to tell you." She paused to catch her breath. "John Henry has finally asked me to marry him. My goodness, the man took his time."

"Oh, Cecilia!" Sara hugged her friend. "I'm so pleased for you both. He was slow because he wasn't sure you'd say yes."

Cecilia looked at her with surprise. "Then not only was he slow to act he must have a ten-dollar hat on a ten-cent brain. I did everything but ask him myself!" They both laughed.

Daniel peered around the corner of a shelf. "Mr. Adams is a smart man if he asked you to marry him, Miss Stewart."

Cecilia smiled. "Thank you, Daniel."

"We've set the wedding for three weeks away when the traveling preacher comes. We saw no reason to wait longer. John Henry wants to wed at the ranch and then have a barbecue for our friends. Nothing fancy. Emmeline offered me her dress, but I plan on wearing a new calico dress suitable for a rancher's wife. Whit and Emmeline seem pleased about the marriage. Emmeline did the sweetest thing, she asked if when her baby comes he or she could call me grandma. I told her I'd be flattered." Cecilia paused, then said, "Sara, remember when I told you I didn't want to settle for someone I didn't love as much as my former fiancé? Well I'm not settling. I love John Henry deeply."

Sara took Cecilia's hands in hers. "I wish you the greatest happiness, dear friend."

On a bright, sunny Sunday just three weeks later, Cecilia and John Henry were ready to pledge their vows, surrounded by a close circle of friends. The T-Lazy-R ranch house was decorated with wildflowers for the occasion. "I don't think there's an Indian paintbrush left within a mile of here," Emmeline said when Sara arrived early to help prepare for the ceremony. "I picked armloads of them yesterday."

Looking around, Sara saw pitchers, vases, and even cups full of the bright, red-and-yellow blooms. "Aren't they pretty! How can I help?"

"Whit and the men have gathered every chair on the ranch and set them up in rows here in the main room for the ceremony. The ladies can sit, and men can stand against the wall. After the ceremony, we'll clear the chairs for dancing. In the afternoon, we'll have dinner on the porch, buffet style. People will have to find places to sit or just juggle their plates. I'll need your help putting the food out. In the meantime, I know Cecilia would like your help getting ready."

Sara found Cecilia in a robe in one of the ranch-house bedrooms. "Good morning to the bride!" Sara said. "How are you feeling this morning?"

"Excited and a bit nervous. Sara, I never thought I'd be marrying. Then I met John Henry and look what happened—I fell in love."

"Today you'll be Mrs. John Henry Adams. I'm so happy for you. He's a fine man, Cecilia."

Cecilia nodded. "That he is."

"How can I help you get ready?"

"My dress buttons up the back. I need help with the buttons. I want to wear my mother's gold locket. It has a tricky fastener that I can't do myself."

There were several crinolines piled on the bed. Sara gestured toward them. "Let's start with these." Once the petticoats were on, Sara helped Cecilia slide her new calico dress over her head and buttoned the buttons. Cecilia had already braided her hair and wound it into a complex pattern of braids pinned on the top and back of her head.

"Your hair looks amazing," Sara said.

"Thank you, I think I'm ready for the locket." She handed Sara an oval locket with a large garnet set in its center. "My mother wore this at her wedding."

Sara positioned the chain and hooked the clasp. "I suspect she'd be thrilled to know you're wearing it for yours. There. You look lovely."

They could hear the sounds of talking coming from the main room and then guitar music filled the ranch house. "We asked the ranch's vaqueros to provide the music for us," Cecilia said, then she laughed. "Not much about this wedding is traditional. We wanted a Texas ranch wedding."

Emmeline poked her head in the door. "About ready?"

"Yes," Cecilia said.

Cecilia's brother-in-law, Michael Butler, was standing outside the door, dressed in a white shirt, thin tie, and pressed, denim pants. His brown hair was slicked back and his shoes polished. "Ready to walk down the aisle, Cecilia? No cold feet?"

"No cold feet, Michael. I'm ready."

Sara kissed her friend's cheek and hurriedly slipped away to find a seat.

Whit and Cecilia's sister, Effie, were standing up for the couple. They were waiting with John Henry and the preacher as Cecilia came down the aisle to the sounds of slow guitar music.

John Henry stood tall in a crisp white shirt, starched denim pants, and shiny new boots. Effie wore a new, full-skirted calico dress, and Wit's outfit echoed John Henry's.

A Texas ranch wedding! This may be the start of a new tradition.

The preacher declared them man and wife and John Henry kissed the bride. The vaqueros, Juan and Carlos, in full Mexican attire, began to play livelier music. As friends crowded around the newlyweds with warm wishes, Jellie and Zollie cleared the chairs. The dancing began.

Benjamin found Sara and swept her into a quick-step waltz. "I'm not sure how else to dance to this lively music," he said.

She laughed. "I like it, but I suspect we'll be worn out pretty fast."

Whit was dancing with the bride when John Henry asked Sara to dance. As he led her through a waltz, he said, "Sara, thank you for encouraging me to propose to Cecilia. I've faced bullets and arrows, but I was more afraid of having her say no. You gave me the courage to ask her to marry me. Thank the good Lord she said yes!"

Sara grinned at him. "I suspect she was afraid you wouldn't ask her. I think you two are meant to be together."

"It sure feels right. I'm mighty happy."

As the dance came to an end, John Henry asked for everyone's attention. He went down on one knee in front of Cecilia and pledged to build her a proper stone-and-clapboard ranch house, with a covered porch and rocking chairs. Cecilia cried and kissed him, and everyone clapped.

Just past noon, Emmeline gestured to Sara, indicating she needed help in the kitchen. Happy to catch her breath after an hour of dancing and visiting, she excused herself from Benjamin and went to help with the food.

"Cecilia and John Henry asked for a typical ranch meal," Emmeline said. "The menu is barbecued beef, beans, cornbread, pickled vegetables, and peach cobbler for dessert. The peaches are fresh from Farmers Branch, just upriver. There's cider, beer, milk, and water to drink."

Sara helped carry plates, utensils, and full bowls and platters to the two tables, which were soon heaped with food. "We have more people than plates," Emmeline said. "We'll have to watch, and as people finish eating, if you'll gather the used plates, knives, and forks, then I'll wash them for the next round of folks to use. If we can feed them a dozen at a time it should work."

"I'll see if I can control the flow of people by inviting them to the buffet tables twelve at a time. If they have to wait, they can visit and dance," Sara said. "I'll keep the bowls and platters filled too. From the looks of the food, there's no danger of running out."

Sure enough, by two thirty all had been fed, leftovers carried back to the kitchen, and dishes done. Emmeline thanked Sara. "I would have been overwhelmed without you."

After eating the crowd began to thin. By three o'clock, Sara finally had a chance to visit with John Henry and Cecilia. "May I hug your groom?" Sara asked Cecilia.

"Oh, Sara, of course."

Sara gave John Henry a hug. "I am so happy for you. You're a lucky man." She stepped back. "I wish you both much happiness—no one deserves it more."

John Henry slid his arm around Cecilia's shoulders and pulled her closer. He smiled down at his new bride. "I can't imagine anything but happiness with this woman." Cecilia smiled back.

"The ranch wedding was perfect," Sara said, as she squeezed Cecilia's hands. With a final kiss on Cecilia's cheek, Sara told them goodbye.

As she stepped out on the porch, Benjamin saw her. "Aaron and Hattie are already in the borrowed wagon. If you're ready we'll head for town."

"I'm ready. What a lovely day and a wonderful wedding."

Sara and Daniel were taking inventory early one morning when two men stepped into the store. Sara set aside an armload of rope to greet them. The first man was slightly dusty, as if he'd come in off the trail. As he entered, he pulled off his wide-brimmed straw hat and ran a hand through a full head of light-brown hair threaded with gray. Even more gray was evident in his mustache and small, pointed beard. He wore black pants and a white shirt with a black tie. Standing straight and tall behind him was a muscular black man with wiry, short-cropped hair and alert eyes. He also wore black pants and a white shirt. His full, strong neck broadcast strength and stamina. It was obvious the shirt's top button would not close.

"Mrs. Darnell?" The first man spoke slowly, with a deep Southern accent. *Alabama or, perhaps, Georgia?*

"Yes. How can I help you?"

"My name is Watson, Henry Watson. I've just arrived from Alabama with my family and my slaves. Sold my cotton plantation back home, because I believe we will have a war of Yankee aggression and my livelihood will be at risk. I've been told Dallas is good cotton country."

"I believe it is."

"Texas will most likely be the Southern state farthest west and, one hopes, farthest from the fightin'. Should we have a war, cotton will finance the South. I believe many cotton planters will soon be following me to Texas."

Sara was uncertain what Henry Watson wanted. "Dallas is a fine place to be, Mr. Watson. Is there something I can help you find in the store?"

"I'm here to ask about your land. I plan to secure a 640-acre land grant, but my land needs are greater. I'm told you have 320 acres not yet under cultivation. Are you interested in leasin' your land for payment or perhaps for a share of the cotton crop? I have references and I assure you that you would be hard pressed to find a more successful planter as a tenant."

"I do want my land under cultivation, Mr. Watson, and I'm certainly willing to talk about it. Could we meet at my attorney Aaron Davis's office and see if we can agree on a lease?"

"Let me get my family settled at the St. Nicholas Hotel. Tomorrow I'll send Jonah, my overseer"—he gestured at the man behind him—"with a message as to when I could meet. I'm eager to finalize an agreement. It's already cotton-plantin' time. Is there a back door to the store?"

"A back door? Yes."

"Jonah will knock on the back door with my message and a list of the immediate supplies we need."

"He can come to the front door, Mr. Watson." Sara looked at Jonah. "The front door is fine."

"No," Watson spoke emphatically, making a horizontal slashing gesture with his hand. "People may resent a slave comin' to the front door. I'm concerned about his safety, and he will be safer comin' to the back door. Thank you, Mrs. Darnell. We will meet soon." With that, Watson and Jonah turned and were out the door.

Watson and Jonah were hardly gone before Ellie came dashing in. "Guess what I just saw? Bloomers! I've read about them but never seen them. Oh, Sara, you should see them."

She stopped to catch her breath and reposition her wire-rimmed glasses, which had slipped down her nose.

Attracted by the noise, Daniel had joined them from the storeroom.

Sara laughed. "Calm down, Ellie. Who was wearing bloomers?"

"A woman and two girls from the wagon train that rolled into town earlier today. I just saw them headed into the St. Nicholas Hotel."

Daniel frowned. "What are bloomers?"

Ellie was quick to reply. "Short skirts worn over pants. Oh, Daniel, you'll know them if you see them. The three of them were wearing bloomers with white stockings and high, laced boots. They look ever so practical. Oh—they had wide-brimmed straw hats too. Imagine being so fashionable on the trail!"

Sara thought about how hard it had been to keep her long, calico dresses clean on the trip to Dallas. "Bloomers do sound practical, Ellie. I hope I'll get to see them."

Daniel thought for a moment. "I hope I do too."

Ellie said a quick goodbye and was off to spread her benign bloomer gossip.

Early the next morning there was a knock at the back door. The slave Jonah stepped in and handed Daniel a note for Sara and a long list of needed supplies.

Daniel looked at the list. "It will take me awhile to pull all these things together. Do you want to wait or come back in about an hour?"

Jonah's voice was a deep rumble. "I'll be back for the supplies and to get Miz Darnell's answer to Mr. Watson's note."

Sara came from the front of the store, where she had heard the conversation. "I'm here, Jonah." Sara read the note Daniel handed her. "Please tell Mr. Watson that I'll meet him at Aaron Davis' office." Midafternoon, Sara walked across the square to Aaron's law office.

"What I propose is pretty straightforward," Watson told them. "For the use of Mrs. Darnell's 320 acres of land, I'll pay her with 30 percent of the resulting cotton bales."

Aaron asked, "All the land will be planted? And is she welcome to send a representative to view the picking, ginning, and baling, if she wishes?"

Watson nodded. "Yes to both questions. However, I'd ask for a half acre to be used for the construction of a log cabin for Jonah, my overseer. Course, I'd reimburse Mrs. Darnell for its construction. We can agree on the budget in advance."

Aaron looked at Sara. "Is that fine with you?"

"That's fine."

"I'll draw up the paperwork. You can both sign later today."

Following their meeting, Watson announced he was off to meet Benjamin Brown, the cotton broker.

The Solomon church had outgrown its building. Until it could be enlarged or replaced, services were being held in a large arbor built in a grove of live oak trees down by the river. The rustic pews were moved from the church into the arbor each Sunday and then moved back after the service. When Sara and Benjamin had arrived, he had taken off his jacket to help move the seating into place. He came back fanning himself with his hat. "It's hot today, but not as hot and humid as Galveston."

"Your momma told me you really like Galveston. Do you miss it?"

"In some ways, yes. In other ways, no. It's a bigger place, so there is more to do. I have relatives there and I miss them. Mostly, I miss the ocean. But the weather can be miserable, and the mosquitoes are awful."

"More mosquitos than here?"

"Yes, more and bigger! The joke in Galveston is that two mosquitoes were talking. One said, 'We better bite this man fast because when the big mosquitoes show up, they'll carry him off.'"

Sara rolled her eyes. "Your momma is the family storyteller, but you are the jokester."

Benjamin grinned, then turned serious. "I'm glad I'm here. I do like Galveston, but Dallas is growing fast, that means opportunity. Momma is here. And, Sara, you are here." Benjamin held Sara's gaze. Before she could collect her thoughts, the hymn singing began, stopping their conversation and sending them scurrying to their seats.

After the service the two returned to Hattie's for the midday meal. As the fried chicken was passed around the table, Hattie said, "Years ago I invited the first Methodist circuit preacher to the boardinghouse for dinner after church. I served fried chicken. Now, y'all know what is involved in fixin' chicken. I killed it, plucked it, disemboweled it, cut it, soaked it in salt water and then in buttermilk to make it tender, floured it, and fried it. That's a lot of work. It came out crispy and golden. A just about perfect Sunday dinner, I thought, until the preacher looked at his plate and announced he didn't like fried chicken. My thoughts were not very Christian. Seemed to me, after all my work, the charitable thing for him to have done was to have thanked me and eaten the chicken. Instead, he had corn bread, pickled green beans, and two pieces of peach pie. Seems my invitation to dinner went to the only man in Texas who didn't like fried chicken."

Benjamin shook his head. "No problem with fried chicken today, Momma." He, Aaron, and Sara each took a second piece.

Sitting together in the upholstered chairs after their meal, while Hattie and Aaron napped upstairs, Sara told Benjamin about her sharecropping agreement with Henry Watson.

Benjamin grinned. "You are full of surprises, Sara. Guess you'll need a cotton-broker to handle your thirty percent of the crop. Do you know a good one?"

"I thought I might talk to my neighbor downstairs. I understand he's in the cotton-brokerage business."

Benjamin laughed, then turned more serious. Leaning forward in his chair he took Sara's hand. "Sara, I'm hopeful I can make a success of the brokerage business and build a life here. I know we haven't known each other long. But please consider whether you would share that life with me as my wife. You don't have to answer me now. But I'll ask again."

Sara didn't understand her own emotions. *Do I love Benjamin, or am I just lonely? I need to be sure.*

Sara nodded and softly said, "It has only been three years since Morgan died. I'm not ready to make a commitment, Benjamin."

Benjamin reached over and squeezed Sara's hand. "I can wait."

Sometime later, John Henry arrived at the store with a special request. "Sara, we are runnin' out of plates and cups at the ranch. It's about reached the point where we're gonna have to eat every meal in shifts."

Sara chuckled. "That wouldn't be good."

"Sure wouldn't. I want to surprise Cecilia with a big, new set of dishes. Just not sure what all it should include. I know I might have to get you to order it, I just don't know what to order. Know more about tin cups than china. I need your help."

"Come with me." Sara led John Henry to the tableware shelf. "I have plates, cups, soup bowls, serving bowls and platters. If you want enough for family and staff, I'd say a set of twelve with two or three each of serving bowls and platters. We just received a new shipment, so I have enough pieces for you."

John Henry scanned the shelf. "Two different kinds?"

"Yes." Holding up a cream-colored cup, Sara said, "This is creamware, also known as queensware. Pretty cream color." Reaching for another cup, Sara held it up beside the first. "This one is ironstone. It's whiter, stronger. Doesn't chip easily." She put a cup in each of his hands.

"Ironstone's a bit heavier, but the queensware is mighty pretty," John Henry said. "What's your opinion?"

"For a working ranch with lots of people using the dishes in multiple settings, I'd say ironstone."

"Then ironstone it is," John Henry said. "A set for twelve with serving pieces just like you suggested."

"I think Cecilia will be thrilled. Let me ask Daniel to wrap all the pieces and box them for you so they don't break on the way home. You came in the ranch wagon, right?"

"Sure did."

"Good. Let me get Daniel started and then I need some advice from you."

As Daniel began wrapping, Sara turned to John Henry. "Let's go for a walk." Stepping out the back door, the heat of the day greeted them. The air was hot and still and smelled of dust. Sara and John Henry turned toward the river.

"What can I help you with, Sara?" John Henry swatted at a mosquito.

"Benjamin has asked me to marry him, but John Henry, I'm afraid."

"Afraid another marriage would turn out like your first?"

"Yes. I loved the man I thought Morgan was. Turned out there were two Morgans, and the second Morgan broke my heart."

"Do you love Benjamin?"

"I think I do."

"Sara, thinking you do isn't enough. You have to be absolutely certain, with no hesitation, no doubts. Sounds like your fear of making' a mistake is holdin' you back. Take your time. If Benjamin loves you he'll wait."

"Do you really think he will?"

"If he loves you. Get to know him better. Over time his words and actions will reveal the man he is. If he is the man you hope he is you'll know if you love him . . . or not. Be patient. You might even let him know you've been disappointed once and you need to be more than certain this time."

On the following Sunday after lunch, Benjamin and Sara pulled two of the wooden chairs from Hattie's table into the shade behind the boardinghouse. As they sat in the cooling breeze, Sara confessed to never having seen the ocean. "You told me you missed the ocean, Benjamin. I've seen paintings of it but can't imagine what it is really like."

"The ocean is different from one day to the next, Sara. When I lived in Galveston, much of my spare time was spent on the beach. This may sound silly, but when I was younger, I'd splash through the surf—barefooted, with pant legs rolled up to my knees—and imagine that I was the god of the waves who had stilled the sea with my conch-shell trumpet."

"God of the waves? Hmm, ambitious little boy."

"I guess. As an adult, I still spent lots of time on the beach. Some days the ocean is calm and blue. Small waves slide across the sand depositing seashells and sending tiny sand crabs scurrying into their holes. Other days, the ocean can be an angry, gray mass of giant, foaming waves that roar onto the beach as if they want to eat the land. You can feel its power. Add the changing skies and every day at the beach is different and beautiful in its own way."

Sara smiled at the watery images Benjamin had conjured up for her. "I didn't imagine you to be so poetic."

"The ocean makes most everyone poetic, Sara. I hope someday you can experience it for yourself."

"I hope so too."

Whit and an obviously pregnant Emmeline were standing in front of the store waiting for the stagecoach to arrive. Emmeline was so excited she couldn't stand still. Sara had stepped out to say hello. "My Niñera Maria will be on the stage," Emmeline said. "Listen, I hear the whip's trumpet. Here it comes!" Sure enough the stage turned onto the square and stopped just past Sara's store. The first passenger to climb down from the stage was a man who turned to lift a tiny lady out. Sara's first thought was that she looked like a little, round, dried prune. Her face was so wrinkled that her eyes were almost lost. The braids that coiled around her ears were as gray as they were brown. When she saw Emmeline, the smile that appeared transformed her into something beautiful.

"*Mi niña hermosa*," she cried and opened her arms to Emmeline, who had tears streaming down her face.

"Niñera Maria, I have missed you!" Emmeline was still crying.

When the two had calmed down, Emmeline led the tiny woman to Sara and said, "This is my Nanny Maria." Emmeline shared a few Spanish words with Nanny Maria, who then grabbed Sara in a strong hug and smiled up at her, shaking her head yes. In the meanwhile, Whit had been unloading Nanny Maria's traveling bag, boxes, and trunks from the stage and was beginning to pack them in the buckboard. Nanny Maria chattered to Emmeline, who turned to Sara and said, "She says she has brought me many things for the baby."

Whit put the last box in the buckboard. "Honey, we'd best be off if we want to be at the ranch by dark."

They told Sara goodbye as Nanny Maria continued to talk to Emmeline. As they left, Nanny Maria pulled her shawl around her shoulders, turned, waved, and said, "Bye-bye."

A few days later, Sarah Cockrell came into the store and asked, "Can we speak privately?" Sara led the way into the storeroom and closed the door. "I'm afraid this thing with Novella Adison has started. Two of our city aldermen have already sold their properties to her and are leaving town. Two other businessmen are considering selling, based on offers that are higher than the true value of their businesses. I understand they will stay and work with her."

"It does sound like she's trying to take control."

"Yes, and she's moving much faster than I thought she would to try to gain control and power in Dallas. I am at a loss as to how to stop her. I have an informer in her organization who tells me Miss Adison has already done this in Kansas. The town she targeted has gone from a nice town to a hotbed of gambling, drinking, violence, and crime. All very profitable for her and for Devil Jack Black. Not good for the citizens. I came to see what, if anything, you've heard about their recent activities."

"Oh my, I haven't heard anything," Sara said, "but I'll keep my ears open."

"I'll do some shopping now. It's wise for me to leave with packages and I do need several things. Thank you, Sara. Remember we need to be discreet. I believe this couple can be dangerous." Sarah Cockrell slipped out of the storeroom to begin her shopping.

Sara realized Novella Adison's activities were a serious threat to her own mercantile store. With Novella and Devil Jack Black running the town, its character would change. Good people would leave, and a lawless community would be no place to run a legitimate business, especially for a woman. Stopping them was important to the town and to her own future.

Later that week, Novella Adison swept into the store. "Mrs. Darnell—or may I call you Sara?"

She didn't wait for an answer. "I have important business to discuss with you. I've engaged a private room at The Crutchfield House Hotel for lunch at noon. Will you join me? I've arranged it so no one need see us together."

Sara said, "Yes, of course." *I need to know what she's up to.*

"Good, I'll see you then. Please come in the side door," Novella said over her shoulder and swept out.

Sara took off her black store apron, folded it, straightened her skirts, put her bonnet on, and crossed over to old man Crutchfield's hotel. *I wonder if she wants to buy the store.*

As she entered the side door, a gruff-looking man with a jagged scar running from the side of his mouth up to the corner of his eye said, "This way, please." Sara knew she hadn't seen him before. As he walked her down a hallway, his unbuttoned coat flapped open enough for Sara to see a holstered gun.

He led her down the hall and opened the door to a small, private room with a table and several chairs. The table was set for two and Novella Adison was already seated. "Sara, thank you for joining me. I've taken the liberty of ordering for us so we can get to business quickly. I hope you like chicken."

"I do, thank you." Sara no sooner had said the words than a waiter arrived and set a plate of roast chicken and fresh, sliced tomatoes in front of her. Water poured, he disappeared through a door.

"I'm sure you are curious as to why I wanted to speak with you." Novella Adison gestured as if she had forgotten something. "Before I tell you, how did the lavender-satin ball gown work out?"

Here comes the price for the gown. "It was lovely. I've been remiss in not returning it promptly, but I was unsure where to send it."

"No, no, dear, I intended for you to keep it. I'm sure there will be other balls in your future. What I wish to talk about is buying your business." Novella took a dainty bite of chicken. Sara imagined she saw sharp teeth.

"My business is only three years old and I've never thought of selling it. The store was a dream my late husband and I shared," Sara said.

"But if the price were right . . . ?" More sharp teeth.

"No, it's not about money." Sara tasted the chicken.

"Not even for four times your total sales in the past twelve months?" The red of the sliced tomato stained the plate.

"No, not even. I appreciate your interest, but I enjoy my business. I'm young and plan to be a storekeeper for a long time. Why not speak with Mr. Virgil West? He has a successful operation, has been at it longer, and might have an interest in selling." Sara took a bite of tomato.

"I have already negotiated a transaction with Mr. West." Novella Adison sipped her water.

"Why would you want two stores?" Sara asked, surprised.

"It would give me a monopoly—as simple as that."

"I see."

"Would you sell me the 320 acres you own near the town? I'll pay you fair value plus 50 percent." Novella Adison put down her fork and leaned toward Sara, waiting for her response.

"That purchase is my long-term investment. I hope to have cotton crops on the acreage in the short term and have very profitable property when Dallas has grown to encompass it. It is not for sale either."

The atmosphere in the room became less cordial.

"So, I can't convince you to sell to me?" Novella Adison asked slowly, in a low voice.

Sara lowered her tone of voice. "No, neither property is for sale. But I appreciate your interest." They continued eating but with very little conversation. Novella Adison seemed lost in thought.

"I have another question," she said, as Sara took her last bite of lunch. "Would you come to work for me? Not in Boggy Bayou, certainly not. I could use a good assistant and would pay you very, very well. I'd set up a downtown office for you. The young man in your store seems capable of running it with a bit of oversight from you. You would manage my calendar, negotiate with vendors, arrange leases, and generally assist me with business matters. Could you do that?"

Sara was flummoxed for a moment. "Work as your assistant? I'm flattered that you think I could do the job, but no, I'm really content with my store."

"These are your final answers?" Novella Adison asked, rising from the chair.

"Yes," Sara answered firmly, rising as well. "Thank you for lunch."

"Well, I hope you won't regret it," Novella Adison said with almost a sneer.

For a moment, Sara thought she meant the chicken.

That night Sara thought about her encounter with Novella Adison. *There will be repercussions.* Novella didn't like being told no and had resources which could harm Sara and her business. Sara's night was sleepless.

The next morning Sara arrived at the store to find Daniel standing in the storeroom, up to his ankles in scattered merchandise. Everything had been swept off the storeroom shelves. Shipping boxes had been torn open and merchandise scattered. A bag of flour had been torn open and flour spread over everything. "The back door was ajar and I found this when I came in," he said. "Why in the dickens would someone do this?"

"Why in the dickens is right! Let's get to work cleaning it up." She and Daniel spent all morning reorganizing the storeroom. Fortunately there was little real damage to merchandise. It was still irritating and frightening. Sara was sure it was a result of saying no to Novella Adison. Concerned that the vandalism might be a warning of something more serious to come, Sara asked Daniel to put an extra bolt on the inside of both doors. "Just to be doubly safe," she told him, "we need to lock and bolt the back door at night. If we are here after hours, we should use the bolt on the front door as well."

As they locked up that night, Sara told Daniel, "I'm going to visit Sarah Cockrell in the morning on business, so I'll be a bit late."

The next day she was at Sarah Cockrell's office first thing with a bag of Mr. Baker's pastries. The news she had to share would not be good, she thought, but the pastries would be. Mrs. Cockrell's assistant led her into the office. "Sara," Mrs. Cockrell stood up, "what a nice surprise."

"I had an unexpected lunch invitation from Novella Adison day before yesterday," Sara said, "and I want to tell you about it."

Over tea and pastries, Sara discussed, in detail, her conversation with Novella Adison, including the fact that Mr. West had apparently contracted to sell his business. She also disclosed the vandalism at her store.

Sarah Cockrell was distressed. "We need to do something, I'm just not sure what."

"I might have an idea," Sara said. "The gossip is that Devil Jack Black is wanted for killing a man over cards. Can your informant find out the details, especially where it happened and who wants him?"

"Yes, I can ask."

"If he is wanted and Novella Adison is hiding him in Dallas, is she breaking the law? Maybe she was involved somehow in the killing? If we can get this information, and if Novella has broken the law, apart from running gambling halls and houses of ill repute—especially if she was an accomplice in the killing, maybe we could turn them in to the Pinkerton National Detective Agency. They bill themselves as a private, national, crime-fighting organization. For a fee, Pinkerton could arrest them and deliver them to the authorities. Hopefully they'd both end up in jail somewhere other than Texas. Let's see if we can put them away!"

"An interesting idea." Sarah Cockrell rubbed her chin thoughtfully. "The new Pinkerton Agency has already made a reputation pursuing outlaws and criminals successfully. The question is, could our rascals buy their way out of trouble with corrupt lawmen or judges. And then what?"

Sarah Cockrell paused and thought again. "We'd need to do it in a way that Novella and Jack Black don't realize we're the ones that turn them in. We don't want a direct connection to Dallas either. Let's think about this. I'll ask my inside informant to help with the answers to your questions, and then we can make a plan. I'm glad you told me all this. Be careful, Sara. Novella Adison obviously doesn't like being told no. I'm uncomfortable putting you in further danger. Would you like to just leave this to me?"

"This is important—if those two get control of Dallas my business will be at risk too. I want to help," Sara said.

"Good, we'll be a team. But make no mistake, they're dangerous. We have to be smart and very, very careful."

Returning to the store after her meeting, Sara was surprised to find Benjamin waiting for her. He was standing with his hands behind him. "I know you are busy, but if I am going to court you I am going to do it properly." He bowed and swept a bouquet of wildflowers from behind his back. "Mrs. Darnell, would you do me the pleasure of joining me tonight for supper at the St. Nicholas Hotel? Chaperoning us will be Mr. and Mrs. Aaron Davis."

Sara buried her nose in the wildflowers and sneezed. "It would be my pleasure, Mr. Brown."

Benjamin smiled. "We will call for you at six o'clock."

Dinner at the new hotel was an impressive event. The table with its white tablecloth was centered with a small vase of summer wildflowers. Creamware plates and shiny cutlery completed the table setting. All four diners selected beefsteak. The meat arrived seared on the outside with a juicy, pink center. Potatoes and carrots completed the entree. As they cut into their steaks, the conversation turned to Galveston's infamous pirate, Jean Lafitte. "Didn't Lafitte operate in the Gulf of Mexico?" Aaron asked.

"Yep. He had a base in Galveston about forty years ago," Benjamin said. "Spent his time raiding ships up and down the Gulf Coast. Legend says that there's still hidden treasure somewhere on Galveston's beaches."

"Pirate stories are certainly romantic, dashing men . . . a life at sea . . . treasure . . . ," Sara's words drifted off.

"What is it about women and pirates?" Benjamin grinned. "You wouldn't have liked him."

"Wasn't he supposed to be handsome, charming, suave, charismatic?"

"Yes, and women adored him because he could sell them most anything at a low cost that merchants couldn't match."

"So, he undercut merchants like me?" Sara laughed. "In that case, you're right. I wouldn't have liked him."

"You know, he still roams the streets of Galveston once a year."

"Wait," Hattie said, "he's long dead."

"True, but at Mardi Gras, half the men in Galveston dress up as the pirate Lafitte. I've even been known to do it myself."

At that moment the waiter arrived to exchange empty plates for spice cake.

"Ah ha," said Aaron. "This evening's treasure has arrived. I love cake."

As the last bites of cake disappeared, Hattie said, "Sara, I finally finished reading *Wuthering Heights*. I stretched it out as long as possible and really enjoyed it. Aaron and I both wanted to read Charles Dicken's *Bleak House*, so we're now reading it out loud to each other after supper. It's very good. Books open the door to other worlds. Thank you."

"I'm pleased you're happy with the books. I'll watch for more."

Walking back to the bank building after supper, Benjamin took Sara's hand. Squeezing it gently, he said, "Thank you for tonight."

Sara looked up at him. "Everything about it was perfect." As she gazed up at him, just above his head, in the sky, she saw a shooting star and made a wish.

Arriving at the store early the next morning, Sara found someone had smeared the front of the building with smashed, rotten eggs. Sara's temper erupted. Red-faced, with hands on hips, she said, "The wrecked storeroom was bad enough, but this is too much! I don't know what I have to do, but this must stop!"

Sara and Daniel worked all day, between customers, to scrub off the stinky, eggy mess. "Do you know who's doing this?" Daniel asked, soapy brush in hand.

"I have a good idea who's responsible," Sara said. *Novella's gang at work.* "I'm just not sure yet what I can do about it."

A few days later, Sarah Cockrell sent a message to Sara saying they needed to talk. The day was busy, and Sara couldn't break away until after closing time. She walked to Mrs. Cockrell's office and found her at her desk. Settling down to talk, Sarah Cockrell told Sara she had gleaned important information from her informant.

"First, what you heard was correct. There is a warrant for the arrest of Jack Black for a murder in Kansas. The victim, Isaac Mizner, was a wealthy man. I'm told Mizner had a taste for the ladies and for gambling. He liked to impress people and was known to carry a very large roll of money. He was friendly with Novella Adison and frequented her gambling dens and bordellos."

"Was she involved in his murder?"

"Yes. Novella arranged a special faro game for Mizner with Jack Black. During the game, Jack Black accused Mizner of cheating. Words were exchanged and Jack Black shot him. My informant said that immediately after Jack Black fired, Novella slipped Mizner's gun from its holster and dropped it on the floor by his chair, making it appear that he had simply been out drawn. Witnesses have testified to Novella's action. Jack Black immediately retrieved Mizner's roll of money, saying he was taking it since he had lost it to the cheating Mizner previously, and therefore it was his. No one was willing to challenge him."

"So Novella Adison was involved."

"I think we can safely say that Novella Adison was an accomplice in the killing. Apparently, the widow was so appalled at the circumstances of her husband's death that she only posted a small reward for Jack Black's apprehension. An amount insufficient to interest the Pinkerton Agency, I suspect. I am willing to pay any difference."

"Is contacting the Pinkerton Agency the next step?"

"I believe so. We can contact Allan Pinkerton, the founder, and see if the Pinkertons will help us. There is a telegraph in Marshal, and from there, a message can be relayed on to the Pinkerton headquarters in Chicago. I'll send someone we can trust the 150 miles to Marshal to send our telegraph message and have them wait for the response. The time involved in communicating is long, and we need to craft the message carefully. It would be easier if we had a telegraph here in Dallas. If we are lucky, there will be a Pinkerton agent closer than Chicago who can help us. We just have to be patient, which is hard to do."

They put their heads together and wrote a message to Allan Pinkerton that they hoped would get the desired result. The sun was setting when Sara was ready to walk home.

"We've worked late enough that I suspect everyone else in the office building has gone home. I plan to work late tonight and sleep in my room here. My staff is caring for my children and they don't expect me home tonight. Will you be all right walking along the square by yourself?" Sarah Cockrell asked.

"I'm sure I'll be fine," Sara answered.

Sara slipped out the door of the Cockrell building and began to walk briskly along the side of the deserted square. As she passed the brick court-house, she was aware of someone behind her. "Keep looking straight ahead," a rough voice instructed. "I'm here to deliver a message. Keep your nose out of Novella Adison's business, or you'll be dealing with more than rotten eggs."

Sara tried to keep her voice calm. "I assume that's a threat."

"You damn well know it is!" the rough voice answered. "Now keep walking and don't look back."

Sara took a few more steps, then took a chance and quickly glanced over her shoulder and saw a small man in a bowler hat limping away. Relieved when she arrived home, she was careful to lock the outside door to the stair-case even before lighting the small whale-oil lamp she kept by the door. She made her way upstairs and locked her entry door as well. Later, slipping into bed, she realized she was trembling. *I'm not sure what mischief we're unleashing.* It was an hour before she finally fell asleep.

The next day was Saturday, and Mr. West and his wife, Lois, crossed the square from West's store to Sara's store with their news. "Mrs. Darnell," West began, "I have sold my store. The buyer offered me so much for it that Lois and I decided we could not afford to say no. We've been happy in Dallas but plan to move to Austin. We wanted to say goodbye to you and let you know you'll have a new competitor."

"Novella Adison," Sara said.

West blinked then opened his eyes wide. "Yes, news certainly travels fast, doesn't it?"

"It does," Sara agreed. "Mr. West, I'm glad we worked through our early problems and became friendlier competitors. I'll miss you and Mrs. West." Sara turned to Lois West. "You are one of the very best dressmakers in town, Mrs. West, so I am just one of many ladies who will miss both you and your sewing skills. Good luck in Austin." Sara reached out and shook West's hand and gave Lois West's hands a quick squeeze. "Safe travels to you and your son."

On Sunday Sara and her friends had organized a July blueberry-picking expe-dition. After the interaction with Novella Adison and the store vandalism,

Sara was happy for the diversion. Armed with buckets, they trooped north of town to find blueberry bushes. "I bet Whit and I can out pick everyone else," Emmeline challenged.

"Challenge accepted," laughed Hattie. "How about the couple with the fewest berries has to bake a pie to serve to everyone else?"

Ellie said, "I make terrible pies, so you better hope Gerard and I gather lots of berries."

With a clear goal established, the four couples spread out to look for berries. As they walked, Sara and Benjamin could hear John Henry and Cecilia's laughter for a while, then all was quiet.

Finding a clump of bushes, they began to fill their bucket. "Here," Benjamin said pushing several blueberries into Sara's mouth.

"Good," she mumbled through berries, "but we can't eat too many or we'll be baking the pie."

"Okay, Miss Competitive, we'll eat one for every ten we pick, how's that?"

"Not sure we can be so disciplined," Sara laughed and pushed several berries at his mouth, managing to smear them on his face as he turned his head.

"You are in trouble now," he said seriously, and the blueberry fight was on. When both faces were sufficiently blue and the laughter had stopped, Benjamin put a hand on either side of Sara's face, pulled her to him, and began to kiss away the blueberries. Soon the blueberries were irrelevant and the kissing more intense. Breathlessly, Sara put her arms around him, and he scooped her up and laid her down gently on the ground. Stretching out beside her, he curled a strand of her hair around his finger and said, "Sara Darnell, I love you." Putting his fingers across her lips, he asked, "Will you say yes and marry me?"

Again, Sara's emotions were conflicting. *I made the wrong choice before. I care for Benjamin, but I'm afraid to say yes. I need to tell him that.*

"I care for you Benjamin. But . . . but I'm afraid to say yes."

"Afraid?"

"I don't want to make a decision I'll regret."

Benjamin studied Sara for a moment. "Did you regret your first marriage, Sara?"

"I rushed into it and didn't really know Morgan. I learned too late that he drank too much and gambled our money away—"

"Oh, Sara, I promise not to do either of those things. You can trust me."

Sara looked into his warm eyes. "Thank you."

Hearing Whit and Emmeline approaching, they stood and dusted themselves off.

"Both your faces are blue," said Emmeline with a giggle. "It doesn't look like the blueberries made it into your buckets. You better get busy or you'll be baking!" She and Whit wandered on, looking for more berry bushes.

At the end of the afternoon, buckets were compared, and Sara and Benjamin were declared the pie bakers. Sara asked Hattie, "May we borrow your kitchen? Or at least a pie pan?" The following Saturday evening was set as the date for a pie party. Declaring the blueberry expedition a success, the couples took a leisurely walk back into town, enjoying the summer sunshine.

Sarah was in Hattie's kitchen rolling out crust for two blueberry pies when Benjamin came in. "You have flour on your chin," he said.

Sara raised her flour-dusted hands, palms facing him. "No, don't even think about it. No flour fights. I've made enough of a mess already. I need to clean it up before your momma sees what a messy cook I am."

"I came to see if I can help. I think this is supposed to be a joint project since we failed the full-bucket-of-berries test together. What can I do?"

"How about whipping the cream? Ever done it?" Sara asked, handing him a bowl and a wooden-handled Monroe eggbeater, then demonstrating how to use it.

"Clever device," Benjamin said and began to whip the cream. They continued to talk while Sara finished the pies. She slipped them into the oven and realized Benjamin was still whipping.

She began to laugh. "Oh Benjamin, you've whipped so long, you've made butter!"

Benjamin looked down. "By George, I have. What do we do now?"

"I guess Hattie and Aaron can have it with their biscuits tomorrow. I'll see if there's more cream."

Later everyone agreed that the blueberry pie was delicious. A perfect way to celebrate summer, even without whipped cream.

Two weeks later, Sara and Mrs. Cockrell met again. "I have received a telegram from Pinkerton. He says the Pinkerton Agency will accept our assignment. Happily, he has a Pinkerton agent in Louisiana, who has just concluded an embezzlement case, and she can come to Dallas. He has sent a second agent who will not arrive as promptly. He believes two agents will be sufficient."

"She?" Sara's eyes widened in shock. "A female detective?"

"Yes, he promises she is one of his very best agents. She will contact us when she arrives."

Over the next several days, Sara busied herself preparing a new merchandise order, and she and Daniel reorganized some shelves and restocked merchandise. Daniel had left to run an errand for Sara when the door opened, and a woman entered. She swayed into the store and looked around. Attired in a tight-fitting, crimson dress with ruffled sleeves, she straightened her feather boa, batted heavily made-up eyes, and said to Sara, "Got any Pears soap?"

"Indeed I do." Sara took a step toward the soap selection on the shelf. As Sara turned around, she gasped as the woman transformed before her eyes. Her posture changed, the expression on her face seemed to alter her very features, and suddenly she was all business.

"Allan Pinkerton sent me. I'm Pinkerton Agent Jette no-middle-name McCaskill. You just saw me as 'Cheyenne.'" Sara was speechless. "I spoke with Mrs. Cockrell this morning, and I'm thinking that as a dance-hall girl, Cheyenne can infiltrate Novella Adison's operations in Boggy Bayou and assess the situation. Just wanted to introduce myself—or ourselves—as the case may be," at this she grinned, "and let you know I'm on the job. Wesley Steinman, my partner, should be here any day now. We will take care of the two villains you've identified, don't worry."

"Thank you and be careful," Sara warned. "Watch out for a small man who limps and wears a bowler hat."

Jette a.k.a. Cheyenne nodded, turned back into a dance-hall girl, plumped up an empty bag to look like a package, and sashayed toward old man Crutchfield's hotel. Sara sat down on the three-legged chair to process what she had just witnessed. She decided that Jette McCaskill was indeed a top Pinkerton agent.

Not knowing what was going on in Boggy Bayou with Cheyenne was worri-some, but Agent Jette McCaskill had given Sarah Cockrell strict instructions not to try to contact her. Nor had they heard from a second Pinkerton agent. "There's nothing we can do but wait," Sarah Cockrell advised.

They had not waited long—though it certainly seemed so—when, somehow, Agent McCaskill got a note delivered to Sarah Cockrell that they would be acting to arrest the two villains when the stage arrived the following day. Novella Adison and Jack Black were taking a trip and planned to catch the stage. Sarah Cockrell alerted Sara to the plan.

Sure enough, Novella and Jack Black arrived on the courthouse lawn, near the spot where the stage generally stopped, half an hour in advance of the usual arrival time. Each carried a carpetbag. Sara saw them arrive as a customer opened the store door to leave. She resisted the temptation to open the door again to look.

About fifteen minutes later, the stage rolled up early and, as usual, stopped just past the store. Sara heard it and opened her door as she usually did for the stage's arrival. She stepped back, viewing the scene from an angle where she didn't think she'd be seen. Sara noticed the stagecoach driver was not the regular whip. The couple on the courthouse lawn walked toward the stage. Jack Black gave Novella's carpetbag to the driver, who turned to put it up top. Before he could do so, a second stage pulled in. Jack Black looked at the second stage and asked, "What is this?"

The first stage driver dropped the carpetbag, pulled a pistol, and said, "You are both under arrest for the murder of Isaac Mizner." Jette McCaskill leaned out of the stage with her pistol drawn and pointed it at Novella Adison. Jack Black hurled his carpetbag at the driver, who stumbled, tripped over the bag, and dropped his gun. Jack Black pointed his gun at Agent McCaskill. It appeared to be a standoff.

Sara moved forward, opened the drawer in the counter, pulled out Morgan's gun, and quickly stepped into the doorway. She pointed it at

Jack Black and said, "Drop it." Jack Black whirled his head around, facing Sara. "I don't think so," he said, raising his gun and firing at Sara. He missed. Sara heard the bullet ricochet off the coffee grinder and heard him say, "Damn!"

Novella screamed, and Agent McCaskill shouted at her, "Don't you *dare* move!"

Jack Black fired again, but Sara, her heart pounding, had ducked behind the counter. Splinters flew, one scratching her on the neck. "Ouch!" *Got to put an end to this!* Praying that there was no one else in the stage behind him, she stood and fired. The gun spun out of his hand.

The first stage driver had retrieved his gun. With three guns pointed at them, Novella and Jack Black were quickly subdued and handcuffed. Soon Jack Black's wounded hand, now missing one finger, was dealt with by Doc Adams, who said Jack Black would be fine in the jail overnight. Doc Adams would then be back to rebandage his hand in the morning before the Texas Rangers were ready to take him to Kansas and justice.

Sara, pale and shaken by the events, collapsed on the three-legged chair. Once Novella and Jack Black were safely locked up, Agents Jette McCaskill and Wesley Steinman came back to the store, and Sarah Cockrell arrived, having seen it all from an upstairs window in the courthouse.

Jette McCaskill said, "You saved the day, Mrs. Darnell. We have a new Women's Division at Pinkerton headed by Kate Warne. How would you like to join?"

Sara shook her head. "I don't think I could stand the excitement."

Sarah Cockrell grinned. "You were amazingly brave and a crack shot."

"We had asked the real stage driver to wait fifteen minutes before pulling into town," Agent Steinman said. "He jumped the gun—pardon the pun—and came early. The best laid plans . . ." He shook his head.

"Well, it worked out fine," Jette McCaskill said, "thanks to Mrs. Darnell."

Sarah Cockrell turned to Agent Steinman. "I'll send the agreed-upon funds to Pinkerton as soon as the prisoners are delivered to the proper authorities in Kansas. In fact, given their slippery nature, I'd like you two to accompany the rangers to Kansas. If that's possible I'll gladly pay the additional fee. Just let me know the amount."

"We can do that, Mrs. Cockrell," Agent McCaskill offered.

Daniel had come out of the store. "I saw it all," he said. "Scared the dickens out of me. It was better than a Waco Kid nickel novel."

"It was worth it," Sara said with a laugh, "if the dickens is gone." No one else understood why Sara and Daniel were laughing. Neither did any of them see the small man in the bowler hat limp away.

Sara was safely home and having a calming cup of tea after the day's excitement when she heard frantic knocking at the outside door to the staircase. Opening the door on the landing, she could hear Benjamin downstairs calling her name. She went downstairs and opened the outside door, only to be immediately encompassed in a bear hug. "Are you okay?" he kept saying.

"Yes, but let me go," she gasped. "You're squeezing the breath out of me."

He loosened his grip but didn't let her go. "The whole town is buzzing. What in the world? Did you really shoot a murderer? What were you thinking? You could have been in danger." He was babbling.

"I was in danger of being shot," Sara said. "Instead I shot the gun out of the man's hand. Everything is fine."

"Fine—fine?" He was almost shouting. "I could have lost you!"

"But you didn't. Come in," Sara invited. "I'll pour you a cup of tea and tell you all about it."

She told him the whole story, from Novella Adison's initial visit and the lavender-satin ball gown to the arrests. Benjamin shook his head.

"I have a million questions, but first, how on earth did you get so good with a gun?" He asked.

"Thanks to my papa. Since he only had girls and I was the oldest, he took me hunting and for target practice. I'm even better with a long gun. He told me once, 'When it comes to self-defense, Samuel Colt makes men and women equal.'"

"Heaven help me, I'm in love with a gunslinger."

"So you'd better behave," Sara said with a wink.

"If you expect me to behave, Mrs. Darnell, I'd best go." He looked around the room. "By the way, what you have done up here is just wonderful. European antiques?"

"Yes, courtesy of departing La Réunion settlers who didn't want to cart things back to Europe."

"It's a home that suits you. Good night, Sara, and thank God you are okay." Benjamin kissed her good night. Sara slipped her arms around his neck. *I do love kissing him.*

"Good night, Benjamin."

As he went down the stairs, he turned. "Be sure to lock up, Sara."

Lock up . . . hmm. Sara knew that Novella and Devil Jack Black were locked up in the jail but she was still uneasy. *What's going on in Boggy Bayou? What's the man in the bowler hat up to? This may not be over.*

Suddenly Sara knew what she needed to do. Rummaging around in a drawer, she found an old shirt and a pair of pants that had been Morgan's. Bundling the clothing up, she lit a tin lantern, walked to the store, and let herself in. She found a billed cap on the shelf of men's clothing. Stepping out the back door, she rubbed the shirt, pants, and cap in the dirt. Back inside, she smudged her face and hands with soot from the stove. She undressed and put the shirt and pants on. The pant legs were too long. *They need to cover my shoes, but I can't have them tripping me.* She took them off and went to work with the scissors. She stepped back into them and used some twine as a belt. *That's better.* Pinning up her hair, she tucked it into the cap and pulled the cap brim down low. *Can I pass for a boy? In lantern light, I think so.* Looking around she saw a stack of Herman's Lizard Oil Medicine Show promotional fliers on the counter. *Perfect! The show starts tomorrow.* She scooped up the stack of fliers, grabbed the tin lantern, and headed on foot towards Boggy Bayou.

Ellie had said Boggy Bayou was south of the courthouse, somewhere along the river. Sara walked along the river for about a mile before finding it. She saw a single street of about a dozen buildings. Some bore gambling-hall signs, while others were identified as saloons or sporting houses. Some were sheds with no signs. Judging by the women in various stages of undress who were hanging out of sporting-house doors and windows, Sara decided a "sporting house" was a bordello.

The street was busy with men coming and going. There were horses tied in front of buildings. A small corral held more horses. *The Dallas square is never this busy.* Sara began to wander, her eyes peeled for the man in the bowler hat, periodically handing out a medicine-show flier to a passerby. Just when she was about to give up, she saw the man she thought of as Scar Face. Keeping him in sight but not getting too close, she followed him to Bagley's Saloon. *Here goes.* She took a deep breath, tucked her lantern behind a bush, pulled her hat brim down, and walked inside behind the man with the scar.

The room she stepped into was dim, smoky, and smelled of whiskey and cigars. A few men stood at an ornate bar along one wall. Above the bar was a painting of a reclining, naked woman. Sara stared for a moment, then quickly began to look around the room. The first familiar face was a man she knew from church. As if he realized he was being observed, he looked up from his drink. "What ya got there, boy?" He reached out his hand. Sara ducked her head, thrust a flier at him, and moved to another table. She had handed out a few fliers before she spotted Scar Face and the man with the bowler hat sitting with two other men at a corner table. She moved along the wall until she was closer to them. She could just hear them, and it sounded like they were having a planning session. Sara let the fliers fall to the floor near their table and slowly began to gather them.

The man in the bowler hat was talking. "The question is, how do we do a jailbreak? Novella and Devil Jack Black are in the jail here tonight, but we don't know when the Texas Rangers will arrive to pick them up, or if the Pinkerton agents are there now with the marshal or his deputies. We need information and we need to move fast."

"Let's get one of us inside the jail, Clay," Scar Face said. "I can be drunk and disorderly and get arrested. I've done it for real enough times."

So the bowler hat man is named Clay.

"That's a good start. Do it," Clay said. "We'll talk through the cell window once you're in and make a plan with Novella and Jack Black." Sara picked up the last flier just as Clay said, "Give me one of those, kid." Sara balled one up, tossed it to him, slipped out the door, and retrieved her lantern.

She ran most of the way to the Cockrell house and banged on the door. Mrs. Cockrell's housekeeper opened the door. "Sally, it's me, Sara Darnell. I need to talk with Mrs. Cockrell, Sally, quickly."

Sally's eyes widened. "Land sakes, it is you."

Sara heard Sarah Cockrell's voice. "Who is it, Sally?"

Sara shouted, "Sarah, there's going to be a jailbreak, we need to find the Pinkerton agents!"

Sarah Cockrell came to the door. "Sara? Why on earth are you dressed like that?"

"I've been to Boggy Bayou and I overheard Novella's gang planning a jailbreak. We have to warn the Pinkertons."

"They are at the St. Nicolas Hotel—you can give me details as we go," Sarah Cockrell said. The ladies hurried to the hotel. Sara shared details of her visit to Boggy Bayou along the way. At the hotel reception desk, Sarah Cockrell asked the clerk to send up a message to Miss Jette McCaskill that she was needed downstairs urgently. In just a few minutes, the three ladies were in a private office at the hotel.

"We don't have much time," Sara told them. "A scar-faced man is going to get himself arrested and jailed as drunk and disorderly so he can plan a jailbreak with Novella and Devil Jack Black."

"I'll get Wesley and we'll head for the jail to let the county sheriff know," Agent McCaskill said. "Once the scar-face man is in jail, we'll spoil the rest of the plan. I can only guess why you're dressed like a boy, Sara." Jette McCaskill grinned. "Good job. Thanks for the warning."

"You are amazing, Sara, but it's time to go home," Sarah Cockrell said. "This could get dangerous."

Sarah Cockrell borrowed a lantern from the hotel and the two ladies said goodnight. Mrs. Cockrell headed home, and Sara made a beeline for the jail. Just before getting there, she snuffed out her lantern and hid it in a bush. There were just two trees by the jail, but one was a large oak with low-hanging branches. *It pays to wear pants.* Sara managed to climb up the tree far enough to be out of sight from the ground, yet still see through the dense leaves to the two cell windows.

Less than half an hour later, Sara saw Scar Face being locked in a cell with Jack Black. When the deputy stepped away, Sara heard Scar Face say, "We are working to get you and Novella out. Do you know who's here?"

Sara could barely hear. She tried to inch closer along a thick branch but lost her balance and sent a flurry of leaves to the ground.

"What was that?" Scar Face said, turning toward the tree. Sara willed herself to be very still. *Don't move, don't move.*

"Nothin'," Jack Black said, "tree's full of squirrels. They've been scramblin' and chasin' each other up and down ever since I've been here."

Thank heavens for squirrels.

Jack Black walked to the window and whispered into the night, "I think there is only one deputy."

"Only one?"

Sara's heart leapt at the sound of the new voice right below her. Clay had just arrived outside the cell's window. "I'll take care of him," Clay said.

"We'll be waiting." Jack Black turned away from the window.

Clay walked around to the front of the jail. When he was out of sight, Sara slipped down, ducked under the cell windows, and quietly moved to the corner of the building. She peeked around the corner.

Clay was walking into the jail carrying a small bag. Once he was inside, she tiptoed across the porch to the door and peeked around the doorframe. Clay walked up to the deputy sitting inside at a desk. Clay spilled the contents of the bag on the desk. Gold coins rolled out. "What's this?" the deputy asked.

"Coffee money."

The deputy frowned. "What?"

"Yes, money for you to go to old man Crutchfield's for a cup of coffee and accidentally leave your keys behind. It will take you awhile to drink your coffee."

The deputy looked up at the man in the bowler hat. "I have a sudden craving for a cup of coffee." He scooped up the gold, put it in the bag, put the bag in his pocket, left a set of keys on the desk, and walked toward the door. *Well, that didn't take much.* Sara disappeared quietly into the shadows.

Sara could hear the rattling of keys as Clay unlocked the cells holding Jack Black, Novella, and Scar Face. "Let's get out of here," Jack Black said. They hurried to the front door and opened it to find they were facing the guns of the Pinkerton agents, the sheriff, his deputy, and two Texas Rangers. "Just where do you think you're goin'?" the sheriff asked. Already in handcuffs were the four men who had been party to the planned escape and had been waiting several blocks away with horses.

"Well, what do you know," said Agent Jette McCaskill. "We've just rounded up more bad guys." The deputy from inside tossed the bag of gold to Agent McCaskill. "Sheriff says this is Dallas County's contribution to the Pinkerton Agency for helping us clean things up."

As the gang was locked up, Sara left the shadows, retrieved her unlit lantern, and quietly found her way back to the store. *The less Novella and her gang know about my involvement, the better.*

The seven prisoners, two Pinkerton agents, and two Texas Rangers left for Kansas the next morning.

Sara and Mrs. Cockrell met over coffee in the Cockrell office. "Thanks to you and the Pinkertons, we are free of Novella Adison, Devil Jack Black, and their gang. The Pinkertons are on their way to Kansas this morning with Novella, Devil Jack Black, and the gang."

"Good," Sara said. "They were a nasty bunch.

"We won't be rid of all the activities going on in Boggy Bayou, but the danger of the bad elements taking over the entire town is gone, for now. Thank you for all you did, Sara. I still can't believe you went to Boggy Bayou."

"Well, it was worth doing. I've worked too hard on my store to risk losing it in a town run by that gang."

"I'm still concerned. We don't know what the future might bring, or if sometime ahead we might have to deal with Novella Adison or Devil Jack Black again. They will be tried in Kansas, where they have contacts. I don't know if they might be able to influence the trial's outcome in some way."

"You think corrupt officials might let them go?"

"We need to assume that it's possible. They have a powerful gang."

"For now, we need to keep you safe. Rumors and multiple versions of the story will run rampant through Dallas County. It's true that it was a coincidence that you just happened to be on the spot with a gun. We need to be sure that is the story that circulates. And your visit to Boggy Bayou must remain a secret. I'm not sure how we can control the story."

Thinking of Ellie and her love for gossip, Sara said, "I think I know how we can circulate a story that's true—but not complete."

"Then I'll leave that to you," Sarah Cockrell said.

Sure enough, Ellie arrived at the store that day eager to talk. "Sara, I am so glad you're safe. There are so many stories flying around town about what happened. The man you shot was a murderer. Did you really have a gunfight with him? People are saying you're actually a Pinkerton agent. Tell me all about it. It is so exciting!"

Benjamin had brought Sara a second chair for behind the counter, and so they sat, Sara taking the three-legged chair. "Goodness, where to start?" Sara began. "To answer your first question, apparently the man was a killer. He had murdered a wealthy man during a card game and stolen his money. Witnesses said the woman was his accomplice. There was a warrant for his arrest, and the family was offering a reward. At least that is what I was told."

"Was the Pinkerton agent really a woman? How did you meet her?" Ellie was all ears.

"Let me just tell you what happened from the beginning. The female Pinkerton agent came into the store and introduced herself. People assume storekeepers know what's going on in a town, I guess. Plus, I am right in front of the stage stop. She asked if I had heard of a man called Devil Jack Black. I told her that there were rumors he was a gambler who had recently arrived on the stage. Remember? That's what you told me."

"Right," Ellie said.

"She said he was wanted for murder in Kansas and asked me to not say anything about our conversation. The next time I saw her was the day of the arrest. The stage came in a bit earlier than usual, and I opened the door as I always do, hoping for a customer or two. I noticed the whip was not the usual driver. As I stood in the doorway, I saw Jack Black and the woman walk up to the stagecoach. Just then, a second stage pulled in. Jack Black must have realized something was wrong. Anyway, guns were pulled and it looked like a standoff."

"Oh my goodness!" Wide-eyed, Ellie was almost vibrating with excitement.

Sara continued, "Almost without thinking, I grabbed Morgan's gun out of the drawer, pointed it at Jack Black, and said, 'Drop it.' I figured that's what he'd do. Instead he raised his gun and shot at me twice. Fortunately he missed, so I shot the gun out of his hand."

"You could have been killed. Weren't you frightened?"

"It all happened very fast. Doc Adams patched up the gambler's hand, and the Pinkerton's took him and his lady friend off to jail. I understand that sometime in the night, some men from Boggy Bayou tried to stage a jailbreak but ended up getting arrested too. You have probably heard more about that than I have."

"How did you learn to shoot like that? You're not really a Pinkerton agent, are you? Will you get the reward?" Ellie was beside herself with excitement.

"No, silly, I'm not an agent. I am just a storekeeper. My papa taught me to shoot. The reward? It rightly belongs to the Pinkertons."

Sara knew Ellie would happily spread this somewhat-edited version of the story.

When the newspaper editor came to ask Sara for an interview, she repeated the edited version, and it appeared as the full story in that week's edition of the *Dallas Herald*.

Mrs. Cockrell invited Sara to tea at the hotel. Sitting in a quiet corner of the dining room, Sara admired the hotel china as she added cream and sugar to her Earl Grey tea.

Mrs. Cockrell stirred sugar into her tea. "You mentioned that you might want to open a second store. Novella has not yet paid Mr. West for his store, although he has trustingly left for Austin. I propose to buy it from him. If I do, would you like to open another store? I'll happily give you the building. It would be my thanks for your help in keeping those two villains from taking control of the town."

A second store?

Sara trusted Mrs. Cockrell, but she had also learned that gifts often come with high prices. "That's too generous of you. Why not rent the build-ing to me and sell me his inventory, all at a reasonable price? I may have to pay you over time. Would you do that?"

"Of course. As soon as I can negotiate a purchase with West, we can agree on rental terms, a price for the inventory, and do the paperwork. Do you know what kind of store you'd want to open?" Sarah Cockrell asked, sipping her tea.

"Not yet, but I'll think about it."

"By the way," Sarah Cockrell said, "Allan Pinkerton has contacted me to say that the gold the sheriff gave them from the county, on top of the family's reward, will more than cover their fee for the pursuit, arrests, and delivery of the prisoners, so they won't bill me anything."

"That's nice news," Sara said.

"Indeed it is."

The two ladies went on to talk of other things and then, with nothing but tea leaves remaining in their cups, said goodbye. As Sara stood to leave, she remembered Grandma saying there were women who could read the future in tea leaves. If that's true, Sara wondered as she glanced back at her cup, what would my tea leaves say?

When Sara told Daniel about the possibility of another store, his eyes lit up. "The girl I'm sweet on, Julianna MacDougal, is the best dressmaker in town. She has an idea that if ladies could buy ready-made dresses and have small alterations done, rather than having to wait to have a dress made, they would prefer it. What about opening a store that sold ready-made dresses in different patterns and colors?"

"Hmm . . . ready-made dresses?"

"Dallas dressmakers could make them. In return for steady work, Julianna thinks the dressmakers could afford to sell dresses to the store for a good price. The store could then resell them for a higher price, a little less than for custom dresses. Plus ladies wouldn't have to wait for custom work."

Sara believed that was probably one of the longest speeches Daniel had ever made. She liked the idea of ready-made dresses but wanted to talk with Julianna before committing to anything. "Interesting idea," She told Daniel. "I'd like to talk to Julianna and learn more about what she might have in mind."

Daniel wasted no time in putting Sara and Julianna together. Daniel's special friend was a slim, dark-haired girl, wearing a dress she had made. Sara noted that it was well made and nicely fitted.

"I've been thinking about this for a long time," Julianna began in a flurry of words. "First, we'd have to approach the better dressmakers in town and get a firm commitment from them for an agreed-upon number of dresses in a certain time period, and then—"

"What would you ask of the dressmakers?"

"They'd just provide the dressmaking skills, and we'd provide all materials and, working with them, we could decide the measurements for several dress sizes to start with. And the dressmakers would be a good source of information for sizing, as they know what they've already been making and—"

"That makes sense," Sara said.

"Yes, and we'd need to decide how much inventory to start with. I'd need help in how to price the dresses in the shop. We could display them hanging on hooks and folded on shelves and maybe even display one or two on dressmaker's dummies. So, what do you think?"

"Who would run the shop?" Sara asked.

"I would," Julianna answered, beaming. "I have enough sisters that my momma could do without me at home, and even though I've never run a shop, I've been asking Daniel lots of questions about the store and how it operates, and I learn fast."

"If we agreed to do this together, what would you want from me?" Sara asked.

"We'd have to work that out. Obviously, the use of the building that was Mr. West's store. I'd need seed money for fabrics and supplies and lots of advice. We could share profits, or I could work off a loan. I'm not sure about the business details. How would you want to arrange it?"

The more Sara talked to Julianna, the more impressed she was. The girl spoke quickly, but intelligently. "Let me think about this for a few days, Julianna. I have to admit I'm attracted to the idea. I'll give some thought to how it might be structured to work for both of us and whether or not I think there really is a market for ready-made frocks."

"That's it!" Julianna cried, her brown eyes wide. "I've been trying and trying to think of a shop name. How about 'Frocks for Ladies' or maybe just 'Frocks'?"

"Hmm . . . A store named Frocks." Sara grinned. "I like it."

"And we could call the dresses 'Frocks,'" Julianna said.

"Hmm . . . that could work." Sara nodded.

They agreed to talk again in a few days.

Later the same day, Sara walked through Mr. West's store and concluded he had been a good shopkeeper. Inventory records appeared clear and complete. She noted that before selling his store, he had placed an order for not-yet-delivered merchandise and paid for it in advance. The storeroom was organized. His accounting books indicated that he had been nicely profitable. All in all, West's store was a good operation. She could easily step in, run it, and be fairly confident that it would continue to make money. On the other hand, she liked Julianna's idea about ready-made dresses. *What to do? The store is profitable now. I'm saving money each month. Should I expand into a new venture? Too risky?*

The next morning she stopped in the office of the cotton brokerage on her way to the store. Trusting Benjamin's good business sense, she explained her quandary to him.

Benjamin thought for a minute and then said, "As a cotton broker, I've learned there is always risk in business. The trick is to reduce that risk. So, what if you keep West's store and fine-tune the merchandise between your two stores? Then you can make some room in Sara's Merchandising Emporium for a special section of ready-made dresses? That way, you can test the 'Frocks' concept."

"That makes sense."

"Can you afford to put Daniel in charge of daily operations at West's former store, assuming you think he can handle it? Then you can bring Julianna in as assistant in your current store. She can help you, as Daniel has been, and you can guide her with the creation of the Frocks department. What do you think?"

"It's brilliant—*you* are brilliant. That's exactly what I need to do."

When Sara got to the store, she found both Daniel and Julianna there. She shared the idea with them.

"You want me to run Mr. West's old store?" Daniel asked, his eyes wide.

"I think you are ready," Sara told him. "Of course, I'll have to pay you more, that all right?" Daniel's smile nearly split his face. "What's it called when you own all of one kind of a business?"

"A monopoly." Sara thought of Novella Adison's desire to own Sara's store as well as West's.

"Guess that's what we'll have," Daniel said, looking downright smug.

Sara turned to the young woman. "Julianna, what do you think about starting with Frocks as a section of my store? I'd pay you as an assistant and for planning and organizing the dress section. You'd also earn a small part of the Frocks profits."

"I understand. Starting as a special section or department in the store makes sense. It's a great idea." Julianna was shaking her head yes so vigorously her bun was unraveling. "If it works then we can expand. If it doesn't, we aren't stuck with an empty store."

Smart girl, Sara thought. Soon Sara was in business with two stores.

"It's definitely fall," Sara murmured as she wrapped her cape tightly around her shoulders. Today was downright chilly, with a gusty wind scattering leaves around her feet and whipping the hem of her cape as she walked. Yesterday had been warm and sunny. *North Texas weather,* she thought, *you never know what to expect from one day to the next.* She was hurrying between her two stores to see how Daniel was coming with reorganizing inventory. She looked up as a rider passed her, leading another horse. Suddenly, she realized there was a body draped over the second horse, head and feet hanging low. Looking closely, she saw the body was Benjamin.

"Benjamin!" She sank to her knees in the road.

The rider halted. "Do you know him, ma'am? I found him on the trail with his horse standin' beside him. Figured I'd bring him into town to the doc. Had a little trouble gettin' him back on his horse. Dead weight, ya know."

No! Sara thought she was going to faint.

"Oh, sorry ma'am, he ain't dead. Horse must of throwed him. I think he's just knocked out."

"Thank God," Sara sighed in relief. "Follow me to Doc Adams."

"You took a nasty crack to your head, young man," Doc Adams said a bit later as he helped Benjamin into a seated position on the examining table. "The headache you have is likely to last awhile. You've rattled your brains pretty good. Try to stay awake for the rest of the day. If you have trouble doing that, somebody let me know. I suggest you go to your momma's house where she can keep an eye on you for a couple of days. This is Friday, so it won't hurt to close your business for the weekend. Just put a sign up. As I recall, this young lady of yours cracked her head good, too, awhile back. Good news is you both have hard heads." Doc Adams laughed at his own joke and sent them out the door.

Benjamin was a bit wobbly, and Sara put her arm around him and led him toward Hattie's. "Thank heavens you are all right. I was scared to death when I saw you draped on your horse, and when the man said you were dead weight, I thought I'd lost you."

"Would you have minded so much if you had?" Benjamin asked.

Sara stopped and looked at him. "Benjamin, I love you."

Benjamin smiled. "Do you love me enough to spend the rest of your life with me?"

Sara smiled. "I do!"

"Then I guess we are engaged." Benjamin let out a whoop of joy, frightening a nearby dog, which began to bark. "That's right hound dog, shout it to the world: Sara and Benjamin are engaged! I'd kiss you, Sara, but the kiss will have to wait. We are on a public street and I must protect my fiancée's reputation. Let's go tell my momma."

When Hattie opened the door, Sara said, "Benjamin's horse threw him, and he cracked his head."

Benjamin added, "And we're engaged!"

Hattie clapped her hands together in delight. "I couldn't be happier. About the engagement, I mean! Guess we have another wedding to plan. Now, let me look at your head, Benjamin."

Benjamin asked Sara for her papa's address in Tennessee. "I want to write and ask for your parents' blessing on our marriage. I want to do this properly, Sara."

"Thank you."

Dear Mr. Pennington,

I hope this letter finds you and your family well. My name is Benjamin Brown. I have fallen in love with your daughter, Sara, and have asked her to marry me. She has said yes. Your blessing on our marriage is important to Sara and to me. I wish I could introduce myself and ask for your blessing in person. Since we are separated by so many miles, I am doing so with this letter.

My mother is Mrs. Hattie Brown Davis, Sara's former landlady here in Dallas. I have recently moved to Dallas from Galveston to establish the town's first cotton-factoring business. I believe my prospects to be good, and the new business is a branch of R. and D. G. Mills, a large cotton factor. I am twenty-six years old and have the benefit of a good education. Most important, I love your daughter. Sara is smart, courageous, sweet, funny, and I want to spend the rest of my life with her. I pledge to you that I will love and take good care of her.

I hope you and Mrs. Pennington will approve of me and give us your blessing. As Sara has told you, letters sent to Dallas are placed in our postal bag based on the initial of our last name. Sara and I will eagerly await your letter.

Sincerely,

Benjamin Brown

Upon hearing news of the engagement, Cecilia said, "Come get married at the T-Lazy-R Ranch. The new stone-and-board house is almost finished and John Henry couldn't resist the temptation to make it really big. We'll have room for a real celebration. Emmeline is due soon, and once the baby comes, we can host the wedding and celebrate a birth, if you don't mind sharing your special day with a new little one."

"I think one is always supposed to have something new, something borrowed, and something blue for a wedding. What would be better than borrowing Emmeline and Whit's new baby for the celebration? If the new baby is a boy the something blue will be covered." Sara chuckled.

On a cloudy, blustery afternoon in late October, Sara could hear people congregating in the square. She opened the door and stepped into the street to see what the commotion was all about. A long-haired, buckskin-clad man Sara didn't recognize was standing on a box on the edge of the courthouse grounds. He was shouting, "Abolitionists have led a slave insurrection in Harpers Ferry, Virginia. I heard the news in Marshall when I came through there. The report came by telegraph." People began muttering and Sarah heard a few curses. A crowd was gathering around the speaker.

"Who is that man?" Sara asked Ira Webster, who had come out of the saddle shop and was standing nearby.

"Never seen him before. Says he's traveling to San Antonio."

The stranger continued, "An armed band of sixteen white abolitionists and five slaves, led by abolitionist John Brown, attacked a federal arsenal. They were tryin' to steal guns. They planned to arm slaves and abolitionists and start a guerrilla war against Virginia's slave owners. Attack was prob'ly funded by rich Bostonians. Abolitionist subversion is growin'."

The muttering and cursing became louder.

The stranger raised his voice. "Federal troops stopped 'em. Brown and six of his followers are sentenced to be hanged. That's all I know." The stranger stepped off the box and hurried to his horse, which was tied nearby.

"Slave uprisings are starting!" one observer yelled.

"We'll be murdered in our beds!" shouted another.

Doc Pryor mounted the box. "Calm down everyone," he shouted. "No need to work yourselves into a conniption fit. We are a long way from Virginia. Instead pray our politicians in Washington can settle the issue of the right of states to decide for themselves whether or not to allow slavery within their borders, as I believe is defined by the Constitution."

There were some jeers at this and some calls of "We can't depend upon politicians!" and "Secession! Texas should leave the Union!"

Doc Pryor didn't give up. "I know most of us have come from the South, yet nine out of ten of you don't even have slaves. So, let's keep cool heads. Texas is proud to have become a state. I believe what Sam Houston believes: the Union is worth saving." Some heads nodded in agreement; others stormed away in frustration.

"We are in perilous times," Ira Webster said to Sara. "It seems that war is inevitable, despite Doc Pryor's optimism."

"I hope not. Surely it won't come to war." But Sara had a sense of foreboding.

That evening Sara and Benjamin went to supper at Aaron and Hattie's. The conversation around the supper table turned to the Harpers Ferry raid. "It would seem the crisis brewing between North and South is becoming more serious," Benjamin said. "What's your opinion, Aaron?"

"When I was in Austin a few weeks back, consulting on a legal case, the discussions I heard were troubling. There is a cultural, economic, and social divide between North and South that does not bode well for the future. The disagreement over states' rights is at the heart of the issue, and slavery is the flash point. To make it worse, Texans are unhappy with the government. Most don't feel the US military has done enough to protect settlers from Comanche raids."

Sara listened with concern. "That's all true, but are the differences really strong enough to lead to war?"

"I think it's likely, although I hope I am wrong," Aaron said. "Other places, like the British Empire, have abolished slavery through negotiation and reimbursement. I don't see that happening here. I'm afraid the North and South have both dug in their heels at opposite ends of the states' rights and slavery issues."

"The national political parties are definitely at each other's throats," Benjamin said.

"Yes," Aaron said. "It seems that the differences will not come to a successful resolution at the negotiating table. Tempers are too high."

"Governor Houston seems to believe it would be possible to resolve differences without secession. Besides, he says we don't have enough men, money, or industrial production to win a war," Sara said.

"That might be true. But there's still a lot of talk about secession. What do you think that would mean for Texas?" Benjamin asked.

"That's the big question, Benjamin. Most Texans have come here from the South. Although the vast majority are not slaveholders, and many will tell you they are opposed to slavery. I think their fear of social change is stronger than their opposition to slavery. You heard our citizens respond to today's news of the Harpers Ferry raid with fears of a slave insurrection."

"The response from the crowd seemed to be based on fear," Sara said.

"Probably. Not much about this entire situation is completely rational on either side. That's what frightens me about what's ahead. In Austin the talk was about states' rights and seceding from the Union. I don't believe the North would allow the southern states to break away."

Benjamin frowned. "In other words, you agree with the editorials in the *Herald*—secession would lead to war?"

"Yes, even though Sara's right that Sam Houston is against secession and believes it would lead to a war the South would lose, the talk of secession is growing in Austin with the legislature. Governor Houston's opinion is in the minority."

"There's talk here in Dallas County that Texas should leave the Union and go back to being an independent republic," Benjamin said.

"There are proponents of that in Austin as well. It's a bit too soon to know which way the wind will blow. At this point, it's an open political question. Personally, I think secession is inevitable."

At the thought of that, everyone grew quiet. After a moment, Hattie said, "Time will tell, but here's a question we can answer right now: Who wants coffee with their dessert?"

John Henry arrived at Sara's early one Sunday morning, leading an extra horse. "Emmeline had a baby boy last night! She and the baby are both fine. Come out to the ranch with me and meet Winston Adams Wainwright. He's just beautiful, Sara!"

Sara changed, was down the stairs, and mounted on her horse in fewer than ten minutes. "Tell me the baby's name again."

"Winston Adams Wainwright. Winston is for Emmeline's father. Adams is for me. I am really honored by that. We're gonna call him 'Win.' He'll call Cecilia and me 'Grandma and Grandpa.' I feel like the luckiest man on Earth. I've been given a second chance with a wonderful family."

"You deserve it, John Henry. You're a good man."

When they arrived at the ranch, they found Emmeline and Cecilia in two rocking chairs in the main room. Dressed in a robe with her hair freshly combed, Emmeline was flushed and beaming. In Emmeline's arms was a tiny, red-faced baby wrapped in a blanket. "A boy, Sara!" There was obvious pride in her voice. "Isn't he wonderful?"

Sara leaned down to look. "I'd forgotten how tiny newborns are. He's beautiful, Emmeline. Congratulations."

Whit walked in wearing a giant smile. "Ah, Sara, I see you've met Win."

"I have, congratulations."

Win began to cry, balling up his tiny fists and getting louder and redder. Niñera Maria appeared, saying, "I take now and change," and lifted him out of Emmeline's arms.

Cecilia said, "Yesterday was a bit of a panic, Sara. Thank heavens for Nanny Maria. Emmeline was sitting on the porch, knitting baby booties, when her water broke and the pains started. I rushed her into the bedroom, calling for Nanny Maria. Whit and John Henry heard the urgency in my voice and came running. Whit was shouting, 'Is the baby coming? Is the baby coming?'"

Whit asked, "I was? I don't remember."

"You were." John Henry laughed.

Whit said, "I do remember that Nanny Maria took charge. She said 'shoo, shoo' and chased us men out and closed the door."

John Henry said, "Sara, I have to admit that we were so upset by the screams coming from the bedroom that we tapped into my whiskey supply. By the time the sky began to lighten, we were both a bit tipsy—"

"We were," Whit said, "but a new baby is a sobering thing. Just as the sun broke over the horizon, we heard the baby cry. After a few minutes, Cecilia opened the door and motioned us in. Emmeline was propped up in bed, and in her arms was our tiny boy, wrapped in a blanket. I sat on the edge of the bed and Emmeline slipped the baby into my arms. One of the best moments of my life. I realized I'll do anything to protect this child."

Later that day, Sara watched as Whit and Emmeline introduced Winston Adams Wainwright to Jellie, Zollie, Juan, Carlos, and Hector and Alonso, the newest vaqueros. All were suitably impressed, although Zollie was concerned about how red and wrinkled the baby was. "It won't be so wrinkled and red when it grows up some," Jellie reassured him.

John Henry escorted Sara back to town and collected his horse. His last words to her were, "Aren't babies wonderful things?"

Sara smiled at him. "Indeed they are, indeed they are."
Someday Benjamin and I hope to have our own.

Benjamin rushed into Sara's Merchandise Emporium waving a letter. Daniel looked up from his work. and pointed. "She's stocking candles down that aisle."

"Sara, your papa has replied," Benjamin called as he turned down the aisle and hurried toward her. He handed her the letter. Sara began to read out loud.

> *Dear Benjamin,*
>
> *Thank you for your letter. Sara has mentioned you several times in her most recent letters and obviously is very fond of both you and your mother, who sounds like a fine woman. The fact that you reached out to us with your letter tells us that you were reared well. As my wife would say, you are mannerly.*
>
> *Sara's mother and I miss her very much and would feel very comfortable knowing that she has a fine young man who loves her and would care for her. We send you our blessing for the marriage and hope that we can see you and Sara at some time in the future. It is difficult to be so many miles away. We will be thinking of you and wishing you a joyous wedding day. If it is possible, please send us a wedding daguerreotype photograph. We would value it. Please give Sara our love and the love of her sisters.*
>
> *Sincerely,*
> *Logan Pennington*

As Sara finished, Daniel peeked around the corner of a shelf. "I can hear the wedding bells now."

Benjamin looked into Sara's eyes. "Wedding bells, Daniel? What a beautiful sound."

Having finally arrived, Win became the center of the ranch household just in time for Thanksgiving. Sara, Benjamin, Hattie, Aaron, Ellie, and Gerard were invited to celebrate the new baby and the holiday at the ranch.

The large, great-room table and a second table, constructed for the occasion, were covered with tablecloths and set for family, friends, and all the ranch employees. Win joined them in a handmade cradle next to the table. They all gathered and sat down to a supper of wild turkey and gravy, corn-bread dressing, sweet potatoes, and pickled peaches followed by both pumpkin and pecan pies. Beef tamales were also served. Emmeline had talked John Henry into bringing Nanny Maria's favorite niece, Juanita, to the ranch to help in the house. She was the ranch's newest arrival. Juanita was slim, with black hair, flashing white teeth, and dark eyes, enhanced by a thick fringe of lashes. Sara wondered how Juanita and tiny, wrinkled Nanny Maria could possibly be related. *Could Maria have looked like this when she was young?* Juanita spoke both Spanish and English. Jellie made it a point to sit beside her.

"Dear Lord," said John Henry, as the supper began. "We are grateful for all our blessings. Most of all for the wonderful family and friends around this table and for a healthy, new baby boy. Thank you for these blessings and bless this food."

Aaron was asked to give a second grace. "Thank you, Lord, for the friendships we have made in Dallas and for the loved ones we've found. We pray for their safety and good health and ask you to bless the friends and family that aren't with us today. We are grateful for this beautiful meal. Amen"

Sincere amens echoed around the table in two languages. As Sara looked up, she realized John Henry's eyebrows were back. *He looks like himself again!*

Emmeline had told Sara that Juanita was an excellent Mexican-food cook. As the food was passed around the table, Sara added two of Juanita's tamales to her plate. The steamy smell of spicy beef rose from the tamales as Sara removed the corn-husk wrapping and took her first bite. The soft beef and the layer of masa covering it seemed to melt in her mouth, leaving the taste of brisket, corn, onion, cumin, and Sara wasn't sure what else, but it was delicious.

"Your tamales are so good, Juanita. I've never had them before. I can identify some of the ingredients, but is there a secret one?"

Juanita laughed. "Two of them—laughter and gossip. At home when we have a *tamalada*, that's what we call it when women come together to make and eat the tamales, there is much laughter and gossip, so we say they are part of a successful recipe."

Emmeline said, "Seems to me laughter and friendly gossip are two ingredients that should be in every kitchen."

Platters of food were passed around a second time. When the pies were gone and everyone agreed they could not eat another bite, Hattie said, "Now that Win Adams Wainwright has arrived, we have a wedding to plan."

Sara and Benjamin smiled at each other, and Gerard said, "Actually, there are two weddings to plan. Ellie has agreed to be the wife of this French carpenter."

"Congratulations, Gerard," Aaron slapped him on the back and everyone chimed in. "Congratulations!"

"Aren't you sneaky," Sara told Ellie. "You haven't said a word."

"We wanted to wait until today to share our announcement with all of you."

"It's a perfect Thanksgiving surprise," Emmeline said.

"My goodness," Cecilia said, "how wonderful. This is a year for weddings!"

Gerard stood up. "As you know, my friend Mr. Mondriel has left La Réunion and started a brewery. I visited there yesterday and have brought some of his beer to toast all of our happy unions and Win's arrival."

The beer was opened; small glasses poured and raised; and toasts made to the accompaniment of laughter.

Sara heard the sound of the horn and the rattle of the stage as it pulled up in front of the store. As she opened the door, she saw Benjamin approaching. As he came even with the stage, the door opened, and a young woman climbed down. Seeing Benjamin, she threw her arms around his neck. "Benjamin, darling, I've missed you so!"

Darling?

An older woman followed the girl out of the stage. "Benjamin, what a surprise! We didn't know you were going to meet us, dear. Elizabeth could hardly wait to see you."

Sara couldn't hear Benjamin's reply. Instead she was focused on the young woman who had now slipped her arm through Benjamin's. The older woman took Benjamin's other arm.

The word "darling" kept echoing in Sara's head. *I don't know what's going on, but I intend to find out.* She took her store apron off, smoothed her hair, put her straw hat on, and walked to where the three were standing.

Benjamin looked up from their conversation. "Oh, let me introduce you to my fiancée." The young woman laughed and said, "Oh Benjamin, are you proposing? I told mother I thought you might."

Benjamin turned red. "No, this is my fiancée, Sara Darnell. I was just coming to see her. Sara, meet Miss Elizabeth Ridley and her mother, Mrs. Ridley, from Galveston."

Mrs. Ridley said, "Well, I never!"

The young woman's face crumpled, and tears began falling down her cheeks. Her mother glared at Sara, grabbed her daughter's hand and pulled her toward Crutchfield's Hotel.

At the same time, Sara wheeled around and hurried toward the store. "Wait, Sara, wait!" Benjamin cried. "I can explain!"

Sara spun around. "I'm sure you can."

Two more steps and she was in the door of the store. She threw the latch. Benjamin knocked.

"Go away. I don't want to talk to you. I don't want to see you. And as for being your fiancée, I am not!"

After a few more knocks, he finally gave up and wandered down the street.

That evening Sara made her way home and found Benjamin was waiting at the stairway door. "Sara."

"Please get out of the way."

"Sara, there is *nothing* between me and Elizabeth Ridley."

"I suppose she calls everyone 'darling.'" Sara pushed past him, unlocked her door, went in, and slammed the door in his face. *How could I have been so wrong? Miss so-and-so must be Benjamin's Galveston's woman. A "lady" in every port, as they say. At least this time, I found out before the wedding.* At the top of the stairs, she started to cry.

Two days later Hattie came to the store. Sara started to speak, but Hattie raised her hands, gesturing for Sara to stop. "Sara, Benjamin told me what happened with the Ridley women. No . . . no, don't say anything until you've seen what I have to show you. Took me awhile to find these." Hattie handed Sara two envelopes addressed to Mrs. Hattie Brown, with a return address of Galveston. "Please read these before you get too angry with Benjamin. Look at the postmarks on the envelopes." Sara looked. Both were postmarked before Benjamin's arrival in Dallas.

Sara took the letters and the three-legged chair to one of the storerooms and sat down to read. She skimmed down to where the name Elizabeth Ridley first appeared.

"Momma, I need your advice. A young woman, Elizabeth Ridley, has set her cap for me, and I'm not interested. I have danced with her at several parties and she has decided that means I am courting her. I am not, nor do I intend to. She is vain and empty headed. A friend of mine told me Mrs. Ridley believes I have good prospects for being successful and wants me for her daughter. I try to avoid them, but they keep popping up wherever I go. Mrs. Ridley keeps pushing her daughter at me. I wish to be rid of them but don't want to earn a reputation as a cad in the process. What can I do? Any advice?"

Sara opened the second letter.

"Remember my frustration with the Ridley mother and daughter? It continues. I tried explaining nicely that I was not interested in marrying, as you suggested. It didn't work. The mother continues to force the girl on me and sing her praises. I have even tried introducing her to other men in hopes someone will fall for her. No luck. At the last dance I attended, I made it a point to not ask her to dance. Her mother actually found me, pushed the girl at me, and said, 'Don't be shy, Benjamin, I know you are eager to dance with Elizabeth.' I begged off, saying I had just twisted my ankle, and left. I may have to leave town. Seriously, I am open to any new suggestions."

Hot tears streamed down Sara's cheeks. *How could I have doubted him?* Clutching the letters in her hand, she ran to the front of the store and out the door, shouting at Daniel, "I'll be back!" She hurried to the cotton-brokerage office and swung open the door. There stood Mrs. Ridley with Benjamin. Sara looked at the woman, collected herself, and said, "Mrs. Ridley, unless you have brokerage business with my fiancée, we'd like for you to leave." Sara took a step closer to the woman, invading her space. "The fact that Benjamin and I are engaged should be evidence enough that he is not, I repeat not, interested in Elizabeth. I'm sure she is charming." Sarah smiled. "She will find a more suitable beau. Have a nice trip back to Galveston. Or wherever you're going. Good day."

With that, Sara took Benjamin's arm and said, "Darling, we have some wedding decisions to make."

Mrs. Ridley blinked once, then twice. "Uhh . . . uhh." Then she turned and fled out the front door.

Benjamin burst into laughter. "That was masterful. Does this mean we are engaged again? Please say yes."

"Yes," Sarah laughed, put her arms around his neck, and kissed him. He gave her a long, lingering kiss in return. Sara said, "Let's go tell your momma that the wedding is back on."

Julianna rushed into the store early in December waving a copy of the week's *Dallas Herald.*

"Guess what I found in the *Herald*—an ad for a Singer's sewing machine!" She thrust the paper into Sara's hand. "Read this . . . ."

> A first-rate number 1, largest size Singer's sewing machine, suitable for all sorts of work. Entirely new and in perfect order. This machine is particularly adapted to tailors' use and, if early application is made, will be sold low. Enquire at the *Herald* office.

"Sara, just think of all we could do with a sewing machine. I know I can learn to use it and could train one or two of our best seamstresses to use it too. Can we please buy it if the price is right?"

Sara could see the value in having the machine. "Go take a look, make sure the condition is good, and see what price you can negotiate. If you can get if for fifty dollars or less, we can buy it."

Julianna was out the door almost before Sara's sentence was completed. Her excited "Thank you!" floated back over her shoulder. Less than an hour later she was back, followed by two of publisher Swindells' helpers. One was weighted down with an armful of sewing machine. The other carried the table and treadle. "Got it for forty-five dollars," Julianna said with a big smile. "I'll take it home and learn how to use it."

Dear Momma and Papa,
 Merry Christmas!
 I am hoping this short note will arrive at the horse farm in time for the holidays. I know, Momma, that you'll have festooned the house with green garlands and candles, and I can almost smell the turkey roasting. Have a wonderful time and know that I am thinking of you all and sending merry wishes and hugs your way.
 By the time you receive this, Benjamin Brown and I will be married. He is wonderful, and I wish that you could meet him and join in our celebration. I don't know that I have ever been happier. We both thank you for your blessing.
 Our wedding has now become a double wedding! John Henry and Cecilia Adams are hosting our wedding at their ranch, and our friends, Ellie and Gerard, have announced their engagement and are marrying at the same time. We will have a Texas-ranch wedding. I'll tell you all about it in my January letter.
 Whit and Emmeline's new baby has arrived, a little boy named Winston Adams Wainwright. They call him Win. They are thrilled and the baby is just darling.
 Hattie has been teaching me to make light yeast biscuits in an iron skillet. Hers are so good that we call them "dough gods." They are favorites of Benjamin and I am determined to master making them. So far, mine are good, but hers are the best. Working with Hattie in the kitchen reminds

me of how much fun we all used to have making cookies—remember how
we'd chase around the kitchen trying to swat each other with the dish towel?
Lots of laughing!

I promise to write a longer letter after the wedding.
I miss you all.
Love and Merry Christmas,
Sara (the future Mrs. Benjamin Brown)

Wedding planning began immediately after Thanksgiving. Sara and Ellie decided on simple, long-sleeved, white dresses with no hoops. Each chose a dress pattern, and Sara asked Julianna to make their dresses. She announced she would make them on their new Singer's sewing machine. John Henry agreed to give Sara and Ellie away as a stand-in for their fathers. "Thank you for asking me," he said. Hattie, Cecilia, and Emmeline said they'd be pleased to be matrons of honor. Niñera Maria and Julianna agreed to be the bridesmaids. Benjamin asked Aaron to be his best man, and Beaulieu said he would be flattered to stand up for Gerard. It was a large wedding party, but all agreed the more participants, the more celebratory it would be.

A December-morning ranch wedding was scheduled—based on the circuit-rider preacher's calendar. Fingers were crossed in hopes that the weather would cooperate. The chosen day arrived, and Texas delivered on the weather. The sun rose, revealing a powder-blue sky. White clouds played peekaboo with the sun, creating shifting shadows on the prairie grasses. The breezes sighed gently, and the temperature was balmy for December.

The ceremony was to be in the ranch house's great room. Garlands of golden grass and bunches of red-berried greenery added festive color. Chairs had been placed in rows, leaving a center aisle down the middle. Women sat, men stood. Musicians were positioned in a corner of the room.

Invited guests included all six ranch hands, Juanita, Daniel, the Websters, the McDougals, the Pollards, the Butlers, Doc Adams and Doc Pryor and their wives, and many other friends. Mr. Baker brought two matching wedding cakes. Mrs. Cockrell arrived with bottles of wine for toasting the brides and grooms.

Ellie and Sara were both nervous as they waited in one of the bedrooms for La Réunion's violinist to give them the musical cue that it was time to join John Henry for the march down the aisle.

"Do I look all right, is everything straight?" Ellie asked.

"That's the third time you've asked. You still look lovely, your dress is still straight, and so is your veil. Everything's still perfect. Don't worry . . . but it does seem to be taking a long time. Do you suppose something's gone wrong?" Sara asked.

"I'm sure everything's fine."

"Listen," Sara said, "there's the music." *I'm nervous and happy all at the same time. Wonder if Ellie feels the same?* She turned and looked at Ellie.

"Well," Ellie flashed a big smile, "here we go at last." The two brides picked up their cascading bouquets of evergreen leaves and holly berries and walked to the great room's doorway where John Henry was waiting.

Sara watched as the three matrons of honor walked down the aisle to join the grooms and the best men at the front of the room. The men were wearing white shirts, denim trousers, and boots. The ladies in the bridal party had each chosen a colorful Frock from the store and carried small bunches of evergreen leaves. Emmeline carried baby Win, who did indeed represent something new, borrowed, and blue (booties). Bridesmaids Julianna and Niñera Maria followed them down the aisle, also in Frocks. *I am blessed with good friends.*

"Win behaved perfectly," his smiling father told the newlyweds after the fact.

Sara and Ellie, in their simple white dresses, looped their arms through John Henry's. Ellie said, "I'm not wearing my glasses, you'll need to guide me."

John Henry nodded. "You're in good hands." Sara could feel her heart beating in her chest. John Henry looked at each of them and said, "Ladies, you look beautiful and your grooms are waiting."

I'm beginning the walk toward my new life.

Gerard and Benjamin stood by the circuit preacher. Both were smiling. As the brides were handed to their future husbands, Benjamin winked and in a whisper, said, "Hello, beautiful."

Four vows were exchanged. Rings given. Benjamin's "I do" was loud as he looked into Sara's eyes.

Sara spoke softly. "I do." A tear slipped out of the corner of her eye. *A happy tear.* The preacher declared each couple to be man and wife. Benjamin folded Sara's veil back and tipped her chin up. "Mrs. Brown," he said. Carefully placing his hands on her shoulders, he leaned in and kissed her.

"I love you," Sara whispered in his ear.

As they walked back down the aisle, mariachi music began, courtesy of Juan and Carlos. The violinist attempted to keep up with the lively Mexican music with his own bouncy spiccato bowing. Win "sang" along. When the music stopped, Doc Adams predicted that with those lungs the baby would obviously grow up to be an opera singer.

As the chairs were cleared Gouhenant announced he was stealing the couples away for just a few minutes to make the wedding photographs. Taking them into a room adjoining the great room, Gouhenant posed them. "Benjamin, you sit, and Sara, please stand beside him with your hand on his shoulder. Yes, that's perfect. Be still, please." After several minutes Gouhenant said, "Excellent, thank you. Ellie, Gerard, you're next. Same pose, please."

Returning to the great room, the two couples were surrounded by friends.

By midafternoon the cakes were gone, the wine bottles had provided many toasts, and guests shared final good wishes and began to leave to be back in town before dark. The newly married couples thanked everyone for making the wedding so special and left for Dallas in Mrs. Cockrell's carriage. Hattie and Aaron stayed to help clean up and planned to spend the night. Everyone agreed it was a Texas ranch wedding to remember.

It was very late when a happy Sara—tangled in the sheets of their moss mattress—gave Benjamin what she expected to be the last kiss of the night.

"That was . . . you are wonderful, Mrs. Brown," Benjamin sighed.

"A night I'll never forget." Sara snuggled against him.

"Oh!" Benjamin grinned. "It's not over yet."

Sara pulled him closer. "Good!" *How I love this man.*

The next day they woke to a flurry of snow.

Sara opened her eyes and realized Benjamin was already awake. Propped up on his elbow beside her, he reached over and curled a strand of her long, brown hair around his finger. He released the resulting curl and said, "I love you, Mrs. Brown."

Sara smiled up at him. "Well, hello husband," she said with a smile. *What could be better than waking up with this man for the rest of my life?*

"Hello, sleepyhead. You are waking up to a winter wonderland—come see." He gathered her up in his arms, carrying her to the window, then setting her on her feet.

"It's beautiful," she said as she looked out at the snow-dusted square. "It hardly ever snows in North Texas."

"It almost never does, but I arranged this just for you on our first morning together. Like it?"

"I love it. You arranged it? That's quite an accomplishment."

"I was up all night negotiating for snow with the weather gods," Benjamin said with a straight face.

Sara said, "That's a fib. I happen to know that's not what you were doing." Flashes of their first night together made her smile.

"Oh, is that so?" Benjamin opened his eyes wide and made a silly face.

"Absolutely. My feet are freezing. Let's crawl back under the covers. I'll show you what you were really up to."

"I thought you'd never ask, Mrs. Brown," he said as he chased her into bed.

Being Texas, there was no sign of snow by midafternoon.

It was just two weeks later when Benjamin said, "It's hard to believe the year is almost over and it is Christmas again." He peered in a small wall mirror as he tied his tie.

"Here, let me straighten that." Sara turned him toward her, redid the knot, and stepped back to assess the result. "That's better. My, you look handsome."

"You don't look too bad yourself, Mrs. Brown. I like your Frock. All you need to be ready for tonight is this." He pulled a small box from his suit pocket and slipped it into her hand. Sara undid the wrapping and opened the box. Inside was a heart-shaped, gold locket etched with flowers. Engraved on the back were their initials and 1859.

"It's beautiful, thank you." A tear ran down her cheek.

"Do you not like it?"

"It's perfect. I love it and I love you."

Benjamin clasped the chain around Sara's neck and kissed her. "We'd better hurry or we'll be late for the Christmas Eve party."

"There's still time for you to open your gift." Sara opened a drawer and handed a small, rectangular box to Benjamin. Unwrapping and opening it, he looked perplexed for a moment.

"Pencils and a sharpener. I can always use more pencils. Wait a minute—" He lifted one out of the box. "There's an eraser on the end of the pencil. What a great idea! I've never seen these before."

"You are always complaining that you can't find your eraser. Now it will be on your pencil. They're a new invention. You just sharpen the bottom of the pencil to reveal the eraser."

"I'll be! Leave it to you to find the perfect gift. Thank you. I can't wait to show off my new pencils. In the meantime, let's get our coats and blow out the lamp. It's time to go. I'll carry your cake—it's a beauty."

"Thank you, but remember that flattery will not convince me to forgive fingerprints in the frosting."

The outside of Adolph Gouhenant's Art Saloon was decorated for the holiday with green garlands and red berries. Music leaked out of the seams around the doors and windows. The soft light of oil lanterns flickered and cast shadows on the ground as they opened the door. They entered to the smiles and laughter of hardworking people happy to have a reason to celebrate.

The music and dancing were already underway as they stepped into the Art Saloon. Gouhenant, their host, greeted them, wishing them Merry Christmas. "What a pretty cake, Sara. There's a table for sweets against the back wall."

As they made their way into the room, greetings came from all directions. Benjamin set the cake on the sweets table. Sara turned toward the crowd and came face-to-face with Mrs. Tanner from the wagon train. "Mrs. Tanner?" she blurted out.

The woman glared at her. "One and the same. How are you, Mrs. Darnell?" There was venom in her voice.

It took Sara a moment to recover. "It's 'Mrs. Brown' now. This is my husband, Benjamin Brown. Benjamin, Mrs. Tanner was on the wagon train to Dallas with me."

Before Benjamin could respond to the introduction, Mrs. Tanner looked at Sara. "Well it didn't take you long, did it? Hope this one's better than the last." She made kissy-kissy sounds and walked away.

"Whoa! What was that all about?" Benjamin asked as the woman retreated. "It's obvious she doesn't like you."

Cecilia rushed up from across the room. "Oh, Sara, I had hoped to warn you before that awful woman found you."

"What on earth is she doing here?" Sara asked.

"She and her husband are on their way from Waco to the town of Palestine. I'm not sure why. They came in yesterday, expecting to make their connection today. Because of the holiday, the stage schedule changed, so their connection from here to Palestine doesn't leave until the twenty-sixth. They're staying at Crutchfield's. Someone on our wagon train ran into them and invited them tonight."

Cecilia turned to Benjamin. "She's not a nice woman and she harbors a grudge against Sara."

"We'll just have to avoid her," he said. "Can't let her spoil the party."

"John Henry and I saved chairs for you, come visit for a minute." As they settled into their chairs, Cecilia said, "Whit and Emmeline decided to skip the party and stay home with Win. You wouldn't believe how he has grown since Thanksgiving. He is starting to smile and reach for things."

"His head seems to be growin' faster than the rest of him," John Henry said. "I believe it's a sign he'll have a big brain and be very smart. But Cecilia and Emmeline say it's normal and the rest of him will grow and catch up with his head."

Cecilia grinned and patted his hand. "I'm sure he'll still be very smart, darlin'."

As the fiddlers struck up a lively polka, the men led their ladies to the dance floor. As they twirled around, Sara glanced over Benjamin's shoulder and saw Mrs. Tanner quickly pick up her cake. Following Sara's glance,

Benjamin and Sara both saw Mrs. Tanner slide the top layer of Sara's cake onto the table and smash it with the bottom of the plate. Benjamin twirled to the table, stopped beside Mrs. Tanner, who was still holding the plate with the bottom layer of the decapitated cake. "Oh my!" he said. "Look what you've done." He took the plate out of her hand, took a stumbling step, and deftly slid the remaining bottom layer onto the front of Mrs. Tanner's dress. Her mouth flew open. "So sorry, cake accidents do happen." He set the plate down, lifted Sara's hand, and they danced away.

"I can't believe you did that." Sara was trying hard not to laugh.

"I was not about to let her spoil the party for you. She made the first move, I just finished it."

"That was sweet," Sara said. "Thank you."

"You're welcome. I'm just sorry I didn't sneak a slice before the party. Pecan cake is one of my favorites."

"I'll make you another one—you've earned it," Sara said, as she watched the Tanners flee the party.

The fiddlers played, and Sara and Benjamin danced and danced.

A bit breathless, they finally collapsed in their chairs. John Henry said, "We're off to the dance floor." Daniel and Julianna slipped into the now-vacant chairs. "Merry Christmas," Benjamin said. "Do you two have big plans for tomorrow?"

"Dinner at the Pollard house," Julianna said.

"And supper at the McDougal house," Daniel said. "We will be up to our eyebrows in roasted wild turkey and sweet-potato pie." He patted his stomach. "Can't wait."

Julianna shook her head. "Sara, you've seen him eat. How can a thin guy eat so much? It's a mystery to me. What are your plans for Christmas?"

"We've already exchanged gifts. Look at the beautiful locket Benjamin gave me."

"Oh, it's engraved," Julianna said. "That makes it really special, doesn't it?"

Sara smiled at Benjamin. "It does."

Benjamin said, "Sara gave me the most practical pencils—with erasers on one end. Never seen them before."

"What a smart idea," Daniel said. "Are you going to your momma's tomorrow, Benjamin?"

"Yep, we're joining Momma and Aaron for Christmas," Benjamin said.

"Ellie and Gerard are coming too," Sara said. "I'll made a pecan cake in the morning, at Benjamin's request, to take with us."

"Well, have a merry, merry Christmas Day," Daniel said. He stood and took Julianna by the hand. "I promised Julianna I'd dance most every waltz." They blended into the crowd of dancers.

Spotting Sarah Cockrell dancing with Edouard Charles Beaulieu, Sara waved.

When the waltz stopped, Sarah Cockrell joined them. "Merry Christmas," Sara said.

"Merry Christmas to you two newlyweds. Your wedding was lovely, by the way."

Sara smiled at her friend. "Thank you for sending the four of us home to Dallas in your carriage. That was so thoughtful."

"You're welcome. I enjoyed riding back to Dallas with Ira and Marilyn Webster. They are such nice people. I just wanted to say happy holidays and good night. It's getting late and I need to head back home to have Christmas Eve with my children. Have a wonderful day tomorrow."

"You too, Sarah. Merry Christmas." Sara stood and gave her friend a hug.

Later Sara whispered to Cecilia and her sister, Effie, what Benjamin had done to Mrs. Tanner.

Cecilia said, "Served her right, the old biddy . . . destroying your cake . . . she really is mean."

Much later Sara and Benjamin climbed the stairs to home. As Sara opened the door, Benjamin pulled out his pocket watch. "It's past midnight—Merry Christmas, darling. May we have many, many more together."

Sara turned to embrace him. "Many, many more! Merry Christmas, Benjamin."

★1860★

Conflagration!

One January morning over coffee and oatmeal for breakfast, Sara asked Benjamin, "What do you have planned for the day?"

"Four meetings with cotton farmers. Your cotton-plantation partner, Henry Watson, was right when he predicted that Texas would see a flow of plantation owners moving from other cotton-growing states to Texas. All four of my meetings are with new arrivals. Dallas is growing and business is good."

"Business is good, but I have to wonder about the growth in the number of slaves. With all these plantation owners moving here, will protecting slavery become such an issue that secession becomes more likely?"

"Probably, but I think we're headed down that path anyway. Aaron agrees."

"I don't like slavery. It just isn't right to own other people. I also think Governor Houston is right when he says the Union is worth protecting. Avoiding a war we most likely can't win just seems like common sense."

"Having common sense can be a problem, Sara."

"Having common sense . . . a problem?"

Benjamin grinned. "Absolutely. Having it means you have to put up with folks who don't."

Sara grimaced and threw her napkin at him.

He stood, walked over to her, leaned down, and kissed her. "See you tonight, sweetheart."

A few minutes later, a warmly dressed Sara pulled her cape around her shoulders and was off to check on her stores. As she walked she wrestled with a contradiction between her own beliefs and actions. *I don't like slavery, yet Mr. Watson's slaves are working cotton on my land. I have to cultivate the land to keep it and I've taken the easy way to do it.* Sarah realized she had fallen into the trap of how things were done in the South. *There are no two ways about it*, she thought. *I'm a hypocrite.*

At the former West store, she found Daniel had arrived early. He had already dusted the shelves and made a list of what they needed to restock. "I've been keeping a list of new items customers have requested in the past few weeks. What do you think?" He handed her a list.

Sara reviewed the short list. "What are your thoughts, Daniel?"

"I do think we need to add more butter churns. It seems not everyone arrives with them. Sardines sell very well, so we might try a few cans of oysters. When I'm asked for more clothes for children, I refer them to our original store. I've also suggested to Julianna that rubber balls might sell. I've had a number of requests for them."

"Draw up an order for what you want to stock, then we'll look at the cost and make sure we can afford it. I'll see what Julianna thinks about rubber balls."

Daniel sure has a good head on his shoulders. I'm lucky to have him.

"Daniel."

"Yes, ma'am?"

"Thank you for doing such a good job." Sara thought his grin was going to split his face.

Sara's original store was now even more focused on the ladies, but Julianna's idea for ready-made dresses was slow to catch on. They had advertised ready-made Frocks in the *Dallas Herald* and ladies had come in to look. A few bought but most hesitated. Sara was concerned that the idea wasn't working and her decline in profits was evidence of the fact.

Early one morning she and Julianna met over Mr. Baker's pastries to talk about it.

"What sells best are the fabrics and styles on the dressmaker's dummy," Julianna said. "Women seem to be able to imagine the dress on themselves if they see it on a dummy. Dummy . . . that's a terrible word, isn't it? Anyway, how can we help them see themselves in our Frocks?"

"We do need to think of something," Sara said, thinking of her declining savings.

"I've been thinkin', " Julianna's words tumbled out faster than a flock of birds scattering. "I just love looking at fashions in *Godey's Lady's Book*. Think most women do. What if we ask five or six well-known Dallas ladies if they'd be willin' to have their portraits made by Adolph Gouhenant, wearing our ready-made Frocks? They'd choose the dress, get a photograph, and keep the dress, with our compliments."

"Go on. I'm liking this idea."

"We'd post the photographs in the store and show Dallas' best-dressed ladies wearing our Frocks. What do you think? Would the women be willin'? Can we even afford to do it?"

"I think so. Let's put pencil to paper and see what it would cost us to do that." Sara was thinking out loud. "How many dresses would we have to sell to equal the expense? Can you talk to Adolph Gouhenant and ask how much he would charge to do six or eight portraits? He might wish to exhibit the photographs too. We want everyone to be excited about doing it."

"I'm already excited," Julianna said. "I'll start workin' on the numbers. I never knew numbers were such an important part of runnin' a store. I'm sure glad I'm good at arithmetic."

Sara realized that having Daniel and Julianna working at the stores had been one of her best decisions. *What would I do without them?*

Benjamin came home one spring evening with important news. "Wesley Arbuckle, a major investor in the Mills cotton-factoring company, is comin' to Dallas this week on the stage from Galveston. He wants to check on the status of the new office. I just received his letter today."

"This week's stage?" Sara asked. "The stage from Galveston comes in tomorrow about midday."

"Midday! Yikes." Benjamin started running his hands through his hair until it was standing on end. "The cleaner, who comes once every two weeks, doesn't come again until day after tomorrow. The account books are in order but only up to last week. I reconcile them on Fridays. Tomorrow is Thursday . . . Arbuckle will want to see every recent transaction. Wouldn't you know the timin' would be wrong?"

"Here's what we'll do," Sara said, smoothing his hair. "I'll get a broom, a mop, and some soapy water and start cleaning. You start on your account books and we'll see how much we can accomplish. We'll take a break midway and eat the beef tamales Emmeline brought us when she came to town today. Juanita made a new batch and Emmeline says they are the best yet. Then we can get back to work. I'll put on some old clothes to clean in and meet you downstairs."

It was late when the two crawled into bed, but the accounts were current, and the office sparkled. "Thanks to you," Benjamin said, as he snuggled up to her, "I'm ready for tomorrow."

"When we work together, darling, we can work miracles," Sara yawned as they drifted off to sleep.

Benjamin and Sara were watching as the stage arrived the next day. "There's Mr. Arbuckle." Benjamin pointed at the compact, balding gentleman stepping out of the stage. As she looked, her first thought was that he must have been quite handsome as a young man. He wore a black frock coat over pinstriped pants. His gold watch chain caught the light as he turned to assist a tidy lady in a full-skirted, navy-blue, silk dress and a large hat with a veil and feathers. She looked at him with affection as he lifted her from the stage, and they stood arm in arm as the whip retrieved two matching carpetbags. "Oh! His wife is with him," Benjamin said in surprise.

"Don't worry, I'll entertain her." *Somehow.*

"Benjamin," Arbuckle said as he spotted him. "Glad to see you, young man." He shook hands and then slipped his arm around the woman beside him. "Let me introduce my wife, Sadie Arbuckle." Mrs. Arbuckle extended her hand to Benjamin who took it gently.

"I'm pleased to meet you, Mrs. Arbuckle, and to see you again, sir. Welcome to Dallas."

He put his hand on Sara's back. She took a step forward. "I've married since I saw you last. This is my wife, Sara Brown."

Arbuckle and his wife said, "Congratulations," at the same time. Crow's-feet appeared in the corners of their eyes as they both smiled.

"Ah, the brokerage landlord, if I recall?" Arbuckle said

"Yes," Sara said. His voice was friendly, and Sara found herself warming to him. "But even happier to be Benjamin's wife."

"Are you staying at the St. Nicholas Hotel?" Benjamin asked.

"We are. We'll be here today, then tomorrow we'll catch the stage on to Nacogdoches where our daughter lives. We plan to spend a week or two with her before returning to Galveston."

"Let's get you settled in," Benjamin said. They began to walk to the hotel.

"My goodness," Sadie Arbuckle said, looking around as they walked, "I expected a bigger town. What is there to do here?"

Sara smiled and said, "I'm sure we can find something to interest you." An idea was forming in her head. *Could Mrs. Arbuckle help them sell Frocks?*

Benjamin and Sara waited in the lobby of the hotel while the Arbuckles spent a few minutes refreshing themselves in their room, and then all four went to dinner, or "lunch" as Arbuckle called it, in the hotel dining room. After lunch Benjamin and Wesley Arbuckle retired to the office. The ladies lingered at the table for a few moments, talking.

"You are a fashionable lady from a much bigger town. I'd appreciate your opinion and expertise about something," Sara said to Sadie Arbuckle.

"Why yes, of course, dear." Sadie Arbuckle raised a questioning eyebrow. "How might I help you?"

"Let's visit my store and I'll explain." The ladies walked to Sara's store. Julianna greeted them at the door. "This is my assistant, Julianna McDougal. Julianna, Mrs. Arbuckle is from Galveston. She is the wife of an investor in Benjamin's firm." Sara explained to Sadie Arbuckle that the store was now carrying ready-made dresses, most needing just minor alterations and perhaps some final hemming to fit perfectly. Julianna gave them a quick tour of the dress section of the store. "This was Julianna's idea," Sara said.

Sadie Arbuckle clasped her hands and said, "What a wonderful idea, Miss McDougal. Not having to wait to have a dress made would be so convenient."

"We are planning to select few of the best-dressed ladies in Dallas and invite them to have their daguerreotype portraits made wearing our ready-made Frocks. The photographs would be made by our well-known photographer, the Frenchman Adolph Gouhenant," Sara explained. "Each woman could choose the dress she wanted for her photograph. Of course, they'd each get a photograph and keep the chosen dress, with our compliments. We'd ask for permission to post the photographs in the store as examples of Dallas' best-dressed ladies wearing our Frocks. What do you think—would women be willing?"

"I'm sure they'd be delighted," Sadie Arbuckle smiled. "I wish someone in Galveston had thought of this."

Sadie Arbuckle's enthusiasm was what Sara had hoped for. Sara caught Julianna's eye and Julianna understood right away. "Mrs. Arbuckle, this may be presumptuous, but would you like to choose a dress and have your daguerreotype made in one of our Frocks? We'd love to display your photograph and label it 'Mrs. Wesley Arbuckle, one of Galveston's best-dressed ladies'."

"My dear, I'd be flattered and delighted to do so."

After long consideration, Sadie Arbuckle finally decided upon a small floral-print calico with a bell skirt and fitted, button-front bodice with smocking and a high neck. With hemming and just a bit of quick tucking because her waist was so small, Julianna had it ready. "You look absolutely charming!" Sara said.

Fortunately, Adolph Gouhenant was available. Soon Sadie Arbuckle was in front of the camera. By late afternoon the photographic session was declared a success.

When the ladies returned to the store, they found Benjamin and Mr. Arbuckle waiting.

"Wesley, you can't imagine what an enjoyable day I've had with Sara and Julianna." Sadie Arbuckle was flushed with pleasure. "I can't wait to tell you and my friends in Galveston all about it. Before we leave tomorrow, I'll have a new portrait to show you." She thanked Julianna for the third time, and the two couples walked across to the hotel for supper.

Over a meal of prairie chicken, Wesley Arbuckle praised Benjamin. "The brokerage's financials are current as of yesterday and the office was clean as a whistle. Couldn't be more pleased," he told the ladies. "Sara, your husband may be the best manager we have. What's more, he was smart enough to marry the Dallas office's landlady." Everybody laughed and Benjamin glowed with the praise.

As Sara and Benjamin walked back to their home above the office, he squeezed Sara's hand. "Thank you."

"For what?"

"For being you and for making Sadie Arbuckle so happy. I have a feeling that if she's happy, Arbuckle is happy too."

The next day Wesley and Sadie Arbuckle caught the stage to Nacogdoches, her daguerreotype portrait and new Frock safely packed in her carpetbag.

Sara and Julianna prominently displayed the daguerreotype image, labeled "Mrs. Wesley Arbuckle, one of Galveston's best-dressed ladies, in a Frock from this shop." It created a positive stir among the women of Dallas; comments included: "All the way from Galveston to buy a Frock!" and "Look how lovely she looks in that dress." A number of Dallas ladies, including Sarah Cockrell, Margaret Bryan, and the mayor's wife, agreed to pose for portraits in Frocks. Sales finally began to increase. At the end of June, the store's books revealed that the pre-made Frocks were finally profitable.

Midday was hot on Sunday, the eighth of July in 1860. The temperature was estimated at over one hundred degrees. Many residents were at dinner or inside trying to avoid the oppressive summer heat. A pile of empty boxes in front of an empty drugstore on the west side of the square began to smolder. Sara and Benjamin ran from their building when they heard the first calls of "Fire! Fire!"

The wind was strong and gusty. They watched as the strong wind caught the flames from the burning boxes and sent them up and outward to the adjoining building. "It's spreading!" Benjamin shouted.

A crowd was gathering. "Bucket brigade!" someone hollered. Men scattered to try to find pails. Soon stores around the old drugstore, including the *Dallas Herald* building and Mrs. Cockrell's St. Nicholas Hotel and its stable, were beginning to burn.

This can't be happening!

The heat intensified and hot ashes danced into the gusting wind. The dry wood of the buildings was ideal fuel for the flames. Dallas had no fire wagon and the small buckets of water moving hand-to-hand from the river seemed to do little good. It wasn't long before the entire west side of Courthouse Square was being licked by the fire and the air was dark with smoke. People stood in shock. Sara heard someone running by shouting, "It's too hot! Can't get close enough to use the water buckets!"

The hungry red-and-amber inferno was not to be stopped. The wind swirled the angry sparks and flames, igniting more buildings. Sara watched helplessly, black smoke burning her eyes, as The Crutchfield House Hotel and its stables on the square's northwest corner disappeared behind a wall of flames. They ran from the heat as a blacksmith's shop on the square's north side burst into flames. Then, on the northeast corner, the cotton brokerage building began to burn. *Oh no, not our home and Benjamin's office!* Sara clutched Benjamin's hand and looked into his eyes through her tears. They stood, mesmerized by the flames.

Sara's store in Mr. West's old location was next. A mighty explosion of the store's gun-powder inventory blew a hole in the building and shook the ground where they were standing. *Thank heavens no one was in there.* Benjamin put his arm around a weeping Sara. The fire roared as if in anger. Sara and Benjamin ran again from the blistering heat as the flames crawled their way up the sides of the remaining buildings and tauntingly flared out of windows. The smoke was thick and black with soot. The grove of trees that adorned the square added fuel to the fire.

The saddlery shop and Sara's Merchandising Emporium on the square's south side joined the fire. *My dream to have a store . . . all my work . . . up in flames.* Sara wept, the tears leaving streaks in the ashes gathering on her face. Joining the gathering crowd, they watched helplessly from a safe distance as each building was consumed. The brick courthouse in the square's center was still standing, but Sara could see flames inside the walls. Tears were streaming down her face as she buried it in Benjamin's shoulder. He held her tightly. "Gone, all gone," she mumbled through her tears.

A man dashed past them. "Hurry, we have to save what we can of the courthouse!" Grass was now burning at the base of the brick building in the center of the square. Benjamin and Sara ran to join the long bucket brigade that had formed from the river to the square. Scores of people joined in, tossing water in an attempt to save the walls of the courthouse and John Neely Bryan's first cabin. For hours they passed buckets of river water down the long line to the courthouse and the small cabin.

By sunset the brick walls of the two-story courthouse were scorched and damaged but still standing. The interior was gutted. Bryan's original cabin had been mostly saved. Smoke and the smoldering ruins of buildings cast an otherworldly orange glow across the sky. Ashes and blackened logs were everywhere. Like everyone else, Sara and Benjamin were black with soot and bone tired. Benjamin was rolling his aching shoulders.

All around them exhausted Dallas residents stood in shock. Flames had consumed the square, the heart of the town. Not a business stood and residences on the square were gone as well. Sara and Benjamin, Hattie and Aaron, Ellie and Gerard—like many others—were homeless. An exhausted Benjamin looked at what was once his office and their home. "Burned, everything burned." His voice trembled.

Sara pointed. "Look!" The Diebold safe sat like a Phoenix—a charred, soot-covered box where the cotton brokerage had been.

Benjamin shook his head. "It's all gone, your stores, my business, our home. We don't have anything left—except each other." They both sank to the ground.

Sara wiped her nose on her sleeve, smearing the black soot on her face, and looked up at him. "Maybe that's all that really matters." Then she began to sob. Benjamin took her in his arms and Sara felt his hot tears on her cheek.

People stood staring at the ruins of their town; others roamed, looking for friends and relatives. Sara and Benjamin pulled themselves up and began to search for Hattie and Aaron. Sara saw Ira Webster on his knees, head bowed, hands over his eyes. Marilyn Webster was leaning down, her arms around his shoulders, trying to comfort him.

Ellie and Gerard stumbled up to them. "I've never seen such a fire," Gerard said. "We've lost almost everything. Ellie's school and our home—gone.

Thank God, my workshop is off the square in my old, two-room cabin so I still have my carpentry tools." Ellie was weeping and couldn't speak.

"You are fortunate, Gerard," Benjamin said. "And we are all alive."

"We're glad you two are safe," Sara said, hugging Ellie.

"There's Momma!" Benjamin grabbed Sara's hand and they hurried to where Hattie and Aaron were standing. Benjamin put his arms around Hattie. "Thank heavens you and Aaron are all right."

"We're fine, son, but the boardinghouse is gone. Aaron's office is off the square and didn't burn, so that's a blessing. But you and Sara lost both stores, the cotton brokerage, and your home. I'm so sorry. What a terrible thing has happened today. I'm just grateful we're all standing here."

Adolph Gouhenant staggered past. Sara heard him muttering, "How can this be? My photographic equipment destroyed, my Art Saloon burned."

Sara scanned the crowd for Sarah Cockrell but couldn't find her. The sight of the flames had brought people from outside the devastated square and the crowd had grown.

"Listen," Aaron said. They could hear shouting outside the square where a crowd was gathering. "Sounds like Mayor Crockett." They followed the wave of people and found Mayor John Crockett standing on a wooden box. Like everyone else, he was wet, soot-stained, and almost unrecognizable.

"Gather round . . . gather round," he said as people began congregating. "Yes, this is a disaster! But thanks to your efforts, the courthouse hasn't been completely destroyed. And we have no reports of serious injury or deaths." There were a few cheers from the crowd. "I understand the horses from the livery stable and the hotel stables also escaped injury." A few more cheers.

"We have suffered the loss of our entire town square. Terrible! But we are Texans. Tough, resilient, determined. We built Dallas once, we can build it again, better than before." Sara heard some grumbles.

"I know, I know . . . it's late, you're exhausted and discouraged. Get some rest. There are kind people from away from the square and from La Réunion who are here offering shelter for the night. If you are offering a place for tonight please come stand beside me so those in need can find you."

Texans band together to help each other!

The mayor continued. "We have had house-raisings in the past, now we need to plan for a town-raising. What is it we teach our children to say?"

He paused, waiting for the crowd to respond. It was quiet. "Come on, what do we say?"

Someone yelled, "Hurray for—" People joined him in the cry. "Hurray for Texas! Hurray for Dallas!"

"Yes," the mayor cried. "We *will* rebuild Dallas and we'll start tomorrow!"

As he stepped down from his box, Hattie said, "Easy to see how he got elected."

"I believe him," Sara said. "We can rebuild bigger and better." Weak with grief and red-eyed, Benjamin and Sara joined Hattie and Aaron sleeping on the floor of Aaron's law office. The next morning Julianna brought breakfast and a washbasin and pitcher from her parents' farm. She also delivered two completed Frocks that had not yet been added to store inventory. She volunteered to take Hattie and Sara's dirty dresses to the laundress to see if they could be salvaged.

"Remember, there's a freight delivery scheduled for the store in four days. We can send an order back with the freighter for the things you need," Julianna said. "Just make a list for me."

Sara hugged Julianna. "You are a lifesaver, Julianna, thank you."

In the light of day, it was confirmed that, miraculously, not a single person had died.

After washing up as best they could with water from Aaron's office rain barrel, Hattie, Aaron, Sara, and Benjamin walked to the square.

"What on earth is going on?" Sara asked. The area that had been the square was full of shouting, sullen men. Waving their fists wildly and talking over each other, they had worked themselves into an angry panic.

Stopping a man running by, Aaron asked, "What's happening?"

"We just got word that there were also large fires in Denton, Pilot Point, Gainesville, and Waxahachie yesterday. A mill was also burned outside Fort Worth. There are unconfirmed reports of more fires in other towns and other mills being burned. There's talk of an abolitionist plot to incite slaves to burn our North Texas towns. People are afraid." He ran toward the courthouse.

"This is on the edge of becoming a mob," Aaron said.

"Look, there's County Judge Burford," Hattie pointed at a distin-guished-looking man with a full mustache blending into a short, most-ly-white beard. He walked ramrod straight, taking long steps. His suit was immaculate and his shirt white and crisp. He had a deep frown on his face. "Maybe he can calm the crowd."

"How can he be so neat and clean after yesterday?" Sara looked down at her own still-grubby fingernails

"He was in court this past week in McKinney, where he lives. Must have just come into town," Aaron said.

Another man, still dirty from the fire, approached Aaron. "Lawyer Davis, we're putting together a committee of about fifty men to investigate the fire and decide what to do—come join us. I know you have a cool head. Judge Burford wants to talk to us in the courthouse."

Aaron looked at Hattie. "I want to know what's going on."

"Go," Hattie said.

Aaron followed the flow of men.

Hours later a somber Aaron found the three of them sitting on rocks by the river, trying to avoid some of the stench left by the fire.

"I don't have good news. Judge Buford talked to us for almost forty-five minutes and cautioned against taking any action without further investiga-tion. Fortunately he was able to calm the crowd."

"That sounds like good news," Benjamin said.

"Yes, but the meeting didn't stop there. Judge Burford left and rumors about other fires continued to come in. Witnesses from yesterday reported that the fire started in empty, cardboard boxes in front of the vacant drugstore."

"Yes," Sara said. "It's true. The boxes piled in front of the drugstore were the source of the fire. We saw that."

"Another theory, conflicting with the slave-revolt theory, was also pro-posed. Because the day was so hot, someone said the new phosphorus matches might have spontaneously ignited. Given the circumstances of the fire and the fact there were other fires at the same time, the match theory was given little credence by the group.

"A farmer, whose barn also burned, said that one of his young slaves had pointed the finger at another slave, Uncle Cato, claiming he had had told him there would be a fire. Uncle Cato was seized and questioned. He implicated two other slaves."

"Oh dear," Hattie said.

"In hopes of preventing further incidents, the committee decided—by majority vote—that stiff punishment was in order and the three slaves should hang. In two days, they'll be taken to the riverbank at the foot of Main Street and hung. I was against it, but it did no good."

"Oh my goodness, that's awful," Sara said.

"At the very least, it's premature. The investigation was too fast and, in my opinion, incomplete. I came away with the feeling that the committee felt public opinion was so inflamed that someone had to be hung." Aaron sighed and shook his head. "There was even discussion that every Dallas slave should be hung. Thank heavens that was rejected. But there is a recommendation that every slave be whipped by his or her master. I suspect there won't be many whippings though."

Sara found the conversation depressing. "I know the South's cotton economy is heavily dependent on slavery, but there must be another way. And I certainly won't go to any hanging!"

The hanging took place as scheduled. Benjamin and Sara stayed away. *A shameful day in Dallas.*

The *Dallas Herald* office was, like all buildings on the square, a complete loss; however, J. W. Swindells, the publisher of the *Herald*, traveled thirty miles to the larger town of McKinney and used the facilities of their paper to print a special "Dallas Conflagration" edition of the newspaper.

Two days after the fire, Mayor Crockett called a meeting of business owners, tenants, and residents of the square in order to develop a rebuilding plan. Sara and Benjamin joined the crowd. "We need organization," the mayor said. After much discussion, priorities were agreed upon and committees established.

The first task facing the residents was short-term housing for those who had lost their homes. Daniel had been asked to serve on the housing committee. He found Sara in front of Aaron's office where she and Benjamin were still staying. "Folks are crammed together in most any structure that has a roof. We have four extra people at our house and a couple more in the barn."

"So, what's the committee thinking?" Sara asked

"A lot of people who came to Dallas, but were not affected by the fire, still have the canvas from their wagons. The canvas is being collected and given to fire victims to be made into tents. The town donated the big tent made for the county fair. It'll be cut up for tenting too."

"Daniel, the store's Singer's sewing machine is heavy duty. It could be used to speed up the tent making."

"It didn't burn?"

"No, The the machine was on rotation with our Frock seamstresses. The woman using it at the time of the fire lives some distance from the square, so the store's sewing machine is safe. Talk to Julianna about organizing a tent-making effort using our machine. She also has a team of seamstresses who could help with tents. It would certainly speed things up."

"Great idea. I'll work with her to come up with a plan to take to the committee. Thank you."

The second task was clean-up. Once the remains of the buildings had cooled, refuse was shoveled into borrowed farm wagons, hauled away, and dumped in a gully a couple of miles away. The land around the square was then raked level. Benjamin joined the men shoveling and raking. At the end of each workday, he came back to Sara so filthy she could hardly recognize him. He bathed in the river.

"I was given the task of finding a good surveyor who would come immediately to survey the land and remark each lot based on the original town plat," Aaron told Sara and Benjamin. "I believe I've found one in Denison. Once the survey is done, we can confirm ownership and rebuilding can start."

"The Cockrell office burned," Sara said. "Weren't the ownership records and city plat map destroyed?"

"Fortunately not. Mrs. Cockrell's assistant was on the square when the fire started and had the presence of mind to run into the office and grab the ownership records and other papers before the office building caught on fire. Otherwise we'd have to have gone to Austin for the registered copies."

Several days after the fire, when the safe had finally cooled, Benjamin opened it to find the contents had survived the heat and flames. The word quickly spread that money and other valuables stored in the cotton brokerage's Diebold safe were fine. "When you are in business again," Sara said, "there will be a run on the cotton brokerage. Not to take money out, to put money in!"

Benjamin nodded. "The new safe will have to be bigger. If our deposits grow, Mr. Arbuckle will sure be happy." John Henry agreed to secure the safe and its contents at the ranch until a new cotton-brokerage building could be built and a safe procured.

In the wake of the fire, only two families left Dallas and their dreams behind. Others—like Sara and Benjamin—decided to stay and dream big. "You know how to open and run a cotton brokerage. You've done it. I can start and operate a store. If we've done it once we can do it again. Our future is in the new Dallas."

The *Dallas Herald,* still being printed in McKinney, interviewed Mrs. Cockrell, who pledged to support the rebuilding in as many ways as she could. The sawmill and lumberyard would work overtime to deliver boards for new construction. Production at the brickworks would increase. She promised to rebuild the hotel and to build an iron bridge across the Trinity.

The *Herald* also reported that it had taken four days for the news of the fire to make it 250 miles to Houston, where the local paper printed a special edition reporting on "The Great Conflagration in Dallas."

La Réunion became a major source of building stone and craftsmen of various types. The city also advertised in other area newspapers for bricklayers, carpenters, and other tradesmen to come to Dallas. Plans were quickly underway to rebuild the courthouse: walls would be repaired, a third story, topped by a tower, would be added to the structure; and the interior rebuilt. New trees would be planted, and an iron fence would be placed around the courthouse square.

"Four people in Aaron's small office is just too cramped," Benjamin said to Sara after several days of squeezing into the small space. "Let's take John Henry up on his offer to stay at the ranch for a few days until we can make other arrangements."

"Yes, let's."

Several days later after a trip into town, Benjamin came back to the T-Lazy-R, where he and Sara had temporarily moved. He found Sara sitting in a rocker on the porch. "Momma and Aaron have decided to keep staying in Aaron's law office for the time being," he said, sitting down in another rocker. "The good news is that Momma insured the boardinghouse with Mayor Crockett, who represents Homestead Fire Insurance Company. Thanks to her insurance policy, she'll have some money for rebuilding." He smiled. "They are already planning the new house."

Insurance . . . good for Hattie! "That's really is good news." Sara was wistful. "I wish I had been as smart as your momma and insured my inventory. Now I know to do that. How are Ellie and Gerard?"

"They're living on one side of his old double cabin and Gerard has cleared out his carpenter shop on the other side of the cabin and set it up for Ellie's school. Today he was building a shed to use as a new workshop. He is overwhelmed with rebuilding requests and has hired the stonemason and other carpenters from La Réunion to help him. He says he'll soon have several building crews. Both couples are coping, considering the situation, and are trying to decide what more-permanent living arrangements to make."

"It sounds like they'll be fine."

"I believe so. The letter to my company describing what has happened should have arrived in Galveston by now. We'll just have to wait and see what instructions we get from them. I also talked to Mr. Wells, our building owner. He's not sure he wants to rebuild. So, we don't really know our options at this point."

"I was hoping he'd—"

"Rebuild? So was I. In the short term, how would you feel about moving into the warehouse I rented for cotton storage? There's a small office located in one end. It has a parlor stove, a desk, and a couple of chairs. We could move the desk out to make room for a mattress. It's not much, but it's close to town, which is important. What do you think?"

"We can make that work. I'll see if we can buy a new Louisiana moss mattress."

Two days later, with thanks and hugs to their friends at the ranch, they prepared to move back to town and into the warehouse. Before they left the ranch, Cecilia and Emmeline gave them three boxes. "There's a box for you, one for Hattie and Aaron, and one for Ellie and Gerard," Emmeline said. "Should be enough provisions in each box for several days of meals."

"And," Cecelia said, "there's a skillet in each box."

"Thank you both. I may be doing campfire cooking again. Thanks to you, Cecilia, I know how."

The next day, Sara called on Mrs. Cockrell at her home. The housekeeper let her into the house. "Awful, awful thing that fire, Miz Sara."

"It was, Sally. How's Mrs. Cockrell?"

"She so strong. She jest say, 'Sally, I can rebuild. My family is fine and that what matters.'"

Sara found Mrs. Cockrell finishing breakfast in her dining room. Sarah Cockrell stood and embraced Sara. She stepped back and said, "Sara, I am so sorry about the loss of your stores and Benjamin's brokerage."

"And you lost the hotel and your office building," Sara said.

"Yes, I especially hated to lose the hotel. Alexander had started it and finishing it was a labor of love for me. So many people had losses because of the fire, but thankfully, no lives were lost."

Consoling each other over tea, Sarah Cockrell asked, "How about you and Benjamin? Where are you staying? And how about Hattie and Aaron and Ellie and Gerard?"

Sara described everyone's temporary housing.

"So you're at the cotton warehouse?"

"Yes, the office there is cozy, to say the least. But we're fine. Just waiting to hear from Benjamin's company about what they want to do about the brokerage business and hoping a letter will come on tomorrow's stage. I'm working to reopen my store in a tent. I'll start by offering limited merchandise. We're optimistic that things will get better. How about you?"

"I'm finalizing rebuilding plans for a new hotel, but a less elaborate one. I'll also rebuild our office building. And another two-story, brick building to rent is in the works. I'm wondering if you'd like to rent the second brick building. You could combine your two stores into one."

"I'd like that, but I'm not sure I can afford it right now."

"Sara, Dallas needs a good mercantile store. You've proven you're an excellent proprietress. I'll work with you to make it affordable."

Sara grinned. *What an amazing friend she is!* "Then I'd be excited and grateful to be your tenant. Thank you!"

Sarah Cockrell's expression turned serious. "Before you go, I have some bad news. As we feared might happen, Novella Adison is free again. She must have used her influence in Kansas because she was not charged with any crime. At least Devil Jack Black is in prison and scheduled to be hanged for murder, but Novella is free."

Free? "Oh, no! Do you think she'll be back in Dallas?"

"Probably not anytime soon. At this point, there's no town for her to control. I think she'll target somewhere else. But in the future, who knows? We just need to be vigilant. I suspect the woman's vindictive."

"I'm sure she is," Sara said. "We need to watch for her and for members of her gang. Boggy Bayou was untouched by the fire. Do you still have your informant there?"

"Yes, if he sees any of them he'll let me know."

"Thank you for telling me. So, Novella's not locked up . . . . Hmm, the question is, where is she and what might she have planned?"

Later that day Benjamin ran into their tiny warehouse space waving a letter. "Sara! It's from the company. They still believe Dallas has potential as an inland cotton market. They want to construct a new building for the cotton-factoring business and they're offering us the top floor as a residence, at least until some future time when the business needs more space."

"Oh, that's wonderful! When will they start building?"

"As soon as the town is resurveyed, they'll find a lot and start. They're also willing to make small loans to some of the businesses that burned, as well as the usual loans for cotton growers. I'm going to be busy reviewing loan requests starting immediately. Yippee! I'm back in business!" He waved the letter in the air.

"I have good news too. The inventory I ordered before the fire—and paid for in advance—will be delivered tomorrow. My new order will go out tomorrow as well. Julianna has finished the tent for me and Gerard delivered the tentpoles. I'll soon be running my store out of the tent."

"Good! I know you've been chomping at the bit to get your tent store open," Benjamin said.

"Even better, Benjamin, I met with Sarah Cockrell today and she is building a two-story, brick building that she will rent to me at a price I can afford. It will be big enough to combine both stores in one building. Soon I'll be fully back in business too!"

Benjamin looked down at Sara. "I love you, Mrs. Brown. I promise you that we will rebuild, and our life here will be a good one. The mayor was right, we Texans are tough, resilient, determined."

Sara, Daniel, and Julianna spent the next several days setting up shop in a tent located where Sara's Mercantile Emporium had been. Gerard had made some shelves and the three stocked them with the basic merchandise Sara had ordered before the fire—soap, salt, sugar, flour, bacon, cornmeal, and a few canned goods. Some clothing, including Frocks collected from the seamstresses who lived outside the square, also found a place on the shelves. Items that did not fit in the tent were stored in the cotton warehouse and could be requested and retrieved as needed.

Many people had lost everything in the fire, so sales were brisk. Sara kept a list of requested items to add to her next order. Requests for credit were considered and carefully extended.

In August, a full month after the Dallas Conflagration, the *Herald* reported that the *New York Times* had finally received word of the fire and printed a story under a slightly exaggerated headline—Great Fire in Texas: THE TOWN OF DALLAS DESTROYED, ALL THE STORES, HOTELS, AND PRIVATE DWELLINGS BURNED.

Even before the *Times* article was printed, a flurry of building activity in Dallas was well underway. Craftsmen and materials flooded into the town. A new lot was purchased on the square at the intersection of Commerce and Jefferson Streets for a two-story, brick, cotton-brokerage building with a residence above. Construction started immediately following the acquisition of the lot. Mrs. Cockrell's two-story, brick building—for Sara's store—began construction a week later on the corner of Commerce and Houston Streets. Early winter dates were targeted for the completion of both.

News in early November created unrest and agitation in Dallas. Sara hurried into the small cotton-warehouse office clutching the *Dallas Herald*. "Benjamin, did you see? Lincoln's been elected president! This week's issue of the *Herald* says the news came by telegraph to Marshall and the newspaper there sent out bulletins by the Overland Stage to all the stops along the mail route."

Benjamin looked up from reviewing the construction receipts for the new brokerage office and their residence, which was almost finished. "Yep, Lincoln's election is already the talk of the town."

"Do you think his election means Texas will secede?" Sara could feel her heart pounding.

"Probably. I know Governor Houston is still against it, but up to now, the talk has been that if Lincoln wins, Texas should leave the Union. If Aaron's right, and I think he is, secession of multiple states would most likely mean war."

Sara frowned. "That's what frightens me. I'm afraid you'll have to leave to fight. Lincoln won't even be inaugurated until early March, but Ira Webster told me that there's already talk of a secessionist convention. Benjamin, I don't want you to go to war."

"I don't want to go, but if it means protecting Texas, Sara, I'll go. I'm not marching off tomorrow, so let's stay calm. Aaron is a Dallas County candidate for the secession convention in Austin. Win or lose, he'll keep up with decisions made in Austin."

Sara sighed. "As I walked by the square a while ago, I saw that someone has already taken the American flag down from the courthouse flagpole and strung up an old Republic of Texas flag in its place. I met Ellie on the square and she said people are calling it an 'independence pole' and talking about Texas becoming a republic again."

"I guess that's a possibility. We'll just have to wait and see what unfolds. In the meantime, I've borrowed a horse and wagon from Cecilia's brother-in-law,

Michael Butler, so we can pick up our new Louisiana moss mattress, along with the one Momma and Aaron bought. This warehouse floor is hard, and I'm looking forward to a good night's sleep tonight on that mattress."

Sara stretched. "A comfortable mattress sounds wonderful, but the uncertainty of war will probably still keep me tossing and turning."

Sara was standing in the tent store filling an order for her laundress, Mrs. Mizell, and wrapping items in brown paper when Margaret Bryan burst in letting the winter wind blow in the open tent flap behind her. "Sara," she cried breathlessly, "oh, you're busy." she came to an abrupt stop.

I'll be right with you Margaret." Tying the final package and placing it in Mrs. Mizell's basket, Sara thanked Mrs. Mizell, told her she'd bring in a new batch of laundry the next day, and bid her goodbye. She then turned to Margaret. "Margaret?"

"Sara, John's home! After six years he's finally back."

Sara hugged her friend. "What good news!"

"Yes it is. Berry Derrit heard him callin' from across the Trinity last night and brought him across in the ferry boat. When he came in the house, the children didn't recognize him. And he has aged. Let's see . . . he's fifteen years older than I am . . . so he's fifty . . . but looks older. I fear his health is not good."

"Now that he's home you can feed him well and bring him back to better health."

"That's just it. He came home talking about the possibility of war and leaving again to join the Confederate army." Margaret sighed. "I feel like I'll never have my husband. I know the town is already buzzing about his return. Some are probably already predicting his departure again." She shook her head and frowned. "I shouldn't complain, but it's tiresome to always be a main source of gossip and speculation. I'm just happy he's home and hopeful he'll stay awhile."

"I hope so for the sake of you and your children."

"Anyway I wanted you to hear it from me first. You're always willing to listen to me talk about my loneliness and I know what I say will stay with you. You're a good friend, Sara. I'll bring John to the store soon to meet you."

"I'd like that Margaret. I'm pleased that he has come home to you."

Margaret gave Sara a goodbye hug and slipped out the door.

Two minutes later Ellie arrived. "Sara have you heard the news? John Neely Bryan came home last night!"

So I've heard," Sara said.

"Wonder how long he'll stay." Ellie raised her eyebrows with the question.

"I guess only time will tell." With that, Sara changed the subject and ended the conversation.

In December the *Dallas Herald* reported, "Within six months of the July fire, Dallas has risen almost like a dream from the ruins."

★ 1861 ★

Dark Storm Coming

O ne sunny day in late January, Sara was standing outside the tent store enjoying the sunshine when her mother-in-law came to shop. "I'm glad Dallas winters are mostly mild," Sara told Hattie as they stepped into the tent. "I'm hopeful we don't have a blue norther before the new brokerage building and my store are finally finished."

Hattie chuckled. "Lived here long enough to know that this time of year we can drop thirty or forty degrees between noon and dark, then bounce back by mid-mornin' the next day. Most predictable thing about Texas is its unpredictable weather. When will the store's new building be ready?"

"Mrs. Cockrell says in about ten days. Then we can move our inventory from the tent and the cotton warehouse and open the store pretty quickly."

"And your home and the brokerage office?"

"Gerard and his bricklayer say the new Mills Brothers' building will take another two weeks. We can hardly wait. How about your new house on Elm Street?"

Hattie rolled her eyes. "Elm's not much of a street yet, more like a path through the field, but there are lots of pretty trees and we figure someday it will be a real road. As for the house, we're about three weeks away from completion. Aaron wanted a stone-and-clapboard house, and the stonemason has been home sick for three days with a nasty cold. He's single, so I took him chicken soup yesterday in hopes of speeding up his recovery."

Sara grinned. "Can't hurt."

Hattie's expression turned serious. "Most likely Aaron will be back from Austin in the next two weeks. He'll have the results from the secession convention."

Ten days later Aaron rode in from Austin tired, dusty, and burdened with the news from Austin. Sarah, Benjamin, Hattie, and Aaron were invited to supper at the T-Lazy-R Ranch to hear his report.

"There's a great deal of news," Aaron said. "Things are moving quickly. You know South Carolina has seceded and that Alabama sent a representative to Governor Houston encouraging Texas to join them in forming a confederacy?" There were nods around the table. "Our special convention to consider secession has now passed an Ordinance of Secession."

"What does that mean, exactly?" Cecilia asked.

"It means Texas would nullify its agreement to join the Union as a state. Most view it as a first step in joining the Confederacy. Governor Houston talked the convention members into submitting the ordinance to voters for ratification. Voting will take place as soon as possible."

"Houston's still against leaving the Union, isn't he?" John Henry asked.

"Yes. Houston continues to argue that would be a disaster for Texas. However, if we leave the Union, he believes we should go it alone as a separate 'Republic of the Lone Star.'"

John Henry frowned. "What was the mood in Austin?"

"The city is full of secessionists who are calling the governor a submissionist or worse. I think the writing's on the wall. Texas will join at least five other states in the new Confederacy."

"So war looks certain?" Sara didn't realize she was wringing her hands.

"I believe so. But Governor Houston hasn't given up. He is traveling the state in a wagon to try to convince Texans to vote against joining the Confederacy. He is well respected as the hero of San Jacinto, but in this case, public sentiment seems to be against him and in favor of joining."

"What happens now?" Whit asked, slipping his hand reassuringly into Emmeline's, who was sitting beside him.

"As I left Austin, there was word that the commander of federal forces in Texas was being forced to surrender the US arsenal in San Antonio to secessionist volunteers, along with all army posts and property in Texas. The three thousand US Army troops stationed in Texas are now marching to the coast to be evacuated. This will clear the state of Union troops."

John Henry's eyebrows dipped down in a frown and he rubbed his chin. "So, once the Ordinance of Secession has been ratified by Texans, the way is clear for the secession convention to vote to secede?"

Aaron shook his head. "Right . . . and I think we'll be at war by spring."

John Henry looked around the table at them. "Then we need to begin making plans." His voice was deep and serious. "Some of us men will be conscripted, and we need to be sure our loved ones are safe while we're gone—"

"Conscripted?" Emmeline asked.

"The Confederacy will need men to fight. We won't have the chance to say no. We'll be sent into battle. We all need to give some thought to how we're gonna prepare for what's ahead."

War! The thought frightened Sara. She looked around the table. *What will war mean for each of us?*

Three weeks later on a cold and misty afternoon, Sara and Benjamin were standing in Sara's tent store when cries of "Here comes Governor Houston!" and "Look, it's 'Old Sam Jacinto!'" drew them into the street. Sure enough, Sara saw Houston climbing out of a flatbed wagon. He was dressed in his famous white duster, layered under an unbuttoned blanket-coat. Houston wrapped a plaid scarf around his neck, picked up his cane, and walked slowly to the courthouse square.

"He looks so tired," Sara said, studying the balding man with a fringe of white hair circling his head, blending into long, fuzzy sideburns. "He's limping."

"He does look tuckered out, but he's sixty-seven, Sara, and he bears wounds from several wars. Stumping across the state like this can't be easy for him."

Houston mounted a box and began to speak to the quickly assembling crowd. Sara and Benjamin looked at each other with wide eyes. "Suddenly, he's like a different man," Sara said. "He's full of energy."

The crowd was quiet as Houston spoke. "Some of you laugh to scorn the idea of bloodshed as the result of secession. But let me tell you what is coming. Your fathers and husbands, your sons and brothers, will be herded at the point of the bayonet—"

A man beside Benjamin booed loudly. Benjamin put his hand on the man's shoulder and quietly said, "Friend, you must be new to Texas. That is the hero of San Jacinto, the first president of the Republic of Texas, please give him the respect he is due."

"But Houston's wrong!"

"Perhaps. But agree or disagree, Texas would still be part of Mexico without him. Let him have his say and be respectful."

Benjamin did the right thing. I'm proud of him.

Both men turned back to Houston.

"You may, after the sacrifice of countless millions in treasure and hundreds of thousands of lives—as a bare possibility—win Southern independence, but I doubt it."

When Houston finished his speech, people swarmed around him, some wanting to shake his hand, others shaking their heads in disagreement. Yet the Dallas crowd remained respectful.

As they watched Houston climb back onto his wagon, Sara said, "I read in the *Herald* that the crowd he drew in Galveston was hostile and there were threats against his life. I'm glad that didn't happen here."

Benjamin smiled at her. "He's a man of his convictions. Agree with him or not, that's to be admired."

"Do you agree with him?" Sara asked. "I mean, that the South would lose a war with the Union."

"I think he's most likely right."

The sun had just set in a rainy sky when Gerard knocked on the door of their temporary home in the cotton warehouse. "The brokerage building is finished." Gerard said, handing them the key. "It's pitch-black outside and very wet, so wait 'til mornin' to visit." Thanking him and looking outside at the rain, they decided to follow his advice.

The sun was just sending its first rays into the morning sky when two planters arrived at the warehouse to finalize cotton deals with the brokerage. "Go ahead, Sara," Benjamin said. "I'll meet you at the new building."

Sara collected paper and pencil to make her list of the furnishings they'd need for their new home, left the cotton warehouse, and carefully picked her way past the puddles in the muddy street. She chuckled as she remembered Daniel calling yesterday's downpour, 'a real frog strangler.' It had lasted most of the night. She thought the size and depth of the remaining puddles confirmed Daniel's description.

Soon she stood in front of the new two-story, brick building on the corner of Main and Jefferson Streets. *It looks like a bank.* The store had kept her busy dawn 'til dusk, and she hadn't seen the building for at least a week. *This will be home and Benjamin's office.* Benjamin had told her the building measured fifty by sixty-five feet. The front door was on the short side of the building, facing Main Street. The double doors were carved wood. Above the doors was a large, semicircular window, which extended well into the second floor and was divided by wood strips into five equal, pie-shaped, frosted panes. *How pretty. We'll see part of that window upstairs.* On either side of the door were two large, rectangular windows. Slightly smaller versions were repeated on the second floor. The top of the building featured a small, decorative balustrade. Limestone blocks had been laid to create a level front porch with two steps leading up from the dirt street. *Impressive!*

She waited for several minutes on the porch until Benjamin came dashing up. He was a bit breathless from hurrying. "Sorry . . . had to wrap up two cotton agreements . . . March begins planting season." He took a deep breath and gave her a big smile. "At any rate, it's time for your tour, Mrs. Brown!" Several weeks before, he had told Sara, "I want to surprise you with the finished building. It will be more exciting if you see the inside completed instead of in all stages of construction."

Sara handed the key to Benjamin and he inserted it into the shiny, brass lock and pushed the door open. Their steps echoed on the plank floors as they walked into a very large main room. Sara took in the high ceiling and the plaster walls, some highlighted with paneling. "It's beautiful, Benjamin." Stepping to the left side of the room, Sara ran her hand over the decorative handrail of the staircase to the second floor. "I really like the paneling and wood trim."

"The Mills brothers sent their joiner all the way from Galveston to do the trim and paneling. He's gone back to Galveston as of yesterday, but he worked with Gerard's group of masons, bricklayers, and carpenters for weeks. Trained one of Gerard's cabinetmakers to help him, so now Dallas has a carpenter with joiner experience. Gerard says he's working on your store now."

"Yes, wait 'til you see it. He's doing a nice job on the trim work."

Turning her attention to the right, Sara saw a long, narrow room separated from the main area by a solid half wall rising about four feet from the floor. It was topped with a wall inset with a series of window frames, each about eighteen inches apart. Sara guessed this partition rose about seven feet in total. The remaining distance to the ceiling was open. There were doors at each end, closing the space.

"What's that room?"

"Think of it as tellers' windows. There is a counter and locked cash drawer at each window. I wanted multiple teller windows to give the brokerage room to grow. There's space for desks in the room behind the tellers."

"That's smart."

"There are two private offices in the back of this main room. The niche between those two offices will house the new Diebold safe. It should arrive sometime this month."

Sara patted Benjamin's arm. "I know, darling, you've been talking about it for six weeks."

Benjamin chuckled. "I shouldn't admit this, but I've even been dreaming about it."

He's actually blushing.

"Guess I just like safes. Especially the fireproof ones."

"Amen," Sara said, thinking about opening the old safe after the fire and finding the contents intact.

"There's shelving under the staircase for tagged cotton samples. The rest of the room has plenty of space for client chairs, maybe more desks, and several long tables where samples from cotton bales can be spread out and examined for quality."

"I think it is as nice as any office I've ever seen. Is it what you wanted?"

"Oh yes! And I can't wait to show you the upstairs." He grabbed her hand, pulling her toward the staircase. They climbed the interior staircase and unlocked the upstairs door to their private rooms. Benjamin put his hands over Sara's eyes. "Take two steps forward." Benjamin removed his hands and Sara opened her eyes. Sara gasped. After camping in the cramped office in the warehouse, Sara felt she'd stepped into a mansion. *There is so much space.* Three large windows, including the top of the semicircular one which began downstairs, flooded the main room with light. Slatted, wooden shutters could be closed over the rectangular windows for privacy. "Oh, Benjamin, it's lovely."

"You're happy with it?" Benjamin asked with a grin, as he slipped his arm around her waist.

Sara smiled up at him. "How could I not be?"

She looked down at the smooth, plank floors. *So much nicer than puncheon.* She wrote parlor carpet or oilcloth floor covering on her list. The joiner who had done the downstairs paneling had also done trim work, the fireplace mantel, and moldings upstairs. Sara ran her hand over the fireplace mantel and imagined how pretty it would be with Christmas garlands. *Momma would know how to decorate this for every season.*

Benjamin had promised her a multiburner, iron cooking stove. "Know where you want your stove?"

Sara pointed. "Probably near that corner."

Sara knew that to transform the corner into her kitchen, she needed a worktable. *Or a big butcher block on legs—maybe both?* She added a hutch, woodbox, and pothooks to her list. A table with at least four chairs joined the list. She showed Benjamin her list. "There's also plenty of room for a parlor settee, three upholstered chairs, and a small table, don't you think? That is if we can afford it."

Benjamin nodded. "We have two more rooms. Which one is our bedroom?" They peered into the two rooms. "The one on the right is bigger and it has a window and a parlor stove, let's use it. Agree?"

"Yes. We'll need a bed, dresser, maybe a small table for a water pitcher and bowl."

"You'll want a mirror, right?" Benjamin asked. "And I'd sure like a chair."

"How should we use the third room?"

"I don't know, honey. Maybe we should think about it. We may not be able to afford furniture for it yet anyway!"

Maybe a baby's room someday?

Benjamin put his arms around Sara and kissed her. "Welcome home."

"What a wonderful home it will be. We are so lucky, Benjamin."

Benjamin nodded and kissed her again.

Edouard Charles Beaulieu had offered to take Sara and Benjamin to La Réunion to purchase furniture from the colony's storehouse. He'd said, "As you know, Sara, many who abandoned La Réunion left furniture behind. The items have been collected and stored. Sales help support the remaining colonists. Many Dallas residents are buying furniture from the warehouse to replace what they lost."

The next morning Beaulieu, Sara, and Benjamin piled into a rented wagon and crossed the bridge to La Réunion. By noon they left the La Réunion warehouse with most everything on Sara's list: a curved-back sofa, two upholstered chairs, a wooden rocker, and a country French accent chest for the parlor; a draw-leaf, oak dining table and six matching chairs with woven seats for the dining area; a tall, six-shelf, mesh-front cupboard and a long, narrow, tavern worktable with a limestone top for the kitchen area; a bed frame with a headboard and footboard, a large wardrobe, and *petite chiffonier* with mirror for their bedroom. In addition, Sara chose two patterned carpets for the parlor and bedroom and an oilcloth for the kitchen floor. "We can use two of the dining chairs in the bedroom," Sara said.

By early evening everything was moved in and they took Beaulieu to supper at the newly completed Crutchfield Hotel to thank him. Over the venison steak, the conversation turned to the political situation.

"I've seen the men already gathering outside of town to join the Confederacy. Will you fight?" Beaulieu asked.

"I will," Benjamin said. "John Henry says we won't have a choice. That we'll be conscripted. What about you?"

"Of course I will fight. I am now a Texan. But war can be—how you say?—brutal. In 1844, when I was ten years old, my father died in the Franco-Moroccan War." He looked down and was silent for a moment. "It will be the same. Men will march away, and many will not return."

Sara felt a strong flash of fear. *I know he's right and I'm afraid for Benjamin . . . for Beaulieu . . . for all our friends.*

"I'm sorry," Beaulieu said. "War is too heavy a topic. This should be a celebration of your new home." He raised his wineglass. "*Trinquons à votre nouvelle maison . . .* Let us drink to your new home!" Glasses were raised and sips taken.

The *Dallas Herald* reported that on the second of March, Texas voters had passed the Ordinance of Secession by a vote of 46,153 for secession and 17,747 against. Three days later the legislature voted to join the Confederate States of America. Subsequently, all state officers were asked to take a loyalty oath to the Confederacy. Reading the article, Sara said, "Benjamin, Governor Houston refused to take the oath. The secession convention declared the office of governor vacant and Lieutenant Governor Clark was sworn in as Houston's replacement. Houston is banished from the government."

"That's sad, Sara. Some people have been calling him a Union man, but I believe he wanted Texas to be an independent republic again. I hope history remembers him as the hero of San Jacinto and the Republic of Texas's first president. He has been a powerful force in Texas."

"Yes, but now he is gone and we're one of the seven states in the Confederacy."

"Yes, with several more states likely to join."

"And war on the horizon."

"Yes, it's inevitable, Sara. Which reminds me, I saw John Henry in town this morning and he is inviting a group of us to the T-Lazy-R, as soon as Aaron returns from Austin, to talk about planning for what's ahead. I told him to just let us know when and we'll be there."

Sara frowned. "Yes, it *is* time to plan."

The next day, finishing the last of her morning coffee, Sara looked at Benjamin across their new dining table as he took his last bite of buttered toast. "I'm meeting Mrs. Cockrell in a few minutes to do the final walk-through on the store's new building. Want to come?"

He wiped a crumb from the corner of his mouth. "I sure do."

Mrs. Cockrell had chosen a lot across from the courthouse on the corner of Commerce and Houston Streets in the block where Sara's old store had been located. The new, two-story, brick building was now complete. Sara and Benjamin found Sarah Cockrell waiting in front of the building. "Hello, you two. The building's finished, clean, and ready for you, Sara. I think it turned out rather well. I hope you like it."

Sara looked up at the classic, square building made of red brick. "I certainly do. My sign will be ready to hang tomorrow—'Sara's Mercantile Emporium.'"

The new store measured almost fifty feet square and was across the square from the new cotton-brokerage building. There were two large display windows on either side of the slightly recessed front door. Sara pointed. "If you look inside, Benjamin, you can see the raised platforms for arranging display items in the windows." On the second floor were three additional windows. Each floor also had a row of high windows along the Houston Street side of the building. All the windows were trimmed in limestone. "I love it that the store has high windows on the side. There's plenty of wall space for shelving, yet those windows mean the store won't be too dark."

Benjamin nodded. "The best of both worlds, shelf space and light."

Sarah Cockrell opened the door, and Sara stepped in first. She smiled and pointed at the plank floors. "No more splinters in my knees from scrubbing puncheon floors." The windows brought in the day's early-spring sunshine and illuminated the room. The twelve-foot-long storekeeper's counter was centered at the front of the store and had glass-fronted display cases. Slightly to one side of the main counter was a small counter that would be devoted to a new, red coffee grinder.

Sara had asked for a wall of shelving along the sides of the room and two rows of double-sided shelves spaced equidistant down the middle of the room. The middle shelves were seven feet high, allowing the light to come in above the shelves of the high-ceilinged room. "We can display so much more merchandise now," Sara said. "And there's enough light to see what we have."

The stairs were located in front of a back wall, which separated the retail area from a storeroom stretching the width of the store. The door to the storeroom was under the staircase. They peeked in. "Lots of storage space," Benjamin said.

Sarah Cockrell asked, "Ready to go upstairs?" Sara and Benjamin nodded.

Again, shelving dominated the layout. "Benjamin, look at what Julianna suggested." Sara pointed at a row of clothes hooks placed between the front windows at about five and a half feet above the floor. "Hanging hooks for displaying our Frocks. So much better than folded on the shelf."

"It will be a wonderful store," Benjamin said, looking at the two ladies.

Sara's smile was so big it squinted her eyes. "The wooden trim work on the cabinets and shelving adds the perfect finishing touch. It's an elegant store." She turned to Sarah Cockrell. "Thank you."

"You're welcome. I look forward to a special opening event. Another tea party, perhaps?"

"The building deserves a party," Benjamin said.

Sara grinned. "Then I'd better start planning!"

Sara, Daniel, and Julianna spent the next week stocking the new store. "I think this is the last box from the cotton warehouse." Daniel sighed as he juggled an over-filled box of pots and pans and set it down on the store's counter. "Which shelf do these go on?"

"I'll show you," Julianna said and led him down an aisle of shelves.

Hours later Julianna announced that the Frocks were hanging on their hooks and the sewing sundries were neatly aligned on their shelf. "I think that's the last of the items that belong upstairs."

Sara replaced loose hairpins in her coiled braids and stood up from arranging tools on a bottom shelf downstairs. Daniel looked around the corner of a shelf and said, "I think we're through downstairs too. What do you think, Sara?"

After a quick walk-through, Sara said. "Thank you, both. The store is ready!"

"Whoopee! We are ready to open!" Daniel crowed. "No more store in a tent."

"It's been a long process," Julianna said, untying her store apron, "but the store has turned out better than before."

As they left the store, Sara locked the door, stepped off the porch, and turned back to look at the new sign that stretched across the entire front of the store below the second-story windows. "Sara's Mercantile Emporium," she whispered, "will be back in business Monday, with me, Sarah Brown, storekeeper."

That Saturday, the great room in the T-Lazy-R Ranch was full. Chairs had been gathered from all over the house for the ladies. Sara sat between Cecilia and Hattie. Benjamin and other men leaned against the wall. A few men sat on the plank floor. Among them, John Neely Bryan. Sara looked at the man and decided Margaret Bryan was right, he looked old and tired.

John Henry was leaning against the wall near the front door. He began the meeting. "We are now part of the Confederacy. As you know, the state has seized the federal arsenal in San Antone and federal troops are starting to abandon the forts and military camps in Texas. Sure looks like war with the Union is on the horizon, so we Texans need to do some plannin'. You've prob'ly seen the men campin' on the edge of town."

"Must be a couple hundred men there," Sara heard Whit say.

John Henry continued, "They're already comin' from all over Dallas County to join the Confederate Army. Doc Pryor tells me he's been appointed to set up a supply depot in Dallas—he calls it a commissary—to provide supplies for the army on this side of the Mississippi. So, things are underway. He woulda been here today but he headed to Austin for his instructions. Aaron knows what's happening in Austin, so let's start by asking him to share his information."

Aaron cleared his throat and moved to the front of the room beside John Henry. "Last night I wandered among the men camping outside of town waiting to enlist. Talk was they wanted to sign up early so as not to miss the chance to fight in the one big battle that will win the war. I worry that they are mistaken. It will not be a short, glorious war. The North has at least three times as many men of military age, more money, and a greater ability to produce needed goods. The government in Austin is beginning to realize this, as are the leaders of the new Confederacy. There's talk that after the initial flood of volunteers, the state will conscript men, probably between the ages of eighteen and thirty-five. That includes many of you, so you need to think about how to provide for your wives and children."

"That also means," John Henry said, "many of our ladies will have to manage farms, businesses, and other endeavors while husbands and sons are at war. It won't be easy."

Sara could hear talking among the crowd. She thought the voices sounded questioning and concerned.

"What about money?" Gerard asked.

"Confederate money will be printed. But I don't know any details." Aaron shrugged. "However, I do know that one of the North's first actions will be to cut supply lines to the South. The Gulf Coast will be a target for a blockade. So, just as the Confederacy will need to lay in as many supplies as possible right now, you'll need to do that personally too."

"I can order what you need until New Orleans and other Gulf Coast cities are blockaded," Sara said. "But understand, there will be high demand for limited goods."

"What about getting cotton to market?" Benjamin asked. "If New Orleans and Galveston are blockaded . . ." Benjamin raised his hands questioningly.

"Mexico," Aaron said. "If the blockade is successful we'll have to get our cotton to a Mexican port on the Gulf Coast. Most likely be Matamoros. The Union won't interfere with Mexican ships. This will be critical. The sale of our cotton to Europe will pay for the war and give us something to barter with for weapons and other military supplies. Without our cotton sales to Europe, especially to Great Britain, the Confederacy will be lost. The hope is that the European demand for cotton will cause Britain and France to support the Confederacy."

Aaron turned to John Henry. "John Henry and I have already agreed that cattle will be about as important as cotton. Texas beef will feed our soldiers and cattle sales will help keep our economy going."

"Will we have to drive our cattle to Mexico to get them to market?" Emmeline asked.

"Yes, if the coast is successfully blockaded."

John Henry furrowed his forehead, bringing his eyebrows down and causing his eyes to crinkle. "This brings us to something important." He paused for a moment. "With men off to fight the war, Texas will be unprotected. I fear the Comanche will increase their marauding all across the state. Others from Indian Territory may come south and start raiding again. Banditry will also increase. Our families will be unprotected."

Sara saw that tears were flowing down Ellie's cheeks. *After what happened to her family it must be frightening to hear of possible Indian attacks.* She watched Gerard put his arm around Ellie's shoulders.

John Henry was still speaking, and Sara shifted her attention back to him. ". . . So I've asked Aaron, along with some Texas Ranger friends of mine, to lobby the legislature to establish a frontier ranger regiment to protect the northern and western frontiers of the state. The regiment could take over our existing frontier forts, set up camps in other vulnerable areas, and protect against Indians and bandits, as well as Union invasion. These men could serve close to home."

Sara heard someone say, "That's for me."

"Now before you get all excited," John Henry said, "understand that a frontier assignment would be dangerous as hell. Uh . . . sorry, ladies. You wouldn't be fightin' farmers and clerks. The Comanche are fierce. They know no mercy and are the best horsemen in the world. They can shoot twenty arrows in the time it takes to reload your gun. They'll do it with complete accuracy from thirty or forty yards while ridin' a horse at full gallop."

Sara heard Beaulieu mutter, *"Ç'est pas possible!"*

"The Comanche have earned the name, 'Lords of the Plains,'" John Henry said. "Anyway, somethin' to think about before you rush off to sign up. Wanted you to know that there may be more than one way to get in the fight." He looked back to Aaron.

"Well, you know as much as we do at this point," Aaron said, with a nod to John Henry. "We need to think about how to prepare our families, our town, and Texas for war."

While many stayed to talk and ask more questions, Sara and Benjamin thanked John Henry and rode home on horses they'd rented from Webster's new livery stable. Both were silent all the way back to town. They returned the horses and walked the few blocks home. Daniel was standing at the door waiting for them. He didn't want to meet Sara's eyes and was digging in the dirt with his left foot. *Why does he look so sheepish?*

"Sara, I have to quit the store."

Sara's eyes widened. "Quit? Whatever for?"

I've enlisted, joined the Confederate Army—one of my brothers and me."

"Oh, Daniel." That was all Sara could think to say.

"I'll be here for a while, 'til they form us into cavalry regiments and transport us to our assignments. I'll come say goodbye when it's time. But I want to thank you for all you've done for me. I hope you'll take me back after the war?"

"Of course I will. Let's not say goodbye until you have to leave." Sara realized she had tears in her eyes. "Have you told Julianna?"

He nodded. "She's angry about it. Won't speak to me."

"Don't leave without saying goodbye to her, Daniel."

"I won't."

Benjamin shook Daniel's hand and said, "Stay safe."

Daniel nodded and was gone.

"Daniel enlisting makes it real, doesn't it?" Sara asked, looking at Benjamin as they stepped inside the new brokerage building and started up the stairs. "And it's just the start." *There will be hard times ahead.* Sara wondered if she'd have to face them with Benjamin gone to war.

"Cotton, cattle, and conflict," Benjamin muttered.

"What?" Sara hadn't heard him clearly.

"Cotton, cattle and conflict. That's what John Henry said our lives will be about for awhile."

"Three challenges," Sara said. "I hope we are strong enough to meet them. I hope Dallas and Texas are strong enough."

With a smile in his eyes, Benjamin took her hand. "Hurray . . ." He waited and started again, "Hurray . . ."

Sara chuckled, joined in, and together they said, "Hurray for Dallas! Hurray for Texas!"

Sara linked her arms around his neck and looked into his eyes. "Hurray for us!" she said.

Smiling, they sealed the thought with a kiss, putting aside—at least for the moment—the threats of war and separation.

The End

Watch for *Cattle, Cotton and Conflict,*
book two in the *Texas Brave and Strong* series

For fascinating tidbits of Texas history you didn't learn in school, checkout my Podcast, *Texas Brave and Strong.*

*Find transcripts of the podcast
(in the form of a blog) on LaurieMooreMoore.com*

★ POST SCRIPT ★

Notes on the story's characters
Best to read after finishing the book
Contains spoilers!

Both Texas history and Dallas history are rich with interesting characters and memorable events. My goal with *Gone to Dallas* (an obvious play on the phrase Gone to Texas) was to weave real characters and actual events into the story of a young widow who arrives to build a new life in Dallas, a tiny village of log cabins on the Three Forks of the Trinity River. While this is Sara's story, it is also the story of Dallas in the 1850s. Early readers asked, "Which characters are real?" So, here is the list. I have imagined their personalities using what historical information I could find. For which events in the book actually happened, visit LaurieMooreMoore.com and go to Bonus Content.

The real characters in the book:

★ **John Neely Bryan** – The frontiersman known as the father of Dallas. Born in Tennessee in 1810, he settled on the Trinity River in 1841. His original cabin (with renovations) sits in downtown Dallas next to "Big Red"—Dallas' former City Hall—now a museum.

★ **Mrs. John Neely Bryan (nee Beeman)** – The John Beeman family was one of the first two families to settle in Dallas. In 1841, Bryan convinced Beeman to move twenty-two miles from Byrd's Fort to the Elm Fork of the Trinity. Margaret was one of ten Beeman children, and was age sixteen at the time of the move. She married Bryan two years later at age eighteen. He was thirty-three.

★ **Alexander Cockrell** – The entrepreneur who purchased rights to Dallas land and the Trinity River ferry in 1852 from Bryan. Cockrell took over the development of Dallas until he was killed by Marshall Andrew Moore in 1858.

★ **Mrs. Alexander Cockrell (nee Horton)** – For decades, Sarah Cockrell was the quiet power behind Dallas' growth. She had been involved in the Cockrell businesses prior to her husband's death. He was brilliant, but illiterate, so his wife handled business finances and correspondence. After he was killed, she dealt with the colony's land grants, established numerous businesses, built office buildings, constructed two grand hotels, managed the toll bridge and ferry crossing, formed the company that built the 1872 Trinity River bridge, and raised four children. She was most likely Dallas' first millionaire. At her death in 1892 (age seventy-three), she owned twenty-five percent of downtown Dallas. She has been referred to as the town's first capitalist.

★ **Adolphe Gouhenant (often spelled phonetically as Gounah)** – French photographer, painter, owner of the Art Saloon.

★ **Dr. Samuel B. Pryor** – Physician, civic leader and first Mayor of Dallas. He arrived in 1846. Known as Old Doc Pryor.

★ **Andrew Moore** – Dallas Marshal who killed Alexander Cockrell in a duel in 1858.

★ **"Old Man" Tom Crutchfield** – Owner of Crutchfield House Hotel.

★ **James Wellington (Weck) Latimer** – Publisher/editor of the *Dallas Herald* from 1849 until his death in 1859

★ **J.W. Swindells** – Latimer's partner. Following Latimer's death, he became publisher of the *Dallas Herald* for the next 17 years.

★ **Victor Considerant** – The French organizer of La Reunion, the communal settlement of Europeans across the Trinity River from Dallas. He subsequently abandoned the colony.

★ **Julien Reverchon** – Naturalist, for whom Dallas' Reverchon Park was named.

★ **R. and D.G. Mills** – Although Benjamin Brown is fictitious, the cotton factoring, commission merchandising, and currency business of R. and D.G. Mills existed in Galveston and operated as described. I found no record of them in business in Dallas. Company owners and brothers Robert and David G. Mills were among the most successful businessmen in the South. "Mills Money" circulated in Texas and New Orleans and was known to be "as good as gold." Reputed to be worth three to five million dollars each, the brothers owned at least two hundred thousand acres scattered across Texas, plus more than 3,300 acres in cultivation. Their ships sailed the world with cotton and sugar. During the Civil War, their steamboats were acquired by the Confederacy and their sailing ships were blockade runners. They ended their lives in bankruptcy.

★ **The Trinity River** – The river weaves through Dallas' history as a major player. It is a significant reason John Neely Bryan chose the location for his town. The river tolerates bridges, then destroys them. It floods. It refuses to be navigable. The river shapes the town and its inhabitants. More than a character in the story, the Trinity River is a story all its own.

★ **The Preston Road** – This early road is also a key element in the story. Coffee's Trading Post and Ferry and Colbert's Ferry on the Red River were strategic crossing points from Indian Territory into north Texas. Eager to facilitate immigration, in 1841, The Republic of Texas built the Preston Road linking these two Red River crossings to the new capital of Austin. The road ran through Dallas and was the route Sara's wagon train followed after crossing into Texas. A few years later, travelers approaching Texas from the East, could also take the Central National Road, which began near the northeast corner of Texas and connected with the Preston Road at Dallas. These roads were merely cleared trails, but they meant Dallas was ultimately on the stage line routes, was a kicking-off point for buffalo hunters, and was on the main road south for travelers. After the Civil War, the Preston Road formed part of both the famed Shawnee and Chisholm cattle trails connecting Texas with cattle markets in Kansas and Missouri. Somewhere along the way, the word "the" preceding Preston Road fell away. Today the road is merely named Preston Road.

Several minor characters simply mentioned in the story were also real:

★ **Berry Derrit** – A Cockrell slave, who tended the Trinity toll bridge and ferry crossing, beginning in the 1850s. When emancipation was declared, Derrit rejected it and asked to remain in charge of the Trinity River ferry crossing. He continued in that role as a free man, retiring only when the new bridge was completed in 1872.

★ **Maxime Guillot** – An early French immigrant to Dallas who established a carriage and wagon making company. His wagons were considered top quality and were in great demand. Owning a Guillot "rig" was an indication of high social standing and buyers came from as far away as 350 miles.

★ **Pocahontas Pryor** – One of the eight children of "Old Doc Pryor," Dallas' first Mayor.

★ **Edward Fitzgerald Beale** – Surveyor. While surveying for a road from New Mexico to the California border, Beale led a caravan of camels from Texas to California to help the military determine if camels were superior to mules for military goods transport. The camels were deemed far superior; however, the Civil War ended the camel corps experiment and it was never revived. Most of the camels remained in their camel khan (corral) at Camp Verde, Texas. Others in remained in California. The last known camel from the experiment, Topsy, died in Los Angeles in 1934 at the age of 80. Interestingly, camel sightings continued to be reported in the West for decades thereafter.

★ **Edward Browder** – District Clerk. He cut the entrance ribbon for the first Dallas County Fair.

★ **Kate Warne** – Head of the Women's Division of The Pinkerton Agency.

★ **Sam Houston** – Hero of the Battle of San Jacinto, President of the Republic of Texas, Governor of the state of Texas.

★ **John Brown** – Abolitionist who led the raid on the Harpers' Ferry Federal Armory.

Comments on some fictional characters:

Many of the fictional characters in the book have been developed around the occupations and businesses which existed at the time of the story. For example, the earliest residents of La Reunion did include a dance master, carpenter, baker, milliner, musicians, butcher, brewer, stone mason, and dressmaker. There were only two farmers in the community! I have provided fictional characters for some of the occupations represented at LaReunion and woven them into the story. The same has been done for some of the occupations present in Dallas at the time.

Novella Adison and Devil Jack Black are fictitious, although there were bordello madams and gamblers in Boggy Bayou. Surprisingly, the Pinkerton Agency did have a division of female agents in the 1850s. As you have probably guessed, the shenanigans of these characters in the story are products of my imagination.

Check out the **Bonus Content** section of LaurieMooreMoore.com for info on which events in the story were real.

From the former CEO of The Alamo to the Director of the Fort Worth Stockyards Museum . . .

Texans rave about *Gone to Dallas, The Storekeeper 1856–1861*

★ ★ ★

"After years of researching Dallas history while heading up the Trinity River Corridor Project, I found the book *Gone to Dallas* riveting in its telling of the earliest days of Dallas city history. What a remarkable feat. **I loved reading this book**."

—Dr. Gail Thomas, Founder and Former President, The Trinity Trust and Co-founder, The Dallas Institute of Humanities and Culture

"The first line where Sara's husband lies dead immediately pulled me into the story. Add the well-researched historical detail to **a plot full of twists and turns** and this was a real page turner for me. I certainly want to read the next book."

—Dr. Sharon Skrobareck, Member of the Daughters of the Republic of Texas; Alamo Citizens Advisory Committee; and Associate Member, Bexar County Historical Commission

"**Sara was fascinating**—a strong and enterprising young woman. She had the grit and moxie that Texas women are known for. A good fictional read with real historical events thrown in—an interesting twist. I come from a long line of strong Texas women so I find Sara and the other women in this story inspiring."

—Teresa Burleson, Director, Stockyards Museum, Fort Worth; Western Music Association Female Poet of the Year, 2017 and 2019

"I was fascinated by this story. Beginning with the wagon train journey to Texas to the challenges of building a new life in a tiny, log-cabin village, it had the right balance of compelling story telling and historical details. I found it to be **a brilliant book!** It left me wanting to know what happens to each of the characters through the Civil War and beyond."

—Sam Tucker, Area Director of Sales and Marketing, The Adolphus Hotel and Hotel Emeline

"Finally! Historical fiction about the early days of Dallas! Though there are many books in this genre, there are few that tell the unique story of Dallas pioneers. **Meticulously researched**, it was such fun to encounter historical names I'd long known but never truly explored. It was refreshing to read about a female shopkeeper, especially knowing Dallas' later history as a shopping destination. It was truly a pleasure to read this story about my home town."

—Melissa Prycer, Historian

"Fiction and fact combine to personalize and to introduce people to history. *Gone to Dallas* is the compelling story of a young widow who must build a new life in the 1850s in Dallas, a tiny log-cabin village. Sara's story is compelling and teaches us—in **a fascinating narrative**—what was actually happening in Dallas at the time. A recommended read to learn Texas history in an enjoyable manner."

—Douglass W. McDonald, Former CEO of The Alamo

CPSIA information can be obtained
at www.ICGtesting.com
Printed in the USA
LVHW102258180722
723829LV00017B/411